REA

D1616261

DALE BAILEY

THE
Resurrection Man's
LEGACY

GOLDEN GRYPHON PRESS • 2003

"Dale Bailey: In His Dominion," copyright © 2003, by Barry N. Malzberg.
"The Resurrection Man's Legacy," first published in *The Magazine of Fantasy & Science Fiction*, July 1995.
"Death and Suffrage," first published in *The Magazine of Fantasy & Science Fiction*, February 2002.
"The Anencephalic Fields," first published in *The Magazine of Fantasy & Science Fiction*, January 2000.
"Home Burial," first published in *The Magazine of Fantasy & Science Fiction*, December 1994.
"Quinn's Way," first published in *The Magazine of Fantasy & Science Fiction*, February 1997.
"Touched," first published in *The Magazine of Fantasy & Science Fiction*, Oct/Nov 1993.
"The Census Taker," forthcoming in *The Magazine of Fantasy & Science Fiction*.
"Exodus," first published in *The Magazine of Fantasy & Science Fiction*, July 1997.
"Cockroach," first published in *The Magazine of Fantasy & Science Fiction*, December 1998.
"Sheep's Clothing," first published in *The Magazine of Fantasy & Science Fiction*, Oct/Nov 1995.
"In Green's Dominion," first published in SCI FICTION, June 2002.

Copyright © 2003 by Dale Bailey

Cover illustration copyright © 2003 by John Picacio

Grateful acknowledgment is made to the following for permission to reprint excerpts from copyrighted material:

Dante's *Inferno*, translated by Mark Musa, copyright © 1971 by Indiana University Press.

"All in green went my love riding," copyright © 1923 by E. E. Cummings. Reprinted from E. E. Cummings: Selected Poems by permission of W. W. Norton & Company, Inc. / Liveright Publishing Corp.

LIBRARY OF CONGRESS CATALOGING-IN-PUBLICATION DATA
Bailey, Dale.
    The resurrection man's legacy : and other stories / Dale Bailey ; with a foreword by Barry N. Malzberg.— 1st ed.
        p.   cm.
    ISBN 1-930846-22-3 (hardcover : alk. paper)
      1. Science fiction, American.   2. Fantasy fiction, American.   I. Title.
PS3602.A54   R47   2003
813'.6—dc21   2003008343

For information address Golden Gryphon Press, 3002 Perkins Road, Urbana, IL 61802.

First Edition.

Contents

For Jean and Carson

Acknowledgments

There's only one name on the cover, but it hardly needs be said that no story is ever written alone. Most of the people who had a hand in *these* stories are acknowledged in the notes at the end of the book, but I'd like to take this chance to single out a few individuals whose contributions were global rather than particular to any one piece. They include my friend and sometime collaborator Jack Slay, Jr.; my teachers and classmates at Clarion East in 1992, especially Jim Kelly and Nathan Ballingrud; my agent, Matt Bialer; my friend Barry Malzberg; my father-in-law Wayne Singley; my parents, Frederick and Lavonne Bailey; my wife, the lovely and talented Jean Singley Bailey; and my daughter, Carson. Finally I'd like to acknowledge the opportunities and expert advice provided by my editors: Kristine Kathryn Rusch, Gordon Van Gelder, and Ellen Datlow, who took their chances on these stories one by one; and, especially, Gary Turner, who took a chance on them all at once. Thanks, Gary.

A Manufacturing Note

Three thousand copies of this book have been printed by the Maple-Vail Book Manufacturing Group, Binghamton, NY, for Golden Gryphon Press, Urbana, IL. The typeset is Electra, printed on 55# Sebago. Typesetting by The Composing Room, Inc., Kimberly, WI.

Dale Bailey: In His Dominion

I THOUGHT THIS WOULD BE EASY.
  Well, why not? I have done my fair share of this kind of polar writing over the decades, starting almost thirty years ago with some remarks in *Science Fiction Review* on Gene Wolfe's short story "Cues," know the turns, the byways, the happenstance and controlled clamor of this matter as well as anyone in the room. Rounds are rounds: earlier this year when Karen Joy Fowler asked me what I was writing I said, "Oh, introductions, commentaries, afterwords, columns, the usual employment of the living dead," which is another way of saying that there is something of a life when the torrent of creation is no more. But this introduction—which I more or less requested, which I would have fought to write had it not been offered—this introduction has not been at all easy. "Daunting" is the word; the days and weeks have eroded immediacy; now the end of the year and the publisher's urgency portend and this seemingly easy work has become monumental to contemplate: I want to do this remarkable writer, probably the finest fantasist to have entered the genre in the 1990s, his full due and yet how, outside the context of the stories, can I do this?

  What I want to say, all that I need to say in effect is "Read this collection. It is absolutely signatory; like John Varley's *The Persistence of Vision* in 1979 or Theodore Sturgeon's *Without Sorcery* in 1948, it announces a completely formed, irreplaceable talent at the beginning of a remarkable career. There is nothing unpolished, nothing unformed in this work; Bailey arrived virtually complete and these novelettes, glittering and exquisitely transmuted, are their own introduction and assurance." That would be a sufficiency.

But it would probably not be a sufficiency for the publisher who has the right to expect a little more. So the days and weeks have expanded to months and into the full sprawl of belatedness and now I must try to say more or give it up. I do not wish to give it up; there are certainly people who could write a more eloquent introduction, but none—outside of his immediate family, I shakily announce— who have for the novelettes of Dale Bailey the admiration that I do. Primacy of place; fervor should count for something. Fervor is not contemptible as John Calvin probably said. Sometimes it can be the making of a man.

But give the author the voice. Here is just a little bit of what Bailey can do:

Higher still, the hawk might have seen the town entire: a small place fast in its bowl of hills, tethered to the bustling world beyond by a few narrow strands of gray concrete, cracked and weather pitted, rent by the deep-thirsting roots of the great trees, the wild wood, the ancient forest rising up to hem the town in, to surround it, to envelop it with the threat and promise of an older world, the powers and dominions of a world that could be beaten back, cut down, that could be paved over and driven into submission with enough vigilance and determination, but that would ever and again reassert its presence, in the shriek of the hawk itself maybe—

—come to me—

—drifting down the wind, or in the first blade of grass to thrust through the frost-heaved macadam of some abandoned parking lot; and, yet higher, reaching now to the very limits of its great wings and peering down through shreds of thin high vapor, might have seen even this disappear, might have seen the very curve of the Earth, might have seen all this and more and still not seen the lie in the old woman's heart. ("In Green's Dominion")

And here a closing peroration:

They demand nothing of us, after all. They seek no end we can perceive or understand. Perhaps they are nothing more than what we make of them, or what they enable us to make of ourselves. And so we go on, mere lodgers in a world of unpeopled graves, subject ever to the remorseless scrutiny of the dead. ("Death and Suffrage")

Raymond Chandler noted in a famous letter (and here I will paraphrase) that editors object to lines in a detective story such as: "Then, as he walked across the street, the sun cast its broken light through the buildings until it pooled into shadows on the concrete" because such sentences in no way seemed to advance the plot. To the contrary, Chandler wrote, it was just this kind of writing which however unknowingly the reader did want . . . fiction lived through its background, through details not directly connected to plot. Any writer who did not understand this was something less than a writer.

And these stories, of course, are precisely to that point; they live, they are flooded by the light of circumstance. It is this circumstance which becomes inextricably bound to characters and situation, which cannot be disentangled. "In Green's Dominion" makes remarkable use of those Andrew Marvell lines—"green thought in a green shade"—and what is perhaps most interesting here is that Walter Tevis's great novel *The Hustler* (1959) uses those lines as epigraph and grafts them to the center of narrative as Dale Bailey has done here, no less compellingly. "Touched" is one of the very few stories I know—Tolstoy's "The Death of Ivan Ilych" in fact may be the only comparison—which trembles with uncertain and terrible implication all the way to its last paragraph, furnishes a last paragraph then which, if it were only one line longer, the reader (or at least this reader) thinks would somehow explain everything . . . but holds back on that line, plants it instead by retrospect in the body of the story so that somehow the true meaning must be extracted by the reader rather than given by the writer. Tour de force? I know of nothing quite like this in the literature of modern fantasy. Nor do I know anything like "Cockroach" which as an anatomization of the anxiety of parturition (I refrain from saying any more) is unduplicable.

Flabbergasting.

Like Buddy Glass faced in Salinger's "Seymour: An Introduction" with the task of somehow explaining his brother, a kind weakness overcomes me; not so much a dereliction or flagging as an utter insufficiency. I withdraw from what Buddy would have called this little whore's cubicle of the introducer, like a stagehand I drag that cubicle from the line of sight. The rest of this volume is naught but Dale Bailey's; he is nothing like anyone who has come before and everyone who comes after will be in his penumbra. Like *The Persistence of Vision* this is a first collection which could be the collection of a lifetime . . . but how wonderful to know that it is not and that the author was not thirty-four when the contents were completed. Oh, the places he (and we) will go!

Barry N. Malzberg
Teaneck, New Jersey
December 2002

The Resurrection Man's Legacy
And Other Stories

❖ ❖ ❖

The Resurrection Man's Legacy

I DID NOT KNOW THE PHRASE "RESURRECTION man" eighteen years ago. I was a boy then; such men were yet uncommon.

I know it now—we all know it—and yet the phrase retains for me a haunting quality, simultaneously wondrous and frightening. I met him only once, *my* resurrection man, on the cusp of a hazy August morning, but he haunts me still in subtle and unspoken ways: when I look in the mirror and see my face, like my father's face; or when I take the diamond, my uniform shining beneath the ranks of floodlights, and hear the infield chatter, like music if you love the game.

And I do. I do.

It was among the things he bequeathed to me, that love, though he could not have known it. We do not understand the consequences of the actions we take, the meaning of the legacies we leave. We cannot.

They are ghosts of sorts, actions in a vacuum where all action has passed, inheritances from the inscrutable dead. Legacies.

They can be gifts and they can be curses. Sometimes they can be both.

My father returned to the States in April of 1948, following the bloody, methodical invasion of Japan, and he married my mother the week he landed. She died in childbirth eleven months later, and

I sometimes wonder if he ever forgave me. One other significant event occurred in '49: Casey Stengel, a ne'er-do-well journeyman manager, led the Yankees to the first of an unprecedented five straight victories in the World Series.

Twelve years later, in 1961, my father died too. That was the year Roger Maris came to bat in the fourth inning of the season's final game and drove his sixty-first home run into the right-field seats at Yankee Stadium, breaking Babe Ruth's record for single-season homers. In Baltimore, we still say that the new record is meaningless, that Maris played in a season six games longer than that of our home-grown hero; but even then, in our hearts, we knew it wasn't true.

Nothing would ever be the same again.

Two days after my father's death, the monorail whisked me from Baltimore to St. Louis. I had never been away from home. The journey was a nightmare journey. The landscape blurred beyond the shining curve of the window, whether through speed or tears, I could not tell.

My great aunt Rachel Powers met me at the station. Previously, I had known her only from a photograph pasted in the family album. A young woman then, she possessed a beauty that seemed to radiate color through the black and white print. She wore an androgynous flat-busted dress and her eyes blazed from above sharpened cheek bones with such unnerving intensity that, even in the photograph, I could not meet them for more than a moment.

The photograph had been taken forty years before my father's death, but I knew her instantly when I saw her on the platform.

"Jake Lamont?" she said.

I nodded, struck speechless. Tall and lean, she wore a billowing white frock and a white hat, like a young bride. The years had not touched her. She might have been sixteen, she might have been twenty. And then she lifted the veil that obscured her face, shattering the illusion of youth. I saw the same high, sharp cheek bones, the same intense eyes—blue; why had I never wondered?—but her flesh was seamed and spotted with age.

"Well, then," she said. "So you're a boy. I don't know much about boys." And then, when I still did not speak, "Are you mute, child?"

My fingers tightened around the handle of my traveling case. "No, ma'am."

"Well, good. Come along, then."

Without sparing me another glance, she disappeared into the throng. Half-fearful of being left in the noisy, crowded station, I lit out after her, dragging my suitcase behind me. Outside, in the clear Midwestern heat, we loaded the suitcase into the trunk of a weary '53 Cadillac, one of those acre-long cars that Detroit began to produce in the fat years after the war.

We drove into farming country, on single-lane blacktop roads where you could cruise for hours and never see another car. We did not speak, though I watched her surreptitiously. Her intense eyes never deviated from the road, unswerving between the endless rows of corn. I cracked the window, and the car filled with the smell of August in Missouri—the smell of moist earth and cow manure, and green, growing things striving toward maturity, and the slow decline into September. That smell was lovely and alien, like nothing I had ever smelled in Baltimore.

At last, we came to the town, Stowes Corners, situated in a region of low, green hills. She took me through wide, tree-shadowed streets. I saw the courthouse, and the broad spacious lawn of the town square. On a quiet street lined with oak, my aunt pointed out the school, an unassuming antique brick, dwarfed by the monstrous edifice I had known in the city.

"That's where your father went to school when he was a boy," my aunt said, and a swift electric surge of anger—

—*how could he abandon me?*—

—jolted along my spine. I closed my eyes, and pressed my face against the cool window. The engine rumbled as the car pulled away from the curb, and when I opened my eyes again, we had turned into a long gravel drive. The caddy mounted a short rise topped by a stand of maples, and emerged from the trees into sunlight and open air. My aunt paused there—in the days to come I would learn that she always paused there, she took a languorous, almost sensual delight in the land—and in the valley below I saw the house.

It had been a fine old farmhouse once, my aunt would later tell me, but that had been years ago; now, the surrounding fields lost to creditors, the house had begun the inevitable slide into genteel decay. Sun-bleached and worn, scabrous with peeling paint, it retained merely a glimmer of its former splendor. Even then, in my clumsy inarticulate fashion, I could see that it was like my aunt, a luminous fragment of a more refined era that had survived diminished into this whirling and cacophonous age.

"This is your home now," my aunt said, and without waiting for me to respond—what could I say?—she touched the gas and the car descended.

Inside, the house was silence and stillness and tattered elegance. The furnishings, though frayed, shone with a hard gloss, as if my aunt had determined, through sheer dint of effort, to hold back the ravages of years. A breeze stirred in the surrounding hills and chased itself through the open windows, bearing to me a faint lemony scent of furniture polish as I followed my aunt upstairs. She walked slowly, painfully, one hand bracing her back, the other clutching the rail. She led me to a small room and watched from the doorway as I placed my suitcase on the narrow bed. I did not look at her as she crossed the room and sat beside me. The springs complained rustily. I opened my suitcase, dug beneath my clothes, and withdrew the photograph I had brought from Baltimore. It was the only picture I had of my father and me together. Tears welled up inside me. I bit my lip and looked out the window, into the long treeless expanse of the backyard, desolate in a cruel fall of sunshine.

Aunt Rachel said, "Jake."

She said, "Jake, this isn't easy for either of us. I am an old woman and I am set in my ways. I have lived alone for thirty-five years, and I can be as ugly and unpleasant as a bear. I don't know the first thing about boys. You must remember this when things are hard between us."

"Yes, ma'am."

I felt her cool fingers touch my face. She took my chin firmly, and we stared into each other's faces for a time. She pressed her mouth into a thin indomitable line.

"You will look at me when I speak to you. Do you understand?"

"Yes, ma'am."

The fingers dropped from my face. "That's one of my rules. This isn't Baltimore, Jake. I'm not your father. He was a good boy, and I'm sure he was a fine man, but it strikes me that young people today are too lenient with their children. I will not tolerate disrespect."

"No, ma'am."

"Good." She smiled and smoothed her dress across her thighs. "I'm glad you've come to me, Jake," she said. "I hope we can be friends."

Before I could speak, she stood and left the room, closing the door behind her. I went around the bed and lifted the window. The breeze swept in, flooding the room with that alien smell of green things growing. I threw myself on the bed and drew my father's picture to my breast.

*   *   *

Among the photographs that are important to me number three relics of my youth. They are arranged across my desk like talismans as I write.

The first photograph, which I have already described to you, is that of my aunt as she must have looked in 1918 or '19, when she was a girl.

The second photograph is of my mother as she was in the days when my father knew her; aside from the photograph I have nothing of her. Perhaps my father felt that in hoarding whatever memories he had of her, he could possess her even in death. Or perhaps he simply could not bring himself to speak of her. I know he must have loved her, for every year on my birthday, the anniversary of her death, he drew into himself, became taciturn and insular in a way that in retrospect seems atypical, for he was a cheerful man, even buoyant. Beyond that I do not know; he was scrupulous in his destruction of every vestige of her. When he died, I found nothing. No photographs, but the one I still possess. No letters. Not even her rings; I suppose she wore them to the grave.

The third photograph I have mentioned also. It is of my father and me, when I was eleven, and it captures a great irony. Though it was taken in a ballpark—Baltimore's Memorial Stadium—my father did not love baseball. I don't remember why we went to that game—perhaps someone gave him the tickets—but we never attended another. That was when I felt it first, my passion for the sport; immediately, it appealed to me—its order and symmetry, its precision. Nothing else in sports rivals the moment when the batter steps into the box and faces the pitcher across sixty feet of shaven green. The entire game is concentrated into that instant, the skills of a lifetime distilled into every pitch; and no one, no one in the world but those two men, has any power to alter the course of the game.

In those days, of course, I did not think of it in such terms; my passion for the sport was nascent, rudimentary. All I knew was that I enjoyed the game, that someday I would like to see another. That much is my father's due.

The rest, indirectly anyway, was the resurrection man's gift, his legacy. But I have no photograph of him.

I slept uneasily that first night in Stowes Corners, unaccustomed to the rural quiet that cradled the house. The nightly symphony of traffic and voices to which I had been accustomed was absent, and the silence imparted a somehow ominous quality to the stealthy mouse-like chitterings of the automaids as they scurried about the sleeping house.

I woke unrested to the sound of voices drifting up from the parlor. Strange voices—my aunt's, only half-familiar yet, and a second voice, utterly unknown, mellifluous and slow and fawningly ingratiating.

This voice was saying, "You *do* realize, Miss Powers, there are limits to what we are permitted to do?"

I eased out of bed in my pajamas and crept along the spacious hall to the head of the stairs, the hardwood floor cool against my bare feet.

My aunt said, "Limits? The advertising gave me the impression you could do most anything."

I seated myself on the landing in the prickly silence that followed. A breeze soughed through the upstairs windows. Through the half-open door in the ornate foyer below, I could see a car parked in the circular drive. Beyond the car, the morning sun gleamed against the stand of maple and sent a drowsy haze of mist steaming away into the open sky.

My aunt was rattling papers below. "It doesn't say anything about limits here."

"No, ma'am, of course not. And I didn't mean to imply that our products were not convincing. Not by any means."

"Then what do you mean by limits?"

The stranger cleared his throat. "Not technological limits, ma'am. Those exist, of course, but they're not the issue here."

"Well, what in heaven's name *is* the issue?"

"It's a legal matter, ma'am—a constitutional matter, even. We're a young company, you know, and our product is new and unfamiliar and there's bound to be some controversy, as you might well imagine." He paused, and I could hear him fumbling about through his paraphernalia. A moment later I heard the sharp distinct *snick* of a lighter.

He smoked, of course. In those days, all men smoked, and the acrid gritty stink of tobacco smoke which now began to drift up the stairs reminded me of my father.

I do not smoke. I never have.

"Our company," he resumed, "we're cognizant of the objections folks might raise to our product. The Church—all the churches— are going to be a problem. And the doctors are going to have a field day with the need to come to terms with grief. We know that—our founder, Mr. Hiram Wallace, he *knows* that, he's an intelligent

man, but he's committed. We're all committed. Do you know anything about Mr. Wallace, ma'am?"

"I'm afraid I don't."

"It's an inspiring story, a story I think you ought to hear. Anybody
who's thinking of contracting with us ought to hear it. Do you
mind?"

My aunt sighed. I heard her adjust herself in her chair, and I
could imagine them in the quaint, spotless parlor I had seen the
night before: my aunt in her white dress, her hands crossed like a
girl's over the advertising packet in her lap; the resurrection man,
leaning forward from the loveseat, a cigarette dangling between his
fingers.

Aunt Rachel said, "Go ahead then."

"It's a tragedy, really," the resurrection man said, "but it ends in
triumph. For you see, Mr. Wallace's first wife, she was hit by a bus
on their honeymoon—"

"Oh, my!"

"Yes, ma'am, that's right, a bus." There was a hardy smack as the
resurrection man slammed his hands together; I could hear it even
at the top of the stairs. "Like that," he said, "so sudden. Mr. Wallace
was heartbroken. He knows what you're feeling, ma'am, he knows
what your boy upstairs is feeling, and he wants to help—"

With these words, an icy net of apprehension closed around my
heart, and the tenor of my eavesdropping swerved abruptly from
mild curiosity to a kind of breathless dread. The resurrection man's
next words came sluggish and dim. I felt as if I had been wrapped
in cotton. The landing had grown oppressively hot.

"The potential applications for this technology are mind-bog-
gling," he was saying. "And I won't lie to you, ma'am, Mr. Wallace
is exploring those avenues. But this, this service to the grief-stricken
and the lonely, this is where his heart lies. That's why we're offering
this service before any other, ma'am, and that's why there are limits
to what we can do."

"But I'm afraid I still don't understand."

"Let me see if I can clarify, ma'am. Of all the forces arrayed
against us—all the people like the churches and the doctors who'd
like to see our enterprise go down the tubes—our single most
dangerous adversary is the government itself. Our senators and
representatives are frankly scared to death of this."

"But why?"

"It's the question of legal status, ma'am. What does it take to
be a human being, that's the question. All the agreements we've

worked out with congressional committees and sub-committees—it seems like a hundred of them—all the agreements boil down to one thing: these, these . . . beings . . . must be recognizably non-human, limited in intellect, artificial in appearance. No one wants to grapple with the big questions, ma'am. No one wants to take on the churches, especially our elected officials. They're all cowards."

Aunt Rachel said, "I see," in a quiet, thoughtful kind of voice, but she didn't say anything more.

In the silence that followed, something of the magnitude of my aunt's devotion came to me. I did not know much about Stowes Corners, but I suspected, with a twelve-year-old's inarticulate sense of such things, that the town was as rigidly provincial in perspective as in appearance. Whatever the stranger below was selling my aunt, he had clearly come a long way to sell it; there could be no need for such controversial . . . beings, as he had called them . . . here—here in a place where my aunt had told me that she was among the few folks in town who owned automaids.

I couldn't really afford them, Jake, she had said last night at supper, *but the work was getting to be too much for me. I'm glad you've come to help me.*

Now, with the sun rising over the maples and throwing sharp glints off the car in the drive, the resurrection man coughed. "I hope you're still interested, Miss Powers."

"Well, I don't know a thing about boys," she said. "And I don't want him growing up without a father. It isn't right that a boy grow up without a man in the house."

That icy net of apprehension drew still tighter about my heart. My stomach executed a slow perfect roll, and the sour tang of bile flooded my mouth. I leaned my head against the newel and shut my eyes.

"I agree entirely, ma'am," came the other voice. "A boy needs a father. You can rest assured we'll do our best."

From below, there came the rustle of people standing, the murmured pleasantries of leave-taking. My aunt asked how long it would take, and the resurrection man said not long, we'll simply modify a pre-fab model along the lines suggested by the photos and recordings—and through all this babble a single thought burst with unbearable clarity:

Nothing, nothing would ever be the same again.

I stood, and fled down the hall, down the back stairs. I slammed through the kitchen and into the gathering heat.

When the front door swung open, I was waiting. As the resurrection man—this stout, balding man dressed in a dark suit, and a wide bright tie; this unprepossessing man, unknowing and unknown, who would shape the course of my existence—as this man rounded the corner of his car, his case in hand, I hurled myself at him. Frenzied, I hurled myself at him, flailing at his chest. "What are you going to do?" I cried.

Strong hands pinned my arms to my sides and lifted me from the ground. The rancid odors of after-shave and tobacco enveloped me, and I saw that sweat stood in a dark ring around his collar. "Calm down!" he shouted. "Just calm down, son! Are you crazy?"

He thrust me from him. Half-blinded by tears, I stumbled away, swiping angrily at my eyes with my knuckles. Without speaking, the resurrection man dusted his suit and retrieved his case. He got in his car and drove away, and though I could not know it then, I would never see him again.

My father's body came by slowtrain several days later. He had returned to Stowes Corners only once in the years after the war, to see my mother into the earth where her family awaited her. Now, at last, he came to join her; we buried him in the sun-dappled obscurity of a Missouri noon.

As the minister quietly recited the ritual, a soft wind lilted through the swallow-thronged trees, bearing to me the sweet fragrances of freshly turned earth and new-mown grass. I watched an intricate pattern of light and leaf-shadow play across my aunt's face, but I saw no tears. Her still, emotionless features mirrored my own. The service seemed appropriate—minimal and isolated, infinitely distant from the places and people my father had known. There was only the minister, my aunt, and myself. No one else attended.

When the minister had finished, I knelt before my mother's tombstone and reached out a single finger to trace her name. And then I clutched a handful of soil and let it trickle through my fingers into my father's grave. I shall never forget the sound it made as it spattered the casket's polished lid.

Several years ago, I chanced upon an archaeologist's account of his experience excavating a ruined city, abandoned beneath the sand for thousands of years. Such a project is an exercise in meticulous drudgery; the Earth does not readily divulge her secrets. Stratum after stratum of sand must be sifted, countless fragments painstakingly extracted and catalogued and fitted together for interpretation. You are in truth excavating not one city, but many cities, each built on the rubble of the one which preceded it.

I am reminded of this now, for recollection, like archaeology, is a matter of sifting through ruins. Memory is frail and untrustworthy, tainted by desire; what evidence remains is fragmentary, shrouded in the mystery of the irretrievable past. You cannot recover history; you can only reconstruct it, build it anew from the shards that have survived, searching always for the seams between the strata, those places of demarcation between the city that was and the city that would be, between the self that you were and the self you have become.

How do you reconstruct a past, when only potsherds and photographs remain?

A moment, then.

An instant from the quiet, hot August day my father was interred—one of those timeless instants that stands like a seam between the geologic strata of a buried city, between the boy I was and the man I have become:

Afternoon.

In the room where I slept, the blinds rattled, but otherwise all was silent. Outside, somewhere, the world moved on. Tiny gusts leavened the heat and lifted the luminous scent of pollen into the afternoon, but through the open window there came only a cloying funerary pall. Far away, the sun shone; it announced its presence here only as an anemic gleam behind the lowered blinds, insufficient to dispel the gloom.

I stood before the closet, fumbling with my tie. My eyes stung and my stomach had drawn into an agonizing knot, but I refused to cry. I was repeating a kind of litany to myself—

—*I will not cry, I will not*—

—when a voice said:

"Hello, Jake."

My spine stiffened. The tiny hairs along my back stirred, as if a dark gust from some October landscape had swept into the room.

It was my father's voice.

I did not turn. Without a word, I shrugged off my jacket and swung open the closet door. In the dim reflection of the mirror hung inside, I could see a quiet figure, preternatural in its stillness, seated in the far shadowy corner by the bed.

I don't want him growing up without a father, my aunt had said. *It isn't right that a boy grow up without a man in the house.*

What in God's name had she done?

The figure said, "Don't be afraid, Jake."

"I'm not afraid," I said. But my hands shook as I fumbled at the buttons on my shirt. I groped for a hanger, draped the shirt around it, and thrust it into the depths of the closet, feeling exposed in my nakedness, vulnerable, but determined not to allow this . . . *being*, the resurrection man had called it . . . to sense that. Kicking away my slacks, I fished a pair of jeans out of the closet.

In the mirror, I saw the figure stand.

I said, "Don't come near me."

And that voice—*my God, that voice*—said, "Don't be afraid."

It smiled and lifted a hand to the window, each precise, economical gesture accompanied by a faint mechanical hum, as though somewhere far down in the depths of its being, flywheels whirred and gears meshed in intricate symphony. I watched as it gripped the cord and raised the blind.

The room seemed to ignite. Sunlight glanced out of the mirror and rippled in the glossy depths of the headboard and night stand. A thousand spinning motes of dust flared, and I winced as my eyes adjusted. Then, my heart pounding, I closed the closet door, and at last, at last I turned around.

It was my father—from the dark hair touched gray at the temples to the slight smiling crinkles around the eyes to the slim athletic build, seeming to radiate poise and grace even in repose—in every detail, it was my father. It sat once again in the wooden chair by the night stand, stiffly erect, its blunt fingers splayed on the thighs of its jeans, and returned my stare from my father's eyes. I felt a quick, hot swell of anger and regret—

—*how could you abandon me?*—

—felt something tear away inside of me. I blinked back tears. "My God, what are you?"

"Jake," it said. It said, "Jake, don't cry."

That swift tide of anger, burning, swept through me, obliterating all. "Don't you tell me what to do."

The thing seemed taken aback. It composed its features into an expression of startled dismay; its mouth moved, but it said nothing. We stared across the room at one another until at last it looked away. It lifted the framed photograph that stood on the night stand. A moment passed, and then another, while it gazed into the picture. I wondered what it saw there, in that tiny image of the man it was pretending to be.

One thick finger caressed the gilded frame. "Is that Memorial Stadium?"

It looked up, smiling tentatively, and I crossed the room in three angry strides. I tore the photograph out of the thing's hands, and then the tears boiled out of me, burning and shameful.

"You don't know anything about it!" I cried, flinging myself on the bed. The creature stood, its hands outstretched, saying, "Jake, Jake—" but I rushed on, I would not listen: "You're not my father! You don't know anything about it! Anything, you hear me? So just go away and leave me alone!" In the end, I was screaming.

The thing straightened. "Okay, Jake. If that's the way you want it." And it crossed the room, and went out into the hall, closing the door softly behind it.

I lay back on the bed. After a while, my aunt called me for supper, but I didn't answer. She didn't call again. Outside, it began to grow dark, and finally a heavy silence enclosed the house. Eventually, I heard tiny mutterings and whisperings as the auto-maids crept from their holes and crannies and began to whisk away the debris of another day, but through it all, I did not move. I lay wide awake, staring blindly at the dark ceiling.

During the days that followed my aunt and I moved about the house like wraiths, mute and insubstantial, imprisoned by the unacknowledged presence of this monstrous being, this creature that was my father and not my father. We did not mention it; I dared not ask, she proffered no explanation. Indeed, I might have imagined the entire episode, except I glimpsed it now and then—trimming the shrubs with garden shears or soaping down the caddy in the heat, and once, in a tableau that haunts me still, standing dumb in the darkened parlor, gazing expressionlessly at the wall with a concentration no human being could muster.

Inexorably the afternoons grew shorter, the maple leaves began to turn, and somehow, somewhere in all the endless moments, August passed into September.

One morning before the sun had burned the fog off the hills, my aunt awoke me. I dressed quietly, and together we walked into the cool morning, the gravel crunching beneath our feet. She drove me to the school my father had attended all those long years ago, a mile away, and as I stepped from the car she pressed a quarter into my hand.

"Come here," she said, and when I came around the car to the open window, she leaned out and kissed me. Her lips were dry and hard, with the texture of withered leaves.

She looked away, through the glare of windshield, where morning was breaking across the town. A bell began to ring, and noisy clusters of children ran by us, shouting laughter, but I did not move. The two of us might have been enclosed in a thin impermeable bubble, isolated from the world around us. Her knuckles had whitened atop the steering wheel.

"You can walk home," she said, "you know the way," and when I did not answer, she cleared her throat. "Well, then, good luck," she said, and I felt a reply—what it might have been, I cannot know—catch in my throat. Before I could dislodge it, the car pulled from the curb.

I turned to the school. The bell continued to ring. Another clump of children swept by, and I drifted along like flotsam in their wake. I mounted the steps to the building slowly and carefully, as if the slightest jolt would destabilize the churning energies that had been compressed within me. I was a bomb, I could have ticked.

My aunt and I were in the kitchen, eating supper, that wall of impregnable silence between us. I ate with studied nonchalance, gazing steadfastly into my plate, or staring off into the dining room beyond the kitchen. The creature that looked like my father sat alone in there, shadowy and imperturbable, its hands folded neatly on the table.

Aunt Rachel said, "Jake, it's time to move on with your life. You must accept your father's death and go on. You cannot grieve forever."

I pushed my vegetables around my plate. Words swollen and poisonous formed in my gut; I could not force them into my throat.

She said, "Jake, I want to be your friend."

Again, I did not answer. I looked off into the dining room. The thing looked back, silent, inscrutable. And then, almost without thought, I began to speak, expelling the words in a deadly emotionless monotone: "You must be crazy. Do you think that thing can replace him?"

Aunt Rachel lowered her fork with shaking fingers. Her lips had gone white. "Of course not. Your father can never be replaced, Jake."

"That's not my father," I said. "It's nothing like him!"

"Jake, I know—"

But she could not finish. I found myself standing, my napkin clenched in one hand. Screaming: "It's not! It's not a thing like him! You must be crazy, you old witch—"

And then I was silent. A deadly calm descended in the kitchen. I felt light-headed, as though I were floating somewhere around the ceiling, tethered to my body by the most tenuous of threads. The things I had said made no sense, I knew, but they felt true. My aunt said, "Look me in the eye, Jake."

I forced my stone-heavy eyes to meet hers.

"You must never speak to me like that again," she said. "Do you understand?"

Biting my lip, I nodded.

"Your father is dead," she told me. "I understand you are in pain, but it is time you face the facts and begin to consider the feelings of others again. You must never run away from the truth, Jake, however unpleasant. Because once you begin running, you can never stop."

She folded her napkin neatly beside her plate and pushed her chair away from the table. "Come here," she said. "Bend over and put your hands on your knees."

Reluctantly, I did as she asked. She struck me three quick painless blows across the backside, and I felt tears of humiliation well up in my eyes. I bit my lip—bit back the tears—and finished my meal in silence, but afterwards I crept upstairs to stretch on the narrow bed and stare at the familiar ceiling. A sharp woodsy odor of burning leaves drifted through the window, and shadows slowly inhabited the room. An orchestra of insects began to warm up in the long flat space behind the house.

I dozed, and woke later in the night to a room spun full of gossamer moonlight. The creature sat in the chair by the night stand, cradling the photograph in its unlined hands. It looked up, something whirring in its neck, and placed the photograph on the night stand where I could see it.

"I'll go if you like," it said.

I sat up, wincing. "Light, please," I told the lamp, and as the room brightened, I gazed into the picture. A boy curiously unlike myself gazed back at me, eyes shining, arm draped about the slim, dark-headed man next to him. My father's lean, beard-shadowed face had already begun to grow unfamiliar. Looking at the photograph, I could see him—how could I not?—but at night, in the darkness, I could not picture him. His lips came to me, or his eyes, or the long curve of his jaw, but they came like pieces of a worn-out jigsaw puzzle—they would not fit together true. And now, of course, he is lost to me utterly; only sometimes, when I look into a mirror, I catch a glimpse of him there and it frightens me.

I reached out a finger to the photograph. Glass. Cold glass, walling me away forever.

I remembered the dirt as it trickled through my fingers; I

remembered the sound it made as it spattered the lid of the casket.

"You're not my father," I said.

"No."

We were quiet for a while. Something small and toothy gnawed away inside me.

"What are you?" I asked.

"I'm a machine."

"That's all? Just a machine, like a car or a radio?"

"Something like that. More complicated. A simulated person, they call me—a sim. I'm a new thing. There aren't many machines in the world like me, though maybe there will be."

"I could cut you off," I said. "I could just cut you off."

"Yes."

"And if I do?"

The sim lifted its hands and shrugged. "Gone," it said. "Erased and irrecoverable. Everything that makes me me."

"Show me. I want to know."

The sim's expression did not change. It merely leaned forward and lifted the thick hair along its neck. And there it was: a tiny switch, like a jewel gleaming in the light. I reached out and touched it, ran my finger through the coarse hair, touched the skin, rubbery and cold, thinking of what he had said: *Erased and irrecoverable*.

"You're a machine," I said. "That's all." And everything—the fear and anger, the hope and despair—everything drained out of me, leaving a crystalline void. I was glass. If you had touched me, I would have shattered into a thousand shining fragments. "My aunt must be crazy."

"Perhaps she only wants to make you happy."

"You can't replace my father."

"I don't want to."

Insects had begun to hurl themselves at the window screen, and I told the light to shut itself off. The darkness seemed much thicker than before, and I could perceive the sim only as a silhouette against the bright moonlit square of the window. It reached out and picked up the photograph again and I thought: *It can see in the dark*.

Who knew what it could do?

The sim said, "Did you go to many games at Memorial Park?"

"You ought to know. You're supposed to be just like him."

"I hardly know a thing about him," the sim said. And then: "Jake, I'm not really a thing like him at all. I just look like him."

"That was the only game we ever went to."

"I see."

All at once that day came flooding back to me—its sights and sounds, its sensations. I wanted to describe the agony of suspense that built with every pitch, the hush of the crowd and the flat audible crack of the bat when a slugger launched the ball clear into the summer void, a pale blur against the vaulted blue. I remembered those things, and more: the oniony smell of the hot dogs and relish my father and I had shared, the bite of an icy Coke in the heat, and through it all the recurrent celebratory strain of the calliope. A thousand things I could not say.

So we sat there in silence, and finally the sim said, "Do you think we could be friends?"

I shrugged, thinking of my aunt. She too had wished to be my friend. Now, in the silent moonlit bedroom, the scene at the table came back to me. An oily rush of shame surged through me. "Is it really so bad, running away?"

"I don't know. I don't know things like that."

"What am I going to do?"

"Maybe you don't have to run away." The sim cocked its head with a mechanical hum. A soft crescent of moonlight illuminated one cheek, and I could see a single eye, flat and depthless as polished tin. But all the rest was shadow. It said, "I'm not your father, Jake. But I could be your friend."

Without speaking, I lay down, pulled the covers up to my chin, and listened for a while to the whispery chatter of the automaids as they scoured the bottom floor. A breeze murmured about the eaves, and somewhere far away in the hills, an owl hooted, comforting and friendly, and that was a sound I had never heard in Baltimore.

I had just begun to doze when the sim spoke again.

"Maybe sometime we can pitch the ball around," it said, and through the thickening web of sleep I thought, for just a moment, that it was my father. But, of course, it wasn't. An unutterable tide of grief washed over me, bearing me to an uneasy shore of dreams.

That October, I sat alone in the sun-drenched parlor and listened to the weekend games of the '61 World Series on my aunt's radio. The Yankee sluggers had gone cold. Mantle, recovering from late-season surgery, batted only six times in the whole series; Maris had spent himself in the chase for Babe Ruth's single-season home run record.

Yankee hurler Whitey Ford took up the slack. I read about his game one shutout in the newspaper. Four days later, when he took the mound again, I listened from hundreds of miles away. In the third inning, the sim came into the room and sat down across from me. It steepled its fingers and closed its eyes. We did not speak.

Ford pitched two more flawless innings before retiring with an injury in the sixth.

I stood up, suddenly angry, and glared at the sim. "You ought to have a name, I guess," I said.

The sim opened its eyes. It did not speak.

"I'll call you Ford," I said bitterly. "That's a machine's name."

Dreams plagued me that year. One night, I seemed to wake in the midst of a cheering crowd at Memorial Stadium. But gradually the park grew hushed. The game halted below, and the players, the bright-clad vendors, the vast silent throng—one by one, they turned upon me their voiceless gaze. I saw that I was surrounded by the dead: my father, the mother I had never known, a thousand others, all the twisted, shrunken dead. A tainted wind gusted among the seats, fanning my hair, and the silent corpses began to crumble. Desiccated flesh sloughed like ash from the bones, whirled in dark funnels through the stands. And then the air cleared, and I saw that the dead were lost to me forever. Silence reigned, and emptiness. Endless empty rows.

Day turned into dream-haunted night and into day again. My father receded in memory, as if I had known him a hundred years ago. My life in Baltimore might have been another boy's life, distant and unreal. I was agreeable but distant with my aunt; I ignored Ford for the most part. I passed long stifling hours in school, staring dreamily, day after day, across the abandoned playground to the baseball diamond, dusty and vacant in the afternoon. I had no interest in studies. Even now, I remember my aunt's crestfallen expression as she inspected my report cards, the rows of D's and F's, or the section reserved for comments, where Mrs. O'Leary wrote, *Jake is well-behaved and has ability, but he is moody and lacks discipline.*

In March of '62, on my birthday, I came home from school to find a hand-stitched regulation baseball, a leather fielder's glove, and a Louisville Slugger, knotted with a shiny ribbon, arranged on my bed. I caressed the soft leather glove.

From the doorway, my aunt said, "Do you like them, Jake?"

I slipped on the glove, turned the ball pensively with my right hand, and flipped it toward the ceiling. It hung there for a moment, spinning like a jewel in the sunlight, and then it plunged toward the floor. My left hand leaped forward, the glove seemed to open of its own accord, and the ball dropped solidly into the pocket.

Nothing had ever felt so right.

I said, "I love them."

My aunt sat on the bed, wincing. Already, the arthritis had

begun its bitter, surreptitious campaign. She smoothed her dress across her knees.

I brought the glove to my face. Closing my eyes, I drew in the deep, leathery aroma. "Gosh," I said, "they're fine . . . I mean, they're *really* fine. How did you ever know?"

My aunt smiled. "We're getting to know you, now. Besides I had some help."

"Help?"

She nodded, and touched the bat. "Only the best," she said. "Ford insisted on it."

"It's . . . well, it's just tremendous. I mean, thank you."

She leaned forward and pressed her lips to my cheek. "Happy birthday, Jake. I'm glad you like them." She lifted her hands to my shoulders and gently pushed me erect. "Now, look me in the eye," she said. "There's something we need to talk about."

"Yes, ma'am?"

"I've made some phone calls. I've talked to Mrs. O'Leary and some other folks at school."

I glanced away, let the baseball slip from my glove into my waiting hand. My aunt touched my chin, lifted my head so that I was looking in her eyes. "Listen, Jake, this is important."

"Okay."

"Mrs. O'Leary says you'll pass and go on to junior high, but it's a close thing. And starting next year your grades will count toward college. Did you know that?"

"No, ma'am."

"Every member of my family for two generations has gone to college. I do not intend for that to change."

I said nothing. Her eyes were a sharp intense blue. Penetrating. So we were family, I thought.

She said, "Ford thinks you might like to try out for baseball next year. Is that true?"

I had never considered the possibility. Now, turning the ball in my hand, I said, "I guess."

"I talked to the junior high baseball coach, too. You have to bring your grades up or you won't be eligible for the team. Can you do that?"

"Yes, ma'am — it's not that I'm dumb or anything. It's just — " I paused, searching for words that would not come. How could I explain? "I don't know."

Aunt Rachel smiled. "But you'll do better, right?"

I nodded.

"Good." She smiled and reached out to squeeze my hand. I

could feel the pressure of her fingers. I could feel the ball's seams dig into my palm. "Oh, that's fine, Jake. Have you ever played ball before?"

"No, ma'am," I said.

"Then you have some catching up to do. I think there's someone outside who'd like to help."

I stood and went to the window. Ford waited below, his shadow stretching across the grass. He wore a glove on his left hand, a baseball cap canted over his eyes. When he saw me, he lifted the glove and hollered, "Hey, Jake! Come on!"

I lifted my hand in a half-reluctant wave and just then Aunt Rachel stepped up behind me. She tugged a cap firmly over my head, and let her fingers fall to my shoulder. "Go ahead, have fun," she whispered. "But remember our deal."

"Yes, ma'am!" I shouted. Scooping up the bat, I ran out of the room. I bounded down the steps, through the kitchen, and into the sunlit backyard where Ford awaited me.

Ford pitched, and I batted.

The sun arced westward. Time and again, the Louisville Slugger whistled impotently in the air, until at last I threw it down in frustration.

"You're swinging wild," Ford said. "You're hacking at the ball."

He picked up the discarded bat, and swung it easily for a moment with his large and capable-looking hands.

"Like this," he told me. He planted his feet, and bounced a little on his knees. He held his elbows away from his body, tilted the bat over his shoulder, and swung smoothly and easily.

"Watch the ball," he said. "You've got to eye the ball in, and meet it smoothly. You want to try?"

I shrugged. Ford handed me the bat and took his position sixty feet away. I bobbed the bat, swung it once or twice the way I had seen the pros do, and relaxed into the stance Ford had shown me, the bat angled over my right shoulder. I tracked the ball as it left his hand, saw it hurtle toward me, but I held back, held back . . .

. . . and at the very last moment, just when it seemed the ball would whip by untouched, I swung.

I felt the concussion all along my shoulders and arms. My mouth fell open, and I tossed the bat into the grass, hooting in delight. Ford clapped his hands as the ball rocketed skyward, disappeared momentarily into the sun, and began to drop into the high grass beyond the yard.

Gone.

"Now we have to find it," Ford said.

I set off across the yard, jogging to keep up with Ford's long strides. My arms and shoulders ached pleasantly. I could taste a slight tang of perspiration on my upper lip. Half-curiously, I looked at the sim. Not a single droplet of sweat clung to his perfect, gleaming flesh. He walked smoothly, and easily, his knees humming with every step.

When we finally found the ball, far back in the field behind the house, I threw myself exhausted in the grass. Ford lowered himself beside me, propping his weight on his elbows, and we remained that way for a while, sucking thoughtfully on sweet blades of grass. An old game my father and I had played came back to me and I began to point out shapes in the clouds—a chariot, a skull, a moose—but the sim did not respond.

"Do you see anything?" I asked him, and when he did not answer I turned to eye him. "Well, do you?"

He chased the grass stalk to the far corner of his mouth and smiled. "Sure I do, when you point them out, Jake. You go ahead, I like to listen."

And so I did, until the charm of the game began to wear thin; after that we just lay quiet and restful for a while. At last, my aunt called me for supper. Inside, for the first time, the sim came into the kitchen and took a chair at the table while we ate. He shot me a glance as he sat down, as if I might have something to say about it, and I almost did. A quick flash of anger, like heat lightning, flickered through me. I looked away.

"Discipline," Ford told me that summer. "In baseball, discipline is everything."

That, too, was a legacy. And though I imagine Ford could not have known it—what could he really know, after all?—perhaps he sensed it somehow: this was a lesson with broader implications. Certainly Aunt Rachel knew it.

"For every hour you spend on baseball," she told me that night, "you must spend an hour reading or doing homework. Agreed?"

And so commenced my central obsessions, those legacies that have shaped my life. From that time onward, my youth was consumed by baseball and books. During that summer and the summers that followed—all through my high school career—Ford and I worked in the quiet isolation of the backyard. I took to baseball with a kind of innate facility, as if an understanding of the game had been encoded in my genes. I relished the sting of a line-drive into well-oiled leather, the inexorable trajectory of a fly ball as it plummeted toward a waiting glove. I relish it still. There is an order and a symmetry to the game which counteracts the chaos that pervades our lives; even then, in some inchoate, inexpressible fashion, I understood this simple truth.

Every pitcher has to have a repertoire, Ford told me one day, a fastball and a curve. Leaning over me, he shaped my fingers along the seams of the ball. Hide it in your glove, he said. Don't tip off the batter.

Summer after summer, until the season broke and winter closed around the town, Ford coached me through the pitch—the grips, the wind-up and pivot, the follow through on the release. I wanted to hurl with my arm. Save your arm, he told me; he showed me how to use my legs.

But it was more than merely physical discipline; Ford had a strategic grasp of the game, as well. He taught me that baseball was a cerebral sport, showed me that a well-coached team could prevail over talent and brawn. Some days we never touched a ball at all. We sat cross-legged in the grass, dissecting games we had heard on the radio or read about in the paper. He fabricated situations out of whole cloth and asked me to coach my way through them, probing my responses with emotionless logic.

Occasionally, in the frustration of the moment, I would stand and walk away from him, turning at last to gaze back to the far distant house, past the sim sitting patiently in the grass, to the back-porch where my aunt waited, watching from the steps that first summer, and later, as the arthritis began to gnaw away inside her, from the hated prison of her powerchair.

In those later years, she preserved her dignity. On our infrequent excursions into town, she insisted on walking upright; she masked her pain and held her head rigidly erect, regal as a queen. She did not give up. Standing there in the open field, I would remember this, and her simple lesson, the litany she lived by, would come back to me: *You must never run away.* Chagrined, I would remember another thing that had been said to me—Ford's voice this time, saying, *Talent is never enough, Jake. Discipline is everything*—and I would walk back and take my place across from him.

Tell me again, I would say.

Tiny motors whirred beneath his flesh, drew a broad smile across his features; he would tell me again. Day after day, through the long summer months, he told me again. We hashed over countless situations, until the strategies came thoughtlessly to my lips, naturally, and I did not walk away in frustration anymore.

During these same years, I spent nights alone in my bedroom, studying during the school year, reading for pleasure in my stolen hours. At first, in a kind of half-conscious rebellion against my aunt's ultimatum, I read only about baseball—strategies and biographies, meditations on the game. But gradually my interests broadened. I read history and fiction and one memorable summer, everything I could find about simulated people. I read about Hiram Wallace and his absurd tragedy. I read his encomiums for the specialized sims he called grief counselors—and opposing editorials from every perspective. The resurrection man had been right about one thing: Wallace had his critics.

But none of them convinced me.

At the school library one fall I researched the matter. I flipped anxiously through news magazines, half-hoping to run upon a picture of the stout, hearty salesman that had come to the house, half-fearing it as well. That night, I lay awake far into the morning, examining in a magazine graphic the wondrous intricacies of Ford's design. I remember being half-afraid the sim would walk in upon me, as if I were doing something vaguely shameful, though why I should have felt this way, I cannot say. After that, during sleepless nights, in the darkness when the image of my father would not cohere, I thought of Ford: I imagined the twisted involutions of his construction, the gears and cogs and whirring motors, the thousand electric impulses that sang along his nested wires, far down through his core, to the crystal-matrixed genius of his brain.

This is what I remember about high school:

Empty stands.

Not truly empty, you understand—the crowds came in droves by my senior year, when I won ten of eleven as a starter. By that time, a few local fellows, short on work, had even started looking in on practice. They lounged in the stands, trimming their nails or glancing through the want ads; every once in a while, if someone got a piece of the ball, they would holler and whistle.

And hundreds showed up for the last game of my high school career, when I gave up the winning run on a botched slider in the seventh. But the stands were empty all the same.

Afterwards, I stood on the mound and watched the crowd disperse. A few teammates patted my shoulder as they headed in to see their families, but I just stood there in the middle of the diamond.

My aunt had never seen me play; she could barely leave the house by then. And Ford? Who would take him to the ballpark?

A jowly, red-faced man awaited me at school the following Monday.

I had seen him in the stands during practice the last week or so, looking on with a kind of absent-minded regard, as if he had more important things on his mind. I assumed him an out-of-work gas jockey or a farmhand with time on his hands.

I was wrong.

He sat across from me in the cluttered office off the locker room, his beat-up oxfords propped carelessly on the corner of Coach Ryan's desk. He wore a shabby suit and a coffee-stained tie; his shirt gapped at the belly. Coach Ryan had introduced him as Gerald Haynes, a scout for the Reds.

"So what happened the other night?" Haynes asked.

I started to speak, but Coach Ryan interrupted. He fiddled with a pencil on his blotter. "Just an off game, Mr. Haynes—an off pitch, actually. The boy played a solid game." He looked at me as if he had just noticed I was there. "You played a solid game, Jake."

Haynes lifted an eyebrow. "What do *you* say, son?"

"I made a bad decision," I replied, when the silence had stretched a moment too long. "I went with the slider when the fastball had been working all day. It hung up on me." I shrugged.

"Jake's got a pretty good slider, actually—" Coach Ryan began, but Haynes held up his hand.

He picked up a paper cup that sat on the floor and dribbled a stream of tobacco juice into it. I could smell the tobacco juice, intermixed with the locker room's familiar stink of mold and sweat. "Why would you make a decision like that, son?"

"I knew there were some college scouts in the stands. I wanted to show them what I had."

Haynes chuckled.

"I didn't know *you* were there," I said.

Coach Ryan said, "I didn't tell him. I didn't want to make him nervous, you know?"

"So you pitched to impress the people watching, am I right?"

My bowels felt loose, like I might be sick, but I met his eyes. "Yes, sir."

Haynes put the cup down and leaned close to me. I could smell his polluted breath. "You pitch to win, Jake. That's the cardinal rule, okay?"

"Yes, sir."

"You aren't ready to throw sliders, and you certainly aren't ready to throw them on a two-three count in the last inning of a tied ballgame. You want to know about sliders, I'll tell you about sliders. A badly thrown slider can throw your arm out of whack for good, ruin your career. I've seen it once, I've seen it a thousand times."

"Yes, sir."

"You want to take care of yourself." Haynes leaned back and crossed his arms over his belly. He stared at me for a while.

I knew I shouldn't ask, but I couldn't help myself. "Why is that, sir?"

Haynes dug a clump of snuff from behind his lip and flipped it into the cup. He stood, wiped his hands on his pants, and extended his arm to me.

I reached out and took his grip. He squeezed hard and smiled. "I've seen better, son," he said. "But you ain't bad. You ain't bad."

Those were the days before ballplayers commanded the astronomical salaries they draw now, as Aunt Rachel quickly pointed out. "I'm entirely against it, Jake," she told me one evening early in July.

I sighed and shifted uncomfortably in one of the claw-footed chairs in the parlor. The Reds had, in fact, extended me an offer, but I had been chosen in the late rounds. My signing bonus was negligible, my proposed salary more so. *You've got talent, all right*, Haynes had told me, *but you ain't no ace, son.*

Not yet, I had thought.

Now, I glanced at Ford. He sat on the loveseat across the room, his back straight, his hands resting flat on his thighs. "Well, Ford," I said. "What do you think?"

The sim tilted his head with a faintly musical hum. He looked to my aunt and then back to me. "I don't know, Jake," he said at last. "I can't answer things like that."

"Well, wouldn't you like me to play pro ball?"

"Sure. I guess so."

"Don't you think he ought to go to college?" Aunt Rachel said dryly.

"Yes, ma'am. I guess so."

I crossed my arms in exasperation and swung my legs over the arm of my chair. I managed to hold the pose for all of thirty seconds before my aunt's silent disapproval compelled me to lower my feet and sit up straight.

"Thank you," Aunt Rachel said. Then, after a brief silence, "Jake, you know that machine can't be a part of this."

I didn't answer.

"I only want what's best for you. You know that." She coughed weakly, grimacing, and straightened herself in the powerchair.

The doctor had told me she was in extraordinary pain, but it was easy to forget. She did not speak of her illness; she refused pain medication.

I felt awful. I wanted to apologize to her. But this was an opportunity that might never again present itself. I said, "College will wait. I can go to college anytime."

"Every member of my family for two generations has been to college."

"I didn't say I wouldn't go. I said it would wait."

My aunt guided her chair to the broad windows that overlooked the front. I could see the caddy out there, more broken-down than ever, and on the knoll at the end of the long drive, the stand of maple overlooking the valley. I wondered what she could be thinking—if, like me, she was remembering the day she had brought me to this place, this home, and how she had paused up there to look out over the house and the land and to let me look out over them for the first time, too. I wondered what it had cost her to take me in, what it might cost her yet.

She said, "There are some things you should understand."

She did not turn around. I could see her gray hair, pulled into a loose bun, and the shawl she had taken to wearing across her shoulders even in July.

"Yes, ma'am?" I sought her eyes in the window, but her reflection shimmered, liquescent in the failing light.

She turned the chair and I cut my eyes to the sim, but he didn't say a word. He merely sat there, implacable and still, inhumanly so, watching.

My aunt cleared her throat. "Your father didn't leave much for you. He was a young man and hadn't much to leave. I don't have much either." She chuckled humorlessly. "I am an old woman, and I am sick. The doctors will have what remains to me. You understand?"

"But I can help. I can send you money. Some ballplayers make great money, more money than you can even imag—"

She held up her hand. "Not in the minors, Jake. What will you do if you injure yourself?"

"I can go to school if that happens."

"But how will you pay for it?"

I glanced at Ford, but the sim was quiet.

My aunt said, "Right now you have scholarship offers from three schools. If you injure yourself so you can't play ball that won't be true."

"And if I injure myself playing ball in school, I'll never play in the majors."

"In that case you'll have something to fall back on."

Again, there was silence. I stared at her resentfully for a

moment, and then I looked away. I studied the faded floral pattern on the rug and nagged at my lower lip with my teeth.

Aunt Rachel said, "It's decided, then?"

Before I could think, the words were out: "Nothing's decided. I'm eighteen. I can do what I want."

My aunt drew her eyebrows together. "Of course, that's true. If that's the way you feel, you'll do whatever you wish." She touched a button on her powerchair, wheeled around, and zoomed out of the room.

"Christ."

I stood, walked through the dining room to the kitchen, and went outside. The sky had begun to grow dark, stippled with the first incandescent points of stars. Somewhere, I knew, players were taking the diamond, uniforms shining in the glare of banked floodlights. I could almost hear the good-natured give and take of the infield chatter, the mercurial chorus of the fans.

Dry grass crackled behind me, and turning, I saw Ford, one half of his face limned yellow in the light from the house. Up close, he smelled of machine oil and rubber, stretched taut over burnished steel.

"Are you okay?"

I stared away into the memory-haunted yard. Here, here was the place where it had begun, my passion for the game. Here, where we had so often thrown the ball around, honing my skills until I could send the ball sizzling over the plate in a single smooth motion, like a dancer.

"I shouldn't have said that about doing whatever I want."

The sim stood beside me. A breeze came up, leavening the night heat. "What are you going to do?" Ford asked.

"I don't know. Go to school, I guess."

"I see."

We were silent for a few moments, watching fireflies stencil glowing trails through the darkness.

I said, "When I'm away, I'll miss you."

Ford cocked his head, something humming in his neck.

I said, "You'll take good care of her?"

"I will."

I raised a hand to the machine's shoulder and squeezed once, softly. I started back to the house. When I was halfway there, Ford said, "I'll miss you, too, Jake."

Smiling in the darkness, I said, "Thanks," and then I turned and went up the stairs and into the kitchen. I lay in my darkened bed-

room for a long while before I heard the whine of the screen door
and the sound of the sim coming into the house below.

The last time I saw the house in Stowes Corners, I was a senior in
college. I have not been back since.

But the moment lingers in my mind, as timeless as the day my
father was buried and Ford came to me in the humid stillness of a
Missouri noon. Once again, I am reminded of the archaeologist, his
search for the seams between the strata of the buried cities, built
pell-mell one atop the rubble of another. This, too, is such a
moment—a seam between the boy I had been, the man I would
become:

I was twenty-three, informed by a grief pervasive in its devastation.
My aunt had died two nights previous. A major stroke. Merciful, her
doctor had called it. Painless. But how could he have known?

Three of us gathered that afternoon—the minister; a probate
lawyer named Holdstock; myself. I had blown two week's work-study
salary on the flowers which stood in ranks about the open grave,
exuding a heady, cheerful perfume that seemed blasphemous. The
sun printed the shadows of the tombstones across the grass, and the
awning above us snapped in the breeze as the minister closed his
book.

Once again, I crumbled dry earth between my fingers. I listened
as it trickled against the coffin. Nothing changes.

I shook hands with the minister, walked the lawyer to his
Lincoln.

"Everything's taken care of?" I asked.

Holdstock smiled at the question, asked twice in as many hours.
"The auction's set for two weeks tomorrow. I'll be in touch."

We shook hands, and he opened his car door. He turned to look
at me, and an odd expression—half embarrassment, half determination—passed over his face. He tugged nervously at the lapels of
his dark jacket.

I knew what was coming.

"Listen," he said. "My boy's a big fan. He loves Tiger baseball. I
was wondering, could I—" He held a pad in his hand.

"Sure." He fished a pen out of his coat, and I scrawled my name
on the page.

"My boy has lots of autographs," he said. "We usually head down
to St. Louis for opening day and—" He shook his head. "Aw hell,
I'm sorry."

He held out his hand again, said, "Best of luck, Jake," and shut the door. The Lincoln pulled away. A drop of perspiration slid between my shoulder blades. I shrugged off my jacket, slung it over my shoulder, and surveyed the cemetery. Everything was still. Yellow earth-moving machinery waited behind a screen of trees; I was delaying the inevitable.

I got in my car and drove away from the town, into a region of summer-painted hills. The house was to be sold, the furnishings auctioned. Medical expenses had taken everything, just as Aunt Rachel had predicted. I'd made a list for Holdstock; the few things I wished to keep had been delivered to the hotel. For reasons I had avoided analyzing, I couldn't bring myself to stay at the house.

Now, however, the funeral behind me, those reasons lingered like uneasy specters in my mind. *You must never run away from the truth*, Aunt Rachel had told me. *Once you begin running, you can never stop.*

Before I had gone twenty-five miles, I cursed and pulled to the side of the road. With a kind of nauseating dread, I swung the car back toward town. There was unfinished business.

A realtor's sign stood at the head of the long drive, but when I emerged from the maples and paused atop the hill, I saw that everything was the same. It seemed as if no time at all had passed. I might have been a boy again. Steeling myself, I touched the gas and started down.

The locks had been freshly oiled, and my key sent the tumblers silently home. As I stepped inside, something whirred at my feet; an automaid sped around the corner, treads blurring. Bulky and low, it looked curiously antiquated; the newer models were sleek, silent, somehow disquieting.

I closed the door. Afternoon sunlight slanted through half-closed blinds. The hardwood shone with a merciless gloss, but everything else seemed faded. The floral-patterned rugs had been drained of color, and pale sheets glimmered over furniture earmarked for auction. I could smell the musty odor of stale air and enclosed spaces, and the lemony ghost of my aunt's furniture polish, somehow disconcerting. It was a house where no one lived anymore.

I found Ford upstairs in my old bedroom. He sat rigidly in the chair by the window, his broad unlined hands flat against his thighs. He looked just the same.

"I wondered if you would come," he said.

I examined the dim room, lit only by an exterior glare cleft into radiant shards by the blinds. An old Orioles pennant dangled from one tack on the far wall, but the room was otherwise devoid of personality. The photo albums where I'd kept my baseball cards were gone, stored now in the shelf over my desk in Columbia. Gone too were the photographs—my aunt, my father, my mother. They stood now on the end tables in my apartment. Nothing remained.

"I've been reading about you in the papers," Ford said.

"I'm the big news, I guess," I said.

"Do you have a contract yet?"

"Soon. We're negotiating." I shrugged.

The sim didn't say anything, so I crossed the room and lifted the blind and gazed into the backyard for a moment. A bird chirped in the eaves.

"When do you graduate?"

"August." I laughed. "She couldn't hang on to see it, you know."

"I'm sure she would have liked to."

"Wouldn't have mattered anyway, I suppose. I'll be on the road in rookie league by August."

"And then?"

"Who knows? I saw Haynes recently. Remember him? He said, 'You ain't an ace yet, son, but you're getting better.' I plan to make it."

"So the old dream is coming true," Ford said.

"I guess. We'll see."

I sat on the denuded mattress. In here, in the room where I had been a boy, the years seemed to have fallen away. I felt as fractured and alone as when I had been twelve years old, as much a stranger to this room and house. I could not help but recall the day the resurrection man had come, could not help but remember his dark suit and garish tie, his unpleasant stink of after-shave and tobacco. *It isn't right that a boy grow up without a man in the house*, Aunt Rachel had said, and now, remembering this I felt ice slide through my veins.

So this is what it all had come to.

I said, "I wanted to thank you. You've done everything for me."

"It's nothing," the sim said. "I understand."

We sat for a moment. Outside, the bird whistled merrily, as if it was the first bird, this the first day.

Ford turned to look at me, his neck swiveling with a hum so slight you could miss it if you weren't paying attention. He smiled, and I could hear tiny flywheels whir inside of him, and it all came back to me. Everything. The long days in the backyard, and Ford's strong hands gentle on my own, curving my fingers along the seams of the ball. The nights alone, here in this very room, when the darkness seemed to whirl and I could not remember my father's face. Ford—his vast intricacies, the thousand complicated mechanisms of his being—Ford had filled the void.

Ford said, "I didn't know about this part. I knew so much. They filled me up with so much knowledge about baseball and King Arthur and pirates and wars—all the things a boy might conceivably wish to know or learn. But they left this part out. I wonder if they knew?"

And then, for the first time, I thought of legacies. And though I did not say it, I thought: *They didn't know. How could they?*

But all I said was, "Nobody told me either."

I looked straight into his eyes, just as my aunt had taught me. "I'll be on the road a lot," I said, "there's nothing I can do. I'm sorry."

The sim smiled and bowed his head. The coarse hair at the base of his neck had neither grown nor been cut. It was the same color it had been always. And when he lifted a thick sheaf of it away, I saw what I knew I would see, what I had seen once before: a colored switch, like a tiny gem. The sunlight fell against it, and shattered into myriad colored fragments along the walls of the room.

Show me. I want to know, I had said all those years ago, and he had shown me, and I had seen that he was not my father, not even a man, but just a machine. A machine.

I reached out to the switch, touched it with trembling fingers, tensed to throw it home—

And if I do? I had asked him once.

Gone, he had told me. *Erased and irrecoverable. Everything that makes me me.*

Ford said, "We had some times, Jake."

"We had some times, Ford," I replied. "That's for sure."

And then I cut him off.

I remember it all. I remember the room as I saw it last, barren of everything that had made it mine. I remember Ford, slumped in the wooden chair, another lost possession—just furniture, awaiting auction. I turned away and walked down the stairs and through the foyer to the porch. I stood there for a long time, my eyes watering in the afternoon glare, and then I walked to the car and drove away.

I didn't look back.

But every day is a backwards glance. When I take the mound, I feel his fingers around my fingers, showing me the grips. And when I'm up by one in the ninth and the tying run is on third, it is his voice that I hear in my head.

I live in a fine house now, with my wife and son, and I play in Memorial Stadium more frequently than I might ever have hoped. My family attends every game.

But I have a recurrent dream.

In the dream, I stand on the mound, clutching a baseball and staring across the grass to the batter. The crowd is wild. If I look to the stands I can see them by the thousands, venting as one a full-throated roar. And with that enhanced acuity that comes to us in dreams, I see all the dead who are lost to me, scattered among the throng. The mother I could not know, the father I can barely re-member. Aunt Rachel. Ford. The resurrection man, who unknowing shaped my destiny, and left for me this legacy, its blessing and its curse.

The game rides on a single pitch. The bases are loaded, one out remains in the final inning, the count stands at three and two. I have to throw a strike.

But even as the pitch leaves my outstretched fingers, I know that it is poorly thrown. A slider, it hangs up on me, seeming almost to float. The batter steps close, shoulders tensing with the pressure as he delays the swing, and then, in the final moment before the ball is over the bag, he whips the bat around in a single blurring motion.

You can hear the impact all over the park.

The ball leaps skyward. The crowd noise surges to a crescendo, and holds there momentarily, battering, contusive. And then, all at once, it is gone.

Silence fills the stadium.

I wheel around to track the progress of the ball, a diminishing speck as it climbs higher, still higher. I watch as it begins its long descent through the quiet air, plunging toward the second deck. And that is when I notice: my mother and father, Aunt Rachel and Ford, the resurrection man himself—gone, all of them, gone. As far as I can see, the empty stands, the endless empty rows.

Death and Suffrage

IT'S FUNNY HOW THINGS HAPPEN, BURTON used to tell me. The very moment you're engaged in some task of mind-numbing insignificance—cutting your toenails, maybe, or fishing in the sofa for the remote—the world is being refashioned around you. You stand before a mirror to brush your teeth, and halfway around the planet flood waters are on the rise. Every minute of every day, the world transforms itself in ways you can hardly imagine, and there you are, sitting in traffic or wondering what's for lunch or just staring blithely out a window. History happens while you're making other plans, Burton always says.

I guess I know that now. I guess we all know that.

Me, I was in a sixth-floor Chicago office suite working on my résumé when it started. The usual chaos swirled around me— phones braying, people scurrying about, the televisions singing exit poll data over the din—but it all had a forced artificial quality. The campaign was over. Our numbers people had told us everything we needed to know: when the polls opened that morning, Stoddard was up seventeen points. So there I sat, dejected and soon to be unemployed, with my feet on a rented desk and my lap-top propped against my knees, mulling over synonyms for *directed*. As in *directed a staff of fifteen*. As in *directed public relations for the Democratic National Committee*. As in *directed a national political campaign straight into the toilet*.

Then CNN started emitting the little overture that means somewhere in the world history is happening, just like Burton always says.

I looked up as Lewis turned off the television.

"What'd you do that for?"

Lewis leaned over to shut my computer down. "I'll show you," he said.

I followed him through the suite, past clumps of people huddled around televisions. Nobody looked my way. Nobody had looked me in the eye since Sunday. I tried to listen, but over the shocked buzz in the room I couldn't catch much more than snatches of un-scripted anchor-speak. I didn't see Burton, and I supposed he was off drafting his concession speech. "No sense delaying the inev-itable," he had told me that morning.

"What gives?" I said to Lewis in the hall, but he only shook his head.

Lewis is a big man, fifty, with the drooping posture and hangdog expression of an adolescent. He stood in the elevator and watched the numbers cycle, rubbing idly at an acne scar. He had lots of them, a whole face pitted from what had to be among the worst teenage years in human history. I had never liked him much, and I liked him even less right then, but you couldn't help admiring the intelligence in his eyes. If Burton had been elected, Lewis would have served him well. Now he'd be looking for work instead.

The doors slid apart, and Lewis steered me through the lobby into a typical November morning in Chicago: a diamond-tipped wind boring in from the lake, a bruised sky spitting something that couldn't decide whether it wanted to be rain or snow. I grew up in southern California—my grandparents raised me—and there's not much I hate more than Chicago weather; but that morning I stood there with my shirt-sleeves rolled to the elbow and my tie whipping over my shoulder, and I didn't feel a thing.

"My God," I said, and for a moment, my mind just locked up. All I could think was that not two hours ago I had stood in this very spot watching Burton work the crowd, and then the world had still been sane. Afterwards, Burton had walked down the street to cast his ballot. When he stepped out of the booth, the press had been wait-ing. Burton charmed them, the consummate politician even in defeat. We could have done great things.

And even then the world had still been sane.

No longer.

It took me a moment to sort it all out—the pedestrians shoul-dering by with wild eyes, the bellhop standing dumbfounded before the hotel on the corner, his chin bobbing at half-mast. Three taxis had tangled up in the street, bleeding steam, and farther up the block loomed an overturned bus the size of a beached plesiosaur. Somewhere a woman was screaming atonally, over and over and over, with staccato hitches for breath. Sirens wailed in the distance. A TV crew was getting it all on tape, and for the first time since I blew Burton's chance to hold the highest office in the land, I stood in the presence of a journalist who wasn't shoving a mike in my face to ask me what had come over me.

I was too stunned even to enjoy it.

Instead, like Lewis beside me, I just stared across the street at the polling place. Dead people had gathered there, fifteen or twenty of them, and more arriving. Even then, there was never any question in my mind that they were dead. You could see it in the way they held their bodies, stiff as marionettes; in their shuffling gaits and the bright haunted glaze of their eyes. You could see it in the lacerations yawning open on the ropy coils of their guts, in their random nakedness, their haphazard clothes—hospital gowns and blood-stained blue jeans and immaculate suits fresh from unsealed caskets. You could see it in the dark patches of decay that blossomed on their flesh. You could just see that they were dead. It was every zombie movie you ever saw, and then some.

Goose flesh erupted along my arms, and it had nothing to do with the wind off Lake Michigan.

"My God," I said again, when I finally managed to unlock my brain. "What do they want?"

"They want to vote," said Lewis.

The dead have been voting in Chicago elections since long before Richard J. Daley took office, one wag wrote in the next morning's *Tribune, but yesterday's events bring a whole new meaning to the tradition.*

I'll say.

The dead had voted, all right, and not just in Chicago. They had risen from hospital gurneys and autopsy slabs, from open coffins and embalming tables in every precinct in the nation, and they had cast their ballots largely without interference. Who was going to stop them? More than half the poll-workers had abandoned ship when the zombies started shambling through the doors, and even workers who stayed at their posts had usually permitted them to do as they pleased. The dead didn't threaten anyone—they didn't do much of anything you'd expect zombies to do, in fact. But most people found that inscrutable gaze unnerving. Better to let them cast their ballots than bear for long the knowing light in those strange eyes.

And when the ballots were counted, we learned something else as well: They voted for Burton. Every last one of them voted for Burton.

"It's your fault," Lewis said at breakfast the next day.

Everyone else agreed with him, I could tell, the entire senior staff, harried and sleep-deprived. They studied their food as he ranted, or scrutinized the conference table or scribbled frantic notes in their day-planners. Anything to avoid looking me in the eye. Even Burton, alone at the head of the table, just munched on a bagel and stared at CNN, the muted screen aflicker with footage of zombies staggering along on their unfathomable errands. Toward dawn, as the final tallies rolled in from the western districts, they had started to gravitate toward cemeteries. No one yet knew why.

"My fault?" I said, but my indignation was manufactured. About five that morning, waking from nightmare in my darkened hotel room, I had arrived at the same conclusion as everyone else.

"The goddamn talk show," Lewis said, as if that explained everything.

And maybe it did.

The goddamn talk show in question was none other than *Crossfire* and the Sunday before the polls opened I got caught in it. I had broken the first commandment of political life, a commandment I had flogged relentlessly for the last year. Stay on message, stick to the talking points.

Thou shalt not speak from the heart.

The occasion of this amateurish mistake was a six-year-old girl named Dana Maguire. Three days before I went on the air, a five-year-old boy gunned Dana down in her after-school program. The kid had found the pistol in his father's night stand, and just as Dana's mother was coming in to pick her up, he tugged it from his insulated lunch sack and shot Dana in the neck. She died in her mother's arms while the five-year-old looked on in tears.

Just your typical day in America, except the first time I saw Dana's photo in the news, I felt something kick a hole in my chest. I can remember the moment to this day: October light slanting through hotel windows, the television on low while I talked to my grandmother in California. I don't have much in the way of family. There had been an uncle on my father's side, but he had drifted out of my life after my folks died, leaving my mother's parents to raise me. There's just the two of us since my grandfather passed on five years ago, and even in the heat of a campaign, I try to check on Gran every day. Mostly she rattles on about old folks in the home, a litany of names and ailments I can barely keep straight at the best of times. And that afternoon, half-watching some glib CNN hardbody do a stand-up in front of Little Tykes Academy, I lost the thread of her words altogether.

Next thing I know, she's saying, "Robert, Robert—" in this troubled voice, and me, I'm sitting on a hotel bed in Dayton, Ohio, weeping for a little girl I never heard of. Grief, shock, you name it— ten years in public life, nothing like that had ever happened to me before. But after that, I couldn't think of it in political terms. After that, Dana Maguire was personal.

Predictably, the whole thing came up on *Crossfire*. Joe Stern, Stoddard's campaign director and a man I've known for years, leaned into the camera and espoused the usual line—you know, the one about the constitutional right to bear arms, as if Jefferson had personally foreseen the rapid-fire semi-automatic with a sixteen-round clip. Coming from the mouth of Joe Stern, a smug, fleshy ideologue who ought to have known better, this line enraged me.

Even so, I hardly recognized the voice that responded to him. I felt as though something else was speaking through me—as though a voice had possessed me, a speaker from that broken hole in the center of my chest.

What it said, that voice, was: "If Grant Burton is elected, he'll see that every handgun in the United States is melted into pig iron. He'll do everything in his power to save the Dana Maguires of this nation."

Joe Stern puffed up like a toad. "This isn't about Dana Maguire—"

The voice interrupted him. "If there's any justice in the universe, Dana Maguire will rise up from her grave to haunt you," the voice said. It said, "If it's not about Dana Maguire, then what on Earth is it about?"

Stoddard had new ads in saturation before the day was out: Burton's face, my words in voice-over. *If Grant Burton is elected, he'll see that every handgun in the United States is melted into pig iron.* By Monday afternoon, we had plummeted six points and Lewis wasn't speaking to me.

I couldn't seem to shut him up now, though.

He leaned across the table and jabbed a thick finger at me, over-turning a Styrofoam cup of coffee. I watched the black pool spread as he shouted. "We were up five points, we had it won before you opened your goddamn—"

Angela Dey, our chief pollster, interrupted him. "Look!" she said, pointing at the television.

Burton touched the volume button on the remote, but the image on the screen was clear enough: a cemetery in upstate New York, one of the new ones where the stones are set flush to the earth to make mowing easier. Three or four zombies had fallen to their knees by a fresh grave.

"Good God," Dey whispered. "What are they doing?"

No one gave her an answer and I suppose she hadn't expected one. She could see as well as the rest of us what was happening. The dead were scrabbling at the earth with their bare hands.

A line from some old poem I had read in college—

—ahh, who's digging on my grave—

—lodged in my head, rattling around like angry candy, and for the first time I had a taste of the hysteria that would possess us all by the time this was done. Graves had opened, the dead walked the Earth. All humanity trembled.

Ahh, who's digging on my grave?

Lewis flung himself back against his chair and glared at me balefully. "This is all your fault."

"At least they voted for us," I said.

Not that we swept into the White House at the head of a triumphal procession of zombies. Anything but, actually. The voting rights of the dead turned out to be a serious constitutional question, and Stoddard lodged a complaint with the Federal Election Commission. Dead people had no say in the affairs of the living, he argued, and besides, none of them were legally registered anyway. Sensing defeat, the Democratic National Committee counter-sued, claiming that the sheer *presence* of the dead may have kept legitimate voters from the polls.

While the courts pondered these issues in silence, the world convulsed. Church attendance soared. The president impaneled experts and blue-ribbon commissions, the Senate held hearings. The CDC convened a task force to search for biological agents. At the UN, the Security Council debated a quarantine against the United States; the stock market lost fifteen percent on the news.

Meanwhile, the dead went unheeding about their business. They never spoke or otherwise attempted to communicate, yet you could sense an intelligence, inhuman and remote, behind their mass resurrection. They spent the next weeks opening fresh graves, releasing the recently buried from entombment. With bare hands, they clawed away the dirt; through sheer numbers, they battered apart the concrete vaults and sealed caskets. You would see them in the streets, stinking of formaldehyde and putrefaction, their hands torn and ragged, the rich earth of the grave impacted under their fingernails.

Their numbers swelled.

People died, but they didn't *stay* dead; the newly resurrected kept busy at their graves.

A week after the balloting, the Supreme Court handed down a decision overturning the election. Congress, meeting in emergency session, set a new date for the first week of January. If nothing else, the year 2000 debacle in Florida had taught us the virtue of speed.

Lewis came to my hotel room at dusk to tell me.

"We're in business," he said.

When I didn't answer, he took a chair across from me. We stared over the fog-shrouded city in silence. Far out above the lake, threads of rain seamed the sky. Good news for the dead. The digging would go easier.

Lewis turned the bottle on the table so he could read the label. I knew what it was: Glenfiddich, a good single malt. I'd been sipping it from a hotel tumbler most of the afternoon.

"Why'nt you turn on some lights in here?" Lewis said.

"I'm fine in the dark."

Lewis grunted. After a moment, he fetched the other glass. He wiped it out with his handkerchief and poured.

"So tell me."

Lewis tilted his glass, grimaced. "January fourth. The president signed the bill twenty minutes ago. Protective cordons fifty yards from polling stations. Only the living can vote. Jesus. I can't believe I'm even saying that." He cradled his long face in his hands. "So you in?"

"Does he want me?"

"Yes."

"What about you, Lewis? Do you want me?"

Lewis said nothing. We just sat there, breathing in the woodsy aroma of the scotch, watching night bleed into the sky.

"You screwed me at staff meeting the other day," I said. "You hung me out to dry in front of everyone. It won't work if you keep cutting the ground out from under my feet."

"Goddamnit, I was *right*. In ten seconds, you destroyed everything we've worked for. We had it won."

"Oh come on, Lewis. If *Crossfire* never happened, it could have gone either way. Five points, that's nothing. We were barely outside the plus and minus, you know that."

"Still. Why'd you have to say that?"

I thought about that strange sense I'd had at the time: another voice speaking through me. Mouthpiece of the dead.

"You ever think about that little girl, Lewis?"

He sighed. "Yeah. Yeah, I do." He lifted his glass. "Look. If you're angling for some kind of apology—"

"I don't want an apology."

"Good," he said. Then, grudgingly: "We need you on this one, Rob. You know that."

"January," I said. "That gives us almost two months."

"We're way up right now."

"Stoddard will make a run. Wait and see."

"Yeah." Lewis touched his face. It was dark, but I could sense the gesture. He'd be fingering his acne scars, I'd spent enough time with him to know that. "I don't know, though," he said. "I think the right might sit this one out. They think it's the fuckin' Rapture, who's got time for politics?"

"We'll see."

He took the rest of his scotch in a gulp and stood. "Yeah. We'll see."

I didn't move as he showed himself out, just watched his reflection in the big plate glass window. He opened the door and turned to look back, a tall man framed in light from the hall, his face lost in shadow.

"Rob?"

"Yeah?"

"You all right?"

I drained my glass and swished the scotch around in my mouth. I'm having a little trouble sleeping these days, I wanted to say. I'm having these dreams.

But all I said was, "I'm fine, Lewis. I'm just fine."

I wasn't, though, not really.

None of us were, I guess, but even now—maybe *especially* now—the thing I remember most about those first weeks is how little the resurrection of the dead altered our everyday lives. Isolated incidents made the news—I remember a serial killer being arrested as his victims heaved themselves bodily from their shallow backyard graves—but mostly people just carried on. After the initial shock, markets stabilized. Stores filled up with Thanksgiving turkeys;

radio stations began counting the shopping days until Christmas. Yet I think the hysteria must have been there all along, like a swift current just beneath the surface of a placid lake. An undertow, the kind of current that'll kill you if you're not careful. Most people looked okay, but scratch the surface and we were all going nuts in a thousand quiet ways.

Ahh, who's digging on my grave, and all that.

Me, I couldn't sleep. The stress of the campaign had been mounting steadily even before my meltdown on *Crossfire,* and in those closing days, with the polls in California—and all those lovely delegates—a hair too close to call, I'd been waking grainy-eyed and yawning every morning. I was feeling guilty, too. Three years ago, Gran broke her hip and landed in a Long Beach nursing home. And while I talked to her daily, I could never manage to steal a day or two to see her, despite all the time we spent campaigning in California.

But the resurrection of the dead marked a new era in my insomnia. Stumbling to bed late on election night, my mind blistered with images of zombies in the streets, I fell into a fevered dream. I found myself wandering through an abandoned city. Everything burned with the tenebrous significance of dreams—every brick and stone, the scraps of newsprint tumbling down high-rise canyons, the darkness pooling in the mouths of desolate subways. But the worst thing of all was the sound, the lone sound in all that sea of silence: the obscurely terrible cadence of a faraway clock, impossibly magnified, echoing down empty alleys and forsaken avenues.

The air rang with it, haunting me, drawing me on at last into a district where the buildings loomed over steep, close streets, admitting only a narrow wedge of sky. An open door beckoned, a black slot in a high, thin house. I pushed open the gate, climbed the broken stairs, paused in the threshold. A colossal grandfather clock towered within, its hands poised a minute short of midnight. Transfixed, I watched the heavy pendulum sweep through its arc, driving home the hour.

The massive hands stood upright.

The air shattered around me. The very stones shook as the clock began to toll. Clapping my hands over my ears, I turned to flee, but there was nowhere to go. In the yard, in the street—as far as I could see—the dead had gathered. They stood there while the clock stroked out the hours, staring up at me with those haunted eyes, and I knew suddenly and absolutely—the way you know things in dreams—that they had come for me at last, that they had always been coming for me, for all of us, if only we had known it.

I woke then, coldly afraid.

The first gray light of morning slit the drapes, but I had a premonition that no dawn was coming, or at least a very different dawn from any I had ever dared imagine.

Stoddard made his run with two weeks to go.

December fourteenth, we're 37,000 feet over the Midwest in a leased Boeing 737, and Angela Dey drops the new numbers on us.

"Gentleman," she says, "we've hit a little turbulence."

It was a turning point, I can see that now. At the time, though, none of us much appreciated her little joke.

The resurrection of the dead had shaken things up—it had put us on top for a month or so—but Stoddard had been clawing his way back for a couple of weeks, crucifying us in the farm belt on a couple of ag bills where Burton cast deciding votes, hammering us in the south on vouchers. We knew that, of course, but I don't think any of us had foreseen just how close things were becoming.

"We're up seven points in California," Dey said. "The gay vote's keeping our heads above water, but the numbers are soft. Stoddard's got momentum."

"Christ," Lewis said, but Dey was already passing around another sheet.

"It gets worse," she said. "Florida, we're up two points. A statistical dead heat. We've got the minorities, Stoddard has the seniors. Everything's riding on turnout."

Libby Dixon, Burton's press secretary, cleared her throat. "We've got a pretty solid network among Hispanics—"

Dey shook her head. "Seniors win that one every time."

"Hispanics *never* vote," Lewis said. "We might as well wrap Florida up with a little bow and send it to Stoddard."

Dey handed around another sheet. She'd orchestrated the moment for maximum impact, doling it out one sheet at a time like that. Lewis slumped in his seat, probing his scars as she worked her way through the list: Michigan, New York, Ohio, all three delegate rich, all three of them neck-and-neck races. Three almost physical blows, too, you could see them in the faces ranged around the table.

"What the hell's going on here?" Lewis muttered as Dey passed out another sheet, and then the news out of Texas rendered even him speechless. Stoddard had us by six points. I ran through a couple of Alamo analogies before deciding that discretion was the better part of wisdom. "I thought we were gaining there," Lewis said.

Dey shrugged. I just read the numbers, I don't make them up.

"Things could be worse," Libby Dixon said.

"Yeah, but Rob's not allowed to do *Crossfire* any more," Lewis said, and a titter ran around the table. Lewis is good, I'll give him that. You could feel the tension ease.

"Suggestions?" Burton said.

Dey said, "I've got some focus group stuff on education. I was thinking maybe some ads clarifying our—"

"Hell with the ads," someone else said, "we've gotta spend more time in Florida. We've got to engage Stoddard on his ground."

"Maybe a series of town meetings?" Lewis said, and they went around like that for a while. I tried to listen, but Lewis's little ice-breaker had reminded me of the dreams. I knew where I was— 37,000 feet of dead air below me, winging my way toward a rally in Virginia—but inside my head I hadn't gone anywhere at all. Inside my head, I was stuck in the threshold of that dream house, staring out into the eyes of the dead.

The world had changed irrevocably, I thought abruptly.

That seems self-evident, I suppose, but at the time it had the quality of genuine revelation. The fact is, we had all—and I mean everyone by that, the entire culture, not just the campaign—we had all been pretending that nothing much had changed. Sure, we had UN debates and a CNN feed right out of a George Romero movie, but the implications of mass resurrection—the spiritual implications—had yet to bear down upon us. We were in denial. In that moment, with the plane rolling underneath me and someone —Tyler O'Neill I think it was, Libby Dixon's mousy assistant— droning on about going negative, I thought of something I'd heard a professor mention back at Northwestern: Copernicus formulated the heliocentric model of the solar system in the mid-1500s, but the Church didn't get around to punishing anyone for it until they threw Galileo in jail nearly a hundred years later. They spent the better part of a century trying to ignore the fact that the fundamental geography of the universe had been altered with a single stroke.

And so it had again.

The dead walked.

Three simple words, but everything else paled beside them— social security, campaign finance reform, education vouchers. *Everything.*

I wadded Dey's sheet into a noisy ball and flung it across the table. Tyler O'Neill stuttered and choked, and for a moment everyone just stared in silence at that wad of paper. You'd have thought

DEATH AND SUFFRAGE   45

I'd hurled a hand grenade, not a two paragraph summary of voter idiocy in the Lonestar state.

Libby Dixon cleared her throat. "I hardly thin—"

"Shut up, Libby," I said. "Listen to yourselves for Christ's sake. We got zombies in the street and you guys are worried about going negative?"

"The whole . . ." Dey flapped her hand. ". . . zombie thing, it's not even on the radar. My numbers—"

"People *lie*, Angela."

Libby Dixon swallowed audibly.

"When it comes to death, sex, and money, everybody lies. A total stranger calls up on the telephone, and you expect some soccer mom to share her feelings about the fact that grandpa's rotten corpse is staggering around in the street?"

I had their attention all right.

For a minute the plane filled up with the muted roar of the engines. No human sound at all. And then Burton—Burton smiled.

"What are you thinking, Rob?"

"A great presidency is a marriage between a man and a moment," I said. "You told me that. Remember?"

"I remember."

"This is your moment, sir. You have to stop running away from it."

"What do you have in mind?" Lewis asked.

I answered the question, but I never even looked Lewis's way as I did it. I just held Grant Burton's gaze. It was like no one else was there at all, like it was just the two of us, and despite everything that's happened since, that's the closest I've ever come to making history.

"I want to find Dana Maguire," I said.

I'd been in politics since my second year at Northwestern. It was nothing I ever intended—who goes off to college hoping to be a senate aide?—but I was idealistic, and I liked the things Grant Burton stood for, so I found myself working the phones that fall as an unpaid volunteer. One thing led to another—an internship on the Hill, a post-graduate job as a research assistant—and somehow I wound up inside the Beltway.

I used to wonder how my life might have turned out had I chosen another path. My senior year at Northwestern, I went out with a girl named Gwen, a junior, freckled and streaky blonde, with the kind of sturdy good looks that fall a hair short of beauty. Partnered in some forgettable lab exercise, we found we had grown up within a half hour of one another. Simple geographic coincidence, two Californians stranded in the frozen north, sustained us throughout the winter and into the spring. But we drifted in the weeks after graduation, and the last I had heard of her was a Christmas card five or six years back. I remember opening it and watching a scrap of paper slip to the floor. Her address and phone number, back home in Laguna Beach, with a little note. *Call me some time*, it said, but I never did.

So there it was.

I was thirty-two years old, I lived alone, I'd never held a relationship together longer than eight months. Gran was my closest friend, and I saw her three times a year if I was lucky. I went to my ten-year class reunion in Evanston, and everybody there was in a different life-place than I was. They all had kids and homes and churches.

Me, I had my job. Twelve hour days, five days a week. Saturdays I spent three or four hours at the office catching up. Sundays I watched the talk shows and then it was time to start all over again. That had been my routine for nearly a decade, and in all those years I never bothered to ask myself how I came to be there. It never even struck me as the kind of thing a person ought to ask.

Four years ago, during Burton's reelection campaign for the Senate, Lewis said a funny thing to me. We're sitting in a hotel bar, drinking Miller Lite and eating peanuts, when he turns to me and says, "You got anyone, Rob?"

"Got anyone?"

"You know, a girl friend, a fiancée, somebody you care about."

Gwen flickered at the edge of my consciousness, but that was all. A flicker, nothing more.

I said, "No."

"That's good," Lewis said.

It was just the kind of thing he always said, sarcastic, a little mean-hearted. Usually I let it pass, but that night I had just enough alcohol zipping through my veins to call him on it.

"What's that supposed to mean?"

Lewis turned to look at me.

"I was going to say, you have someone you really care about—somebody you want to spend your life with—you might want to walk away from all this."

"Why's that?"

"This job doesn't leave enough room for relationships."

He finished his beer and pushed the bottle away, his gaze steady and clear. In the dim light his scars were invisible, and I saw him then as he could have been in a better world. For maybe a moment, Lewis was one step short of handsome.

And then the moment broke.

"Good night," he said, and turned away.

A few months after that—not long before Burton won his second six-year Senate term—Libby Dixon told me Lewis was getting a divorce. I suppose he must have known the marriage was coming apart around him.

But at the time nothing like that even occurred to me.

After Lewis left, I just sat at the bar running those words over in my mind. *This job doesn't leave much room for relationships*, he had said, and I knew he had intended it as a warning. But what I felt instead was a bottomless sense of relief. I was perfectly content to be alone.

Burton was doing an event in St. Louis when the nursing home called to say that Gran had fallen again. Eighty-one-year-old bones are fragile, and the last time I had been out there—just after the convention—Gran's case manager had privately informed me that another fall would probably do it.

"Do what?" I had asked.

The case manager looked away. She shuffled papers on her desk while her meaning bore in on me: another fall would kill her.

I suppose I must have known this at some level, but to hear it articulated so baldly shook me. From the time I was four, Gran had been the single stable institution in my life. I had been visiting in Long Beach, half a continent from home, when my family—my parents and sister—died in the car crash. It took the state police back in Pennsylvania nearly a day to track me down. I still remember the moment: Gran's masklike expression as she hung up the phone, her hands cold against my face as she knelt before me.

She made no sound as she wept. Tears spilled down her cheeks, leaving muddy tracks in her make-up, but she made no sound at all. "I love you, Robert," she said. She said, "You must be strong."

That's my first true memory.

Of my parents, my sister, I remember nothing at all. I have a snapshot of them at a beach somewhere, maybe six months before I was born: my father lean and smoking, my mother smiling, her abdomen just beginning to swell. In the picture, Alice—she would have been four then—stands just in front of them, a happy blond child cradling a plastic shovel. When I was a kid I used to stare at that photo, wondering how you can miss people you never even knew. I did though, an almost physical ache way down inside me, the kind of phantom pain amputees must feel.

A ghost of that old pain squeezed my heart as the case manager told me about Gran's fall. "We got lucky," she said. "She's going to be in a wheelchair a month or two, but she's going to be okay."

Afterwards, I talked to Gran herself, her voice thin and querulous, addled with pain killers. "Robert," she said, "I want you to come out here. I want to see you."

"I want to see you, too," I said, "but I can't get away right now. As soon as the election's over—"

"I'm an old woman," she told me crossly. "I may not be here after the election."

I managed a laugh at that, but the laugh sounded hollow even in my own ears. The words had started a grim little movie unreeling in my head—a snippet of Gran's cold body staggering to its feet, that somehow inhuman tomb light shining out from behind its eyes. I suppose most of us must have imagined something like that during those weeks, but it unnerved me all the same. It reminded me too much of the dreams. It felt like I was there again, gazing out into the faces of the implacable dead, that enormous clock banging out the hours.

"Robert—" Gran was saying, and I could hear the Demerol singing in her voice. "Are you there, Ro—"

And for no reason at all, I said:

"Did my parents have a clock, Gran?"

"A clock?"

"A grandfather clock."

She was silent so long I thought maybe *she* had hung up.

"That was your uncle's clock," she said finally, her voice thick and distant.

"My uncle?"

"Don," she said. "On your father's side."

"What happened to the clock?"

"Robert, I want you to come out he—"

"*What happened to the clock, Gran?*"

"Well, how would I know?" she said. "He couldn't keep it, could he? I suppose he must have sold it."

"What do you mean?"

But she didn't answer.

I listened to the swell and fall of Demerol sleep for a moment, and then the voice of the case manager filled my ear. "She's drifted off. If you want, I can call back later—"

I looked up as a shadow fell across me. Lewis stood in the doorway.

"No, that's okay. I'll call her in the morning."

I hung up the phone and stared over the desk at him. He had a strange expression on his face.

"What?" I said.

"It's Dana Maguire."

"What about her?"

"They've found her."

Eight hours later, I touched down at Logan under a cloudy midnight sky. We had hired a private security firm to find her, and one of their agents—an expressionless man with the build of an ex-athlete—met me at the gate.

"You hook up with the ad people all right?" I asked in the car, and from the way he answered, a monosyllabic "Fine," you could tell what he thought of ad people.

"The crew's in place?"

"They're already rigging the lights."

"How'd you find her?"

He glanced at me, streetlight shadow rippling across his face like water. "Dead people ain't got much imagination. Soon's we get the fresh ones in the ground, they're out there digging." He laughed humorlessly. "You'd think people'd stop burying 'em."

"It's the ritual, I guess."

"Maybe." He paused. Then: "Finding her, we put some guys on the cemeteries and kept our eyes open, that's all."

"Why'd it take so long?"

For a moment there was no sound in the car but the hum of tires on pavement and somewhere far away a siren railing against the night. The agent rolled down his window and spat emphatically into the slipstream. "City the size of Boston," he said, "it has a lot of fucking cemeteries."

The cemetery in question turned out to be everything I could have hoped for: remote and unkempt, with weathered Gothic tombstones right off a Hollywood back lot. And wouldn't it be comforting to think so, I remember thinking as I got out of the car— the ring of lights atop the hill nothing more than stage dressing, the old world as it had been always. But it wasn't, of course, and the ragged figures digging at the grave weren't actors, either. You could smell them for one, the stomach-wrenching stench of decay. A light rain had begun to fall, too, and it had the feel of a genuine Boston drizzle, cold and steady toward the bleak fag end of December.

Andy, the director, turned when he heard me.

"Any trouble?" I asked.

"No. They don't care much what we're about, long as we don't interfere."

"Good."

Andy pointed. "There she is, see?"

"Yeah, I see her."

She was on her knees in the grass, still wearing the dress she had been buried in. She dug with single-minded intensity, her arms caked with mud to the elbow, her face empty of anything remotely human. I stood and stared at her for a while, trying to decide what it was I was feeling.

"You all right?" Andy said.

"What?"

"I said, are you all right? For a second there, I thought you were crying."

"No," I said. "I'm fine. It's the rain, that's all."

"Right."

So I stood there and half-listened while he filled me in. He had several cameras running, multiple filters and angles, he was playing with the lights. He told me all this and none of it meant anything at all to me. None of it mattered as long as I got the footage I wanted. Until then, there was nothing for me here.

He must have been thinking along the same lines, for when I turned to go, he called after me: "Say, Rob, you needn't have come out tonight, you know."

I looked back at him, the rain pasting my hair against my forehead and running down into my eyes. I shivered. "I know," I said. A moment later, I added: "I just—I wanted to see her somehow."

But Andy had already turned away.

I still remember the campaign ad, my own private nightmare dressed up in cinematic finery. Andy and I cobbled it together on Christmas Eve, and just after midnight in a darkened Boston studio, we cracked open a bottle of bourbon in celebration and sat back to view the final cut. I felt a wave of nausea roll over me as the first images flickered across the monitor. Andy had shot the whole thing from distorted angles in grainy black and white, the film just a hair over-exposed to sharpen the contrast. Sixty seconds of derivative expressionism, some media critic dismissed it, but even he conceded it possessed a certain power.

You've seen it, too, I suppose. Who hasn't?

She will rise from her grave to haunt you, the opening title card reads, and the image holds in utter silence for maybe half a second too long. Long enough to be unsettling, Andy said, and you could imagine distracted viewers all across the heartland perking up, wondering what the hell was wrong with the sound.

The words dissolve into an image of hands, bloodless and pale, gouging at moist black earth. The hands of a child, battered and raw and smeared with the filth and corruption of the grave, digging, digging. There's something remorseless about them, something relentless and terrible. They could dig forever, and they might, you can see that. And now, gradually, you awaken to sound: rain hissing from a midnight sky, the steady slither of wet earth underhand, and something else, a sound so perfectly lacking that it's almost palpable in its absence, the unearthly silence of the dead. Freeze frame on a tableau out of Goya or Bosch: seven or eight zombies, half-dressed and rotting, laboring tirelessly over a fresh grave.

Fade to black, another slug line, another slow dissolve.

Dana Maguire came back.

The words melt into a long shot of the child, on her knees in the poison muck of the grave. Her dress clings to her thighs, and it's a dress someone has taken some care about—white and lacy, the kind of dress you'd bury your little girl in if you had to do it—and it's ruined. All the care and heartache that went into that dress, utterly ruined. Torn and fouled and sopping. Rain slicks her blond hair black against her skull. And as the camera glides in upon Dana Maguire's face, half-shadowed and filling three-quarters of the screen, you can glimpse the wound at her throat, flushed clean and pale. Dark roses of rot bloom along the high ridge of her cheekbone. Her eyes burn with the cold hard light of vistas you never want to see, not even in your dreams.

The image holds for an instant, a mute imperative, and then, mercifully, fades. Words appear and deliquesce on an ebon screen, three phrases, one by one:

The dead have spoken.

Now it's your turn.

Burton for president.

Andy touched a button. A reel caught and reversed itself. The screen went gray, and I realized I had forgotten to breathe. I sipped at my drink.

The whiskey burned in my throat, it made me feel alive.

"What do you think?" Andy said.

"I don't know. I don't know what to think."

Grinning, he ejected the tape and tossed it in my lap. "Merry Christmas," he said, raising his glass. "To our savior born."

And so we drank again.

Dizzy with exhaustion, I made my way back to my hotel and slept for eleven hours straight. I woke around noon on Christmas day. An hour later, I was on a plane.

By the time I caught up to the campaign in Richmond, Lewis was in a rage, pale and apoplectic, his acne scars flaring an angry red. "You seen these?" he said, thrusting a sheaf of papers at me.

I glanced through them quickly—more bad news from Angela Dey, Burton slipping further in the polls—and then I set them aside. "Maybe this'll help," I said, holding up the tape Andy and I had cobbled together.

We watched it together, all of us, Lewis and I, the entire senior staff, Burton himself, his face grim as the first images flickered across the screen. Even now, viewing it for the second time, I could feel its impact. And I could see it in the faces of the others as well—Dey's jaw dropping open, Lewis snorting in disbelief. As the screen froze on the penultimate image—Dana Maguire's decay-ravaged face—Libby Dixon turned away.

"There's no way we can run that," she said.

"We've got—" I began, but Dey interrupted me.

"She's right, Rob. It's not a campaign ad, it's a horror movie." She turned to Burton, drumming his fingers quietly at the head of the table. "You put this out there, you'll drop ten points, I guarantee it."

"Lewis?" Burton asked.

Lewis pondered the issue for a moment, rubbing his pitted cheek with one crooked finger. "I agree," he said finally. "The ad's a frigging nightmare. It's not the answer."

"The ad's revolting," Libby said. "The media will eat us alive for politicizing the kid's death."

"We *ought* to be politicizing it," I said. "We ought to make it mean something."

"You run that ad, Rob," Lewis said, "every redneck in America is going to remember you threatening to take away their guns. You want to make that mistake twice?"

"Is it a mistake? For Christ's sake, the dead are walking, Lewis.

The old rules don't apply." I turned to Libby. "What's Stoddard say, Libby, can you tell me that?"

"He hasn't touched it since Election Day."

"Exactly. He hasn't said a thing, not about Dana Maguire, not about the dead people staggering around in the street. Ever since the FEC overturned the election, he's been dodging the issue—"

"Because it's political suicide," Dey said. "He's been dodging it because it's the right thing to do."

"Bullshit," I snapped. "It's *not* the right thing to do. It's pandering and it's cowardice—it's moral cowardice—and if we do it we deserve to lose."

You could hear everything in the long silence that ensued—cars passing in the street, a local staffer talking on the phone in the next room, the faint tattoo of Burton's fingers against the Formica table top. I studied him for a moment, and once again I had that sense of something else speaking through me, as though I were merely a conduit for another voice.

"What do you think about guns, sir?" I asked. "What do you really think?"

Burton didn't answer for a long moment. When he did, I think he surprised everyone at the table. "The death rate by handguns in this country is triple that for every other industrialized nation on the planet," he said. "They ought to be melted into pig iron, just like Rob said. Let's go with the ad."

"Sir—" Dey was standing.

"I've made up my mind," Burton said. He picked up the sheaf of papers at his elbow and shuffled through them. "We're down in Texas and California, we're slipping in Michigan and Ohio." He tossed the papers down in disgust. "Stoddard looks good in the south, Angela. What do we got to lose?"

We couldn't have timed it better.

The new ad went into national saturation on December 30th, in the shadow of a strange new year. I was watching a bowl game in my hotel room the first time I saw it on the air. It chilled me all over, as though I'd never seen it before. Afterwards, the room filled with the sound of the ball game, but now it all seemed hollow. The cheers of the fans rang with a labored gaiety, the crack of pads had the crisp sharpness of movie sound effects. A barb of loneliness pierced me. I would have called someone, but I had no one to call.

Snapping off the television, I pocketed my key-card.

Downstairs, the same football game was playing, but at least there was liquor and a ring of conversation in the air. A few media folks from Burton's entourage clustered around the bar, but I begged off when they invited me to join them. I sat at a table in the corner instead, staring blindly at the television and drinking scotch without any hurry, but without any effort to keep track either. I don't know how much I drank that night, but I was a little unsteady when I stood to go.

I had a bad moment on the way back to my room. When the elevator doors slid apart, I found I couldn't remember my room number. I couldn't say for sure I had even chosen the right floor. The hotel corridor stretched away before me, bland and anonymous, a hallway of locked doors behind which only strangers slept. The endless weary grind of the campaign swept over me, and suddenly I was sick of it all—the long midnight flights and the hotel laundries, the relentless blur of cities and smiling faces. I wanted more than anything else in the world to go home. Not my cramped apartment in the District either.

Home. Wherever that was.

Independent of my brain, my fingers had found my key-card. I tugged it from my pocket and studied it grimly. I had chosen the right floor after all.

Still in my clothes, I collapsed across my bed and fell asleep. I don't remember any dreams, but sometime in the long cold hour before dawn, the phone yanked me awake. "Turn on CNN," Lewis said. I listened to him breathe as I fumbled for the remote and cycled through the channels.

I punched up the volume.

"—unsubstantiated reports out of China concerning newly awakened dead in remote regions of the Tibetan Plateau—"

I was awake now, fully awake. My head pounded. I had to work up some spit before I could speak.

"Anyone got anything solid?" I asked.

"I'm working with a guy in State for confirmation. So far we got nothing but rumor."

"If it's true—"

"If it's true," Lewis said, "you're gonna look like a fucking genius."

Our numbers were soft in the morning, but things were looking up by mid-afternoon. The Chinese weren't talking and no one yet had footage of the Tibetan dead—but rumors were trickling in from around the globe. Unconfirmed reports from U.N. Peacekeepers in

Kosovo told of women and children clawing their way free from previously unknown mass graves.

By New Year's Day, rumors gave away to established fact. The television flickered with grainy images from Groznyy and Addis Ababa. The dead were arising in scattered locales around the world. And here at home, the polls were shifting. Burton's crowds grew larger and more enthusiastic at every rally, and as our jet winged down through the night toward Pittsburgh, I watched Stoddard answering questions about the crisis on a satellite feed from C-SPAN. He looked gray and tired, his long face brimming with uncertainty. He was too late, we owned the issue now, and watching him, I could see he knew it, too. He was going through the motions, that's all.

There was a celebratory hum in the air as the plane settled to the tarmac. Burton spoke for a few minutes at the airport, and then the Secret Service people tightened the bubble, moving us en masse toward the motorcade. Just before he ducked into the limo, Burton dismissed his entourage. His hand closed about my shoulder. "You're with me," he said.

He was silent as the limo slid away into the night, but as the downtown towers loomed up before us he turned to look at me. "I wanted to thank you," he said.

"There's no—"

He held up his hand. "I wouldn't have had the courage to run that ad, not without you pushing me. I've wondered about that, you know. It was like you knew something, like you knew the story was getting ready to break again."

I could sense the question behind his words—*Did you know, Rob? Did you?*—but I didn't have any answers. Just that impression of a voice speaking through me from beyond, from somewhere else, and that didn't make any sense, or none that I was able to share.

"When I first got started in this business," Burton was saying, "there was a local pol back in Chicago, kind of a mentor. He told me once you could tell what kind of man you were dealing with by the people he chose to surround himself with. When I think about that, I feel good, Rob." He sighed. "The world's gone crazy, that's for sure, but with people like you on our side, I think we'll be all right. I just wanted to tell you that."

"Thank you, sir."

He nodded. I could feel him studying me as I gazed out the window, but suddenly I could find nothing to say. I just sat there and watched the city slide by, the past welling up inside me. Unpleasant truths lurked like rocks just beneath the visible surface. I could sense them somehow.

"You all right, Rob?"

"Just thinking," I said. "Being in Pittsburgh, it brings back memories."

"I thought you grew up in California."

"I did. I was born here, though. I lived here until my parents died."

"How old were you?"

"Four. I was four years old."

We were at the hotel by then. As the motorcade swung across two empty lanes into the driveway, Gran's words—

—*that was your uncle's clock, he couldn't keep it*—

—sounded in my head. The limo eased to the curb. Doors slammed. Agents slid past outside, putting a protective cordon around the car. The door opened, and cold January air swept in. Burton was gathering his things.

"Sir—"

He paused, looking back.

"Tomorrow morning, could I have some time alone?"

He frowned. "I don't know, Rob, the schedule's pretty tight—"

"No, sir. I mean—I mean a few hours off."

"Something wrong?"

"There's a couple of things I'd like to look into. My parents and all that. Just an hour or two if you can spare me."

He held my gaze a moment longer.

Then: "That's fine, Rob." He reached out and squeezed my shoulder. "Just be at the airport by two."

That night I dreamed of a place that wasn't quite Dana Maguire's daycare. It *looked* like a daycare—half a dozen squealing kids, big plastic toys, an indestructible grade of carpet—but certain details didn't fit: the massive grandfather clock, my uncle's clock, standing in one corner; my parents, dancing to big band music that seemed to emanate from nowhere.

I was trying to puzzle this through when I saw the kid clutching the lunch sack. There was an odd expression on his face, a haunted heart-broken expression, and too late I understood what was about to happen. I tried to move, to scream, anything, as he dragged the pistol out of the bag. But my lips were sealed, I couldn't speak. Glancing down, I saw that I was rooted to the floor. Literally *rooted*. My bare feet had grown these long knotted tendrils. The carpet was twisted and raveled where they had driven themselves into the floor. My parents whirled about in an athletic fox-trot, their faces manic with laughter. The music was building to an awful crescendo, percussives bleeding seamlessly together, the snap of the snare drums, the terrible booming tones of the clock, the quick sharp report of the gun.

I saw the girl go over backwards, her hands clawing at her throat as she convulsed. Blood drenched me, a spurting arterial fountain —I could feel it hot against my skin—and in the same moment this five-year-old kid turned to stare at me. Tears streamed down his cheeks, and this kid—this child really, and that's all I could seem to think—

—*he's just a child he's only a child*—

—he had my face.

I woke then, stifling a scream. Silence gripped the room and the corridor beyond it, and beyond that the city. I felt as if the world itself were drowning, sunk fathoms deep in the fine and private silence of the grave.

I stood, brushing the curtains aside. An anonymous grid of lights burned beyond the glass, an alien hieroglyph pulsing with enigmatic significance. Staring out at it, I was seized by an impression of how fragile everything is, how thin the barrier that separates us from the abyss. I shrank from the window, terrified by a sense that the world was far larger—and immeasurably stranger—than the world I'd known before, a sense of vast and formless energies churning out there in the dark.

I spent the next morning in the Carnegie Library in Oakland, reeling through back issues of the *Post-Gazette*. It didn't take long to dig up the article about the accident—I knew the date well enough— but I wasn't quite prepared for what I found there. Gran had always been reticent about the wreck—about everything to do with my life in Pittsburgh, actually—but I'd never really paused to give that much thought. She'd lost her family, too, after all—a granddaughter, a son-in-law, her only child—and even as a kid, I could see why she might not want to talk about it.

The headline flickering on the microfilm reader rocked me, though. *Two die in fiery collision*, it read, and before I could properly formulate the question in my mind—

—*there were three of them*—

—I was scanning the paragraphs below. Disconnected phrases seemed to hover above the cramped columns—bridge abutment, high speed, alcohol-related—and halfway through the article, the following words leapt out at me:

> Friends speculate that the accident may have been
> the product of a suicide pact. The couple were
> said to be grief-stricken following the death of
> their daughter, Alice, nine, in a bizarre shooting
> accident three weeks ago.

I stood, abruptly nauseated, afraid to read any further. A docent approached—

"Sir, are you all—"

—but I thrust her away.

Outside, traffic lumbered by, stirring the slush on Forbes Avenue. I sat on a bench and fought the nausea for a long time, cradling my face in my hands while I waited for it to pass. A storm was drifting in, and when I felt better I lifted my face to the sky, anxious for the icy burn of snow against my cheeks. Somewhere in the city, Grant Burton was speaking. Somewhere, reanimated corpses scrabbled at frozen graves.

The world lurched on.

I stood, belting my coat. I had a plane to catch.

I held myself together for two days, during our final campaign swing through the Midwest on January 3 and the election that followed, but I think I had already arrived at a decision. Most of the senior staff sensed it, as well, I think. They congratulated me on persuading Burton to run the ad, but they didn't come to me for advice much in those final hours. I seemed set-apart somehow, isolated, contagious.

Lewis clapped me on the back as we watched the returns roll in. "Jesus, Rob," he said, "you're supposed to be happy right now."

"Are you, Lewis?"

I looked up at him, his tall figure slumped, his face a fiery map of scars.

"What did you give up to get us here?" I asked, but he didn't answer. I hadn't expected him to.

The election unfolded without a hitch. Leaving off their work in the grave yards, the dead gathered about the polling stations, but even they seemed to sense that the rules had changed this time around. They made no attempt to cast their ballots. They just stood behind the cordons the National Guard had set up, still and silent, regarding the proceedings with flat, remorseless eyes. Voters scurried past them with bowed heads, their faces pinched against the stench of decay. On *Nightline*, Ted Koppel noted that the balloting had drawn the highest turnout in American history, something like ninety-three percent.

"Any idea why so many voters came out today?" he asked the panel.

"Maybe they were afraid not to," Cokie Roberts replied, and I felt an answering chord vibrate within me. Trust Cokie to get it right.

Stoddard conceded soon after the polls closed in the west. It was obvious by then. In his victory speech, Burton talked about a mandate for change. "The people have spoken," he said, and they had, but I couldn't help wondering what might be speaking through them, and what it might be trying to say. Some commentators speculated that it was over now. The dead would return to the graves, the world would be the old world we had known.

But that's not the way it happened.

On January 5th, the dead were digging once again, their numbers always swelling. CNN was carrying the story when I handed Burton my resignation. He read it slowly and then he lifted his gaze to my face.

"I can't accept this, Rob," he said. "We need you now. The hard work's just getting underway."

"I'm sorry, sir. I haven't any choice."

"Surely we can work something out."

"I wish we could."

We went through several iterations of this exchange before he nodded. "We'll miss you," he said. "You'll always have a place here, whenever you're ready to get back in the game."

I was at the door when he called to me again.

"Is there anything I can do to help, Rob?"

"No, sir," I said. "I have to take care of this myself."

I spent a week in Pittsburgh, walking the precipitous streets of neighborhoods I remembered only in my dreams. I passed a morning hunting up the house where my parents had lived, and one bright, cold afternoon I drove out 76 and pulled my rental to the side of the interstate, a hundred yards short of the bridge where they died. Eighteen wheelers thundered past, throwing up glittering arcs of spray, and the smell of the highway enveloped me, diesel and iron. It was pretty much what I had expected, a slab of faceless concrete, nothing more.

Evenings, I took solitary meals in diners and talked to Gran on the telephone—tranquil gossip about the old folks in the home mostly, empty of anything real. Afterwards, I drank Iron City and watched cable movies until I got drunk enough to sleep. I ignored the news as best I could, but I couldn't help catching glimpses as I buzzed through the channels. All around the world, the dead were walking.

They walked in my dreams, as well, stirring memories better left forgotten. Mornings, I woke with a sense of dread, thinking of Galileo, thinking of the Church. I had urged Burton to engage this brave new world, yet the thought of embracing such a fundamental transformation of my own history—of following through on the article in the *Post-Gazette*, the portents within my dreams—paralyzed me utterly. I suppose it was by then a matter mostly of verifying my own fears and suspicions—suppose I already knew, at some level, what I had yet to confirm. But the lingering possibility of doubt was precious, safe, and I clung to it for a few days longer, unwilling to surrender.

Finally, I could put it off no longer.

I drove down to the Old Public Safety Building on Grant Street. Upstairs, a grizzled receptionist brought out the file I requested. It was all there in untutored bureaucratic prose. There was a sheaf of official photos, too, glossy black and white prints. I didn't want to look at them, but I did anyway. I felt it was something I ought to do.

A little while later, someone touched my shoulder. It was the receptionist, her broad face creased with concern. Her spectacles swung at the end of a little silver chain as she bent over me. "You all right?" she asked.

"Yes, ma'am, I'm fine."

I stood, closing the file, and thanked her for her time.

I left Pittsburgh the next day, shedding the cold as the plane nosed above a lid of cloud. From LAX, I caught the 405 South to Long Beach. I drove with the window down, grateful for the warmth upon my arm, the spike of palm fronds against the sky. The slipstream carried the scent of a world blossoming and fresh, a future yet unmade, a landscape less scarred by history than the blighted industrial streets I'd left behind.

Yet even here the past lingered. It was the past that had brought me here, after all.

The nursing home was a sprawl of landscaped grounds and low-slung stucco buildings, faintly Spanish in design. I found Gran in a garden overlooking the Pacific, and I paused, studying her, before she noticed me in the doorway. She held a paperback in her lap, but she had left off reading to stare out across the water. A salt-laden breeze lifted her gray hair in wisps, and for a moment, looking at her, her eyes clear in her distinctly boned face, I could find my way back to the woman I had known as a boy.

But the years intervened, the way they always do. In the end, I couldn't help noticing her wasted body, or the glittering geometry of the wheelchair that enclosed her. Her injured leg jutted before her.

I must have sighed, for she looked up, adjusting the angle of the chair. "Robert!"

"Gran."

I sat by her, on a concrete bench. The morning overcast was breaking, and the sun struck sparks from the wave-tops.

"I'd have thought you were too busy to visit," she said, "now that your man has won the election."

"I'm not so busy these days. I don't work for him anymore."

"What do you mean—"

"I mean I quit my job."

"Why?" she said.

"I spent some time in Pittsburgh. I've been looking into things."

"Looking into things? Whatever on Earth is there to look *into*, Robert?" She smoothed the Afghan covering her thighs, her fingers trembling.

I laid my hand across them, but she pulled away. "Gran, we need to talk."

"Talk?" She laughed, a bark of forced gaiety. "We talk every day."

"Look at me," I said, and after a long moment, she did. I could see the fear in her eyes, then. I wondered how long it had been there, and why I'd never noticed it before. "We need to talk about the past."

"The past is dead, Robert."

Now it was my turn to laugh. "Nothing's dead, Gran. Turn on the television sometime. Nothing stays dead anymore. *Nothing.*"

"I don't want to talk about that."

"Then what do you want to talk about?" I waved an arm at the building behind us, the ammonia-scented corridors and the endless numbered rooms inhabited by faded old people, already ghosts of the dead they would become. "You want to talk about Cora in 203 and the way her son never visits her or Jerry in 147 whose emphysema has been giving him trouble or all the—"

"All the what?" she snapped, suddenly fierce.

"All the fucking minutia we always talk about!"

"I won't have you speak to me like that! I raised you, I made you what you are today!"

"I know," I said. And then, more quietly, I said it again. "I know."

Her hands twisted in her lap. "The doctors told me you'd forget, it happens that way sometimes with trauma. You were so *young*. It seemed best somehow to just . . . let it go."

"But you lied."

"I didn't choose any of this," she said. "After it happened, your parents sent you out to me. Just for a little while, they said. They needed time to think things through."

She fell silent, squinting at the surf foaming on the rocks below. The sun bore down upon us, a heartbreaking disk of white in the faraway sky.

"I never thought they'd do what they did," she said, "and then it was too late. After that . . . how could I tell you?" She clenched my hand. "You seemed okay, Robert. You seemed like you were fine."

I stood, pulling away. "How could you know?"

"Robert—"

I turned at the door. She'd wheeled the chair around to face me. Her leg thrust toward me in its cast, like the prow of a ship. She was in tears. "Why, Robert? Why couldn't you just leave everything alone?"

"I don't know," I said, but even then I was thinking of Lewis, that habit he has of probing at his face where the acne left it pitted—as if someday he'll find his flesh smooth and handsome once again, and it's through his hands he'll know it. I guess that's it, you know: we've all been wounded, every one of us.

And we just can't keep our hands off the scars.

I drifted for the next day or two, living out of hotel rooms and haunting the places I'd known growing up. They'd changed like everything changes, the world always hurrying us along, but I didn't know what else to do, where else to go. I couldn't leave Long Beach, not till I made things up with Gran, but something held me back.

I felt ill at ease, restless. And then, as I fished through my wallet in a bar one afternoon, I saw a tiny slip of paper eddy to the floor. I knew what it was, of course, but I picked it up anyway. My fingers shook as I opened it up and stared at the message written there, *Call me some time*, with the address and phone number printed neatly below.

I made it to Laguna Beach in fifty minutes. The address was a mile or so east of the water, a manicured duplex on a corner lot. She had moved no doubt—five years had passed—and if she hadn't moved she had married at the very least. But I left my car at the curb and walked up the sidewalk all the same. I could hear the bell through an open window, footsteps approaching, soft music lilting from the back of the house. Then the door opened and she was there, wiping her hands on a towel.

"Gwen," I said.

She didn't smile, but she didn't close the door either.

It was a start.

The house was small but light, with wide windows in the kitchen overlooking a lush back lawn. A breeze slipped past the screens, infusing the kitchen with the scent of fresh-cut grass and the faraway smell of ocean.

"This isn't a bad time, is it?" I asked.

"Well, it's unexpected to say the least," she told me, lifting one eyebrow doubtfully, and in the gesture I caught a glimpse of the girl I'd known at Northwestern, rueful and wry and always faintly amused.

As she made coffee, I studied her, still freckled and faintly gamine, but not unchanged. Her eyes had a wary light in them, and fresh lines caged her thin upper lip. When she sat across from me at the table, toying with her coffee cup, I noticed a faint pale circle around her finger where a ring might have been.

Maybe I looked older too, for Gwen glanced up at me from beneath a fringe of streaky blonde bangs, her mouth arcing in a crooked smile. "You look younger on television," she said, and it was enough to get us started.

Gwen knew a fair bit of my story—my role in Burton's presidential campaign had bought me that much notoriety at least—and hers had a familiar ring to it. Law school at UCLA, five or six years billing hours in one of the big LA firms before the cutthroat culture got to her and she threw it over for a job with the ACLU, trading long days and a handsome wage for still longer ones and almost no wage at all. Her marriage had come apart around the same time. "Not out of any real animosity," she said. "More like a mutual lack of interest."

"And now? Are you seeing anyone?"

The question came out with a weight I hadn't intended.

She hesitated. "No one special." She lifted the eyebrow once again. "A habit I picked up as a litigator. Risk aversion."

By this time, the light beyond the windows had softened into twilight and our coffee had grown cold. As shadows lengthened in the little kitchen, I caught Gwen glancing at the clock.

She had plans.

I stood. "I should go."

"Right."

She took my hand at the door, a simple handshake, that's all, but I felt something pass between us, an old connection close with a kind of electric spark. Maybe it wasn't there at all, maybe I only wanted to feel it—Gwen certainly seemed willing to let me walk out of her life once again—but a kind of desperation seized me.

Call it nostalgia or loneliness. Call it whatever you want. But suddenly the image of her wry glance from beneath the slant of hair leaped into mind.

I wanted to see her again.

"Listen," I said, "I know this is kind of out of the blue, but you wouldn't be free for dinner would you?"

She paused a moment. The shadow of the door had fallen across her face. I couldn't see her eyes. She laughed uncertainly, and when she spoke, her voice was husky and uncertain. "I don't know, Rob. That was a long time ago. Like I said, I'm a little risk averse these days."

"Right. Well, then, listen—it was really great seeing you."

I nodded and started across the lawn. I had the door of the rental open, when she spoke again.

"What the hell," she said. "Let me make a call. It's only dinner, right?"

I went back to Washington for the inauguration.

Lewis and I stood together as we waited for the ceremony to begin, looking out at the dead. They had been on the move for days, legions of them, gathering on the mall as far as the eye could see. A cluster of the living, maybe a couple hundred strong, had been herded onto the lawn before the bandstand—a token crowd of warm bodies for the television cameras—but I couldn't help thinking that Burton's true constituency waited beyond the cordons, still and silent and unutterably patient, the melting pot made flesh: folk of every color, race, creed, and age, in every stage of decay that would allow them to stand upright. Dana Maguire might be out there somewhere. She probably was.

The smell was palpable.

Privately, Lewis had told me that the dead had begun gathering elsewhere in the world, as well. Our satellites had confirmed it. In Cuba and North Korea, in Yugoslavia and Rwanda, the dead were on the move, implacable and slow, their purposes unknown and maybe unknowable.

"We need you, Rob," he had said. "Worse than ever."

"I'm not ready yet," I replied.

He had turned to me then, his long pitted face sagging. "What happened to you?" he asked.

And so I told him.

It was the first time I had spoken of it aloud, and I felt a burden sliding from my shoulders as the words slipped out. I told him all of it: Gran's evasions and my reaction to Dana Maguire that day on CNN and the sense I'd had on *Crossfire* that something else, something vast and remote and impersonal, was speaking through me, calling them back from the grave. I told him about the police report, too, how the memories had come crashing back upon me as I sat at the scarred table, staring into a file nearly three decades old.

"It was a party," I said. "My uncle was throwing a party and Mom and Dad's baby sitter had canceled at the last minute, so Don told them just to bring us along. He lived alone, you know. He didn't have kids and he never thought about kids in the house."

"So the gun wasn't locked up?"

"No. It was late. It must have been close to midnight by then. People were getting drunk and the music was loud and Alice didn't seem to want much to do with me. I was in my uncle's bedroom, just fooling around the way kids do, and the gun was in the drawer of his night stand."

I paused, memory surging through me, and suddenly I was there again, a child in my uncle's upstairs bedroom. Music thumped downstairs, jazzy big band music. I knew the grown-ups would be dancing and my dad would be nuzzling Mom's neck, and that night when he kissed me good night, I'd be able to smell him, the exotic aromas of bourbon and tobacco, shot through with the faint floral essence of Mom's perfume. Then my eyes fell upon the gun in the drawer. The light from the hall summoned unsuspected depths from the blued barrel.

I picked it up, heavy and cold.

All I wanted to do was show Alice. I just wanted to show her. I never meant to hurt anyone. I never meant to hurt Alice.

I said it to Lewis—"I never meant to hurt her"—and he looked away, unable to meet my eyes.

I remember carrying the gun downstairs to the foyer, Mom and

Dad dancing beyond the frame of the doorway, Alice standing there watching. "I remember everything," I said to Lewis. "Everything but pulling the trigger. I remember the music screeching to a halt, somebody dragging the needle across the record, my mother screaming. I remember Alice lying on the floor and the blood and the weight of the gun in my hand. But the weird thing is, the thing I remember best is the way I felt at that moment."

"The way you felt," Lewis said.

"Yeah. A bullet had smashed the face of the clock, this big grandfather clock my uncle had in the foyer. It was chiming over and over, as though the bullet had wrecked the mechanism. That's what I remember most. The clock. I was afraid my uncle was going to be mad about the clock."

Lewis did something odd then. Reaching out, he clasped my shoulder—the first time he'd ever touched me, really *touched* me, I mean—and I realized how strange it was that this man, this scarred, bitter man, had somehow become the only friend I have. I realized something else, too: how rarely I'd known the touch of another human hand, how much I hungered for it.

"You were a kid, Rob."

"I know. It's not my fault."

"It's no reason for you to leave, not now, not when we need you. Burton would have you back in a minute. He owes this election to you, he knows that. Come back."

"Not yet," I said, "I'm not ready."

But now, staring out across the upturned faces of the dead as a cold January wind whipped across the mall, I felt the lure and pull of the old life, sure as gravity. The game, Burton had called it, and it was a game, politics, the biggest Monopoly set in the world and I loved it and for the first time I understood *why* I loved it. For the first time I understood something else, too: why I had waited years to ring Gwen's doorbell, why even then it had taken an active effort of will not to turn away. It was the same reason: Because it was a game, a game with clear winners and losers, with rules as complex and arcane as a cotillion, and most of all because it partook so little of the messy turmoil of real life. The stakes seemed high, but they weren't. It was ritual, that's all—movement without action, a dance of spin and strategy designed to preserve the status quo. I fell in love with politics because it was safe. You get so involved in pushing your token around the board that you forget the ideals that brought you to the table in the first place. You forget to speak from the heart. Someday maybe, for the right reasons, I'd come back. But not yet.

I must have said it aloud for Lewis suddenly looked over at me. "What?" he asked.

I just shook my head and gazed out over the handful of living people, stirring as the ceremony got underway. The dead waited beyond them, rank upon rank of them with the earth of the grave under their nails and that cold shining in their eyes.

And then I *did* turn to Lewis. "What do you think they want?" I asked.

Lewis sighed. "Justice, I suppose," he said.

"And when they have it?"

"Maybe they'll rest."

A year has passed, and those words—*justice, I suppose*—still haunt me. I returned to D.C. in the fall, just as the leaves began turning along the Potomac. Gwen came with me, and sometimes, as I lie wakeful in the shelter of her warmth, my mind turns to the past.

It was Gran that brought me back. The cast had come off in February, and one afternoon in March, Gwen and I stopped by, surprised to see her on her feet. She looked frail, but her eyes glinted with determination as she toiled along the corridors behind her walker.

"Let's sit down and rest," I said when she got winded, but she merely shook her head and kept moving.

"Bones knit, Rob," she told me. "Wounds heal, if you let them."

Those words haunt me, too.

By the time she died in August, she'd moved from the walker to a cane. Another month, her case manager told me with admiration, and she might have relinquished even that. We buried her in the plot where we laid my grandfather to rest, but I never went back after the interment. I know what I would find.

The dead do not sleep.

They shamble in silence through the cities of our world, their bodies slack and stinking of the grave, their eyes coldly ablaze. Baghdad fell in September, vanquished by battalions of revolutionaries, rallying behind a vanguard of the dead. State teems with similar rumors, and CNN is on the story. Unrest in Pyongyang, turmoil in Belgrade.

In some views, Burton's has been the most successful administration in history. All around the world, our enemies are falling. Yet more and more these days, I catch the president staring uneasily into the streets of Washington, aswarm with zombies. "Our conscience," he's taken to calling them, but I'm not sure I agree. They demand nothing of us, after all. They seek no end we can perceive or understand. Perhaps they are nothing more than what we make of them, or what they enable us to make of ourselves. And so we go on, mere lodgers in a world of unpeopled graves, subject ever to the remorseless scrutiny of the dead.

❖　❖　❖

The Anencephalic Fields

DADDY LEFT WITH A BIG-CITY DOLLYMOP when I wasn't but six years old, and Mama got a job tending the corpse gardens outside of Scary, Kentucky. By the time I was twelve, a tow-headed not-quite boy in his daddy's hand-me-down jeans, I remembered the dollymop better than I did the man himself. She was a loud, brash redhead with tits like jugs and a mouth like a wound, but Daddy had faded to a dull blur of memory. I couldn't for the life of me remember how he looked and Mama said the resemblance was minimal; but I could remember how it felt when he touched me, and if I tried I could still smell his jackleg whiskey and the black-market smoke that always hung about him. Mostly, though, I could recollect his hands. I used to lie awake nights, fingering over that memory in my mind, like a miser with a bag full of gold—the memory of those big, callused hands against my face and the sound of his voice when he said, "You're the man of the house now, Kemp. You've got to take care of your mama." That was just before he left—I remember the dollymop waiting in her car, while Mama cussed them both in the background—and I hadn't seen either one of them since.

Mama claimed this particular memory was a lie, but when it came to Daddy, Mama had her own issues, and I'd learned not to press her on them. I took what I had—the dollymop and her tits, Daddy and his hands—and let Mama do her own grieving.

Meanwhile we moved to Scary, Kentucky.

The good folks of Scary didn't cotton to outsiders, so Mama and I were pretty much alone out there with six acres of the not-quite dead. Rust-dimpled NO TRESPASSING signs hung on the razor-wire fence surrounding the compound.

DANGER!
BIOGENE RESEARCH FACILITY
AUTHORIZED PERSONNEL ONLY
BEWARE ATTACK DOGS

they read, but I never knew of any dogs. Not that it much mattered. Mostly this all happened during the crash and people had more important things on their minds, like food. Our land was too hard-scrabble to make it worth stealing, and nobody wanted to eat what we were raising anyway. The rumors were enough to keep anyone else away. When I was little, I always expected to look out the front windows one night and see a line of torches winding out of the surrounding hills, like the villagers in a flat-screen Frankenstein, but the worst trouble we ever had was townies throwing rocks at the signs on Halloween—and even that came to an end when Mama accidentally left a gate open and a couple of the kids got a glimpse into one of the growing sheds.

Me, I've never been superstitious, so the meat didn't bother me one way or the other. That was the word I used around the house, meat, mainly to bug Mama, who mostly used another term. I used to see it in the reports she sent to BioGene every month or two: anencephalic. Mama had an education—a lot of education—and I suppose that was one of the things I held against her. Mama never let me join up at the school in Scary; she said she wasn't paying her hard-earned dollar to see some second-rate hillbilly corrupt her son with nonsense. I didn't see how she reckoned her dollar hard-earned; she never did anything but tend the meat and zombie down the cyber-highways as far as I could see. But the long and short of it was that I was pretty much stuck out there in the corpse gardens with six acres of meat and one ball-busting bitch who didn't have a use for any man, much less one that sprang from the loins of her dear departed.

The way I figured it, Daddy had a lot to answer for.

The man named Smee came to our little corner of paradise in my twelfth summer. I watched the dust trail draw near from a ridge not far outside the fence-line. Most of the vehicles that came that way—and there weren't many in those days—took the branch that leads by an old logging road south to Beauty. But this one came straight on, and by the time I glimpsed the humvee itself, a dull metal flash motoring along through the trees below, I had worked out exactly what that meant.

Once upon a time Mama and I had entertained our fair share of visitors. There had been her friends from the college where she used to teach for one, and a worse bunch of cackling hens I never hope to see, but that pretty much came to an end during the crash, when it wasn't a good idea for a woman to travel alone. BioGene reps had stopped in three or four times a year as well, high profile corporate drones most of them, with faces impervious as glass and their big-city dollymops along for a squeeze. But that petered out during the crash, too. Mama said that BioGene had shifted into bio-warfare research big time by then, and we figured they'd forgotten all about their little experiment—though I suppose someone must have remembered because corporate continued to download Mama's check regular as clockwork.

Mama thought we were safer in Scary than we might be in lots of other places, so we stayed put and tended the meat because that's what we'd always done—or at least since Daddy had left, which was as close to always as I could figure when I was twelve years old. But BioGene hadn't sent one of their drones around for over four years at this point, so when I saw the humvee rumbling through the trees below I figured the stranger to be a bandit, and I lit out for home.

Mama was a bitch all right, but I'd long since decided that if anyone was going to kill her, it was going to be me.

I nearly got myself killed instead. Mama stood on the front porch with Daddy's old Mossberg in her arms and as I cornered the last of the growing sheds, she spun like a high-strung cat and leveled the shotgun right at me. Maybe I didn't really sense her finger tightening about the trigger, but I sure thought I did, and for a single frozen heartbeat I couldn't see a thing but the enormous barrel of that shotgun, hateful and deadly as a borehole to hell.

Then she kind of nodded. "Kemp," she said, and all the air went out of me in a whoosh.

"What's going on?" I said. "Who's—"

Already she'd swung the shotgun away from me. "Shut up, Kemp," she said, and someone else added, conversationally,

"Yes, lad, do shut the hell up, would you?"

I glanced into the yard and that's when I got my first look at Shamus Smee. He looked like nothing more than a drowned sewer rat, thin faced and delicate boned, with a three day beard running to gray, and furtive eyes the color of lead. He wore combat boots and a sweat-stained camo jumper, and his corded hands hung at his thighs, flexing with nervous tension. He projected a sense of contained energy, like a coiled steel spring, and when he spoke again, his clipped northern accent sounded wheedling and hostile:

"Now then, you were saying—"

"I was explaining to you and your slut how you had taken a wrong turn in Scary," Mama said. "Less you have ID."

Said slut—a waiflike twenty-something with a close-cropped head of dirty blonde and a torso-hugging mood shirt—gasped. "Shamus—" she began, the T-shirt flaring an angry red, but Smee interrupted.

"Shut up, Lush. True is true. Back to the car with you."

"Shamus—"

"Back to the car with you, I said!" He turned on her and something electric passed between them. I could feel it, sizzling in the August heat.

The blonde edged toward the humvee, parked carelessly fifteen meters from the house. Its doors stood open, internal alarms bleating like a sickly cow. Smee stood his ground.

"As I was telling you," Smee said, "BioGene has—"

"Nobody informed me that you were coming."

"I have come to relieve you. And frankly, I couldn't give two shits whether you were informed."

Mama didn't answer. She just set her mouth in a grim line and started down the steps, gesturing with the shotgun. Smee backed away, lifting his hands, palms outspread before him.

Then all hell broke loose. The blonde darted toward the humvee, her shirt flickering with anxiety, and Mama swung the Mossberg around. The shotgun jerked, spitting fire, and thunder smashed the air into millions of glittering shards. Shot kicked up dust at the blonde's heels as Smee surged toward Mama, his corded hands outstretched. Mama stepped up to meet him, reversing the shotgun like a club. And even as I realized that they'd forgotten all about me—all of them, Mama, Smee, even Smee's slinky blonde dollymop—I was moving. Not toward Smee, but toward the blonde and the humvee and whatever it was that she might have hidden inside it.

She had the head start, I had speed. I got there maybe a split second behind her, but even as she lifted the pistol from between the seats, I hurled myself through the driver's side door and grabbed for the barrel. In the enclosed space, the detonation was deafening. The barrel bulged and heat passed through my clenched fist. The bullet banged off the armored ceiling, ricocheting through the interior of the humvee like a speed-crazed bee. For a single instant, the blonde and I stared dumbfounded at one another, the pistol caught between us. Everything seemed grotesquely heightened, super real. I could feel sweat tickling between my shoulder blades, I could see the wild pulse at her temple. Mostly though, I could smell her perfume, so sweet it made my mouth water, like nothing in my life up to then.

Yanking the gun away from her, I jammed the barrel into her face and backed her out of the humvee, scrambling across the seats to follow her through the passenger-side door. My heart was racing, my breath ragged. I could hardly keep the gun steady on her.

"Don't," she whispered, and her shirt went gray with fear. She caught her lower lip beneath her teeth and her eyes widened in their orbits, but I didn't trust myself to speak. I backed away a step, angling my body so that I could see the entire yard. Smee was climbing to his feet before Mama, cradling his jaw in one hand. Mama pumped a fresh shell into the empty chamber and leveled the shotgun at Shamus Smee with a pleasant smile. "Now, then," she said, "I think you were fixing to show me some ID."

At night I walked the rows.

During the day, the corpse gardens had nothing to offer me, just endless aisles of pale emerald bodies erupting from soil-sunk pods, slick and stinking with insecticides from the overhead sprinklers. The growing sheds themselves were long narrow buildings like covered bridges, banged together from corrugated tin with Plexiglas skylights open to the Kentucky sun. Within, the bodies grew in rows, the soft inhaling, exhaling, farting, moist life of them obscured by the clatter of machinery—air conditioners and wheezers, pumps and fans. But in the night . . . in the night, you could *hear* them—the not-quite dead, anencephalic, brain-deprived vegetable (Oh, how rich a term!) corpse meat to which my mother had devoted her life—

You could hear them breathing.

Maybe that's how it started—just a small boy, nine, ten years old, fleeing the Kentucky farmhouse where his father did not live and where his mother bent her every waking hour to the six acres of meat beyond the peeling clapboard walls. I used to move through the moon-splashed rows, gazing down at them, their breasts heaving with the half-lives Mama had thrust upon them. Just listening, comforted somehow by the steady sigh of respiration, the slow reflexive shiftings of their mindless slumber.

Transplants.

That had been Mama's original plan, all those years ago when she had gotten the first BioGene grant—before the corpse gardens themselves took root, before the disorders and the crash that followed. Before Daddy abandoned her to feast on the juicy sweetmeats of his downtown whore. But no one had ever come to harvest the organs, and now, with the world winding down around us—Mama's metaphor, not mine—maybe no one ever would.

In the meantime, I found another use for them.

And so we come to a part of my tale I don't much like to think on. But I was twelve years old—think of it, twelve!—and my dreams burned like fever with half-imagined images of Daddy's dollymop, and the pleasures such a woman might confer upon me. Oh yes, I took solace among the dead.

I found her in the spring of that year, in the strange half-light of a cloud-gauzed moon that hid the color of her flesh. I must have walked past her a thousand times without paying her any attention, but that night the play of light and shadow across her body drew me to her. I stood there looking down at her, heavy breasted with dark-rouged nipples, and farther below, beyond a sweet smooth curve of belly where no umbilical knot winked its solitary eye, the honey patch that hid her sex. Like Daddy's jug-meloned grope, I remember thinking, and what I did next I did without a moment's conscious thought. Bursting with the kind of groaning lust only a twelve-year-old can know, I shucked my clothes and stood engorged in the moon-washed silence. I felt as if I had stepped over the edge of an enormous precipice. Like I was falling.

On my knees, between her falling thighs, I drove myself to the hot, wet core of her. Her ripe vegetable scent enveloped me—the moist verdure of rich soil and green things growing and sweat—and her body moved beneath me reflexively. When I brushed away the tangle of leaves that lay across her face, I saw her vacant eyes snap open to stare into the still Kentucky night, and in the same moment I felt something give way inside me. I closed my eyes as I came, and when I opened them again, the world had changed forever.

After that I tried to stay away from there, but I could not. The growing sheds and their promise of sweet, slick sin drew me back; it left me gasping, that sin, my fingers tangled in the leaf-grown tubers which bore the meat life. But it left me full. And that moonlit

August night when Shamus Smee arrived in Scary, Kentucky, I found myself drawn to my accustomed place, to the corpse that so reminded me of the brassy tart who had lured my daddy into another life.

And, oh, my friends, it *was* sweet. It was velvet and roses, it was wine and song, and when I threw my head back and dug my fingers into the black, black loam to either side of her heaving breasts, caught in that moment of equipoise when the floodgates tremble within you—in that moment, it was sweeter still. Then the floodgates burst. I cried aloud as the shudders tore through me and I emptied myself within her. Then I opened my eyes, and that was when I saw him, silhouetted against the moonlight, watching from the open door of the growing shed, his corded hands dangling beside him:

Smee. Shamus Smee.

"Smoke, boy?" said Shamus Smee.

He spun a home-rolled bone across his knuckles like a trick wizard and magicked it into nothing before my eyes; it reappeared between his grizzled lips, conjured from the very air. He dug out a lighter, and the tent—their tent, I'd watched them set it up a hundred meters from the house in the heat of the summer afternoon—filled with the heady tang of black-market smoke.

Shamus Smee exhaled a blistering cloud of gray, sipped bourbon from the neck of the bottle, and smiled gingerly. The smile was knowing and ironic, a smile of shared secrets, a smile between men. It reminded me of our encounter in the growing shed, his figure limned against the moonlit night.

"My name's not boy."

"Isn't that cute, Lush? His name's not boy. Pray tell, what could his name be?"

"What's your name, kid?" said Lush, recumbent on a mattress of home-blown air, not looking at me, not looking at anything as far as I could see.

But I was looking.

I studied the lines of her body under her clothes. All sinew and bone, Lush was, with her helmet of bleached blonde hair and her tits mere bumps under the frayed green fabric of her T-shirt. The shirt said, *Ask me, I might*.

"Kemp," I said, and I said it to her, but she only yawned.

Smee leaned toward me in his canvas chair. When I glanced at him, I could see the purple shadow Mama's Mossberg had left across his stubbled jaw. "Well, if it's not smoke," he said, "and it's not booze, then whatever have you come for, *Kemp*?" He drew the last word into a mocking parody.

I did not—I could not—speak.

"What do you want, lad? You want to ask me something, is that it? You want to talk?"

"Sure."

Smee uttered an ugly little laugh, like stones trickling into a dry well. "To talk, Lush, you hear that?"

"Mmmm," said Lush.

And Smee said, "So talk."

He rubbed his bruised jaw with one hand. His hands were big and callused and didn't go with the rest of him, like he'd been sewn together from leftover parts and someone had tried to make do.

"Nothing to say? Then let me ask you this: how do you like it here in hillbilly heaven?"

"I'm not a hillbilly. Mama—"

"I know about your mother. Your mother was a big-league brain once upon a time. And I know where you came from and I know why. And I know your father left you and I know you're here alone. And I know we've got a stalemate. Your mother has the guns, but Shamus Smee has all the time in the world. You hear that, Kemp Chamberlain? All the time in the world. And I'm. Not. Going. Anywhere."

He winked at me and lifted the bottle. I watched his hands, those big hands, and smelled the smell of him—the stink of whiskey and smoke—and I tasted something ashen and hateful in my mouth.

"She won't back down. Not unless the company tells her to, and maybe not then."

"The company sent me. I am their trusted emissary."

Lush snorted and turned her back to us.

"Alas," said Smee, "Lush has grown cynical in the ways of corporate America. Forgive her. My purpose here is not the point. The point is this: do you like Scary, Kemp?"

I hesitated. "All right, I guess."

"Not much company is there? A young man like yourself, I think he might get lonely." He gazed at me through a cloud of malodorous smoke, his eyes like flat and knowing stones. "Do you get lonely, Kemp?"

"Some—" I cleared my throat. "Sometimes."

"The world has changed since your mother brought you here,

you know. Chaos, but for a resourceful young man chaos presents opportunities. And you have proven that you're resourceful. Lush can testify to that. You ever think about the world out there, Kemp?"

"Sometimes," I said, and even as the word slipped away, I wanted to draw it back. I wanted to tell Shamus Smee the truth—that I was burning inside, that I was burning with a hunger for the great wide world beyond Mama and her precious dead, beyond the growing sheds and the meat which could not contain forever the cravings which consumed me. But I didn't say another word.

Smee stubbed out his smoke and conjured up another. I watched his knowing fingers roll it and place it in his mouth unlit. "I thought so."

"What kind of opportunities?"

He leaned forward, so close that his whiskey stench of breath washed over me, and when he spoke again, his voice fairly pulsed with intensity. "I can make it real for you, boy. No more play acting, no more pretend. I can make it real," he said. He said, "Think about it," and then he leaned back, lifted his lighter, and ignited the home-rolled butt. He puffed at it for a moment, and then he extended it toward me between two blunt nicotine-yellowed fingers. "It's the real thing, lad," he said, and almost against my will I reached out and plucked it from him. I took it and wedged it between lips that had gone so dry they felt like they would crack, and I inhaled it like a drowning man. And, oh, the taste was sweet.

"Now run along," he said. "I have things to do."

But I stood outside the tent and watched their shadows on the taut canvas—watched Lush pout and stare, and Smee smoke another cigarette before he rose to extinguish the lights, one by one, until only a single lamp burned within, like a beacon shining out at me from another world. Afterwards, I watched their shadows tangle, Smee wiry and small with those big hands grasping, and Lush jerky with a kind of joyless haste, grinding her boyish hips atop their mattress of home-blown air. Toward the end she cried out, a muffled lament of grief and despair, somehow lonely, a cry a woodland creature might have uttered. But Smee didn't say a word. Me? I stood there watching long after the tent had gone dark. And when I turned away I spat into the grass. There was a foul taste in my mouth. I had smoked Shamus Smee's black-market bone until it burned to a cindered roach between my fingers.

Mama had waited up. She sat in the black living room, smoking a

denatured cigarette and gazing out the back window at the score or
so of growing sheds, the rolling acres of the not-quite dead.

"Where have you been, Kemp?" she asked.

I stood by the stairwell and said nothing, my heart all tangled in
the stink of Smee's black-market smoke—in the burnt-wood fragrance of jackleg whiskey, the memory of corded hands.

She said, "You think I don't know what you do nights?"

I flushed. "But I—"

She waved her hand as if to swat away a fly.

"You've been out there with Smee, have you? Listening to his
lies."

"Are they?"

"Lies?" She shrugged. "I'm checking into that." She turned to
look at me, the cigarette flaring, so that her face seemed to grow and
shift and retreat into the gloom. "What's he want, did he say?"

I shrugged. "Said he wasn't leaving."

"Didn't think he would."

"I told him you wouldn't back down unless the company told
you. Maybe not then."

"What did he offer you, Kemp?"

And now I thought of her again, my pale green dollymop, my
mindless, brain-stripped grope writhing underneath me, impaled
on the shank of need. *I can make it real*, he'd said, and what had that
meant? What could I ever say to Mama, how could I explain? He
offered me the world, I could say, he offered me the whole wide
world—and, oh, I long for it. But all I said was nothing.

"Well," Mama said lightly. "Something, I'm sure."

I turned and started up the stairs, but halfway to the top I turned
around. "You ever want to get away? You ever want to see the world?"

"I've seen it, Kemp. It's overrated."

"That's not what Daddy thought," I told her, and then I started
up again. When I reached the landing, I heard her speak again,
hardly more than a whisper, but in the silence whispers carried. I
thought there might be tears in her voice, but I didn't think I was
supposed to hear them. And besides, I didn't care.

"Why do you hate me, Kemp?" she said.

But I could think of no reply.

Dreams fractured my sleep: nightmarish flights through endless
dark, here and there punctuated by glimpses of eerily distorted
faces, somehow more terrifying still—Mama, her lips set against
some fate I could not yet perceive; narrow-faced Lush, her blue eyes
hooded with mysterious intent; and the dead, acre after acre of the

silent and accusing dead. And then, in one of those bizarre trans-
formations that come to us in dreams, I found myself in the growing shed, found myself staring down at my daddy's redheaded
squeeze, found myself kneeling between her parted thighs. My
friends, I threw back my head and cried out loud for the joy of it,
for the sweet, slick rapture of her body under mine. And only at the
end did I see what was happening to her face: it was changing, melting somehow, transforming itself into the rat-faced visage of Shamus
Smee—

   —*I can make it real for you*—

   —as I spurted in her depths. Horrified, I scuttled away. The
body—Smee and not Smee, my daddy's jug-meloned dollymop and
the verdant corpse into whom I emptied all my dreams—capered
and howled, hurling itself against the medusa coils of foliage that
bound it to the earth. I screamed and tried to wake, but there was
no waking, only terror. And so I backed away, my eyes fixed before
me, until an abrupt arresting surface, unyielding as a stone, drew
me up erect.

   All the world suspended in a single breath, I turned and gazed
at the thing that had obstructed me: the scuffed combat boots and
the sweat-stained camo jumper, the big and callused hands. They
reached out to gentle me, those hands, and it was like a lock had
opened in my heart. A rush of feeling overwhelmed me as I looked
into his face. It was a face I had never once been able to recall, a
face I had never even seen in dreams.

   It was my daddy's face.

   And then I woke. I lay there in the tangled sheets for the longest
time, but no matter how hard I tried, I couldn't bring that face into
my mind again. Nothing at all remained. Only the silent bedroom,
the vacant mirror of my memory, the stain of hot Kentucky sun
against my sleep-stunned eyes.

I found the house brain armed, the house itself locked down, with
Mama hunkered at her board. A single glance at her sight-glazed
orbs and I knew that she'd gone zombie, searching out the cyber-
highways for answers to whatever questions haunted her. I break-
fasted on a day-old crust of bread and let myself out, re-arming the
house behind me. Smee's tent was empty, but out by the fence-line
I saw Lush, clad in bone-colored rags and a T-shirt that flashed her
vital signs in neon random. She stood with her back to me and her
fingers laced in the links, gazing off through the woods at the road
that wound south to Scary.

   She glanced up when I stopped beside her. "Where's the dogs?"

"Never was any. It's just a sign."

"Too bad," she said. "I like dogs."

She ambled along the fence-line, glancing off into the woods now and then. Heat shimmered over the ridges, and the whole world looked wilted. I gazed with numb fascination at a single bead of sweat glistening at Lush's temple. *Lush*, I said to myself, and the name conjured up images of steaming jungle, of fevered efflorescence. I said it again, *"Lush,"* rolling the single syllable off my tongue, recollecting the way her eyes had widened when I pointed the gun at her, the scent of her perfume. Only this time I must have said it just above my breath, for she glanced over at me, lifting her eyebrows, and said, "How's your hand?"

"My hand?"

She aimed her finger at me and dropped her thumb like the hammer of a gun. "Bang," she said, and I thought of the pistol's breathtaking concussion, the barrel bulging in my clenched fist as it spat the bullet into the humvee. "Well?"

"Oh, it's fine." I hesitated. "I wouldn't have shot you, you know."

"I would have shot you."

"You *tried* to shoot me."

"Well, what'd you want me to do? Shamus was pissed, you know, said if I wasn't such a lousy shot—" She shrugged.

"Where is he?"

"Out and about." She gestured vaguely at a cluster of growing sheds. "You know, he's more interested in all those bodies than in you and your mom. Or even me." She laughed, and added wryly, "He wants to give me to you. Thinks it'll bring you around."

"Do what?"

"Give me to you." She thrust her index finger into the hollow cylinder of her left fist.

I could feel the heat behind my face.

"Jesus," she said. "I didn't mean to embarrass you." She began to grind her hips suggestively, and I turned on her, thrusting her away. She stumbled, and laughed aloud, her eyes aglitter with meanness.

"It's not like that—"

"Then what's it like? You think they enjoy it, kid? You think they're having big screaming orgasms? Well, I got news for you, they're just glorified fuck dolls."

"Yeah, and what are you?"

She didn't answer for a moment, and then she laughed again, a strange bitter little laugh. "Maybe you're right."

She turned her back and stalked away along the fence-line. She hadn't gone far before she began to pick up speed, and finally she ran blindly, her coltish limbs falling into an aimless awkward gait, like she didn't know whether she was running away from something or into the arms of something else, some mysterious fate she could not even imagine yet, let alone see.

The thing was, I *knew* how she felt. I'd felt that way about a thousand times myself, thinking about Mama and Daddy and the dairy-rich whore he'd followed over the far horizon, like a dog with a hard-on for a bitch in heat. See, I too had walked that fence, and this is what I learned: no matter how hard you run, you always end up in the same place you started. And so I thought of Lush, Lush and her stupid T-shirts and the way her eyes had widened when I leveled the pistol at her, Lush and the faint aroma of her perfume and the first word she had ever said to me—

—*Don't*—

—and somehow I was running too.

"Wait!" I cried, but she did not wait, and my breath was coming hard when I saw her stumble at the crest of a knoll and tumble down the other side. She was still lying there, half laughing but mostly crying, when I arrived, sweaty and out of breath. I stood over her, watching her heartwave race across her T-shirt in a jagged line.

I wanted to apologize, but I couldn't begin to guess how, so I settled for not saying anything at all. I only stood there, staring down at her and her idiot T-shirt, her pulse rate blinking like a moronic beacon over the bump of her left breast.

"Well?" she said.

"Do you like him?"

"You really don't get it, do you? It's not about liking him or disliking him, it's about survival: long as he gets his dick wet, that's how long he takes care of me. That's the way the world goes round."

"Why don't you leave?"

"Where am I gonna go? Not all of us can live behind fences, Kemp. Who's gonna take care of me? You?"

"I might."

We were silent then. Lush sat up, her head hanging, her arms draped over her knees, her breath coming in shallow gasps. After a while, she glanced up at me from beneath her cap of dirty blonde hair. "You're sweet," she said. "Maybe I won't shoot you after all."

"Your mother let you out today?" said Shamus Smee.

"She going to stop me?"

He measured me with one eye, squinting away smoke from his black-market bone. "I think she might at that, lad."

He pinched out the smoke, tucking the butt into his pocket

before he turned back to his work. What that work was I couldn't say, but his hands charmed me, so dexterous and quick. He brushed a flickering red jewel on the belly of a spidery-looking thing made of wire and chrome; its claws flexed, extruding filaments of shining silver. When he let it go, it scuttled off beneath the foliage, through the rows of meat.

Smee grunted thoughtfully, tapped at his wafer board for a moment, then fished another spiderclaw from a cardboard box. The growing shed seemed alien and strange, aswim in the emerald light of a failing sun, ripe with the stinks of fertilizer and sweat and greenhouse foliage healthy to the edge of rot. I could hear the far-away chuff of the wheezers and Smee's pensive grunts whenever one of the spiderclaws stole humming into the rows. If I listened close, I could hear something else, too—the inspiration and expiration, the respiration of the slumbering dead. Like music, a siren song or symphony borne from a distant shore.

Said Smee, "So you've spoken to Lush, have you?"

"That's right."

"You like her?"

"Why? You planning to give her to me?"

"Does the idea offend you?" Smee asked.

He'd been hunkered over a supine spiderclaw, studying it through a jeweler's loupe and using a tiny screwdriver to tinker with its guts. Now he flipped closed the little metal breastplate and lifted the loupe with its elastic band onto his forehead. "Well?"

But I had to think about his question. The fact was I *did* want Lush—the taste and scent and look of her, not the secondhand allure of her perfume or the dime-shop charm of the T-shirts she affected, but the spare, sinewy reality I sensed beneath the T-shirts, under the perfume, on the far side of her skin itself. Lush. *Herself.* But I had a notion that Smee couldn't give me that, and probably hadn't any right to try—that maybe only Lush could, and only if she were willing.

"It doesn't seem right."

"*Right?*" Smee threw his head back and laughed. "I couldn't care less about that, my friend. The point is, I *can.* I *can* give her to you."

He stood and nudged the squirming spiderclaw onto its feet with the toe of his boot. The thing scurried away into the failing light.

"Under certain terms," Smee said. "You'll enjoy Lush," he added. "And I won't mind, there's a thousand like her."

"Terms?"

"Terms. Guns, for one. I want the guns. And you'll have to disarm the fucking house, won't you?"

"What about Mama?"

"What about her?"

"You'll hurt her."

"Would you mind so much, Kemp?"

"Maybe," I said. I said, "Maybe not." And after a moment, I added: "She might hurt you instead."

Smee laughed out loud. "Me? Hurt me? I don't think so, boy. Your mother's weak. She has no taste for cruelty. So I'll do as I please."

"And what's that? What is it that you've come for?"

"Ah," Smee said, "that's the question, isn't it?" And now he stopped before me, the jeweler's loupe cocked atop his forehead like a third eye, his breath a reek of nicotine and whiskey. Tiny blisters of sweat clung to the gray stubble of his beard, and his teeth were mossy and crooked in his ratlike face. His eyes shone in their intensity, and when he reached out to lay a hand against my cheek, his touch was gentle. His touch was a caress. "We're two of a kind, we are, my friend," he whispered. "You want it to be real, and I— *I've* come to make it so."

He laughed again and turned away from me, hunkered over his wafer board, his thick fingers flying across the keys. And what I felt was rage—at Shamus Smee and at my mama, too, at my long-gone daddy and the smiling slut with her mouth like a wound and the gatefold tits who had stolen him away from me. At all of them, all of the adults and the complex world they had made for me to understand. "Mama beat you once," I said. "She could beat you again."

"Not again," said Shamus Smee, and he punched a final key with one blunt finger.

Behind me, in the gloom of the growing shed, a rustle erupted among the rows of slumbering dead. My heart banged against the cage of my chest as I spun to face it, my mind abruptly flooded with the backwash from my dream—my pale green dollymop arisen from the dead. And friends, it was true, true—

I saw her heave herself up, saw her shrug away the life-bearing tubers that entangled her, smelled the ripe complaint of bruised foliage as she came toward me through the rows—erect, alive, *real*, my half-dead squeeze with her tits like jugs, my grope, my fuck doll, my goddess. Mine. Just as Smee had said. I stood there, rooted to the ground as surely as if *I* had grown there, companion to the numberless dead. Fear gripped my throat and heart, but I did not, I could not flee.

And then she took me in her arms and pressed her lips to mine. I could feel the swollen tips of her breasts through the thin fabric of my shirt, could smell her cloying green fragrance. I could even taste her, like raw spinach and spit and a faraway hint of fecund earth. My cock throbbed inside my daddy's cast-off jeans. A stricken rat clawed in my constricted throat. Fear and desire, that's all it came to, wound like snakes about the caduceus of my spine.

I thought of Lush, fraught and hurting Lush—

—*you think they like it, kid?*—

—chasing herself around the compound's fence only to arrive back where she started, but then my half-dead dollymop pressed her groin against me, and friends, I could not say her no. I thrust my tongue deeper into her mouth, lifted my arms to embrace her, ran my fingers over the knobby, root-woven terrain of her sap-slick back. At last I pressed my hand to her neck to draw her face still closer to my own, and that's when I felt it: the spiderclaw, pulsing with internal heat, its attenuated strands of silver plunged into the warm flesh that encased her spinal cord—

Smee laughed and from the corner of my eye, I saw his fingers dance across the wafer board.

Abruptly, my dollymop slumped against me, dead weight, her tongue an extruded chunk of flesh, slack between my lips. I screamed and stumbled back as she slid to the floor in a boneless heap, and knowledge pealed inside my brain like a bell:

Dead, dead, dead. Just so much meat.

"Sometimes," said Shamus Smee, "cruelty is necessary."

I found Mama in her study, a dark shape against the surrounding darkness, staring silently at her board. For a moment I thought she hadn't returned, that she was still out there somewhere, another lost soul roaming the cyber-byways. Then she moved, the slightest adjustment of her head and shoulders, but enough to show me that she was here after all, at home in her body. Awake. Crying. I don't know how I knew that, but I didn't doubt it for a moment: it was after midnight, and Mama was sitting in her study, weeping. The simple fact of it touched something in me that I had locked away six long ages past, when we first came to Scary, Kentucky. In all those years I'd never seen Mama cry; now I had seen it twice in as many days, and just that suddenly the whole cloth of my life had started to unravel. I could hardly imagine a change more disturbing—not if the sun had failed to rise that morning, not if all the stars had fallen from the midnight sky.

What would I do if I didn't have Mama to hate?

But there it was, and maybe Mama sensed it, too, for when she spoke I heard a certain stillness in her voice, a gentleness I had not known before.

"So you've been out there again, have you?"

"Yes."

"All day?"

"Most of it."

"And what do you think of him, Kemp, our friend Shamus Smee?"

Once upon a time, I'd have replied with sarcasm if I bothered to answer her at all, but that strangely gentle tone gave me pause. After a moment, I said, "He scares me, Mama."

"Me, too," she said. She said, "And yet you're drawn to him, aren't you?"

I said nothing.

"What does he want, Kemp?"

"I don't know."

Mama laughed. "You're lying, but it doesn't matter anymore."

She touched a button on her board and a screen sprang alight, limning her face in shifting green. A numbing wave of memory crashed over me; involuntarily, I retreated into the shadowed doorway, my heart lurching as the green woman staggered toward me once again.

"Smee's legit," Mama said. "But he's a lying sack of shit."

"What do you mean?"

"I raided BioGene's data banks. His records were buried, but I snuck past the data-sentry."

"Who is he?"

"Just who he says he is, Shamus Smee, an ace BioGene brain. Six weeks ago he melted down—burned his project memory, threatened his supervisor. He claimed BioGene was trying to steal his work."

"Were they?"

Mama thought for a moment. "Probably. But those are the terms going in. They bankroll you and give you free rein. In return, they get any commercial applications of your work."

"What happened then?"

"He went freelance. He's been heading south ever since, trying not to make his destination obvious. I backtracked him for a few weeks before I lost him, and BioGene's probably doing the same. The Feds, too, but the Feds are spread too thin with the insurrections out west to do much good." She paused, adding, "BioGene, though, they'll be along."

"Here?"

"Oh, yes."

"But why?"

"Well, that's the million dollar question, isn't it? I stole his project file, as much as BioGene could recover from the fried memory. You recognize this?"

She punched a button and the shifting green luminescence on the screen gave way to a three-dee diagram of pale blue lines. The board turned it this way and that, giving us the view from all angles. I didn't have to watch but a minute before I knew what it was: a spiderclaw. I recognized the queerly elongated thorax, the razor-edged claws and their attenuated silver wires. A chill ran through me. My pale green anencephalic grope lurched from the swamp of memory, her full breasts bobbing, her lips warm against my own.

"Do you know what it is?"

"No," I said through a throat so parched of moisture that it hurt to swallow.

Mama said, "I don't suppose BioGene's brains have sussed it out yet. But they'll put it together soon enough and then they'll know he's here."

"What is it?"

"God, I never would have imagined this, Kemp." She shook her head. "Healthy, inexpensive organ donors, that's all I ever intended. And then the crash came along and suddenly my research ground to a halt. Suddenly I'm just maintaining meat."

"That's my word for them."

"I never liked it, either. But God knows it's accurate. Anencephalic, right? Brainless shells. Cheap life-support systems for donor organs, that's all I ever had in mind."

"The spider . . . That thing, what's it do?"

"It's a brain. Smee can program the initial parameters, probably control it, but unless I'm mistaken, it has the capacity for growth. It can develop self-awareness. It's pretty crude, but give it a generation or two and . . ."

We shared an uneasy silence and then Mama said, "What an ass I've been not to see this coming. Can you imagine the applications? Armies of cannon fodder. Mining. Any shitty job we can't bring ourselves to do . . ."

"But why's that so bad? Why should we have to do that stuff?"

"Because we should, that's why. We were just starting to come out of the dark ages, Kemp. We were just starting to grow up as a species." She stabbed angrily at the board and the screen went black, plunging the room into darkness.

She said, "I know what you do out there at night."

"Mama, I—"

"It doesn't matter. It's natural, I suppose. You're twelve years old and that's hard enough in the best of times. But that doesn't make it right. You understand? It's not right to use another living being—"

"Isn't it? Is it so different from what you had in mind for them? Slicing them up and distributing their organs?"

"Maybe so," she said, "but this changes everything. I won't let him enslave them, Kemp." Her voice held an adamantine anger like nothing I had ever heard before, not even when Daddy abandoned us for his jug-meloned whore.

"What are you going to do?"

"I did some damage to Biogene's system. I burned Smee's file and fried every record I could find of my own research. I won't let them pervert my work, Kemp. Smee and I, we're just alike in that respect, I guess."

"He asked me to disarm the house," I said. "He asked me to steal back his guns."

"And in return?"

"Lush. He said he would give me Lush."

"Is that the kind of gift you want, Kemp?"

"I don't know what I want."

"I've got a feeling you don't have the luxury of time. BioGene reps will be arriving here soon and they'll scare you more than Smee does. You're going to have to make some choices, and you're going to have to live with them. It's worth thinking about what they might be."

She was silent for a long time after that, and then she started speaking in this strange, toneless voice. "I used to wonder if I made the right choice, coming out here and living in the middle of nowhere. You were a smart kid, and I figured we'd be okay together. But somewhere along the line you started hating me. And now it looks as though I'm going to lose the work, too. Smee's come to take it away from me, and if he can't, BioGene will."

I wanted to answer her, but I didn't know what to say. Mostly, I was just glad for the dark and the way it hid her from my sight. I felt stranger than I'd ever felt in my life—bloated with emptiness, disconnected from the world I'd known, but embarrassed at the same time, like I'd walked in and seen Mama naked.

"What I think now," Mama said, "is that I was probably wrong. You can't run away. You have to live in the world." She repeated that, like it was something I ought to remember—"You have to live in the world, Kemp"—and then she sighed. I heard her fumbling in the dark, and a moment later the room flickered with the light of a denatured cigarette.

"Smee smokes real cigarettes," I said.

"Coffin nails," she said. "That's what we used to call those things."

"Daddy smoked them, too."

Mama laughed. "So he did. Sometimes I wonder. Maybe if I hadn't been so driven he wouldn't have left. Maybe then you wouldn't hate me. Do you think about him often, Kemp?"

I stood there for a long moment trying to decide, but I couldn't seem to think on it clearly like I wanted to. All my thoughts kept getting tangled up in the smell of him, the woodsy aroma of jack-leg whiskey and black-market smoke; that, and the feel of his big hands, gentle against my face, and the sound of his voice when he said it: "You're the man of the house now, Kemp. You've got to take care of your mama."

But for the life of me, I couldn't recollect his face.

"All the time," I said.

Lush came to me that night, in a scattering of pebbles against my window. I threw aside the covers and gazed down at her, a small, pale figure in the clearing before the growing sheds, black and dimensionless against the blue hills beyond, like painted flats propped against the stars. I stole through the night rooms to the kitchen door, punching in the code to disarm the house.

In my silent bedroom, she stood naked before me, her body fuller than I had imagined, high-breasted and muscular, with a dearth of excess flesh. My hand trembled as I lifted it to touch her face, to trace the moonlit shadow of a bruise beneath her eye. She sighed, flinching, and I felt a swift rill of excitement tumble through me.

"Smee," she whispered, and I could see him in the eye of my imagination. I could see those strong hands raining blows upon her.

"Did he send you to me?" I asked. "Because I wouldn't want it, not that way."

"I came because I wanted to," she said. She said, "Are you gonna take care of me now, Kemp?"

The words detonated in my brain, triggering a flash of memory—his big hands against my face, his warm voice saying, "You've got to take care of your mama." That had been a vow, I knew, and I thought of Mama, forlorn in her darkened study, and I saw that I had failed in keeping it.

"I'll try," I said, knowing that this also was a vow, knowing too that I would fail in keeping it, knowing that I had to make it anyway. "We'll take care of each other," I said, and then the tears came, swift, silent tears for all that I had lost and all that I would lose, now or someday—my daddy and my mama and the only world I had ever known, the corpse gardens, the growing sheds and their acres of meat, all of it drifting inexorably out of my grasp in the moment I had finally reached out to embrace it.

Lush drew me to her breast. "Shhh," she said, and she made some other sounds, wordless murmurs meant to solace me, and they did. We stayed that way for a long time, I don't know how long, and then we found our way to the bed. Her mouth was warm and moist, her body flushed, her small breasts like ripe fruit, the nipples quickening beneath my tongue.

A strange and sudden hunger filled me up, and the first time I cried out before she even touched me. But Lush just laughed softly and cradled me in her arms, and after a while her hands found me. "It's okay," she whispered. "Slow down, don't rush it."

The second time was sweeter.

A foghorn called in the darkness. I plunged deeper into fathomless sleep, but the foghorn followed me, a note of panic in its broken voice; finally I rose to meet it, toward a faraway light. I broke the surface of consciousness with a shock as the foghorn's cry metamorphosed into something else. A scream.

I sat up abruptly—

—*Mama*—

—aware of a touch, tentative as the wings of a moth. Glancing into Lush's narrow-planed face, I suddenly came fully awake. A tsunami of guilt crashed over me—Lush, the kitchen, Shamus Smee. The house. I'd disarmed the house.

Mama screamed again, and I heard a gunshot, the sharp, abrupt crack of a pistol.

"Kemp—"

I spun on her. "What have you done?"

I didn't stop to listen to her response. I stumbled up, reaching for my jeans, and that's when I caught a glimpse of the scene beyond the window, lurid in the blood-red light of dawn. Time slipped out of sequence. For a moment, I could do nothing but gape at the nightmare below, the growing sheds vomiting forth their freight of meat. The dead, everywhere the dead—upright, aware, awake, dead no longer if not quite alive, and striding with dumb purpose toward the house, toward *me*, their bodies root-shrouded and shining with sap, their green locks adrift like seaweed about their naked shoulders. And silent. Oh my friends, that was the worst of it, their silence. Not a single shout of joy, nary a cry of hope or hatred or despair. Just icy, implacable silence, just nothing. That's when I truly understood the vile miracle they had wrought between them, Mama and Shamus Smee. Light from the darkness, form from the abyss, they had conceived a new creation, they had served as midwives to its birth—and, my friends, I was afraid.

"My God," Lush said at my shoulder, and I turned in that timeless moment to gaze at her. I wanted to scream and strike her, to tear her limb from limb. She must have seen the violence in my eyes, for she when spoke again, her voice was hushed and pleading. "I didn't know," she said. "Kemp, I promise you I didn't know."

Then Mama's pistol went off once again and I fell back into the moment.

"Don't," Lush said, but I shrugged away her grasping hands. The hall was full of corpses. Half a dozen of the things turned to stare at me, their eyes aglitter in their slack gray faces as the door banged against the outer wall. Simultaneously, Mama appeared in the doorway of her bedroom, clutching the blue-steel automatic I had taken from Lush. The corpses wheeled between us for a moment, like cattle in a slaughter chute, and then, inexorable as compass needles seeking the magnetic pole, they swung back to Mama. "Get back!" she screamed, and a gout of orange flame leapt from the barrel of the pistol. A body dropped, convulsing in a fountain of sap and blood, and the spiderclaw astride the thing's neck shorted out in a torrent of sparks. The stench of singed flesh—ripe eggplant shriveling in heat—permeated the narrow hallway.

Still they came on, two more in the hallway and a third mounting to the landing, with a shadowy fourth beyond. Mama squeezed off another shot and another body dropped in a spray of sparks and sap. I launched myself at the emerald shadow behind it, driving the thing over the railing. It tumbled in eerie silence to the floor below, but another of the things was already upon us.

Mama squeezed off a shot that went wide, blowing out a chunk of plaster; and still the thing advanced, stepping deliberately over the husks of its fallen comrades, charged with the implacable purpose of a machine. I slunk away, trying to conceal myself in the shadows, but the thing merely glanced at me, its flat eyes passing over me like I didn't even exist.

And maybe I didn't.

The thought triggered an eidetic montage, pregnant with mysterious significance, in my stunned brain. Again, I watched Smee finger his wafer board, again I saw my root-woven grope heave herself free of the foliage that bound her to the earth. Like I had slipped out of time, from the nightmare of one moment into the horror of another, I watched the scene replay—tasted once more the pressure of her lips against my own, caught a glimpse of Smee as his fingers flew across the wafer board, felt my pale green dollymop sag in my arms and fall boneless to the floor.

Dead, dead, dead. Just so much meat—

A gunshot shattered my reverie. I saw the bullet punch into the thing's shoulder, staggering it, but leaving the spiderclaw astride its neck intact. Regaining its balance, the creature advanced, first among a silent onslaught of the dead. Mama sighted down the barrel at it, her legs braced in a shooter's stance, her face above the pistol's bore like a strained white flag as she squeezed off another shot.

The hammer fell upon an empty chamber.

That sterile click reverberated in the gloomy hallway, loud as doom. I watched Mama pull the trigger again and saw the hammer fall on yet another empty chamber—

—*click!*—

—as the thing bore her screaming to the floor. And then she disappeared in a crashing tide of gray-green meat.

"Mama!" I stumbled toward her, my mind serving up an image of my daddy, those big hands of his gentle against my face—

—*you've got to take care*—

—as a red haze enveloped me. And then I was among the dead. I could hear her screaming as I clawed and scratched at the pliant flesh, dragging the things from her writhing body. I heard a sound like a length of stove wood being snapped, and I caught a glimpse of her face—still, pale, dead—through the tangled limbs of green, and I knew that it had ended, but the screaming did not stop. And then Lush was there, coaxing me from the squirming mass of the not-quite dead, from the hot vegetable stench of them, and their fingers grasping. I knew then that Mama wasn't screaming—knew that Mama was forever past screaming, knew that maybe I never would be. But Lush held me, rocking me until my screaming *did* stop, and the enigma of that eidetic montage of images—Smee and his wafer board, my pale green dollymop boneless in my arms—at last snapped clear inside my head: You couldn't stop the things. You had to stop the man behind them.

Too late. Too late.

I found the shotgun locked up in Mama's study. The man himself I found inside one of the growing sheds, crouched over his wafer board and studying the projection of a spiderclaw which hung above it, dissolving into static and reconstituting itself with every whim of humid air. Prone beside him lay a shell of brain-deprived meat, its back and flaccid buttocks overgrown with soil-clotted roots. Every now and then, Smee turned and hunkered over the thing, peering through his jeweler's loupe as he probed with a tiny screwdriver at the spiderclaw astride its neck.

Me? I just stood there in the doorway for the longest time, trying to decide how to feel. I had passed two dozen brain-stunned corpses in the yard, wandering aimlessly, most of them, now that Mama—

I closed my eyes, dragging in a breath of heavy morning air, trying not to remember. But there it was: the image of Mama's broken body as the things drifted away from her, their eyes flickering without recognition over Lush and me, huddled there in the doorway to my bedroom. I thought I might be seeing that image for a long time yet, maybe every time I closed my eyes. But the dead—they took no interest in me and Lush. Crude, Mama had called the spiderclaw brains, and I suppose they were, bereft of Smee's ill will. But I couldn't help remembering something else she'd said, that they possessed the capacity for self-awareness. Maybe I could see the first vestiges of that, as well. For they didn't just stop, did they, once they had finished with Mama? They wandered instead, aimless-like, but maybe not entirely aimless. Like a newborn baby, maybe, drinking in the whole wide world.

A pair of them drifted through the emerald reaches of the growing shed, cocking their heads when the wheezers kicked on to flush the interior with nutrient-enriched air. That was my chance.

I crossed the growing shed quickly, careful of the root-bound meat still growing there. I saw holes and mashed-up foliage among the rows where the spiderclaws had done their work, waking the things from mindless slumber to do Smee's bidding. But Smee himself never looked up, never turned to see me coming, didn't even hear me over the whir and bluster of the wheezers.

I cocked the Mossberg and pressed the cold iron to his neck.

About where a spiderclaw might sink its silver wires if one ever got the chance.

And Smee? Smee didn't even flinch.

"Ah, my boy," he said after a moment. "You've decided to join me. I've been wondering when you might happen by."

"You killed Mama."

"Did I, then? How unfortunate."

Now he moved. Slowly, I thought, backing away a step and holding the shotgun steady. Slowly, I thought—and found that I had said it aloud.

"Oh, yes, slowly," he said. "It wouldn't do to blow my head off, would it?" His fingers skated across the wafer board, and the hologram spiderclaw sizzled into nothingness. "I wasn't under the impression that you much cared for your mother, my boy."

"You killed her."

"Not me. *They* did it." He jerked a thumb at the two corpses adrift in the twilight reaches of the growing shed. They had wandered closer, their green shades blurring into mere suggestions of motion, human shapes abroad the verdant green.

"Because you told them too."

"Well, there's that." And he stood, those big hands clenching and unclenching at his thighs. In readiness, I thought. And I backed away another step. "Question is," said Shamus Smee, "what do you intend to do about it, boy?"

My arms ached from holding the gun like that, but I never looked away from Shamus Smee. I saw his eyes drop, calculating his odds, and my finger tightened across the trigger. We hung there for a moment before Smee decided. I could see the tension go out of his body.

"I think I'm going to kill you," I said.

"Will you, lad? I don't think you've got the balls. You're a little like your mother in that respect, I'd say."

"I will—"

"Fine, then. Whatever." He waved a hand dismissively. "What did you think of Lush, my young friend? How did it feel to fuck someone who could fuck you back for a change? Hmmm?"

"You hit her, she wanted to come to me, she—"

"Did she?"

I broke off, inundated with memory: Lush at my window and Lush inside the kitchen door, the way she had kissed me there . . . distracting me just long enough that I forgot to arm the house again. Lush, saying, *I didn't know, I promise you I didn't know.*

But did she?

I glanced up, caught a glimpse of the pair of dead men maybe twenty meters away, and turned back to Smee.

"Where is Lush, by the way?" he asked.

"This isn't about Lu—"

"Not a pleasant one to have behind your back, I'd say. She's a dream between the sheets, that one, but a vixen otherwise. And it's worth remembering she has a reason to begrudge you."

"Lush—"

"I always kept a weather eye when I was fucking her, but you, you're different aren't you? You think she gives a damn about you, don't you? Boy?"

I'll never know why I spun when I did. Maybe it was a shift in Smee's eyes, though I don't remember it happening that way. Or maybe it was a tiny sound, some infinitesimal change in the pressure of the air. Or maybe it was luck. I kind of think it was.

But spin I did, the name rising like an accusation to my lips—

—"Lush"—

—and dying there, for it was not Lush. It was my pale green dollymop, my root-woven, sap-slick fuck doll with her gatefold tits and her mouth like a wound, my anencephalic grope, with a spiderclaw brain programmed by Shamus Smee and murder in her flat, cold eyes.

At the same time, I realized that the pair of corpses had flanked me, moving now with purpose, and suddenly it all came clear in my mind—Smee caressing the wafer board, the spiderclaw projection winking into nothing, and something else. He'd used the opportunity, hadn't he? He had called them to him, one and all. That's when the whole interior of the growing shed exploded into movement—dozens of the things, row after row of the unquiet dead, tearing themselves from their graves and standing erect, to stagger toward me.

I jerked the shotgun up and blasted a hole in the air half a meter above Smee's head. He dropped to his knees, covering his head with his forearms; in the same motion I levered another round into the breech and stepped forward, leveling the shotgun a half a meter in front of his face. My voice, when I spoke, throbbed with terror.

"Call them off!"

But Smee's gaze, when he met my own, was steady. "I would have let you go, you stupid child. You and that stupid whore. All you had to do was walk away."

Foliage rustled as the closer of the pair of dead men closed upon me. I swung to face it, yanking the trigger hard. The spread took the thing square in the throat and threw it half a dozen meters. It hit the ground, expelling a verdant spray of sap and blood. Already I was spinning back to Smee—

Too late.

I sensed more than saw his corded hand dart out. I tried to step away, but he moved with the speed of a striking copperhead. In a crashing succession of moments his thick hand closed like a vise around my ankle, the growing shed whirled and tilted under me, my face smashed into the fragrant earth. I'd lost the shotgun somehow. Smee rose to his knees, those big hands opening to choke the life out of me. I rolled to my left, kicking. My foot caught him square in the face and he stumbled back, flailing for balance.

I clawed my way through the dirt on hands and knees, scanning the foliage for the fallen Mossberg. I could hear Smee cursing behind me as he stumbled to his feet, but I didn't bother glancing back. Breath burned in my lungs. Sweat blistered my forehead, slipping down to blind me. Any minute I expected Smee to fall upon me, that viselike grip to close around my neck.

And then I saw it, a glint of oiled gunmetal, a hint of walnut stock, half-hidden in the overlapping leaves. I dove forward, fingers scrabbling in the dirt—

And then she fell upon me.

Oh yes, my friends, my moss-green fuck doll, my tit-swollen anencephalic grope, a jealous lover to the last—she snapped me up. I felt her fingers close about my shoulders like iron bands. She dragged me up against her, so close that I could smell her, raw vegetables and sweat and earth. And then she started to squeeze, emptying my lungs. Breath exploded out of me in a gust. Wrenching my head around, I caught a glimpse of Smee, his face a blood-streaked mess beneath his shattered nose. I watched him stagger toward the shotgun as black dots began to swarm across my vision.

With the last of my strength I buried my hands in the thing's hair and yanked, trying to snap her neck. My fingers trailed over something cold and hard—

—*the spiderclaw*—

—and I clutched at it desperately, tearing it from her flesh. Those attenuated silver strands whipped back and forth like the antennae of a crazed insect, and my dollymop collapsed. I caught a glimpse of her face as we went down, and for a single vertiginous moment I wasn't sure where I was. Her face shifted, malleable, a quicksilver mirror of other faces, lost faces—my daddy's big-city whore and my mother in the last moment I had seen her, just after that terrible wrenching snap, when her face went gray and restful.

Rage filled me as I scrambled away, scrabbling at the foliage-tangled earth with one hand and stumbling to my feet. Smee whirled to face me, holding the shotgun dead level at my guts. I flung the spiderclaw in his face. He flinched, and I bowled into him at a dead run. We went over in a pile, the spiderclaw skittering away into the empty rows, and then I had slipped free of his grasping hands and rolled to my feet, clutching the Mossberg.

I backed away as the dead closed around me.

"Call them off!" I screamed, and what I saw before me in that moment was not Shamus Smee or the encircling legions of the not-quite dead, but only that strange overlay of faces—my brain-deprived anencephalic grope, my daddy's redheaded whore, and my mama. Mama, her lips set as the dead things overwhelmed her. Mama, lying broken there in the hallway by her bedroom door, her face grim and gray and empty.

Dead. Dead. Dead.

Raw, red hatred enveloped me as I advanced upon him, screaming that he'd better call them off or I'd blow him straight to hell.

Smee backed away, but even then I think he knew it was too late. He must have seen the change in my eyes, he must have known that he had finally overreached himself. In the last moments, he stumbled to his knees, scooping up the wafer board in those big hands of his. His fingers skated across the keys as I closed on him, pumping a fresh round into the breech. I didn't even realize I had pulled the trigger until the spread caught him in the chest. He jerked suddenly, bee stung, and a bright arterial stain blossomed on his camo jumper. His mouth worked for a moment, but nothing came out. Then he collapsed into the pit of a vacant grave.

He must have keyed in the final command as the gunshot took him, for all about me the dead abruptly dropped into the fecund soil that had grown them. The sound of it, that soft boneless collapse, took me back. Superimposed across my tear-glazed vision, I saw her once again, my verdant green dollymop, my lovely, lovely grope, so like my daddy's big-city whore. I felt her lips go slack against my own, I saw her slip away from between my clutching arms. And Smee's words echoed in my head: *Sometimes cruelty is necessary.*

Maybe so, I wanted to tell him.

But that doesn't make it right.

It took nearly a week to clean the place up. The whole time I kept my ears pricked for the thrum of engines winding up the ridge from

Scary. I'd never known Mama to be wrong—not about something like that, anyway—and I figured it was only a matter of time before BioGene showed up in force, and maybe the Feds, too. I didn't want to be around when that happened, but I didn't want to leave anything behind if I could help it. Mama had given her life to keep Smee from enslaving the meat, and the more I thought about it, the more I thought she might have been right.

Lush helped me gather the bodies. The ones Smee hadn't got to yet, growing mindless in the rows Mama made for them, we saved for later. We found the others, two or three dozen of them, scattered in clumps about the yard, in the house, just everywhere, wherever Smee had dropped them. We dragged them one by one into the clearing in front of the house and made an enormous pile of them, fly-swarmed and stinking of rot beneath the August sun. Last of all, we threw Smee on the pile, his chest all ragged from the shot, but his ratlike face unchanged. Then we drained some diesel off the wheezers out back of the growing sheds and soaked the whole pile down. And then we watched them burn.

I dug Mama's grave myself, off in a sun-drenched glade beyond the fence. You could see a whole stretch of purple ridges from there, winding south into the hazy distance of Tennessee, and I couldn't think of a prettier spot. I didn't reckon Mama would get much pleasure from the view, but I didn't want to give her cause for sorrow on the off chance I was wrong. It wouldn't have been the first time, and God knows I had plenty to make up to her.

Lush and I, we had a little service over the grave and I tried to pray some, but I didn't do much good at it. I drove a homemade cross into the mound because it seemed like I probably should, and then we just stood there for a while and watched the sky turn smoky and red as the swollen sun dropped behind the hills. In the blue twilight, Lush said, "I didn't betray you, Kemp. I came to you because I wanted to. Because I didn't think I could take it anymore."

I didn't answer her for a while. I was thinking about something Mama had said, about how we make our choices and how we have to abide by them. I didn't know whether or not Lush was telling the truth, but I decided to believe her, partly because nobody else was left, but mostly because she was wearing that stupid mood shirt once again, and as I studied her in the falling light it seemed to me that it really had gone black with sorrow. It seemed as good a reason as any other, and I guess it still does because Lush and I, we're together yet, and this all happened ten years ago, plus change.

That night Lush and I slept together in my narrow bed, but neither of us felt much like fucking, so we just laid there in one another's arms. I suppose I cried some, and then we talked and before we knew what happened it had gotten so late that even the moon had fallen. We dozed off, but I grew restless toward dawn. I opened my eyes and watched the morning steal across her face, all restful-like. I could taste her breath, sour with sleep, but kind of sweet at the same time, and it occurred to me that the thing I was feeling right then was pretty fine, better maybe than fucking after all. Then Lush woke up, too, and tried to convince me otherwise, and my friends I have to tell you, she just about persuaded me.

Afterwards, I cleaned up in Mama's bathroom. I was still feeling weird inside, the way I'd been feeling for nigh a week now, and I drifted into a kind of daze. Lush found me there, just staring at my face in the mirror.

"What are you doing?" she asked.

"Nothing," I told her, but actually I was wondering who I looked like. If I turned my head just right I could see a hint of Mama's lean, thin-lipped features, but I could see a hint of someone else, too, some stranger looking back at me. I couldn't say whether that was the daddy I hadn't seen in six long years or whether it was the man I was turning out to be. It doesn't matter, I suppose, because I won't ever know the truth. Almost no one ever does.

It took us most of the day to finish up there. I used a sledge-hammer to smash Mama's computer equipment into little pieces, and then I crushed those pieces into smaller pieces still. We carried a bunch of stuff out to the humvee, and then we soaked down the house with more diesel fuel. I never thought I'd be sad to see the place go, but it was only the thought of BioGene drones combing through our lives that made me follow through and set the place alight. That's the way Mama would have wanted it, I suppose.

After that we hit the growing sheds, using the last of the diesel from the wheezers to soak down the structures themselves, not to mention the bodies—the restless, farting, brain-deprived bodies that Smee had never got to. That was hard to do, but it was harder still to set the things alight. The whole sky lit up red with flames as evening fell, and I stood by the last of the sheds for the longest time before I could bring myself to strike the match. And then I stood there a while longer and watched it burn. The bodies writhed as the fire devoured them, and the heat lunged out at me, and for the first time I had some doubts about the course I'd chosen. Slaves can always get their freedom, but the dead—well, they're just dead, aren't they?

I'm still thinking on that one, and I doubt I'll ever really suss it out. But the bodies writhing as they burn—well, that's an image that haunts my dreams even now. And I wouldn't be surprised if it always did.

And then we were done.

Lush and I stowed the last of our salvage and then I wandered off a piece into the burning compound and stood there for a time, just trying to say goodbye. As I walked back to the humvee, I couldn't help thinking of Mama's words to me on the night Smee and Lush had first arrived. It wasn't more than a week ago, but it felt like centuries.

Back then, I'd asked Mama if she ever longed to see the world, and what she'd said in response had puzzled me. *I've seen it, Kemp,* she'd told me. *It's overrated.*

I didn't have much doubt that she was right. But all the same, I thought, I probably ought to find out for myself.

Home Burial

FEBRUARY GRIPPED THE FARM LIKE A FIST, and the baby would not let her rest. Rachel lay wakeful by her sleeping husband and listened. The baby's cry came to her as a faint protest from the burying ground, patient and mournful as the keen of wind about the clapboard house.

"Breece," she whispered, shaking him gently. "Breece, listen."

Breece mumbled, rolled over, and dragged her into his embrace, but he did not wake. Outside, the wind gusted, rattling the knotted fingers of the skeletal oak that stood by the house and chasing watery moon-cast shadows through the bedroom. The barn door banged. Gray specks of snow spat beyond the pale square of the window.

The wind grew louder, drowning out the baby's racket, and Rachel felt a quick surge of relief that Breece had not awakened. She pulled the rough woolen blanket close against her breasts, still heavy and sore with milk, and admonished herself for imagining things. *Breece Casey is a practical man*, her mama had told her the week preceding the wedding. *He won't tolerate your daydreaming and nonsense!*

That had been almost a year ago. Sighing, Rachel knotted herself about the lingering tenderness between her legs. In the chill of the midnight bedroom, there came to her a series of stark inviolable memories: sweltering summer nights when Breece had lovingly assembled the tiny crib, hardly a real bed at all, and she had sewn the unborn child a tiny flannel night dress; another night, more recent, rank with the doctor's whiskey-stench, the fever vision of his face distorted by a haze of pain and morphine.

Rachel choked back tears. Squirming from beneath the dead weight of Breece's arm, she settled herself more comfortably in the goose-down mattress. Quills pricked her side and back. Every night for two weeks now, the baby's patient mournful wail had pierced through to her from the burying ground. Imagination, she told herself, but tonight she was glad for the clamorous fury of the storm. Wind shrieked through the barren hollows about the house and drove snow against the window panes with a gravelly spatter.

Presently, Rachel began to drift. Swept gradually into the tidal rhythms of Breece's respiration, she dreamed of a sun-dappled forest clearing, the warm bundle of a breathing child against her breasts, ribbons woven into its fine hair.

A sound woke her. Her heart pounded against her ribs; frigid air needled her lungs. Breece slept restlessly beside her, his scored knuckles curved beneath his chin, his breath sour. Big downy-looking snowflakes swirled beyond the window. The storm had abated, the wind died down. Rachel held her breath and listened.

Nothing.

And then, just as she began to breathe, there it was again—the shrill cry of the child cutting through the night from the burying ground. Panic knotted Rachel's throat. She pushed aside the covers and crossed the icy floor to stand in the chill radiance of the window.

Through her faint homely reflection, twisted by the brittle skin of ice that had grown over the glass, Rachel looked out at a world rounded and dimensionless beneath a dingy lid of snow. The oak tree loomed against the moonlit sky like a shaggy grandfather, bearded gray by the storm. Farther away, on a hill that would turn gentle and green come spring, lay the burying ground. Three roughly carven wooden markers and a single wooden cross, knotted about with rawhide strips, leaned like jagged teeth from the frozen earth. The markers indicated the graves of Breece's folks, dead two decades, and his first wife, Shelley, dead near upon three years now. The cross wasn't even two weeks old; it marked the spot where Rachel's child had been buried.

"Rachel?" Breece said, and she turned to see him sitting upright in a tangle of blankets. He watched her alertly.

"Listen," she said. "Can you hear it?"

She looked back out the window and the sound of the baby came to her with the icy clarity of undiluted pain. Rachel felt as if a knitting needle had been plunged into her heart.

"Hear what?"

Rachel wrapped herself in an embrace and saw that tiny goose bumps had erupted along her forearms. "The baby."

Breece sighed. She heard the covers shift, his bare feet against the floorboards. "Come to bed now," he said, appearing in the window as a ghostly reflection. "Ain't nothing out there."

"Don't you *hear* it?"

"I don't hear a thing except you talking foolishness." His hands closed about her arms. "Ain't nothing to hear."

"Our baby's crying, Breece."

"Baby's dead, Rachel," he said gently. "You know that."

Anger boiled out of some poisoned well within her. "I don't know that," she said. "I never saw the baby. You buried him without me ever seeing him. I don't know that."

Breece's rough hand came up to smooth hair from her forehead. "Nothing out there, Rachel. Nothing at all." He guided her back to the bed.

For a long time Rachel lay awake, staring at the ceiling and listening to the baby cry through the darkness. Very clearly, in her mind's eye, she could see the tiny flannel night dress, hand-sewn against the cold. "You buried him naked, didn't you, Breece?" she asked. "You buried him naked and now he's about to freeze."

But Breece was already sleeping, and he didn't answer.

"I'm going to see about hiring a man in Copperhead tomorrow," Breece said at breakfast. "I'm going to need a fellow come spring."

The small kitchen was chilly, despite the fire blazing in the stove. Rachel sipped at her coffee before she answered. "You never had to hire anyone before."

Breece probed at his eggs with his fork. Thick dry yolk clogged the tines. Rachel still hadn't mastered the technique of getting the whites solid and keeping the yolks runny, the way Breece liked them.

"There's too much work around the place," he said. "It ain't getting any easier, old as I am."

"You ain't all that old."

Breece grunted as if to say, sixteen years older than you, Rachel. But all he said aloud was, "Maybe I'll just hire a boy. I could use an extra hand."

Unbidden, an image flashed through Rachel's mind: the cross Breece had driven into the cold earth over the child's grave. She shook her head, gathered up her dishes, and moved to the wash basin. The water was pleasantly warm from the stove, and she liked the clean, biting smell of the soap. She imagined a fresh-bathed baby girl might smell that way.

A few minutes passed, and Rachel had begun to hope that Breece wouldn't say anything more when he spoke again. "How you feeling?" he asked.

A plate slipped out of her hand, bobbed to the surface without breaking, and Rachel felt tears start up behind her eyes. "Just fine, Breece."

"Turn around here and look at me."

Rachel dipped the plate into the rinse water, and turned to face him.

Breece gestured vaguely with his fork. "You know what I mean. How do you feel down there?"

Rachel stared at the floor. "Well, I don't know, Breece."

"Are you hurting any?"

"A little, I guess."

Breece shook his head. "You'll be all right soon," he said gruffly, and a minute later she heard his fork clatter to his plate and the door bang shut behind him.

An immense silence followed. For a moment, Rachel imagined she could hear the faint ghostly sound of a baby crying, and then she shook her head again.

Imagination.

Still, she could not get the matter out of her head. Breece was over forty now, anxious for a child. Last July, when he had taken her down to Sauls Run for the fireworks, he had almost said as much. *You can't take care of that farm when I'm gone*, he had said then. Skyrockets exploded into radiant showers behind him, and Rachel felt sweep through her a wave of sympathy for all that beauty. Breece glanced shyly at her belly, which had barely begun to swell, and when he met her eyes, she saw that his face was all ashine with fierce joy. *Our boy*, he had said, *he'll take care of it*.

And that was the problem, Rachel thought, as she slid the last dish into the cupboard. For Breece, a child was just a means to an end; he wouldn't care that the next child would not be the same as the first. As long as it was a boy, everything would be fine as far as Breece was concerned, and already he was after her to try again.

✳   ✳   ✳

Rachel was heating a pot of stew for dinner when the stranger arrived. When the knock sounded at the front door, Breece set aside the newspaper he had picked up last week in Copperhead, stood, and went out into the hall. He returned a moment later, followed by a dark-headed man clad in a black linen suit, and a great overcoat that hung to his shiny boots. He clasped a scuffed leather case in one hand, and extended his other to Rachel as he crossed the kitchen. In the instant before her hand was engulfed in his firm grip, Rachel looked up and found herself staring into a pleasant, clean-shaven face split by a wide mouth.

"Evening, ma'am."

Rachel tried to speak, but her mouth had gone dry. She cleared her throat and felt a hot flush mount her cheeks. "Evening," she managed. Flustered, she turned to the stove, and discovered that her spoon had slipped into the stew.

"This here is Rowe Montgomery," Breece said. He sat down at the table and nodded at Rachel. "My wife."

Rachel nodded politely, and watched as Montgomery draped his great coat over the back of a chair. "My horse slipped and lamed himself up the valley aways," he said. "Your husband said you all could put me up for the evening."

"Pleased to have you," Rachel said.

"I thought I'd run him down Copperhead come morning, since I was going anyway." Breece looked at Montgomery. "You can catch a train there, or buy yourself another horse."

Rachel placed bowls around the table, setting the chipped one at her own place and turning it to hide the flaw. She served the stew with cool milk from the cellar and fresh-baked bread. Breece devoured his food as though he was afraid some one would take it away from him. Rachel ate with embarrassed delicacy, keeping a covert watch over Montgomery.

"Good stew," Montgomery remarked at one point, and once again Rachel felt a hot flush mount her cheeks. She nodded, and stared at the table. She could feel Breece eyeing her.

After the meal, Breece lifted his rifle from the pegs above the door and shrugged into his old coat.

"Where are you off to?" Rachel asked.

"We got to see about Mr. Montgomery's horse."

"You're not aiming to kill it, are you?"

"I don't know," Breece said. He looked at Montgomery. "He's all lamed up, ain't he?"

Montgomery nodded, and Breece turned to meet Rachel's gaze. His eyes gleamed in the light from the stove, and all at once, as if her mama was standing right there and had spoken into her ear, Rachel again heard the words she had last night remembered: *Breece Casey is a practical man.*

"We better see to that horse," Breece said to Montgomery, and then they were gone.

"What is it that you do for a living, Mr. Montgomery?" Rachel asked when they returned. She looked up from her knitting, and gazed at the two men by the stove. Breece slouched in a kitchen chair and whittled, his thin face shadowed with gray stubble, his eyes hooded. Montgomery sat with his back straight and his white sleeves rolled back over forearms thick with dark corkscrews of hair. He had remarkable posture, Rachel thought.

"I'm a salesman, Mrs. Casey."

Breece paused in his whittling. "What is it you sell?"

"Books. I sell the Fellowship House Bible by subscription." Montgomery met Rachel's eyes and smiled.

Rachel glanced away. She saw that she had dropped a stitch and she set aside the knitting in frustration. "I would imagine most everybody owned a Bible already."

"Yes, ma'am, that's a fact." Montgomery laced his fingers behind his head and stared through the grate at the fire. Flames danced and licked at the hollows of his face.

"What makes your Bibles so special that people would want to buy them?" Rachel asked.

"I sure am glad you asked that, ma'am." Montgomery stood, retrieved his leather case, and returned to his seat. "All I have here are samples," he said, extracting a bundle of cardboard sheets from the case, "but it would be a real pleasure to put you folks down for one, seeing as you've been so kind and all."

Breece straightened up in his chair a little and put aside his whittling.

"Now the missus asked what it is that makes our Bible so special," Rowe Montgomery said, "and that's a good place to start." He flipped over the first of the cardboard sheets, and Rachel saw that a printed page had been pasted there.

"The first thing that makes our Bible different, is that the words of our Lord Jesus Christ—blessed be his name—are printed in red ink. That way you can see them real easy."

Breece leaned forward to study the cardboard sheet. Montgomery indicated the red print, and Rachel saw that his cuticles formed perfect little half-moons beneath his nails.

Breece said, "I reckon it reads the same no matter what color the ink is," and a stiff embarrassed silence followed. Rachel sighed and looked away, painfully aware of the little kitchen's shabbiness. The floorboards had long since faded to a dingy gray and it seemed to her that the whole room stank of soot and bacon grease. They didn't even have a proper fireplace, just that old iron cook stove. All at once it occurred to her to wonder why she had ever married Breece, and just as suddenly a sharp voice that sounded suspiciously like that of her mama spoke up. *You didn't really have a choice, did you Rachel?* said the nasty little voice. *Twenty-five years old, and not a single proposal!*

Rachel glanced around the rundown kitchen again and felt a wave of sorrow ebb through her. No place for a little girl, anyway, she thought, and grief twisted through her guts. For a little while, in the excitement of having a real live visitor, she had managed to forget it.

"Well, now, Mr. Casey," Montgomery said, "you're right about that—the words read just the same. But they stand out, you see, the way the words of our Lord Jesus ought to."

Breece nodded, and Rachel saw that he had retreated into his customary reticence.

"But that's not all that makes the Fellowship House Bible unique," Montgomery continued.

"What else is there?" Rachel asked.

"Pictures," said Rowe Montgomery. "The Fellowship House Bible has the finest illustrations of any such volume on the market, ma'am. There are seventy illustrations total—one for every book, and two for each of the gospels. Each one is guaranteed to be historically accurate."

"Can I see them?" Rachel asked.

Montgomery passed the sheaf of cardboard sheets to her, and Rachel began to page through them. From the dark mouth of a tomb, a man wrapped in dirty rags staggered toward the figure of a mystically glowing Christ, who stood with his head thrown back and his arms lifted to the heavens. The caption below the picture read: *Lazarus came forth, bound hand and foot with graveclothes.*

Rachel pursed her lips and flipped the next sheet of cardboard. Vertigo tore through her. Mounted soldiers exploded from the painting, and a slaughter-house stench of blood and sweat flooded the room. As the horsemen swept past, Rachel flattened herself against a stone wall and clutched her screaming baby to her breasts. Thick dust clogged her lungs. The thunder of hooves and the panic-stricken shrieks of women and children choked the dense air.

Sobbing, Rachel turned to flee, but she hadn't gone more than a few steps before a horseman materialized out of the dust and snatched the infant from her arms.

"No!" Rachel screamed.

She threw herself against the rearing stallion, but already she was too late. With a look of withering disdain, the horseman drew back the gore-stained blade of his knife, plunged it once again into the child's breast, and—

Rachel gasped.

She felt as if all the air had been sucked out of the room, as if she could not draw breath. *Then Herod was exceeding wroth,* the caption read, *and sent forth, and slew all the children that were in Bethlehem.* Her fingers loosened. The cardboard sheets slid to the floor in a heap, and Rachel felt tears start down her cheeks. A gentle touch caressed her jaw, and for a moment she allowed herself to hope that Rowe Montgomery had crossed the room to comfort her, but when she looked up, it was, of course, only Breece.

Upstairs, as Rachel changed into her gown, she could not help but run a finger over the tiny flannel night dress she had placed in the cedar-scented drawer where she kept her underthings. Shadows hovered in the flickering light, and for a moment Rachel could believe that dark horsemen tarried beyond the oil-lamp's dim pool of radiance. Distant as the trickle of water in an underground creek-bed, she heard the muffled thunder of hooves. Somewhere far away, a woman wept, and the screams of dying children filled the air.

Rachel shivered, folded the small night dress, and shut the drawer. She blew out the bedside lamp and eased herself into the corona of Breece's animal heat.

Another storm had closed in. Gray snow, silent as a midnight intruder, spun outside the window. The wind was hushed, the quiet so encompassing that it seemed to her that the snow had smothered every noise in the world.

Outside, the baby began to cry.

Rachel stiffened beside her husband. Imagination, she thought, and she closed her eyes, but words leapt into the void of thought: *Lazarus came forth, bound hand and foot with graveclothes.*

Rachel remembered the long hours of labor. Agony like a dagger twisted in her guts, sweat stood on her brow as she fought to expel the child—

—*the girl, the baby girl*—

—from her body.

And then, suddenly, the pain was gone. It was if she had fallen into a well. A dim circle of awareness receded above her until at last it disappeared and she plunged, not sleeping but not awake, into the subterranean depths of unconsciousness. When next she became aware, the pain, the sweat-soiled bedclothes, and the desire, the reflexive *need*, to thrust the child from her body—all these were gone. A faraway circle of radiance, shiny as a new coin, gradually took shape above her; centered in that circle, she saw the doctor's grim visage. She could smell his familiar whiskey stink. Somehow, she had known that he was packing his instruments for the ride to Copperhead, known, too, that in the vast reach of darkness between the two glimpses of light, she had given birth to a child.

She felt a dull pinch in her upper arm, and darkness edged in around her.

When it once again retreated, Breece stood before her. *The baby was born dead*, he had said.

And perhaps that was true. Except . . .

Except that she could hear it during the long hours of darkness when sleep would not come. She could hear it, the patient mournful cry of a child in the night. With astonishing clarity, that strange vision loomed up before her: the horseman rearing up and away from her as he drove the gore-stained knife into her baby's breast.

Why couldn't the baby rest?

A terrible suspicion blossomed within her.

After breakfast, Breece headed out to the barn to hitch up the wagon for the ride into Copperhead. Rachel watched him tramp away through the ice-sheathed lens of the kitchen window. She turned back to her dishes. Exhaustion stitched her eyelids, and sour nausea coiled through her guts. The baby had not let up last night. Rachel had not slept.

Behind her, Rowe Montgomery cleared his throat. Rachel turned, wiping her hands on a dish towel. Montgomery stood by the kitchen table, muffled in his boots and great coat.

"I'm sorry about last night, Mrs. Casey," he said. "I didn't know those pictures would upset you."

Rachel set the towel aside. "There ain't no way you could have known. You oughtn't feel responsible."

"I'm mighty sorry about your loss." He paused as if he expected Rachel to speak. When she did not, he went on. "I went ahead and put you down for one of the Bibles—"

"Breece and I, we can't afford no fancy books."

"Think of it as a gift," he said. He glanced at the case by his feet. "It's just my way of saying thanks for all you folks done for me. It's my way of saying I'm sorry."

Rachel smiled. Warmth radiated from the core of her being. "Thank you, Mr. Montgomery, that's right nice." She glanced out the window and saw Breece emerge from the barn, leading the horse and wagon. "Breece is coming," she said. "He'll be anxious to get started."

Montgomery nodded and picked up his case.

"Goodbye, Mr. Montgomery," Rachel said. She turned back to her washing.

A moment passed. "Mrs. Casey?"

"Yes?"

"I thought I heard something last night."

Rachel's heart quickened. She felt suspended in the moment, trapped, like an insect she had once seen preserved in a square of amber. She tried to speak, but her throat had rusted closed like an old pipe, and the moment stretched, an elastic interval in which it seemed all time and movement had ceased except for the blood pounding through her brain. At last she managed to work up enough spit to say, "What did you think you heard?"—and time lurched forward again.

She dipped a plate into the soapy water and began to scrub dried egg yolk away. The kitchen smelled of coffee and wood smoke. Breece's whip snapped as he urged the horse through the snow toward the house.

"Sounded like a baby," said Rowe Montgomery.

The plate slipped from her soapy fingers and smashed on the edge of the metal tub. The sound was very loud in the small room. Clay shards skimmed across the floor.

"Probably just a bobcat," Rachel said. "They sound like a child sometimes." She turned to look at him.

He had not moved. He held the leather case in one hand. His face formed a pale smear beyond the dark folds of his upturned collar. He smiled suddenly, and when he spoke his voice boomed with forced gaiety. "Of course," he said. "Probably just a bobcat. I spend so much time on the road, you know. My imagination, it gets carried away with me."

Still smiling, he started to move toward the door.

"Do you believe in ghosts?" Rachel asked.

Montgomery stopped and fixed her with his clear gaze. "Well, ma'am, I don't rightly know."

Rachel heard the wagon rattle to a halt outside. The horse whickered and stamped. Breece yelled Montgomery's name.

"I reckon you ought to go," Rachel said.

Rowe Montgomery stepped to the door, paused with his hand on the latch, and looked back at her. "My grandma, now, she used to say that spirits lingered, if you hadn't done them right." He stared at Rachel, but she had the feeling that he did not see her. She thought he had the look of a man staring way off into the past, or into himself, and she felt as if she stood at the verge of some vast mystery that with his next words would be revealed.

Outside, Breece hollered again, his voice impatient.

Montgomery shook his head and smiled. "That's just an old wives tale," he said. "As for myself, I don't know what to believe." He dipped his head, and opened the door.

The frigid breath of February illuminated the small kitchen. Rachel caught a glimpse of the wagon and the snow-covered yard beyond, and then the door closed with a bang and Rowe Montgomery was gone.

Rachel had not been alone for more than an hour when the crying began. She tightened her lips and resolved to ignore it. *Idle hands are devil's tools!* her mama had frequently told her, and remembering that, Rachel swept through the house in a virtual frenzy, as if, in the mind-deadening industry of scoured floors and straightened cupboards, she could somehow submerge the patient clamor of the child.

And then, without even an awareness of how she had come to be there, Rachel found herself in the bedroom. She was sitting on the bed with the baby's tiny night dress cradled in her hands. The complaint of the buried child—conspicuous as a single dark thread woven through a swatch of shining white—pierced all through the stillness of the abandoned house. Tears carved icy runnels through her flesh. There fell over her the shadow of that awful suspicion which had last night taken root in the soil of her heart.

This was what she most feared, most believed:

Breece Casey had killed her baby daughter.

Even as she allowed this insight to frame itself in her mind, she told herself that it was not true, that it could not be true. And yet she could not help but believe it.

For Breece Casey was a practical man. Her mama had told her that, and if Rachel had learned anything in the last year, it was the truth of that statement. Breece Casey was a practical man.

His was the kind of practicality that hesitated not for one moment to shoot a lamed horse, his the kind of practicality that sought a spinster for a wife—not for love and certainly not for beauty, but for the simple peasant strength of her large-boned body and the inescapable utility of her wide-slung hips, through which might issue ruddy strong-limbed heirs, their tiny fists already clenched in anticipation of the long labors that awaited them. And when those wide hips delivered forth not the first of those ruddy-faced little boys, but a pink and screaming baby girl—what then? His was the kind of practicality that would not hesitate to place a pillow over that child's face and hold it there until her screaming stopped.

Such things were not uncommon, Rachel knew, and it would have been a simple matter to buy the doctor's silence. An occasional bottle of whiskey would have done it—infinitely cheaper than the cost of raising a daughter.

Rachel Casey, married for eleven interminable months, stood and folded the little night dress against her breasts.

Spirits linger, if you haven't done them right, Rowe Montgomery had said, and all at once Rachel saw what had to be done.

For Breece Casey's was the kind of practicality that would bury a little girl naked to save his wife the labor of sewing a new night dress when the next child—

—*a boy, a little boy*—

—was born, and Rachel could not allow it.

Rachel drove the spade into the frozen earth with all her weight; the muscles in her shoulders and arms tensed with the effort. Heavy flakes of snow, gray with the pollution of the coal mines down Copperhead, drifted through her field of vision. With every shovelful of earth, the child's crying ratcheted up a notch or two.

Rachel emptied the spade onto the mound of dirt by the grave, wiped perspiration from her forehead with cold-numbed fingers, and reached once again into the pocket of Breece's woolen work coat. The flannel night dress was still there. She paused to catch her breath, propping her weight against the smooth haft of the shovel.

A low-slung leaden sky brooded over the mountains. To her left, white smoke curled from the ramshackle chimney of the farmhouse, and for a single bitterly amused instant, she wondered why she had ever found the kitchen chilly. Then, with a glance toward the stark tree-lined ridges that rose in steep ranks to her right, she got back to work.

The blade clanged as it smashed against the wooden coffin. The clamorous bellow of the child grew still louder.

She shook her head to dislodge tears before they froze to her cheeks, and began to dig with renewed vigor. Before twenty minutes passed she had widened the hole sufficiently to scramble down, grasp the tiny coffin by the burlap handles at either end, and wrestle it from the ground. The crying was very loud now. She saw that the box was not a proper coffin at all—merely a big loose-boarded shipping crate from the commissary down Copperhead—and a swift arrow of hatred for Breece lodged within her.

Rachel collapsed beside the coffin. The empty grave gaped like an open gate into some undiscovered country. She fought off a bout of hysterical laughter. The baby's noise had evolved into a fortress of sound, walling her away from even the most immediate perceptions—the darkening sky as the dull copper blur of the sun inched below the high western ridges, the knife-edged gust of the wind as it poured out of the high passes into the bleak bowl of Breece Casey's farm, her own fingers, curled into frozen talons.

None of this mattered. None of it.

Rachel flung back the wooden lid. Rusty hinges squealed; the lid shuddered against the mounded soil.

Rachel was shocked to see that the child had been wrapped in a thick woolen blanket. Tiny fingers curled beneath its chin, and its face wrinkled in an expression of boundless noisy energy. For the briefest possible instant, Rachel believed the child alive; then she saw that it had merely been preserved by the icy weather. She lifted the baby with trembling fingers and clasped it to her chest. Cold, so cold. That terrific bawling complaint continued to pour from its frozen lungs. Her heart pounding, she fumbled beneath the blanket to check.

A boy, she thought, a boy, *it's a boy, it's a—*

"Rachel!"

Blood hammered through her veins. Clasping the baby against her breasts, she stumbled to her feet and wheeled around to face the house. A figure emerged from the swirling snow. Rachel staggered back, believing that a grinning horseman loomed out of the storm before her, his knife arm drawn back to strike the fatal blow. Then, as quickly as it had possessed her, the illusion passed. A man on foot walked toward her, his head bowed against the intensifying storm.

Breece, she thought. Breece.

Rachel clutched the tiny corpse to herself. The baby shrieked. "You murderer!" she screamed. Cradling the child with one hand, she drew back the other, frozen into a twisted talon, to batter Breece away. "Son of a bitch! Murderer!"

Breece caught her arm even as it swung toward him. Frost rimed the whiskers around his lips. His eyes flashed out at her in a way she had not seen since that long-ago July 4th, shiny with strong emotion, grief and fear and maybe—

—maybe love.

Breece Casey is a practical man, hissed that insistent voice.

"No! You've got it wrong, all wrong!"

"Then how? How?"

"It was an accident," he whispered hoarsely. "The doctor, that goddamned drunken doctor."

Rachel stumbled away and went to her knees. She felt as if the Earth had abruptly shifted on its axis, and for a single vertiginous instant, she thought she might be sick. Snow soaked the fabric of her skirt. When she lifted her head to look at Breece, hair whipped about her face. His eyes had filled with tears. Rachel saw then how it must have been for him—the guilt and anger, the burden of a grief that surpassed his meager store of words. Most of all, the knowledge he had tried to save her: the baby could have lived. All at once, there passed before her the memory of that distant July— skyrockets raining down glory all about them; Breece's face, aglow with fierce joy. An incandescent blaze of feeling brighter than anything she had known illuminated her, and her callow fantasies of Rowe Montgomery ignited like a heap of cardboard images.

"Help me," Rachel said. "Help me dress him."

She fumbled the tiny night dress from her pocket, and Breece helped her tug it around the baby's stiffened limbs. The wailing began to die away, to stutter off into hiccoughs and gasps, and finally silence. Rachel held the child against her for a moment, pressed her lips to its icy flesh, and placed it into the wooden crate. She tucked the blanket in tight around it, and together, they lowered the crate into the earth.

"Go, now," Breece said, "you go on. I'll finish here." Rachel hesitated, hearing in her mind the baby's terrible draining cry. But that was over now; it was time to trust. Clutching the woolen coat close, Rachel turned and walked downhill to the house. She heard the rasp of the shovel, the rattle of dirt against the coffin, but after a few more steps even those sounds faded. She walked on through a deep easy silence that seemed to fill up the world.

Quinn's Way

JEMMY E. USED TO SAY THAT SAULS RUN WAS
so small that if you farted on the east side of town, they'd be talking about it on the west side before the stink even died. By the time
I was twelve years old, I knew this to be a lie. These days it has
become fashionable for folks to claim they have been abused: physically, mentally, sexually, you name it, I've seen it all and litigated
most of it. But in those days—the good old days, a few of the treas-
ured relics I call friends like to term them—no one claimed anything of the sort, under any circumstances. Ever. Which is not to say
that it didn't exist—though most of the aforementioned relics would
say it didn't—or that most people weren't aware of it either. Such
atrocities have always been more common than most folks like to
think about, and good people everywhere have mastered the art of
not seeing what's plain before their eyes, and maybe that's okay, too.
In my bleaker moments, I've often thought that our illusions
alone—our cherished, beloved illusions—enable us to wake up
each morning without stuffing the barrel of a revolver in our col-
lective mouths.

But such philosophical abstractions don't help much when
you're twelve years old and in almost constant pain—physical or
mental, or both more often than you want to think about. By the
time I was twelve, I knew that the town of Sauls Run stank, literally
(of the coal slag forever smoldering in the hills above town) and

figuratively (we'll get to that). I knew also that the stink was a miasma more oppressive than any mere intestinal gas. And I had begun dimly and with horror to perceive that it just might not be limited to Sauls Run; it might be present everywhere. But one thing I knew and knew for certain: Jemmy E. had it wrong when he said that Sauls Run was so small that everybody in town was sure to gossip about the latest stink. The truth was that nobody in town would say a word about the things that really stank in Sauls Run, West Virginia.

But we both knew that everyone could smell them.

In forty years as a lawyer, I have learned one true thing about stories, real stories as opposed to fictional ones. They have no true beginnings. There is an irony in this, I suppose, for if I have learned even one other true thing, it is that more than anything else, people want their stories to be shapely as the stories of fiction are shapely. Clear beginnings, problematic middles, sensible resolutions.

This accounts for the fascination most folks have with the law, for a court of law is designed to create beginnings where none are visible, to force problems to unnatural resolutions. The law tells us a lie we want to believe: that past history is inadmissible. It does not matter if the thief who stole your wallet only wanted to feed his hungry children. It does not matter if the drunk driver who killed your daughter had no control over the disease coded into his genes. Beginnings lead to moral distinctions; and moral distinctions . . . well, we'll come to them too, I guess.

Thousands of facts are relevant, of course, and past history always counts, but I'm enough of a lawyer to know that still we must begin. So. This story starts in the bright, hopeful summer of a long-ago year when a good war had ended in victory, when a famine of want had drawn to a prosperous conclusion, when the nation turned its face to a future unblemished by presentiment of disaster. It begins in an age of innocence, in a day when children—even twelve-year-old boys—could still believe in magic. It begins here, with the sound of a train whistle.

Listen:

Darkness shrouded the town of Sauls Run, West Virginia, and everyone was sleeping. Nothing stirred but the wind, which chased ragged scraps of newspaper through streets of dew-settled dust. The dew had been early and generous; it glinted from every surface, from every blade of grass and leaf; it hung like jewels in the silken webs of fat and drowsy spiders. Here and there, electric night-lights shown dimly in the windows of the shuttered houses, but many homes still depended on gas and kerosene for heat and light. The great war was over, and mushroom clouds over Hiroshima and Nagasaki had ushered in an age of anxiety, but Sauls Run lingered still, only three years short of the middle of the century, in the innocent moment between the agrarian past and the industrial future. If anyone had been awake to observe it (no one was), he could have noted the juxtaposition of these worlds: in the hills above town, the mines had long since been mechanized. Great machines gnawed coal out of the earth and sometimes the arms and legs of miners, too. Here, alone of all the places near the town, men were awake and the night jostled with the noise of trucks and chain-driven cars. Elsewhere, it might have been 1897 instead of 1947. Hitching posts still stood outside most public buildings; many homes still had an outhouse in the backyard; and at three-thirty in the morning, everyone in town still slept. Cats dozed in open windows, dreaming of mice; chained up in the vacant lot by the Grand Hotel, a monkey slumbered atop a locust post, dreaming of the moist verdant jungle he used to know; even the presses of the *Daily Telegraph* were still, dreaming their unfathomable dreams—that quiet, that hushed, that peaceful.

In a ground-floor bedroom of a rambling structure near the courthouse lay a dark, fragile-looking boy named Henry Sleep— ironic, this name, for of all the people in the town, Henry Sleep alone hovered in that dreamful state between sleep and wakefulness. He alone thrashed in his bedclothes, his ears pricked to detect the slightest noise at the open window.

Listen:

The howling siren song of a locomotive broke across the sleeping town, suddenly and clear. Henry's eyelids sprang up like window shades. In the moment before he came fully awake, he dreamily recalled the poster he had first seen three endless weeks ago, tacked up among the sun-bleached war-bond placards and faded ads for patent medicines that thronged the Grand Hotel bulletin board: a tiger, a flaming hoop, these bright proclaiming words:

BITTERROOT & CRABBE'S WORLD FAMOUS
CIRCUS AND MENAGERIE!
DIRECT FROM A COMMAND PERFORMANCE
BEFORE THE CROWNED HEADS OF EUROPE FOR
A SPECIAL LIMITED ENGAGEMENT!!
3 DAYS ONLY: JUNE 7–10!!!

The train roared again, shredding the poster into streams of vivid colors. *Wake up!* it screamed. *Wake up!* Henry sat up in bed, his heart thundering. Again, the whistle shouted, and this time it blew open all the closed doors in his heart. Who cared if the whole damn town was sleeping?

Henry kicked the bedclothes aside and reached for his trousers. He slid his shoes on and lifted the window sash. Night air flooded the room, freighted with the scent of lilac. Every cell in his body screamed itself awake as he slid his leg over the windowsill and into the blackness.

Just then, just there, he experienced a single twinge of doubt. If his father found out—

Away over the folded hills and sleeping houses of Sauls Run, the whistle bellowed again. The hell with it, he thought. Ducking through the window, he dropped to the ground and headed off through the dark to find Jemmy E. The whistle blasted again as the circus train came roaring into town.

Through the deserted streets they ran: Henry Sleep and the black cowlick his mother couldn't tame, dark eyes and furtive, fearful smile; Jemmy E., wild-eyed and pale, his spiky hair ashimmer with a jack-o-lantern glow. Breathless through the dirty streets—past the monkey, scolding from his post; past the Stull house, broken window-shards like jagged hungry teeth; past the Bluehole, depthless in the moonlight, lair of serpents carnivorous and dread.

To Cinder Bottom they raced, row after row of burnished rails strewn with castoff spikes and coal. Their leather shoes pounded the ties. Smells of dirt and diesel and oiled iron hovered in the air. The train whistle shattered the stillness and harried them across the tracks to a switch-plate above the yards. Here a single track on a mounded hillock curved away to the county fairgrounds.

"Let's go!" Henry shouted. "Hurry! It's coming!"

He glanced over his shoulder. Jemmy E. had dropped to the tracks behind him. Henry paused, his breath burning in his lungs.

"What are you *doing?*"

Jemmy E. lifted his hand for silence. Henry fidgeted impatiently. The Stone Bridge loomed over the yards, black against the graying sky. Here and there a light blazed in a lonely window. Along the ridge to the west, the milkman's headlights made fitful progress from house to house. Henry's stomach growled.

"Come on!" he hollered.

"Quiet, you dope," said Jemmy E. "Listen."

Henry dropped to his knees beside the tracks. Cinders ground into the knees of his trousers; too late he regretted his carelessness. A shadow like a summer cloud slid across his heart. Then he pressed his ear to the dew-chilled rail and all shadows were forgotten. The iron bucked with tidings of the onrushing locomotive. *Bitterroot and Crabbe!* the rail screamed. *Circus! Menagerie! Coming! Coming!*

He had almost forgotten the trousers when he felt a hand at his shoulder. He twisted around, his heart rattling in its cage of ribs. Jemmy E. stood limned against the pale sky. He grinned like Old Nick himself: a grin crooked and charming, and just a little dangerous.

"Let's go!" he said.

He went, a pale blur, a wraith against the lifting dark. Henry trailed his fingers along the rail—it sang with greetings—and watched the soles of Jemmy's shoes flashing in the murk. Jemmy E.'s voice floated back to him—gently mocking—and took substance in the air: "Can't catch me!"

Henry, shouting laughter, leaped forward, his feet scrabbling for purchase in the cinders. Off like a rocket, like a bullet from a gun, sucking in lungfuls of the sweet, sweet morning air, until the other boy appeared before him. The tracks curved still farther from the Cinder Bottom railyards, dove through a crepuscular stand of birch—white trunks like sentinels in the gloom—and emerged into the open fields that bordered the fair grounds.

Bitterroot and Crabbe! sang the locomotive in a voice that filled the world. *Menagerie! Circus! Bitterroot and Crabbe!*

Out of nowhere, it bore down upon them. Henry felt its hot breath upon his shoulder; its iron wheels screamed like banshees. He lowered his head. His legs pumped furiously. His feet found the ties as if by magic. He risked a glance behind him, and the train—train?—the monster—the fury—the dragon—encompassed his entire field of vision. Still Jemmy E. fled on, an arm's length before him, his legs rising and falling as if all the demons of hell had been loosed upon his heels. The locomotive screamed like some terrible beast from the prehistoric past.

"Jemmy!" Henry screamed. "Jemmy!"

But the clangor, the din, the sheer preposterous world-shattering pandemonium of the monster sweeping down upon them, drowned out his little cry.

His feet flashed over the ties. He willed them to move faster, faster. A deadly vision hovered before him: a badly placed foot, a moment of vertigo, and then the train, the train, hungry wheels gnawing at his flesh. Henry risked another backward glance. The locomotive roared and surged after him. He screamed in exhilaration and ran as he had never run before. A little wind touched him, tugged at him. He reached out for Jemmy in the last moment before the train devoured them; together, shrieking gales of joyous laughter, they leapt from the tracks. He seemed to fall forever, and then the soft, sweet-smelling grass reached up for him with a thousand eager hands. He skidded into the marshy soil at the base of the declivity and opened one eye as the train blurred by above him in a rage of sparks and thunder.

"Damn! Did you see that? Did you? *Did you?*" Jemmy E. popped out of the weeds beside him, pounding his chest and chortling with delight. He pounced on Henry, braying demented laughter, and they wrestled with the simple joy and exhilaration of survival. At last, exhausted, they parted.

Henry plucked a long blade of grass, and sucked on it meditatively as he watched the train slow, disgorging billows of steam. An elephant trumpeted; roustabouts leapt from open cars in groups of two and three. Jemmy E. turned his face to the sky and let loose a wordless shout of delight. As if in answer, the elephant trumpeted again.

"God," said Jemmy E. "Don't you wish it could be like this forever?"

The sheer absurdity of the idea set them off again. By the time the laughter ceased, a fat crescent of orange had appeared over the eastern ridges. Henry studied his pants—so soiled with cinders and grass stains that he could only surmise their original color—and once again, that shadow passed over his heart. He glanced at Jemmy E. Now, visible in the spreading light, he saw the puffy bruise that discolored the other boy's cheek. He thought of Jemmy E.'s father, sullen drunk and down with the black lung. Not too long ago—no more than a year—Jemmy's dad had smashed him with a whiskey bottle. It took seven stitches to close that wound.

If only it didn't have to be this way, he thought. If only it could be like Jemmy E. had said: *Don't you wish it could be like this forever?* And he did, he did. Henry tilted his head against the slope, and chewed thoughtfully at the blade of grass. He closed his eyes. An inexpressible longing to extend this moment endlessly possessed him. He could not say why tears trembled at the corners of his eyes.

The hearse slid up behind Henry three blocks from home—no

longer technically a hearse, but forbidding nonetheless; long and low, forever stamped with the imprimatur of death. The county had picked it up cheap and pressed it into service as a police car, but the insignia on the door—*Sheriff*—could not wholly dispel the vehicle's macabre associations.

Once a vehicle for the dead, now the car itself was dying. The engine ran with a halting chop, and the tailpipes choked out clouds of malodorous blue smoke. But Henry trudged along the dusty street unawares, his head down, preoccupied with his thoughts. They continued thus—Henry first, the hearse lumbering after him like a cancerous mutt—for a block before the car abruptly sped up and passed him. A sooty cloud of smoke and dust engulfed Henry as the driver angled the hearse into a driveway, blocking his path.

"Henry!"

Henry licked his lips. He swallowed.

"Henry!"

"Yes, sir."

His father didn't answer. The hearse idled raggedly in the driveway, and Henry stood before it like a sinner called to judgment, his pants soiled and his suspenders dangling at his knees.

"Hello, Sheriff," someone called from down the street.

His father turned. Sunlight flashed off the badge pinned to his cap.

"Morning, Mrs. Vellner," his father hollered in that voice he had—Henry's mother called it his "people voice," mellifluous and charming. "Charlie doing okay?" He used the smile that went with the voice. Without looking at Henry, he said, "Get in the car, son."

Henry climbed in, swinging the door closed on its rusty hinges. It latched with a fatal thunk. His father backed the hearse into the street. The car sputtered, coughing smoke as they started slowly home.

"You weren't in your room this morning, son."

"No, sir."

"Circus train come in this morning. A fellow down the fairgrounds told me it near killed a couple kids on the track out there. You know anything about that?"

Henry didn't answer.

"I drove down t'other side of town. Seems Jemmy E. wasn't in his room this morning either."

Henry stared out the window and did not speak. The air felt cool against his face. At the intersection near the courthouse, ten or twelve cattle milled. Three boys with switches hustled about, urging them on. His father cut left to avoid the back-up.

"You know what I think of that boy."

"Yes, sir."

"Well, what then?"

Henry blinked twice. "He's no account. Him nor his family."

His father didn't answer. They made another cut and the house came into view, a sprawling clapboard structure built by three generations of Sleeps of uncertain architectural competence. It stood at the corner, bordered on the east by a brick belonging to the Millers and on the west by fields that climbed to the rim of the valley and the ridge beyond. Last summer, Henry and his father had painted the house, or Henry had painted it while his father limped along behind him, offering advice.

The limp was what the Germans had done to him, that and something more: for the man who came back from the war could be grim and cruel in a way that the man who left never had been. Henry still remembered the first time he had seen the archipelago of scars rising from the dense hair on his father's calf—like the humped spine of a serpent breaking the surface of a black, black sea. Even now, when his father wasn't home, he occasionally sneaked upstairs to gaze at his father's medals, arrayed as casually as a pocketful of change atop the dresser. His father had served in the war and he was a hero, Henry's mother liked to say. But he had seen some awful things, and now he was a little broken inside and they had to love him anyway. Henry tried to imagine what it was like to be broken inside—he had an image of sharp little pieces of glass poking into everything—but his father had started to speak again:

"That ain't all is it, Henry?"

"No, sir."

"Well go on, then."

Henry swallowed. "He ain't no account and you don't want me running around with him. They ain't—they aren't—" That was his mother's voice, that correction. "They aren't our kind of folks."

His father braked in front of the house. He turned the car off. "Your mother ain't going to be happy when she sees those trousers."

"No, sir."

"Go on in the house and get them off. Maybe your Mom can wash them before the stains set."

"Yes, sir." Henry opened the door and started toward the house. His father said:

"I'll be along directly, Henry. We got some business together."

"Yes, sir."

"Go on, then. I'll be along."

Henry's mother waited in the kitchen. When she saw him, she

said, "Oh, Henry," but he sped by without speaking, through the living room, past the kitchen and dining room, and down the hall to his bedroom. He stripped off the soiled pants and left them in the hall for his mother. He could hear her out there, saying, "Asa, please—"

"Leave me alone, Lil," his father said. "The boy has to learn."

"He doesn't have to learn. He's a child. He'll learn soon enou—"

A quick sharp sound like a handclap stilled her, and Henry didn't have to be there to see the expression on her face. He had seen it before, her lips in a narrow whitened line, her large eyes swimming as she turned away. Henry clenched his fists and stared out the window. The sun stood straight overhead and the world looked hard-edged and sharp, without shadow. The full heat of the day had begun to bear down and a stillness had settled over the town. Dust from the streets gathered on the windowsill and on the stone walk to the disused privy; it coated even the grass and leaves, so that everything seemed less alive and green than it had that morning, as if all the magic had drained out of the world.

From the doorway, his father said, "Henry."

He still wore his uniform, blue slacks, gray shirt, gun-laden belt. He had taken off his cap. Henry could see tiny beads of sweat on his forehead. His scalp was chafed pink by his hatband where his hair had started to thin. He carried a willow switch, green where he had cut it.

"Now, then," his father said, without raising his voice. He came into the room and closed the door. He moved with an awkward gait, lunging with his good leg and sweeping the other one along behind it, so you could hear it and know he was coming—a thump and a long sweep, like somebody dragging a body across a wooden floor.

Henry lowered his underwear. He braced himself against the mattress and dragged a pillow close so he could bite down on it if he had to. He had learned not to cry out.

"This hurts me more than it does you, son."

Henry clenched his jaws as the willow switch descended with a hiss, but you could not prepare yourself for the pain. Fire raced along his bottom. His father grunted with the effort of it. Again. Again. Again. Each blow so painful that it seemed you could not experience such hurt and live.

Henry squeezed his eyes shut so hard that tears streamed down his face. His father was a good man. *He was!* He was a hero. Henry tried to picture the medals arrayed across the dresser and tried to remember his mother's words: *It was the war that had made him this way. It was the war, it was—*

But then he couldn't think that anymore. He couldn't think anything. It was all he could do not to scream—

His father paused, breathing hard. "Okay, son."

Henry collapsed against the bed. A moment passed, and when he thought he could stand without falling, he eased the undershorts over the welts. The brassy clamor of the circus band drifted through the open window; they were tuning up in the square by the courthouse.

"Parade's fixing to get underway," his father said. He shook his head. "You're grounded, son. You got to learn."

His father dragged him from the sprawling circus tent, saying over and over in his gentle voice, "You got to learn. You got to learn." The voice had a bizarre, sinister quality that puzzled Henry until he realized that it wasn't his father speaking at all. It was a clown, a capering, grinning harlequin with hair that jutted out in three comical tufts; he wore gigantic, floppy pantaloons, and shoes six sizes too big. The clown seized his collar and dragged him through the muck. Henry thrashed in desperation, but the clown just clutched him tighter. At last it paused, moonlight like teeth in those unruly tufts of hair. It leaned into his face. If the voice—

—his father's voice—

—had been unsettling, this was worse. Shadows slid like oil over the thing's face, and in this oleaginous play of dark and light, Henry saw that the bulbous rubber nose had come askew, and the colorful greasepaint had started to run. Underneath, he thought he saw another face, lupine and cruel, but in the mercurial light, he couldn't be sure. The clown moved closer, his breath a contagion in the air. He lifted Henry higher, and only then, dangling helpless above the ground, did Henry see the willow switch. The clown whipped it around in vicious, whispering circles. Henry could feel the wind of its passage. "You got to learn," the clown chanted. "You got to learn, you—"

"—dope! Come on! *Wake up!*"

Henry opened his eyes. Twilight shimmered among the trees, insubstantial as gauze. Jemmy E. stood at the window, his hair wildly aspike. He had a fresh bruise on his cheek, and a light in his eyes like Henry had never seen before.

"Come *on*," he said. "It'll be starting soon."

Henry rubbed at his eyes. Mocking rags of dream—

—got to learn!—

—drifted in the still air. "What?" he said. He sat up too fast, and sharp little barbs sizzled along his back and rear. Then he remembered. The circus had come to town at last. "I can't. My dad."

"The hell with your dad," said Jemmy E. "The hell with him and his whole damn town. Come on!"

"I can't."

But there it was, clear and beckoning through the evening air, the voice of the circus: the honeyed charm of cotton candy and magicians, the monstrous chortle of the freaks. There it was: the joyous shout of the calliope, the basso trumpet of the elephant, the brassy jig of the band, the snap of canvas in a summer breeze. The voice of all wild, untamed things, calling out to his boy's heart. He would not let this be taken from him. He could not.

Out then, out through the window to the welcoming dark, to streets lit fitfully by fireflies and moonlight. Out and away, his father's house eclipsed by night. To Cinder Bottom and the fairgrounds beyond, to the midway thronged with townsfolk in their grays and browns. You could see the coal in the lines of their tired faces and their knotty, bruise-knuckled hands, in their clothes and hair and in their eyes, hungry for wonder. The circus folk flitted like spirits among them—hucksters and acrobats, dwarves and clowns, their faces burnished and shiny beneath the electric lights strung hastily overhead. Alleys and alleys full of such people—jugglers, vendors, freaks and fortune-tellers—talking and yelling and selling all at once in glorious pandemonium. And such smells! Hot dogs and cotton candy and good old-fashioned sweat, and over all, the wild, earthy exhalation of the animals, caged and tawny in their alley beyond the tent.

A trumpet sounded, and a barker cried out in the dark. "This way," said Jemmy E. He grabbed Henry's hand, and led him through the twisting crowds that shuffled toward the tent, their faces slack and eager, like the faces of pilgrims or of children. They ducked through the slow-crawling line to the ticket booth; ran along a track of garishly painted boxcars, shuttered now and dim; and emerged into the lane where the animal cages had been parked. Smells hung heavy in the air here—smells of wet fur and old straw and rotting meat; and the unfettered stink of the animals themselves, tigers astalk in their cages, goats huddled in their pen, elephants all in line, hooked trunk to tail as they waited with sad, patient eyes for the show to get underway. Just ahead, in the pool of radiance beneath an electric bulb, three roustabouts struggled to control a balky horse. Jemmy E. clutched at Henry.

"Now," he whispered fiercely, and for the second time that night, Henry saw a light in his eyes that he'd never seen before. A crazed shine of joy or fear or maybe both.

They ducked into a narrow space between two cages. A heavy paw swiped the air over their heads, and Jemmy chuckled fearlessly. Beyond the cages, the crawl space ended at a wall of taut canvas.

"Here," said Jemmy E., tugging at the base of the tent. He lifted it a foot while Henry crawled beneath it, and then he followed. The vast space within was garishly illuminated. Henry saw towering many-peopled stands, three vacant rings in the center of the earthen floor, and everywhere troupes of ebullient clowns. Then the lights went out, plunging them into impenetrable dark. There was a sound as of a thousand in-drawn breaths.

The circus had begun.

The lights blazed up with a flourish of trumpets. In marched the circus folk, led by a tall, cadaverous ringmaster clad in tails, his gray hair in a fan across his collar. Acrobats tumbled, clowns capered, elephants marched in lockstep with exotic women astride their broad heads. Around the tent they went, big cats roaring in their cages, horses prancing, jugglers juggling.

A flame of joy sprang alight in the heart of Henry Sleep. He flipped a hank of hair from his eyes, and watched hungrily, needfully. Around and around the circus people marched while the crowd cheered them on . . . and then the show began. The ringmaster appeared and disappeared as if by magic, in the darkness of the first ring or in the brilliance of the third or in the towering reaches of the tent itself, on a platform high atop the center post. Act after act he introduced in a rich-timbred voice that filled the airy reaches of the big top: Knife Throwing! Frank Buck and the Lions of Darkest Africa! The Soaring Marconi Brothers and the Never-Before-Attempted Triple Somersault!

On and on it went, act after fabulous act, a seizure of delight that Henry hoped would never end. But at last the tent fell dark. With a flourish, the ringmaster appeared in a spotlight. He bowed deeply and wished them a good night.

Jemmy E. tugged at Henry's sleeve. Out they went, under the canvas into the space between the cages, down the reeking alley to the lane of shuttered boxcars. As they merged into the crowd, Henry's heart jumped into his throat. He had seen his father.

"Run!" screamed Jemmy E.

But it was too late. Jemmy's face had gone slack; the bruises stood out lividly against his pale flesh. "We have to run, Henry," he whispered. "We have to!" Emotion seized his features. "Come on," he said. Henry took half a step toward him.

"Henry," his father said.

"*Please*," said Jemmy E.

Henry swallowed. "Let's go," he said.

They fled. People milled across the grounds, gathering in clusters to chat or smoke. Long lines wound from the concession and souvenir stands. Jemmy E. dodged through them recklessly, Henry close behind him.

He didn't see what arrested his flight, but it felt like running full-tilt into a down mattress. Something big and soft and smelling of lavender soap gathered him up. "Why Henry Sleep!" it said, and his heart fell.

"Evening, Miss Wickasham," he said. He tried to move past her, but her wrinkled fingers clamped like talons over his shoulders.

"I haven't seen you in ages—look how you've grown!" Miss Wickasham said. "How is your dear father? Such a shame about his leg, and him such a brave man. I haven't seen him in ages, but I voted for him in the—" She blushed. "Why Sheriff Sleep, I was just asking about you!"

Henry subsided.

"Miss Wickasham." His father doffed his cap. "The boy and I were just having a bit of quarrel, I'm afraid."

"Henry?"

"That's right, ma'am."

She drew Henry close and pinched his cheeks. "Have you been bad? You know what happens to boys who misbehave."

He knew all right. He'd seen the fresh and livid bruise on Jemmy's cheek. Every time he moved, he felt thin stripes of agony erupt across his back and buttocks. Oh, yes, he knew—but he didn't know what he intended to say until the words were out, fatal and irrevocable: "I don't give a damn." He tore himself away, but his father clutched him and spun him around. Henry looked up just in time to catch the slap full across the face.

"You apologize to Miss Wica—" his father began, but he didn't finish for a flat stone whizzed past Henry's shoulder and caught his father square in the forehead. He staggered. Henry wrenched loose, sending Miss Wickasham sprawling. She rolled on her back like an upended turtle, lunging after him as he passed.

"Murder!" she shrieked.

Heads turned as Henry sprinted by.

"Murder! Murder!" shrieked Miss Wickasham. She jabbed a claw after Henry. "Get that child!"

"What did she say?" someone asked.

"Murder," said someone else.

The crowd picked it up. "Murder, murder, murder." A torrent of accusations flooded the throng. Someone grabbed for Henry, but he slipped away. He followed the arc of the tent at a dead run and collided head-on with Jemmy E. They went down in a tangle of limbs, struggled up, and dashed off into the maze of cages and boxcars beyond the midway. Henry risked a glance back at the mob as they flew down the line of cages behind the tent.

"You didn't have to throw the rock," he gasped.

"You didn't have to push the fat lady down."

They ducked between the cages opposite the tent, into a lane of garish boxcars.

"Here!" someone shouted. "There they go!"

"He's going to beat us within an inch of our lives," Henry said. "He's going to kill us."

"That's what I'm afraid of."

"Why'd you throw that rock?"

They turned a corner into another line of cars. Back here, far behind the main concourse, few lights had been strung. Minatory shadows loomed up, and for a moment Henry wasn't certain what was worse: getting lost in the maze of circus vehicles or facing the pursuing crowd.

"I'm just sick of it," said Jemmy E. He started to say something else and then stopped abruptly, panting. They had reached a dead end. Boxcars crowded in on three sides. A single light gleamed at the far end of the lane, but here the night pressed down thick and unyielding. Henry thought he heard things moving—slithering maybe—in the tenebrous depths under the cars.

"We've got to do something," Jemmy said. "If they catch us they'll hang me."

"Hang you? Are you crazy?" Henry stared, but he could see only a shadowed wedge of Jemmy's face.

Jemmy turned away. "I threw the rock because I wanted a chance to say goodbye."

"Goodbye?"

"I'm leaving. I'm running away."

"What happened?"

Jemmy was silent for a long moment. Henry could hear the pursuing mob, drawing closer. He could hear something moving under the boxcars. He was so afraid that he hardly dared to draw breath. Jemmy E. said:

"I think I killed my old man."

"Killed him? What are you talking about?"

"When I got home, he'd been drinking all morning. He said your dad had been hassling him." Jemmy laughed bitterly. "He beat the hell out of me. You think my face looks bad, you should see my ribs." He paused, and Henry thought of the red welts on his back and bottom. While they had been running, he had felt them cracking, breaking open.

Jemmy said: "After a while, he passed out and I . . . I was so mad, Henry. I've never been that mad. The whiskey bottle was still half full, but I didn't care. That's how mad I was. I just smashed it over his head without even thinking. There was so much blood."

Henry didn't speak. The crowd had drawn nearer. He could hear them shouting, "Murder! Murder!" If only they knew, he thought, and fine hairs prickled at the back of his neck.

"I hid out all day. I didn't know what to do. I just wanted to say goodbye. I didn't mean to get you in trouble."

"It's okay."

"You don't think less of me, do you? Do you?"

"No."

The crowd sounded very close indeed.

"You've got to get away," Henry said. A sickening image had come into his mind: Jemmy E., his face blue and puffy, his black tongue extruding from his mouth. Jemmy E. swinging at the end of a hangman's rope. He didn't know if they hanged kids, but he didn't want to chance it.

"What are we going to do?" said Jemmy E., and it was the first time in all the years they had known each other that *he* had asked that question instead of Henry Sleep.

Henry thought he heard a moist slithering sound in the dark spaces beneath the cars. But it didn't matter. He *knew* he heard the crowd, shouting angrily. Any minute they would appear at the end of the lane.

"The boxcars," Henry said. "We'll go under them."

Just then a door opened in a nearby car, and a wedge of light fell out, shattering the gloom. Henry swallowed as a long, bony arm clad all in black extended from within. A single gaunt finger with a yellow nail curled itself into an inviting crook. A calm, mellifluous voice said, "Why don't you boys step inside?"

*   *   *

Like drinking with Livingstone from the fabled wellsprings of the Nile, or opening long-dead pharaoh's tomb, mouth agape at the wonders there but fitfully revealed. That was what stepping into that car was like.

A suit of armor glimmered dully in one dim corner. In another, the calcified tusks of some prehistoric monster had been propped as carelessly as tent-posts. Amid the clutter piled atop the table along the far wall stood an abacus, a crystal ball, a shrunken head. Jemmy E. gasped. Henry executed an awe-stricken revolution, choking back a cry as a rattlesnake struck down at him from a shelf. He stumbled back and saw that the snake had been expertly stuffed—stilled forever in mid-strike, its eyes glassy and blind.

The door slammed shut behind them.

"Now then," said the ringmaster. He sat at the far end of the car in a chair as ornately carven as a throne. At the circus he had seemed vibrant, youthful. Close up, he looked like a man past death and into the first stages of decay. His long fingers steepled before his gaunt and bony face; his iron-gray hair swept back from a pronounced widow's peak and fell loose about his shoulders. He regarded them with obsidian eyes. After a moment, he reached out to the table beside his chair and adjusted a kerosene lantern. Skeletal shadows capered around the room.

Henry swallowed audibly. Paper rustled near his foot; a dun-colored rat the size of a loaf of bread emerged from a stack of disintegrating magazines and began to nose around the cluttered perimeter of the room. Henry saw that the abacus hadn't moved in days or weeks. A layer of dust clung like dandruff to the shrunken head. The ringmaster's tuxedo was frayed about the sleeves and shoulders; it had the threadbare sheen of clothes too often worn.

"Let's see," said the ringmaster. "You—" he leveled a gnarled finger at Jemmy E. "—must be Jemmy—Jemmy E., the locals call you, your name defies them. And you—" he nodded at Henry, "—must be Henry Sleep."

"How did you—" said Jemmy E.

"I spoke with your father this morning," the ringmaster said to Henry. "Charming man." He picked up a snifter of greenish fluid. Steam curled from it in wisps as he passed it under his hooked nose and sniffed delicately.

No one said a word. After a while, the tramp of heavy feet and voices raised in anger broke the silence. The sounds continued for a few moments—"I swear they went this way," "Murderous little wretches"—and then faded back the way they had come.

"I fear you are in dreadful trouble."

"What's going on here?" said Jemmy E. "Who are you?"

"I am Quinn. This is my circus. This is my car."

"What about Bitterroot?" said Jemmy E. "What about Crabbe?"

"Bitterroot and Crabbe are pompous little ledger-keepers and number-toters. Mere conveniences. This is Quinn's circus, Quinn's place, Quinn's way. Quinn is master here."

"Lots of neat stuff you've got," said Henry.

"Trinkets," said the ringmaster. "Rubbish, trinkets, and junk." He leaned forward. "I want to talk about you."

Henry looked up. Jemmy E. stepped forward, his face half in shadow, that crazed gleam of fear or anger in his eyes.

"We have to get back," Henry said.

"Get back where, my young friend? Your father will hide you when you return. *His* father—" He nodded at Jemmy E. "—lies dead in a shack with blood drying on his face. Stay awhile. The circus has only just begun."

Quinn stood. He towered over them in the flickering light, clad all in black with his crimson bow tie like a daub of blood at the base of his neck. He drained the snifter of vile fluid, and it seemed to Henry that the deep furrows in his face softened just a touch, that his gray hair had grown almost imperceptibly darker.

Then, with something like shock, he felt the impact of the ring-master's words: Dead, *dead in a shack*. Then it was true. He saw the bone-weary shack where Jemmy E. lived with his father, desolate above a stream that ran black with coal dust. It seemed then that he stepped forward, stepped somehow through a doorway into the shack itself, and there he saw it for himself: Jemmy E.'s father, cheek to splintered table, his arms dangling, a froth of blood and snot caked on his chin.

He screamed and stumbled back. Wrenching his gaze from the crystal ball—

—*how did I come to look in there?*—

—he saw that he was in the ringmaster's cluttered car. "Dad?" Jemmy E. said, and Henry saw that he too had been in the broken shack, that still he lingered there, that maybe he would never leave. A spark of hatred tumbled into the dry kindling of his heart—hatred that Jemmy E. had been driven to this, hatred that such men existed. The stripes on his back burned. His mind churned with incoherent thoughts—*he's a good man, he's a good*—

"Dad?" Jemmy E. sobbed. "I'm sorry, Dad." He sank to his knees, his yearning hands uplifted. "I'm sorry."

"Stop it," Henry said. "Stop it! You're killing him!" He snatched the crystal from the table. It threw off crazed, maniacal reflections as he hurled it away. The rat squealed and burrowed into the debris. Jemmy E. fell forward on his face, his thin shoulders heaving.

"I can take this pain from you," Quinn said into the silence. "I can make it go away."

Jemmy E. looked up.

They watched as Quinn knelt and threw back the lid of an oaken casket that alone of all the mysterious rubbish in the room lay free of dust. Hinges glided noiselessly in their sleeves as the lid fell open, revealing half a hundred glittering vials cradled in velvet collars. Quinn turned to look at them. The light flickered in the hollows around his eyes. It danced along the polished edge of the casket and fired the many-faceted vials with luminescent beauty.

"Come to me," Quinn said, and they came. In fear and voiceless longing, they came. In eight willing steps apiece, they crossed that room.

Quinn retrieved a vial and held it aloft, its contents splashing motes of ruby light around the car. He loosened its little cork, and tipped a droplet into each of two tiny snifters, which he then held out to them. "Here is the essence of the thing," he said, though what thing he meant Henry could not say. He did not pause to wonder. He brought the snifter to his nostrils, inhaled the smell rising from within, like garlic and blood, and tilted it to his dry lips.

It lifted him out of himself, it swirled him away. He found himself at a window he had not seen before, gazing at a stricken desert landscape. The sun had fallen behind the distant mountains and evening scrabbled at the rocks with shadowy fingers. He was filled with terrible knowing: this day had been exactly as empty as the last and tomorrow would be the same. This is what it is to be old, Henry thought.

"Abalone, Arizona," Quinn said. "She sought me out when she saw that the world had died for her, that never again in her little span of days would she know passion."

Quinn said, "Here, now." Henry turned as the ringmaster tipped into his snifter a droplet of bitter yellow bile. "Selma, Alabama," Quinn was saying. "He sought me out—"

But Henry was not listening. He lifted the snifter to his lips and tasted almonds and bitter coffee. He stood in a rain-swept street beneath a flickering neon sign. There was an ashen flavor in his mouth that Henry could not know, but which he somehow recognized as the aftertaste of cigarettes and bourbon. I will never see her again, he thought—

Quinn was saying, "An old man from Hannibal, Missouri, left me this," and he let fall into the outstretched snifter a single droplet of clear blue river water.

Henry tipped it to his lips. Tears sprang to his eyes, for this pain he knew, though he had not known he knew it. He knew it in his heart or in his bones. Time held him green and dying; nothing gold could stay.

The snifter slipped from his nerveless fingers. Again Henry seemed to hear the long, low whistle of the locomotive break across the town where he alone lay sleepless; and now its voice was mournful, full of grief for all things passed and passing. No more the joy of circus trains. No more the joy of sunlit, drowsy afternoons. Just the endless toil of life in these hard mountains. He thought of his mother, the gentle way she had, and how she would not meet your eyes; he thought of his father, who had gone to war a whole man and come back with the shards of his broken self sawing at his heart. All of them—his parents; Jemmy E.'s sad father, alone in his shack with his black lungs and his whiskey; the weary folk who had thronged the midway, their faces gray with coal that would not wash away and their eyes hollow with a hunger for some transitory wonder—all of them, somehow lost and broken. Young, he thought desperately, to be young and hopeful in spite of everything. *Don't you wish it could be like this forever?* Jemmy E. had said. And he did. He did.

Jemmy E. said, "Who are you? What are you?" His voice was dim with fear or wonder. Henry turned to look at him, and saw him, really *saw* him for the first time ever—helpless and afraid. It was as if a fog had been lifted from his eyes, or as if he had for all these years been gazing through a film of waxen paper, perceiving the larger shapes of the world, but blind to the details that made the vision whole and true. *I do not want truth*, he thought, and a hollow pain went through his belly, a kind of longing for a state forever lost to him.

Jemmy E. stood looking up at Quinn, the little snifter empty in his veined and ragged hands. His clothes hung too large about his frame—old castoffs Henry saw—and his hair stood blond and spikey about his head. He thought of Jemmy's father, slack and lifeless against the beat-up table where he had done his drinking. His heart was like a coal, white-hot with hatred.

Quinn sighed as he closed the oaken chest; he shuffled to his throne-like chair, neither as tall nor as looming as Henry had thought. "I am just an old, old man," he said, and the way he said it you knew that it was true. "But I can take this pain from you. I can leave you as you are or were. Young, free, hopeful." He waved a hand. "A boy's will is the wind's will," he said, and he seemed almost to envy them.

"How?" said Henry.

Quinn stroked the sinewy flesh between his finger and thumb. When he spoke, he seemed almost to be talking to himself. "Old," he said, "older than old, not seventy years or a hundred and seventy, but older still. Decades now I've feasted on the pain of others, but found no one to relieve me of my own." He chuckled under his breath and shook his head.

What fear had shackled Henry's heart now fell away, for it was true, he saw: Quinn had no power over them unless they surrendered it themselves. And if they did? He thought of the anticipation that had seized him when the circus train bellowed out across the sleeping town. A child alone could feel such joy. If Quinn could give them that—childhood everlasting, forever free of pain—was that so bad? Why not?

"And then?" said Jemmy E.

"You join the circus. Or you go off on your own, a boy that will not grow. 'Then' is up to you."

Jemmy E. stepped forward. When he spoke there was a hopeful and defiant note that Henry had never heard in his voice before. As if he feared this chance would somehow get away. "Please." His voice broke, and so Henry knew what was in his mind and heart: the dilapidated shack where lay his father's corpse. He could never leave that room, Henry knew, not unless Quinn could make him whole again.

"And you, Henry Sleep?" said Quinn, surprising him.

Across the stillness in the room, Henry's eyes sought Jemmy's face. *Don't you wish it could be like this forever?* Jemmy E. had said. And it could be. It could be.

The welts along his back flared red with agony. It did not have to be that way anymore, he thought. Hope surged up within him as he thought of himself and Jemmy E., how he had always envied the other boy—his quick, sardonic wit, and the daring that was nothing more than the freedom of nothing left to lose. I can be like him, Henry thought, I can be like him. And another thought occurred to him, an image from his dream: the clown who was not a clown, but his father, and the father who was not his father, but a creature wolfish and cruel. That was true, he knew—except . . . except that his father never raised his voice. Except that he could be kind. Except that he was a hero—and if he was broken inside, that wasn't really his fault, was it? Henry knew this to be true, as well. His mother had told him it was so.

And now he saw his mother as he knew she would be: her face lined with worry for him, and with grief. He thought of the way she slicked his cowlick down on Sunday mornings, of the way she looked away when she spoke, and would not meet your eyes. He thought: I *cannot leave her to him.*

"I am not evil, Henry Sleep," Quinn said kindly. "I can make you whole again."

But he had never been broken, or if he had been he would mend himself. He would be strong at the broken places.

"I have to get home," he said. Again, he met Jemmy E.'s eyes, and because they were boys and didn't know how to say goodbye, they did not hug or shake hands. But Henry could feel the loss of it; he knew that Jemmy E. could feel it too.

"See you around," he said.

"You know it, you dope," said Jemmy E.

Without another word, he slipped out of the car and off into the night. The town slept—the cats in their windows, the monkey chained atop his post, the presses in their gloomy subterranean chamber. It had grown chill and as he hurried through the desolate streets a million million stars gazed down from watchful skies, and could not be troubled to care that never in all the years of his life would Henry Sleep see his one true friend again.

By the time Henry reached home, the moon had fallen and the long front porch lay in shadow under its shingled canopy. From the fragrant darkness by the lilacs, he heard the steady rhythm of the rocker against the porch's slatted floor and he knew that his father had waited up for him. For a moment, he thought of turning, fleeing back through the sleeping streets to Quinn and Jemmy E. and the solace that they offered.

And then he resolved himself. He walked across the yard and mounted the stairs to the porch, deliberately treading on the creaking step. A lamp glowed thinly inside the house and dim light fell through the window by which his father rocked, his face ascending into light and retreating into darkness with chill regularity. They waited like that for a time. Light gleamed against his father's badge and along the edge of the gun-belt, which he had removed and placed beside his chair. He rocked and rocked, and Henry warmed himself at the white-hot coal that was his heart and watched the light steal across his father's features and retreat before the encroaching mask of darkness.

"I don't want you to run away from me like that, Henry."

"Yes, sir."

Silence then, and more waiting. A shadow passed in the living room, occluding the light, and Henry knew that his mother too was awake. He could picture her clearly, sitting on the sofa, her hands twisting in her lap until nerves got the better of her and she had to stand and pace.

"I need to know where he is."

Henry didn't speak.

His father rocked awhile and Sauls Run slept around them and did not acknowledge them.

His father said: "You got to grow up, son. You got to grow up and see what it's all about."

"I know," Henry said.

"I only want what's best for you."

"I know you do, Dad."

An owl called softly in the darkness, and then there was only the sound of the rocker; his father's face loomed out of the shadows and retreated.

"I want to tell you a story," his father said. "This happened to me in the war. I was in a German POW camp. It was pretty bad there. The Germans were too busy trying to keep the war going on two fronts to care much what happened to us. We were so hungry that we ate the leather from our shoes. When they would let us into the yard for exercise—maybe once a day for fifteen minutes—we would spend the whole time looking for something to eat. Grass . . . worms . . . bugs. Just anything, you understand?"

Henry nodded, and then he thought: *He can't see me*, so he said aloud, "Yes, sir."

"A lot of men were very sick. From hunger, exposure, whatever. They would die pretty frequently, and the Germans would drag them out of the barrack where they kept us and bury them somewhere. I saw lots of dead men, and a lot of them were men I called friends."

His father fell silent then, for a very long time, and Henry waited. He could sense that his mother was listening through the screen, and he didn't think she had heard this story either, though he didn't know. His father didn't talk much, and one of the things he didn't talk about most was the war and what had happened to him in it.

When he began to speak again, his voice was pitched low and without emotion. "One night, a man I knew woke me up—an American, another prisoner of war. He woke me up, and I could see that his face was covered with blood. That blood was smeared around his face and around his mouth especially. And he said, 'Rabkin's dead.' He said, 'Come on, you have to eat if you're going to survive. Rabkin wouldn't mind,' he told me. So I got up, but I couldn't do it. I couldn't do it. I went back to bed and early in the morning, it was just starting to get light, German soldiers woke us up and marched us into the yard. They had built a gallows and five men I knew were hanging dead there, and one of them was the man who had woken me up. They had painted on the gallows in English, 'Here are five brave American cannibals,' and they let those bodies hang there until they had rotted almost to skeletons. As a reminder, they said."

"I'm sorry," Henry said, and then he didn't say anything because when the light slid across his father's face he saw the tears that glinted there. What could he say? What could anyone?

"Don't be. You have to understand. The Germans were awful, they were often evil. But they were right in what they did that night, because those men, they had broken a taboo that should not ever be broken. And they had to be punished because unless you punish the people who do wrong, society falls apart. You can understand why those men did what they did, but people have to be punished or we'll have chaos."

"Okay," Henry said. But he wasn't sure it was okay. He didn't think he understood at all.

His father said, "That's why you have to tell me where he is, Henry. Even if you understand why he did it. You have to tell me where he is."

Henry said nothing. He felt as if the world had slipped from beneath his feet, as if gravity had been reversed, unshackling him from the Earth and all things earthly he had known. Everything had changed so swiftly, so completely. He reached out and took the rail that ran along the edge of the porch, as if by gripping it he could reestablish contact with the world he had lost: a world where creatures like Quinn could not exist, where fathers were fathers and not clowns or wolves or shattered and unhappy men.

"You have to tell me where he is."

Far, far away from here, Henry thought. He thought: I don't

know where he's gone or how he's getting there. And a fierce longing seized him. *I should not have chosen this path. I should have chosen Quinn's way, I should have stayed with Jemmy E.*

"Henry." His father stood, dark against the light from the living room. He moved toward Henry.

Henry backed away. "He's gone. You won't find him."

From the screen door, his mother said, "Let the boy be, Asa. He hasn't done anything."

"This is between me and Henry. You stay out of it."

"I won't."

She opened the screen and stepped onto the porch. The wooden screen whined closed on its spring, striking the door frame with a bang. Henry stood there, caught between them.

"Don't you understand?" his father said. His voice had begun to rise. "A man has been murdered. Murdered, Lil. Beat to death with a whiskey bottle. Henry has to tell me."

His mother took a second hesitant step onto the porch. When she spoke, her voice quavered. She would not look up, and Henry saw then how it was for her and knew something of her courage.

"Asa, I'm sorry that happened to you. I'm sorry you had to experience that. But you're home now, and Henry and I—we love you, and we want you to be better. Just let him be."

"Goddammit, Lil, don't you see! A man died!"

Henry saw lights come on at the Miller's. A face appeared at a window, but his parents didn't seem to care.

"—not a good man," his mother was saying. "He had it coming. He beat that boy constantly and the whole town knew it, Asa!"

"That don't matter, Lil! It ain't our place to judge. You can't just go around killing people you don't approve of! Now Henry is going to tell me where that boy is!"

"I can't," Henry said. "I'm sorry, but I can't." He moved away, but he wasn't quick enough. He never saw the blow, but all at once the left side of his face went entirely numb, and a thousand bells began to peal in his head. He staggered against the rail. Half the world had gone dim and blurry. The light shifted and distorted in his left eye.

Through the incessant clangor of the bells, Henry heard his mother scream. He tried to reach out for her to tell her it was okay—his daddy was broken inside and he couldn't help being this way—but he couldn't seem to get his legs to move. He realized he had slumped over somehow. His legs stuck out in front of him like broken sticks.

He was crying, and his mother was crying. He watched the two of them struggle in the half-light there before him, his father trying to get at him, saying, "He's got to tell me," and his mother sobbing and screaming through her sobs, "You're no better than he is, you son of a bitch, you're no better than he is!"

His head hurt so he closed his eyes, and when he opened them again, he saw that his mother had curled herself into a knot on the porch. She held her hands cupped over her face. Her legs kicked helplessly beneath her. A dark animal shape crouched over her, massive fist upraised. Henry heard the dull thud of flesh on flesh as it descended. He blinked. He felt like he was underwater. In the wavering light he seemed to confuse this moment with his dream—the clown drew back its fist for yet another blow, and Henry saw that the rubber nose had come askew. The greasepaint had started to run. He caught a glimpse of something thin and lupine, unremitting in its hatred and despair.

"No, please—" he said through thick lips. He tried to push himself to his feet and sagged back against the rail.

His mother had stopped kicking. He could hear nothing but the sound of the wolf-thing, panting over her. He began to crawl toward the rocker. He heard the thumps of two more heavy blows before he made it there, and the detonation of a third as he fumbled at the gun-belt. At last, he dragged the revolver free. He pulled himself erect, using the rocker as a crutch. He almost dropped the pistol. It was unbelievably heavy, the heaviest thing he had ever touched. He staggered toward them—his unmoving mother and the wolfish thing that hunkered over her—and dragged back the hammer. Using both hands, he leveled the gun and pressed the icy barrel to the wolf-thing's temple.

"Stop," he said, as the thing drew back its fist for yet another blow. "Stop or I'll kill you."

The fist dropped to the porch. It became a hand. His mother drew a weak breath and began to cry. The wolf-thing looked up to meet his eyes, and in the light from the living room its face was pale and drawn, blanched by grief and fear. It was a human face and the tears it shed were human tears. It was his father's face. In that moment, Henry Sleep did not know whom he pitied most: the broken man or the huddled woman or the little boy with the gun who stood over them and wept. In the long run, he supposed, it didn't matter.

He said: "If you ever lay another hand on her, I'll kill you."

He said: "If you ever touch me again, I'll kill you."

He said: "The Germans were wrong to hang those men. They were wrong because they drove those men to do what they did."

Very softly, then, he lowered the hammer on the revolver and heaved it with every ounce of his strength into the dark yard. He glanced at the Miller house and saw that the lights were on and that there were faces in the window. He looked back along the broad, dirty street and in every house as far as he could see, lights gleamed and faces peered out the windows. No one had come to help them. No one had cared.

Henry turned and went through the door into the house. He turned off the light in the living room and walked through the familiar dark, past the kitchen and dining room and down the long hall to his bedroom. He slept soundly that night, and without dreams. He slept that way for many nights, and if he dreamed he could not remember what dreams they were. But sometimes, waking in darkness, he would hear across the valley and the sleeping houses of the town, the lonesome, mournful exhalation of a locomotive, and on those nights he thought of Quinn and Jemmy E. He could not say whether the path he had chosen was right or wrong. But these things he knew: He had been broken. And he was strong at the broken places.

The past is treacherous, memory deceitful. But I do not lie when I say that this story is a true one.

I am Henry Sleep.

I recall these events at such length not out of some misguided nostalgia, but because of the boy who showed up in my office the other day: a slim redheaded child with eyes the size of saucers, and a ragged bear he clutched white-knuckled, like a talisman. No more than seven, he had the wide prominent bone structure of the woman who accompanied him, and a touch of her frail beauty, too: his mother, of course, also a redhead. She wore that expression you sometimes see on the faces of broken women: a wide-eyed look I've glimpsed in the eyes of headlight dazzled deer. It was especially distressing on her, not only because of the lucid intelligence in her eyes, but because she reminded me of my mother. The furtive way she had of moving, maybe, like a dog that's been too often kicked; or the way she wouldn't meet my eyes when she talked.

"Redhead, deadhead, five cents a cabbage head," I told the boy, and I leaned forward to pluck a quarter from behind his ear.

I've picked up a few such tricks. They're helpful in this line of work. My hands are age-spotted now, not as swift as they used to be. But I still believe in magic.

This boy, this Eric—he was having nothing of it. He flinched when I extended my hand, and he would not take the coin when I proffered it. So I placed the quarter on the edge of my desk, where he could get it if he wanted it, and I listened to the story his mother had to tell.

I'd heard the story a thousand times or so—you have too, though maybe you didn't listen like you should have—but I listened anyway and it moved me, like it always does. When she finished, I made a phone call or two; I found her a place to stay in the shelter over in Princeton, and I promised her that Jesse wouldn't find her, though that's probably a lie.

When they stood to leave, I leaned over the desk once more. "Hey carrot-top," I said. "What's that bear's name? If I'm going to be your lawyer, see, I got to know the names of all the folks with an interest in your case."

They paused by the door, looking back at me. I turned my head so I could see them better—out of the good eye, the right one.

"Go ahead, Eric," his mother said.

But still the boy didn't answer me. We just looked at one another until we came to an understanding. He had eyes like bright gems, I remember thinking. Eyes like bright gems in dark settings.

"That bear's name is Fred Howard," he said. He took a step forward when he said it. His features had taken on a set, defiant look I thought I'd seen before.

"Fred Howard, huh?"

"That's right."

"Well you and Fred Howard come back and see me, okay?"

The boy gazed at me fixedly for another moment, and then his mother twitched his hand. They turned and saw themselves out, and that's when I noticed: the boy had hooked the coin off my desk, all right. He'd done it slicker than owl shit.

But his eyes—those eyes like bright gems—they lingered after him and seemed to illuminate my shabby office. I thought again of that look in his face, that look I knew I'd seen before. I didn't remember where at the time, but that night it came to me. It was the look in Jemmy E.'s face the last time I saw him: a look of defiance and hope and just a touch of desperation. It was the look of an opportunist who thinks that maybe, just maybe, he's found the way out. But mostly it was the look of fear.

Jemmy E. was right about one thing: talk travels fast in a place as small as Sauls Run. But he was wrong as well. My father served as sheriff of our county until he was sixty-three years old; he was reelected to that office four times, an unprecedented run. To this day, he remains fondly remembered in these parts. A brass plaque in the courthouse commemorates him: *war hero, sheriff, beloved husband and father.* I stop to look at the plaque almost every day— my duties take me there—and every day I cannot help but wonder: How could they reelect him year after year? How could they reelect him when they knew?

Jemmy E. was wrong. Talk travels quickly in a town the size of Sauls Run—but only sometimes. People never talk about the things that really matter, about the things that really stink. They cling to their illusions—that the child fell from the swing-set, that the mother hit herself with the corner of a kitchen cabinet. Without their illusions, they cannot survive.

A list of the guilty:

Miss Wickasham, my fifth grade teacher, who saw bruises and never said a word. The Millers, who lived next door. Casey Burroughs, my father's deputy. Reverend Wells, our church's pastor. Merrick Kennedy, who ran the pharmacy. Bill Honaker, my pediatrician. All the fellows who used to sit out front of the Grand Hotel, whittling and chewing the fat: J. C. Cade, Ed Goode, Tosack Burdette, Tillo, Luke Harvey, Wimpy Holland, Mack Asbury, Jack Catarussa. Slick the shoeshine man, who called me "Mistah Henry." The Widow Baumgarten, who taught piano. Deke Burton. Lucy James. Fanny Anderson. Lyle Nottingham. Francis Welland. All of them. All of them are guilty.

I am guilty.

You are.

A few years ago I decided to track down the circus that came to our town in that long-distant summer. I checked every reference book I could think to look at. I talked to every two-bit carny and circus roustabout I could find. I called a professor up at West Virginia University, who knows about such matters. Nothing. Bitterroot and Crabbe never existed according to any official register. No one has ever heard of a man named Quinn who was something more than a man.

The past is treacherous, memory deceitful. But I know that it is true.

Whenever a circus or a carnival comes to Sauls Run—whenever one comes near—I haunt the place. I seek it out. It's become known about town as an eccentricity of mine, on the order of the peculiar law practice I have built, if perhaps not quite as odd or inexplicable.

My law practice caters almost exclusively to victims of abuse, women and children who rarely have a dime to meet my fees, who have left me impoverished, and wealthy beyond my wildest dreams of riches. Such a practice is entirely inexplicable to the people of this town; my penchant for haunting freak shows and circuses and carnivals and other such disreputable places is somewhat less so, but it too has been noted, and held as a mark against me.

But that's okay. I love the midway. I love the smell of exotic animals borne on a summer wind. I love the clowns and the jugglers and the bears on unicycles. I love them all. But that's not the reason I haunt such places. This is the reason:

I'm looking for a certain blond-haired child. I'm looking for Jemmy E. I have something I want to tell him.

Are you out there Jemmy E.?

Listen:

I didn't run away, Jemmy E. I didn't take Quinn's way. I stayed when it was hardest. I stayed and fought. And it has made all the difference to me.

Touched

OH, MAMA, YOU SAY. AND AGAIN: OH, MAMA. Your chest hurts with a dull unceasing ache, but you say it quiet-like, half-afraid she'll hear you.

Mama wishes you would die.

And anyway, she mostly listens to Cade, when Cade is here. Pap, too, and Gramma sometimes.

Gramma now, rocking here in her place by the stove, saying: That one's a half-wit. That one's touched. The old woman lowers a trembling finger at you, huddled beside her, here by the stove.

Coughing the steady, hacking cough that has been with you for days, you move closer to the firebox, but even here you feel the draft from the broken window pane, like icy fingers beneath your clothes. Mama's asked the company to patch up that hole maybe a thousand times, but the company takes its time about things. And the cardboard—well, it doesn't do much good. So you huddle closer to the firebox and watch Mama like you do sometimes when she doesn't think you're looking. Mama is churning butter. And every once in a while, if she thinks you're not watching, she steals a glance at you.

The coughing's got her hopeful.

Touched, Gramma says again, and Mama's pretty face twists up like she just bit into a green apple.

She stops churning and wipes at her forehead with her hand. What do you mean, old woman? she says. Touched?

But Gramma just rocks, back and forth, back and forth. Her rocker squeaks against the floor, squeak, squeak, a noise like a mouse might make. This sound, the cold draft, the heavy scent of beans simmering atop the stove, and Gramma looming over you. Her mouth caves in, wrinkled as a prune. White hairs poke out of her chin.

Mama starts to churn again. The dasher thumps against the wooden crock.

Out the window, pallid winter light climbs the high ridges. Evening coming on. Cade will be home from school soon. And in a little while Pap will be back too, carrying his tool poke across his shoulder, his face black with coal dust.

Gramma says, Touched. Touched by the hand of God. Idiot child'll have a talent.

Mama snorts, and crosses the room to stir the beans. Then she hunkers down beside you and her rough fingers touch your face. Jorey, Mama says. Her voice is cold and hollow-sounding. Jorey doesn't have a talent, old woman. Jorey doesn't have anything at all.

Your coughing starts again, but just then the plank door swings open. Cade sweeps into the room, sweeping in the cold.

Cade, Mama says, her voice filling up. You're home.

Mama stands and you cough hard, jarring congestion loose in your chest. You inch closer to the firebox, almost against the cast iron stove.

Oh, Mama, you say.

But Mama, she doesn't even look around.

High above the number five hole, the chill silence folds around you like a blanket. No shrill voices jeer you; no fingers point. Up here, no one sneaks along behind you to throw you to the frozen ground.

Just the cold, your breath smoky in the still air, and the gaunt trees, dark against the ridges as far as you can see. In the stillness, electric cars clank out of the shaft beneath you, bearing load after rattling load of coal. Far below, railroad tracks veer away from the coal tipple into the steep-walled valley. And if you squint your eyes you can just see the tar-paper roofs of the Copperhead coal camp, black squares against the barren earth.

Home. Mama's waiting.

You jingle the scrip in your pocket, rocking a little in your flannel coat to keep warm. Somehow you can't quite bring yourself to go. It's not the other kids so much as it is your pap, down there somewhere, deep under the mountain. That and the sun, falling against your face as it sets toward the rim of the valley, and a squirrel, perched at the edge of the precipice, gnawing at a frozen nut. You used to bring chunks of bread to feed that squirrel, but you haven't done that since Mama whipped you for stealing bread.

With a rustle of dry leaves, Cade appears at the edge of the woods. He hunkers down beside you, resting his elbows on his thighs. The squirrel hurries into the safety of a looming hickory to scold him, but you just laugh.

Pretty funny, huh, Jorey, Cade says.

But the laughter turns to coughing, the coughing into the hot shameful sting of tears.

Them kids been giving you a hard time again? Cade asks.

You nod, ashamed for Cade to see you cry. Boys aren't supposed to cry.

But Cade just squats there, peers out into the sky, and lets you have your cry. After a while you stop crying and look up at his slim brown face, his blue eyes narrowed against the sun. Nobody's got blue eyes like my Cade, Mama says. And it's true. Cade's face is so handsome and regular that you almost want to reach out and touch it. Perhaps that is what you are extending your short fingers to do when he turns abruptly to look at you.

Feel better? Cade asks. He breaks into a wide smile and reaches out to ruffle your hair.

Okay, you say. What Mama says don't work.

What's Mama say? Cade asks.

Tell them to go jump in a lake.

Cade laughs and sits down. His breath hangs in the cold air.

You laugh, too. Everybody laughs when Cade laughs, except Pap. Maybe because Mama specially likes Cade, but you're not sure. You wish Mama talked to you the way she talks to Cade, her voice all full up instead of thin and sorry-sounding.

Nah, Cade says, pulling his legs up against his chest and resting his chin on his knees. I reckon telling them to go jump in a lake wouldn't do much good.

You say nothing, like you always do, mostly because you don't know what to say. It's okay to be quiet though, especially with Cade. He showed you this place, Cade did. Said it was his special place for thinking, and now it's your special place, too, though you don't think much.

Cade is humming a snatch of something under his breath when you speak again. Mama send you to find me? you ask.

Mama said you done run off with the lamp oil money, that's all, Cade says. I reckoned you were up here.

Mama's going to be mad, you say. You jingle the scrip in your pocket.

Mama ain't going to be mad, Cade says. I'll take care of Mama. She don't understand you, that's all.

Understand me how, you ask.

Cade turns to study you with his clear blue eyes. Mama's funny that way, Jorey. Sometimes, she forgets how special you are.

I ain't special, you say. Stupid, maybe.

Cade chuckles. Well, you ain't no professor, Jorey, that's for sure. But you're special all right.

Cade tousles your hair and laughs again and stands. But you don't move, not for a long moment. Cade's words jolt some memory: Gramma saying, That one's touched. Those words rattling around in your head.

C'mon, lazy, Cade says, prodding you with his boot. C'mon, we gotta get back.

You stand and the scrip jingles in your pocket again. You think of the lamp oil, and the commissary, closed till morning, and you say, Mama's going to be mad.

But Cade says, Don't you worry. Company's sending in some Baldwin-Felts men on the afternoon train. Mama's got plenty to worry her tonight without bothering about you.

He laughs again, but this time there's something underneath the laugh, something shrill and excited and maybe a little scared— something you can't quite put a name to. An uneasy feeling swirls through your belly.

Then Cade says, shivering, Let's go. It's cold out here.

He throws his arm around your shoulders and together you strike off into the woods, angling away from the mine, down toward the tracks and home. Looking back, you see the squirrel come down out of the hickory to sniff around on the rock. Something warm and pleasant opens up inside you, and that uneasy feeling is gone, for a little while anyway.

It's worse at night, the coughing is, and with it a kind of tightness that closes in around your lungs. But no one really notices, not tonight.

Pap, Mama, and Cade are deep in talk, hunched around the table, the kerosene lamp between them. Their long twisting shadows skulk away behind them. The shack is a fitful menagerie of shadows. Gramma's snakes along the floor here by the stove, and your's rocks close beside it: a small boy's shadow, just like any other.

Mama's face is pale in the red gleam, saying, with a tremble in her voice you've never heard there, The boy's too young, Jack.

Pap, his gray hair thin, dark lines of coal dust beneath his eyes, Pap says, We ain't got any choice. Copperhead won't stop at nothing to keep the union out of West Virginia. We got to make a show of force.

Cade leans forward and places his big hands, knotting and unknotting, against the table. His shadow seems to follow him, up along the rough wall and ceiling, looming over him. Cade says, He's right, Mama.

What do you mean, he's right? What about school?

It's only one day, Pap says.

Cade isn't a miner, says Mama.

Ain't nothing else you can be in these parts, Gramma says from her rocker. You ought to know that, Lilla.

Them Baldwin-Felts men coming up from Bluefield tomorrow, Pap says. They're bringing scabs with them.

Let them come, Mama says, but my boy is going to school.

Goddammit, Pap says, he ain't no boy anymore. He's near sixteen years old.

He's fifteen, Mama says. Just a boy. I won't let you use him. People might die there tomorrow. Cade might die.

Pap curses and stands, his chair clattering to the floor behind him. He strides to the window with long angry steps. In the silence, Cade looks into Mama's eyes with that way he has. Cade could charm a snake, Mama says sometimes, and she looks back at him now with shiny, fearful eyes.

Mama, you want to live in them tents again? Cade asks with a voice smooth like syrup.

Mama sniffles and shakes her head. Pap turns from the window to watch, and in the flickering light you can see his eyes are wet, too. Suddenly, without knowing why, you want to go to him, to press your face against his rough shirt, but you hold your peace here by the stove, watching.

Cade says, The strike's going to happen, Mama. There ain't nothing we can do about it. Tomorrow them Baldwin-Felts men are going to throw us out of here and we'll be in those tents again.

You want to live in them goddamned tents all winter? Pap says from across the room. Half-starved and freezing, with Jorey coughing like he is?

Mama doesn't even look at you.

What about Ma, Pap says, jabbing his finger at the old woman.

Cade silences him with a look. For a moment, the only sounds are Gramma's rocker, squeaking, and the lamp, sputtering, nearly dry. Cade says, They'll throw us out, Mama. Put niggers to work in the mines, let niggers live in our houses.

Pap says, Anybody going to take that coal out of the mountain, it's going to be us. It's only right.

But why Cade? Take Jorey if you have to, but not Cade, Mama says. She starts to cry.

Pap laughs. Jorey, he says. You know better, Lilla.

And Cade says, Mama, we got to stand up to them tomorrow. And every man as can help ought to help.

Just then, the kerosene is gone. The lamp flickers and dies. In the half-darkness, the room red with the gleam of the stove, Mama says, Stupid child. That's all the lamp oil. Pap curses and moves to the door. You follow, the room suddenly too close with the smell of kerosene and burning coal, with Mama crying in the gloom. You slip out behind Pap, out into a cutting wind, somehow pure in its iciness. The door slams behind you.

Dark mountains loom against the sky. It has begun to snow, tiny wind-driven flakes, like grains of sand flung against your face. You shiver.

Pap, standing out on the other side of the road, at the edge of an icy creek, turns to face you. Jorey, he says.

Yes sir, Pap, you say.

What are you doing out here, boy? Too cold for you, with that cough.

You cross the road, scuffing your feet against the dirt. Too hot inside, you say. I want to be with you.

Pap shrugs out of his flannel coat and drapes it around your shoulders. He stands there for a minute, then says, Let's walk.

Together, Pap's arm heavy across your shoulders, you head down into the coal camp. Beyond the stream, dark woods press close. The other side of the road is lined with shacks, shuttered against the cold, trailing wind-blown streams of smoke. The stench of burning coal hangs like a pall over the valley.

Wish I could help tomorrow, you say.

I know, Pap says.

You walk in silence for a while. The stream chatters along beside you. In daylight, it runs black with coal dust, that stream, but now it shines silvery in the falling snow, clean-looking. The blackness is still there. You just can't see it.

Mama wants me to help, you say.

Pap sighs, his breath gray and cloudy in the darkness. Your mama don't know what she wants, most of the time, he says. You ain't to judge her, Jorey.

At last, the stream turns away into the woods. You emerge into a rutted street, bordered on this side by a network of railroad tracks that runs the length of the camp. Beyond them, a weather-beaten line of buildings, black behind the shifting curtain of snow, straggles along the dirt lane.

Together, you and Pap cross the tracks and mount the steps to the commissary porch. A single electric lamp glows within the store, casting a narrow rectangle of light across the porch and the wooden walkway that fronts the street. Pap lowers himself to the oaken bench in one shadowy corner, and cradles his face in cupped palms. You move close against him, against his heat.

Shouts and piano music drift up the street from Janey's Saloon, two blocks away. After a while, Pap raises his head and says, You hear me, Jorey? You ain't to judge your Mama.

Okay, you say.

She ain't from these parts, Pap says. She's from down Bluefield, and that ain't mining country. You remember Bluefield.

And you do. A long time ago, three, four years maybe, that was. Pap said you needed a real doctor, not a coal field quack, so he and Mama saved up for a while, and then one spring morning you and Mama took the morning train to Bluefield, nearly an hour away. But the doctor, he just shook his head. Nothing I can do, the doctor said. Boy's a mongoloid. Nothing anybody can do.

Afterwards, Mama showed you the house where your grandpa lived. It was a big house with columns, all shining white, and you wanted to go in and see Grandpa. You hadn't ever seen him. But Mama tightened her lips till they turned white and led you away. On the train back to Copperhead, Mama wept. You just sat there, watching the mountains roll by.

No one has ever said a word about that trip, not ever. But Mama hasn't been the same.

Ahh, Jorey, Pap says now. These mountains call you back. You can't never get away.

You don't know what Pap means by this, so you don't say a word. Just shiver, listen to the music from Janey's, and watch the snow spit heavier out of the night sky. It's beginning to stick, the snow is, a gray shroud across all of Copperhead. After a while, you hear the muffled beat of footsteps against the wooden sidewalk. A long figure ambles in front of the commissary, but you and Pap, submerged in shadow, don't say a word until the cough betrays you.

Then Pap stands, pulling you up with him, pulling you into the light. Evening, Granville, Pap says.

Granville Snidow tips a finger to his black hat and crosses his arms against the porch railing. He wears pearl-handled revolvers strapped low to either hip. At home, Pap calls Snidow a Baldwin-Felts S.O.B., but up here on the porch of the commissary, he just smiles in a private kind of way.

Snidow laughs, a harsh sound. The star pinned to his overcoat glints in the light from the electric lamp. His lips widen beneath his mustache—a handsome affair, your mama calls it—thick and bristling, with ends coiled into tight circles. Well, Jack, Snidow says, how come you ain't down at Janey's drinking up some courage?

I don't need to drink my courage, Granville, Pap says. I ain't a drinking man.

Kind of cold for you all to be out tonight, ain't it?

We was just leaving, Pap says. He grips your shoulder tightly and steers you down to the sidewalk. Together, you cross the tracks and start up the dirt road toward home.

Hey, Jack! Snidow shouts a minute later.

You feel Pap tense as he turns. Granville Snidow is almost lost in the snow that pelts down now out of the sky.

Hey, Jack! Snidow calls. It's a good thing you're heading in! I wouldn't want your half-wit to catch cold!

But Pap doesn't say a word. He just turns away and leads you home. Inside, the tiny shack seems warm after the cold night. In the red glow of the firebox, it is a relief to crawl into the warm bed with Cade, stealing his heat.

Gramma snores in the dark and you hear Pap shuck his clothes before he crawls in bed with Mama. Then the room falls quiet and you sleep.

Sometime in the night, the coughing wakes you. The whole room is bright with moonlight. Outside, the snow has stopped, but you don't pay it much mind. You just lie there, watching Pap. He sits by the window in a cane-backed chair and his long johns seem to shine in the moonlight. He's humming quietly to himself, Pap is, humming as he cleans his rifle.

You wake again to the chill glow that precedes dawn, your nerves tingling with the awareness of someone watching you: Gramma, awake, though the others still sleep. The old woman eyes you word-lessly from her place by the stove as you clamber away from Cade's heat, out into the cold air. She doesn't speak as you dress. And when you offer her a hunk of bread to breakfast on, she merely shakes her head and sucks at her toothless gums.

She just watches you with her pale eyes, and never says a word. Perhaps it's because you're touched.

Touched.

That word, and all its vast mystery, rattles around in your head like a seed in a dry gourd. And together with Gramma's unflinching gaze, somehow awful in the sleeping cabin, it is at last enough to chase you out into the frigid dawn, still holding a half-eaten chunk of bread.

Silent as a wraith, you flee through row after row of squalid shacks. With every step your feet punch through frozen drifts and gray snow clutches at your ankles. Gramma's stare seems to follow you, that word—

—touched—

—to linger in your mind.

Only when you reach the edge of the coal camp and turn up the tracks toward the mines, does your hunger come back. Gramma's persistent stare seems to fall away behind you, and you start to gnaw at the bread. Then the memory of the squirrel probing hungrily about the edge of the precipice returns. A kind of warm feeling opens up in your belly, and you tuck the dry crust into a pocket.

But when at last you reach the special place, up above the number five hole, the squirrel is dead, curled into a frozen knot at the edge of the cliff.

For a moment, standing there, a terrible sense of vertigo sweeps through you—as if you are falling, falling back into a well of memory. Last winter. An explosion in the number three hole. Fifteen miners dead.

You won't ever forget those bodies, stiff and bloody, beginning to stink when they were finally dragged from the rubble. You won't ever forget the funeral: the sound of shovels scraping at mounds of frozen earth; the voices of the miners and their families rising in song together, dry and lonely sounding as night wind in the hollers. Death is real to you, palpable, though you can never understand it.

Now, remembering, Mama's words return to you: *People might die there. Cade might die.*

Today.

And then that endless moment snaps; the world settles into place around you. A sob escapes you, and you step forward, falling to your knees, the crust of bread dropped on the ground behind you, forgotten.

The squirrel is rigid and cold to the touch. Frost rimes its whiskers. Its small skull is cracked as neatly as you have seen Pap crack an acorn beneath his heel, and a single dark streak of blood mats the stiff fur above one eye. Perhaps it has fallen from the icy branches of the overhanging hickory. You don't know.

Somehow, though, in the midst of large griefs which surpass your understanding, this small grief touches you. Loss suffuses you, and for a time you clasp the tiny corpse to your chest, unawares.

When you finally look up again, the pale glow of dawn has given way to the broad luster of mid-morning. The chill has crept beneath your flannel coat. It clings close about your feet, wet from the long hike up the mountain. You feel as stiff and cold as the corpse you cradle in your hands.

As the squirrel. Dead.

You cannot help but recall how the squirrel would nuzzle your empty fingers when the bread was gone, and with that memory a dry emptiness yawns within you. Almost without realizing it, you speak, a single word, whispered in the stillness of morning: No. Something surges within you, a power almost electric. That one word seems to blow away the fog of confusion that clouds your mind. That one word seems to fill you up.

Your fingers, numb with cold mere moments before, grow suddenly warm and flex of their own accord. Your hands flare with sharp, sudden pain. The squirrel twists in your grasp, twists again, and tiny jaws clamp around your finger. Sharp teeth grind your flesh, drawing a sudden welter of blood, dark against your pale flesh.

With a cry of fear and astonishment, you release the squirrel's writhing body. It springs away, turns to scold you briefly, and then escapes into the overhanging hickory. You do not move, not even to lift the bleeding finger to your lips.

A sense of mystery and awe you can never articulate rushes through you. That power, that moment of stunning clarity is again eclipsed by fog and confusion. For long hours you turn all your will to dispel that fog, to try to understand. But it is no use. You can never understand anything.

Through all the fog that fills your mind, there is only this mystery: Gramma's voice, saying, *Touched. Touched by the hand of God. Idiot child'll have a talent.*

Though you cannot understand those words, you think of them over and over through the morning. And despite the cold, you do not move again, not till the long rising whine of the afternoon train calls you out of your torpor.

Cade, you think.

And then you are running down the mountain toward the rail-road tracks and home.

By the time you reach Copperhead, clouds have settled in and gray snow spits from the lowering sky.

Standing breathlessly in the street across from the commissary, you watch Pap and three other men stride down the tracks toward the railway station by Janey's Saloon. They carry long rifles cradled in their arms. Twenty yards behind them follows a ragged crescent of ten or eleven armed men. Cade is among them, his face pale and thin, so young-looking. From the other direction, a loose band of men led by Granville Snidow walks up the tracks. Snidow's palms rest easily on the pearl-handled revolvers that ride low on his hips. His hatchet face is still and expressionless.

When they are ten or fifteen yards apart, the two camps stop to study one another. Both groups of men shift restlessly about. Fingers curl white around the stocks of shotguns and rifles. Pap and Snidow alone stand motionless, facing one another.

In the stillness, you can hear the wind sough among the trees in the hollers. Across the street, a curtain twitches in the commissary window and your eyes are drawn to your mama's face, peering through the glass at the gloomy afternoon.

And then Pap's voice, loud in the silence, draws your attention back to the cluster of men in the street.

Granville, Pap says. He inclines his head, the barest nod.

Well, Granville says. To listen to the talk at Janey's last night, I'd have thought there'd have been more of you today.

I reckon there's enough of us, Pap says. We don't want no trouble. But we don't aim to leave our homes—

Those are the last words spoken. You're not sure who has fired the first shot, or why, but suddenly the afternoon is shattered by a staccato burst of gunfire: the deep-throated boom of shotguns intermixed with the long flat cracks of rifles and the sharp reports of Granville Snidow's pistols, popping over and over again.

The two clumps of men seem to explode in all directions. Men dive to the earth and dart away to the edges of the street. In the confusion of smoke and gunfire and moving bodies, you search for Cade, but you don't see him.

And then, as suddenly as it began, it is over. The acrid tang of burned powder hangs in the air. Granville Snidow stands alone in the midst of the crumpled bodies, a pistol in either hand. Smoke drifts along the silent street.

Pap! you cry. Cade!

The shout decays into a long rattling cough and then you are running toward the middle of the street. Your short legs plow through the gray snow. Pap writhes on the tracks by his rifle, cursing and clutching at his leg. But Cade is still. He lies several yards beyond Pap, flat on his back with his arms flung wide as if to embrace you. His face is the color of ashes against the leaden snow and blood bubbles at his lips.

Cade! you cry again, your voice breaking.

You go to your knees in the snow beside him, cradle his head in your lap. Blood boils out of a ragged hole in his chest. Every time he sucks in a breath, the hole whistles like a tea kettle when the water begins to boil.

Cade, you say. Cade.

And Cade opens his eyes, those eyes so blue they are like the clear blue ice that forms along the edge of the commissary roof. Well now, Jorey, Cade says, lifting his head. Don't this beat all?

He tries to laugh, but the laugh turns into an explosive cough. A thin spray of blood coats your flannel jacket, and Cade's head drops back, his eyes going dark.

Dead as the eyes of the squirrel.

Just then you hear the crack of heels against the ties behind you, and Mama screams from the commissary porch, No! No!

You twist your head around to see Granville Snidow, still clutching a pistol in either hand, wearing a kind of terrible expression like you've never seen on any adult's face. He is so pale and haggard that even his mustache seems to droop. His eyes gleam from dark hollows.

No! Mama screams.

But Granville Snidow lurches a step closer. Oh, Christ, kid, he whispers. Oh, Christ, I'm sorry, I—

He raises his arms to the sky, and a bloody flower blossoms in the center of his chest. There is a hollow echoing boom and Granville Snidow pitches forward, his body thrashing in the snow. Behind him, you see Pap, half-upright, his wounded leg drawn up beneath him, still clutching his smoking rifle.

Jesus, Pap says, and then he, too, pitches forward, dropping the rifle and curling tight around his leg.

Jorey! Mama screams. Jorey!

Looking back around, you see her descend the porch steps. You glance down at Cade, remembering all those days when he sat with you in your special place, just being with you the way he always was, not even caring that you were stupid the way the other kids cared, the way Mama cared. That was the way Cade was. Just Cade.

No, you whisper, and the memory of the squirrel, twisting and twisting in your hands, returns to you.

You can feel it again, that power, that touch. It surges through your body until your nerves sing, tingles down your arms and through your hands. Your fingers flush with electric heat, so hot they seem to glow, and then, almost of their own accord, they flex in Cade's blond hair. The touch jerks through them. Cade's eyelids twitch and flicker open, and you know you can do it.

You can bring him back. You know you can.

But just then, you hear Mama, her voice shrill in the silence as she crosses the rutted street, Mama, crying, Cade! Cade!

The sour taste of bile floods your mouth, and you jerk away from Cade, your hands and fingers going suddenly numb in the cold. His eyelids close again and his head lolls back along his shoulder. Blood drips from his open mouth, melting the gray snow.

Then Mama is standing before you.

Cade's dead, you say.

Mama sobs.

For the rest of your life, this moment will stand apart in time, as stark and memorable as a glimpse of wind-lashed trees along the ridge-tops, frozen against the sky by a sudden flash of lightning. In that timeless instant, you sob out your grief and joy—for some new loneliness, some irrevocable loss that you will never understand no matter how hard you try; for some old hollowness within you, forever filled. At last, the sob breaks, becomes the unceasing cough that has been with you for days now. And coughing, you stand. Stand and step over Cade's body to clutch her fiercely, to press your face tight into her warm skirts.

Oh, Mama, you say. And again: Oh, Mama.

❖   ❖   ❖

The Census Taker

SWAMP EAT ANYTHING, GIVE IT ENOUGH TIME,
my daddy used to say, and soon as I heard the census taker's
automobile outside my store, I knew that it would wind up swamp
food before all was said and done. Take a fool to bring a car this
deep into the Atchafalaya—a fool or a Yankee, one—and after the
trouble we'd had with Billy Go that morning, I wasn't in the mood
to deal with either one. But when I stepped out on the porch of my
store and saw the boy sitting behind the wheel, I knew that he was
both.

He was a colored boy, this one. His face gleamed the shade of
swamp water when you sweep the duckweed back, and his eyes
were calm behind his wire-rimmed spectacles as he gazed out at us.
Folks had already started gathering round, half of them gaping at
the road, the other half at the car itself. Somebody reached out and
touched the fender, yanking his hand back quick, like he'd been
burned. One of Janie Halloway's younguns, it was, Odile, a no-
count seventeen-year-old with a cap of bristly hair and skin the color
of mud. He oughta been busy at something this time of day—it was
getting on toward four—and I made a mental note to have a word
with Janie. Just now, though, I had bigger fish to fry.

"Ya'll go on," I said quietly, and the crowd—there must have
been a dozen of them, colored folks and white ones too—kind of
jumped like they'd been caught stealing. "Get on, now," I said. "You
heard me."

I clapped my hands and then they jumped all right. Just like that the street was empty. I stood there in the heat, staring past the car at the road, two narrow gravel ruts and a hummock of wire grass winding away through a sunshot dapple of tree and scrub. The car itself wasn't much more impressive—just a rust-eaten old heap—but it was more car than folks here in Sulphur Creek had ever seen. Then I saw the sign affixed to the driver's side door, and my heart kind of sank within me.

What it said, that sign, was *Doom*.

What it said was, *United States Census*.

The colored boy turned off his motor and got out. He wore a pair of linen pants and a clean button-down shirt. He reached back inside for a leather valise and then shut the door. My old hound tore out from under the house at the sound, barking his stupid head off. "Hist Booger," I shouted, "settle down now," and he pulled up short, grinning like an idiot. He stood there a moment, his tongue hanging out, and then he flopped over on his side in the grass. I glanced at the stranger by way of apology. "Fool animal's bout worthless," I said. "Take him a month of Sundays to work his courage up."

The colored boy didn't say anything. He just stared at the sign above the porch. GENERAL MERCHANDISE. ULYSSES DECOTEAU, PROPRIETOR, it says, in fancy letters weathered almost the shade of the wood they're painted on. "Are you Mr. Decoteau?" he asked, and right away I saw I was right about him being a Yankee. He had a way of swallowing his vowels before he'd hardly got a taste of them. It had no music, that voice.

"Yes and no," I said. "Ulysses Decoteau—that was my father—died in '61. My name's Armand. I run the place now."

The colored boy studied on this for a minute. He looked up the street in a way that let me see it through his eyes: not a street at all, really, just a couple of ruts winding between a cluster of weather-beaten shanties on stilts, the way folks build in these parts on account of the rainy season. The swamp encroached everywhere, sending vines of Virginia creeper shooting up the sides of our houses and festooning our eaves with dangling gray shrouds of Spanish moss. Coco grass and palmetto choked our door yards. If we didn't hack the stuff back every now and then, Sulphur Creek would just disappear, swallowed up in a slow-rising emerald tide. Appetite, that's all the swamp is. And this colored boy just stood there, taking it all in with a look on his face that told me he didn't know places this backwards still existed in those proud United States of his.

"And you?" I said. "What's your name?"

He glanced up, startled, and smiled the shiniest smile I ever saw, like a bright crescent moon waxing slowly toward full in the middle of his face. "I didn't mean to be rude, Mr. Decoteau. My name is Lucas Dixon. I'm pleased to make your acquaintance." He took the stairs in a bound and shook my hand, smiling the whole time and looking me right in the eye, like a white man. Then he turned to gaze back at his car and the gravel road beyond it, tunneling off through the swamp like a mirage, green tinted and improbably dry. "I don't know how I ended up here. I was trying to reach Evangeline, I came up 31 from New Iberia—"

"You a long way from Evangeline and New Iberia both, boy."

"I can tell that. Question is: where *am* I?"

I didn't know what to say to that, so I just stood there in the heat. Sweat trickled into my eyes and when I went to brush it away, my hand trembled. A dark foreboding filled me. I sighed, cursing this Yankee nigger and his government job and whatever fate had seen fit to bring him here. And then I did what I knew I had to do.

"Sulphur Creek," I said. "I reckon you better come inside."

When we stepped inside the store, Lucas Dixon paused, emitting a slow rising whistle, like a tea kettle just coming to a boil. "Wow," he said in a voice pitched just above a whisper, and I had that queer sense that I was seeing Sulphur Creek through his eyes again, a sepia-toned snapshot out of some lost past. Everything swam in green twilight: the bright moted squares of the windows, the sagging shelves of canned goods and tools, Hiram behind the counter, a shadow amid shadows. A ceiling fan shoved the smells of cheese and dust around.

Maybe a decade ago, I hauled a diesel generator back from Morgan City, dragging a scrap of the twentieth century home to Sulphur Creek just as the rest of the world lurched headlong toward the twenty-first. My daddy would have disapproved, but that fan felt just fine on a hot summer day. Even then, with everything else weighing on my mind, I couldn't help lifting my head to catch the air against my face.

I paused at the hardware counter to tell Hiram to fetch us a couple cold drinks from the cooler. When I turned around, I saw that Dixon had wandered over toward drygoods, where he was rubbing a bolt of cloth between two fingers and gazing about with an expression of thunderstruck delight on his face. "Wow!" he said again. He pivoted on his heels like a weathercock, uncurtaining all those shiny teeth. "I hope you won't take offense, Mr. Decoteau, but this place is a time capsule."

I didn't know what to say to that either, so I just ushered him in the direction of the rockers that sit back by the grocery counter. By the time I got him settled, Hiram had turned up with the sodas. We sat there sipping while Hiram stepped out to sweep off the front porch. "Nothin beats an ice-cold Coca-Cola on a hot day, does it," I said.

Dixon tilted his soda to his lips and took a long swig. "That's true, Mr. Decoteau. And it does get hot down here."

"Where bouts you from, then?"

"Albany, New York." He turned to face me. "I really *do* hope you don't take offense, Mr. Decoteau, but your store—" He gazed around appreciatively once again. "—your store is like a dream come true. I'm working on my Ph.D. over at LSU, specializing in the rural economy during Reconstruction, and this place, well, it's like stepping inside my dissertation."

"Your dissertation."

"That's right. History." He gave me a shy smile. "It sounds ridiculous, I guess, but I *do* love history."

"Sign on your car says you work for the United States Census Bureau."

"That's just summer work. I track down non-responders, see if I can get them to answer a few questions. Did you fill out your census form, Mr. Decoteau?"

"Well, I—"

Lucas Dixon waved his hand. "Don't tell me. You thought it was an invasion of your privacy."

"Well—"

"The thing people fail to understand," Dixon said, "is that the government uses that data to help people. Take that street out front. Using census data, you could probably get the funding to pave that street, put in some proper drainage." He'd been digging in his briefcase while he talked. Now he produced a thick file and began thumbing through it. "I know it's just summer work," he was saying, "but I like to think of the service I'm doing for history, gathering all these facts. I like to imagine some future historian . . ." He trailed off, his brow furrowing. "That's funny. Did you say the name of this place is Sulphur Creek?"

"That's right."

He studied the page for another moment and then looked up.

"Sulphur Creek's not listed here. Did you even *get* a census form, Mr. Decoteau?"

"That's what I wanted to talk to you about, Mr. Di—"

"Lucas. Why don't you call me Lucas?"

"We *do* value our privacy here in Sulphur Creek, Mr. Dixon. Lucas. That's what I brought you in here to tell you."

"I understand that, Mr. Decoteau. But census data is completely confiden—"

"We're just very private folk—"

Dixon rolled on over me. "I have some forms. We could take them around town, have people fill them out—"

"Mr. Dixon," I said sharply.

He paused, a little startled I think.

"Mr. Dixon," I said, softer now. "Lucas. I'm trying to make you understand something, see?"

"I'm just trying to help."

"I know. I know you are. But what would be best, what would be best for you and me both, is if you would just get in your car and get on out of here now. That's what I'm trying to say, you understand."

Lucas Dixon wavered. I could see him trying to work it out—not just my words, but the words behind my words, if you take my meaning—and for a moment I thought I had persuaded him. He slid his papers back into his briefcase, and just for the space it took him to latch the cover I let myself believe that I had managed everything just that neatly. A vivid little fantasy took hold of me. In the fantasy, Lucas Dixon thanked me for the Coke, walked out to his car, and drove back down the gravel road that had brought him here. I stood on the porch and listened as the sound of his engine faded, swallowed up in the sleepy buzz of the swamp.

But it was too late for that.

I heard the sound of boots on the porch, and the front screen whined on its hinges. Stelly Broussard and Avery Verrett came in. Their white faces hung disembodied in the gloom as they stared the length of the store.

"We came soon's we heard," Stelly said.

I got to my feet, nodding. "Stelly," I said. "Avery. This here is Lucas Dixon."

Dixon stood, still clutching his satchel, and went to meet them. He held out his hand. Avery hesitated a moment—he never was too bright, Avery—and then he took the hand and shook it, ginger-like, the way a man picks up something that might be dead and then again might not be, something with teeth. Stelly just stood there, the moment spinning out awkwardly until Dixon at last drew his hand back. The whole thing like to make me sick.

"What the hell we gonna do, Armand?" Stelly said.

"Now just listen—" I started, but Dixon interrupted me.

"Maybe, you're right, Mr. Decoteau. Maybe I'll just go after all."

Stelly Broussard didn't like the sound of that. His face kind of pinched in on itself, growing still harder and more hateful, and it had been plenty of both to begin with. He looked like a man who went to bite into a rind of sweet watermelon, and got a mouthful of lemon instead. Stelly's an old-timer like me, but his years in the swamp haven't worn him down the way they do some folks. Five decades of running traplines for nutria and muskrat had left him rangy and quick, impervious to injury. I've seen him take colored boys apart, they get the least bit uppity. He's got a way with those big hands of his, Stelly Broussard has.

"Now don't be hasty," I said.

They just stood there, staring at me. Stelly was mad, and when Stelly was mad Avery didn't know any better than to be mad, too. But Dixon . . . well, Dixon just seemed puzzled. A little nervous, maybe, but mainly puzzled. In his way, I think, Lucas Dixon was as dense as Avery Verrett ever thought about being.

Me, I was thinking that if I could get Stelly alone, calm him down a little, I might find a way out of this yet. I didn't want to like Lucas Dixon, but somehow I couldn't help it. His words kept coming back to me—

—*it sounds ridiculous, Mr. Decoteau, but I do* love history—

—and getting tangled up inside my head with that gravel road cutting through the Atchafalaya, so clean and dry that God himself might have put it there, and maybe he did. And then it came to me—not a solution, exactly, but a way to buy a little time.

"I've reconsidered your proposal, Mr. Dixon," I said, "seein as you're so dedicated and all." I turned to Stelly. "Mr. Dixon here says he might be able to get us a little money, maybe we can pave the street out front. He just needs to ask a few questions."

"What the hell we need with a paved street—"

"I was thinking maybe Avery could show him around a bit, let him ask a few questions, while you and me, Stelly, we have us a little talk."

I let my eyes bore into him, summoning up my daddy's ghost inside me. After a minute, Stelly turned away.

"You heard the man, Avery," he said.

"Where you want I should take him?"

"You take him round the better sort of folks for now," Stelly said. Dixon frowned. "I need to count everyone, Mr. Decoteau."

"By and by. You let Avery show you around, you catch up with the rest this evening."

"This evening?"

"We havin a little *fais-dodo*. A little country dance, you know. History buff like yourself, you'll enjoy it. Avery'll bring you round."

Avery nodded. He pushed the door open, but Dixon held back, still clutching that bag of his. "Mr. Decoteau—"

"Don't you fret, Mr. Dixon. You go on and ask your questions. We'll get you on the right road soon enough."

He held my gaze a moment longer before he turned away. The screen door banged behind shut behind him, and then Stelly Broussard and I were alone.

Stelly stood there a moment, staring after them. The sun slanting through the screen tattooed a grid of fine lines on his face. The air had that still, sleepy quality it gets late in the afternoon. The heat comes off the water in waves then, gilding everything with a faint damp sheen you can almost taste. The fan creaked. Hiram's broom made a steady rasp in the silence.

Stelly grunted. He turned and came the length of the room, his boots calling up echoes in the stillness. "You see that road out there?"

"I seen it."

"A road." He shook his head. "A goddamn road."

I lowered myself gingerly into my rocker. I had never felt older or wearier. I could have curled up and slept right there in my chair and never woke up again, and glad to do it, too. But Stelly wouldn't let me.

"What we gonna do, Armand?"

"I don't know, Stelly. I'm thinkin on it, don't you see."

"Thinkin!" He laughed, a short ugly bark, without humor.

"Why don't you sit down?"

"Sit down," he said. He leveled one blunt finger at me, right in my face. The finger shook. "You know what, Armand? I'm right tired of you tellin everybody what to do."

"What are you doin here, then?"

Stelly cursed and turned away. The silence held for a while. I could feel the pulse beating at my temple.

Stelly sighed. "Hell, Armand. I've known you all my life. All I'm sayin is that maybe you're losin your heart to do what you have to do. Take this business with Billy Go—"

"I did what was necessary, didn't I?"

"You *let* it be done. You didn't have the stomach to do it yourself."

I didn't have any answer to that. I just sat there, rocking a little, lifting my face to the fan. I closed my eyes, willing it all away. But it wouldn't go, and I knew it wouldn't go. For sixty-odd years now, I'd been closing my eyes and willing it all away, and it wouldn't ever go. It was always there around me: the store that had been my daddy's store and his daddy's store and on and on all the way back to the day of Mr. Jefferson Davis himself and before that even, each successive generation of Decoteaus treading deeper the groove that ran behind the grocery counter and down either side of the store to drygoods and hardware. The store was always there, and beyond that the town, and beyond that the swamp, huge and dangerous and stranger than most anyone could know or guess. And beyond that? Another world, that's what. Now a little piece of that world named Lucas Dixon had settled here among us, blown willy nilly down that gravel road from nowhere, and I would have to decide what to do about him.

All I wanted to do was shut my eyes.

But Sulphur Creek kept crashing in. In the ring of Stelly Broussard's boots on the floor Hiram had polished to a high gloss that very morning and in the labored sigh he made as he settled into the rocker beside me and in the faint stale odor of his breath, like a still pool that has lain too long in the shadow of a willow, where the sun can't reach—in all that and more, Sulphur Creek came crashing in upon me.

Stelly plucked at my sleeve. "I knew your daddy, Armand—"

"You leave him out of this."

"Well he wouldn't have approved, you can be sure enough of that." He studied the floor for a minute. Then, lifting his face so that the light fell across it, he said, "Maybe you done enough, Armand, that's all I'm sayin. Maybe it's time to let this burden pass to someone else."

"You volunteerin, Stelly?"

He didn't answer.

"Because if you're volunteerin, you might want to ask yourself what it is you're volunteerin for. It's more than keepin the likes of Odile Halloway in line and organizin the *fais-dodo* come Saturday night."

"I spent my life in the swamp."

"I ain't talkin about your piss-ant nutria and muskrat lines, Stelly. I'm talkin about seein that everybody has a little somethin to eat come nightfall. I'm talkin about the supply run down Morgan City, the long run through the deep, strange water farther out than you ever dared to go. The night closes in around you out there, Stelly. You hear things like no other man ever heard before, and sometimes you see them too. Eight or ten times a year, I make that run, and it ain't never the same."

"I ain't afraid of nothin."

"You're a bigger fool than I took you for, then."

Stelly jerked his head up, his eyes blazing, and his fingers tightened on the arms of his chair until I thought the wood might splinter under the pressure. He got to his feet stiffly. He wiped his mouth with the back of his hand. "I'll leave it to you for now, Armand. But we both know what has to be done. Mark my words: if you ain't willin to see it through, there's some who will."

He didn't look back as he strode to the door.

The screen swung shut behind him. I felt wrung out and weary, and when I lifted my Coke to my lips I found it had gone brackish and warm. After a time, I realized that the sound of Hiram's sweeping had died away. I got to my feet and went to the door. Hiram sat on the steps with the broom propped between his knees, staring out at Lucas Dixon's motor car and the gravel road beyond it, veering off through the swamp to a place Hiram had never seen. "Now look here, Hiram," I started, but when he lifted his face to mine, I just let the words trail off. I couldn't find it in my heart to scold him.

Night never leaves the Atchafalaya, she just lies up through the heat of the day, same as the rest of the swamp creatures. Live in the swamp long enough, you'll see her pooled in the deep cypress groves or hiding out in the black depths of a mangrove thicket, patient and sure, biding her time. Now and then, you'll catch a glimpse of her in mid-day, in the wind-driven shudder of a palmetto leaf or in the languid dapple of Spanish moss, draping the trees like cast-off wedding finery, ivory veils aging slowly to an antique gray. Then the sun starts down. Slowly, imperceptibly, night takes hold. She steals invisibly across the water, like smoke; she spills out from the wells of shadow beneath our houses. Night's like love. She creeps in and takes possession of everything you ever knew or hoped to know without so much as a by-your-leave. She takes dominion of your heart before you ever know she's there.

I woke in darkness, relieved, thinking I had dreamed it all—that crazy road appearing out of nowhere and Lucas Dixon and the sign stuck on the door of his car, that one that spelled doom sure as I could feel the blood coursing in my veins. The windows were black and the intermittent gusts from the fan carried a chill that hadn't been there before. Night had claimed Sulphur Creek, carrying with it faint strains of music.

The *fais-dodo* had gotten underway. I heaved myself out of my chair and ambled over to look through the screen. At the edge of the porch, Booger lifted his head and yawned. The music was louder here, a fiddle and a ting-a-ling and Louis Mayard's high tenor, lifted in some old Cajun song. Down the street a way, Ruby Lafitte's place was lit up like a jack-o'-lantern. Folks gathered on the porch, drinking and talking in the smoky radiance from within.

I yawned and gave myself a good scratching. Then I opened the screen door, letting it bang shut behind me. Startled voices rose out of the shadows below the porch, a tangle of words in which a single phrase—

—"*shit*, Odile—"

—stood out unmistakably. A car door slammed and boys scattered into darkness like a covey of startled quail. I caught a glimpse of Odile Halloway and I felt a little twinge of sorrow, knowing that he was starting down the same doomed path Billy Go had taken before him. It sickened me a little, to tell you the truth. And it sickened me even more to know that I hadn't been dreaming after all. That gravel road was still there, and so was Lucas Dixon's car. One door still stood open where them boys had been peering in at the dash. A light was shining inside.

I stepped down off the porch and shut the door, and then I stood there, staring up the street toward Ruby's place. I felt strange and haunted, somehow. Someone stood at my shoulder, but I didn't turn around. I knew better than that.

"Daddy," I said by way of greeting.

Words came in response and I couldn't say whether they were coming out of memory, or from some other place, some cold, cold place where words formed slow and hard as diamonds if they formed at all. They were daddy's words, though, and I remembered when he said them. He was already an old man, then, and I think we both knew he didn't have much time.

They'll come a day, he said, *you'll have to do somethin you won't want to do, Armand. But you'll have to do it, anyway, because that's what a man does.*

I sighed and started up the street toward Ruby's place.

As I drew near Ruby's, I could pick out the words in Louis's song, an old Cajun lament. Someone spotted me from the porch and called out, "Hey there, Armand," and a chorus of greetings followed. The regulars had gathered on the porch to play cards, same as always. Oil lanterns flickered atop Ruby's faded porch furniture and Eunice Ray bustled around freshening drinks, her dark skin glossy with sweat. The air smelled of whiskey and tobacco, smells that reminded me of my daddy, rocking there on the front porch of the store, staring out across Sulphur Creek like he owned the place. I caught a glimpse of Stelly, his chair cocked back against the wall with its front legs off the ground. He nodded over his cards.

"Deal you in, Armand?" someone asked.

"Thank you, no."

As I started toward the stairs, somebody plucked at my sleeve. Turning, I saw Hiram's long face peering around the corner. I let him draw me into the shadows at the side of the house. Through the windows, I watched Eduis Frugé pumping away on his squeeze box. They'd pushed Ruby's furniture back along the walls. Dancers whirled in the clear space, their faces shiny as new money.

"You ain't got enough to do, you gotta skulk around out here, Hiram?"

"I been waitin for you."

"Waitin? You know where to find me."

"I'se ascared to come back down the store, Mistah Armand."

The light from inside touched up half his face, leaving the other side in shadow. I couldn't see much but the angle of his jaw, and the white of his eye above it, marbled and weepy looking in the darkness. His lower lip trembled.

"Scared. Why's that?"

"Odile and them others. If I'se to say anything, they said they'd whip up on me."

I took a step toward him. "What are you talkin about?"

"They gonna steal that colored man's automobile." He stumbled a little over the unfamiliar word. "Said they's done sick and tired of Sulphur Creek, said they's gonna break Billy Go loose and just drive on outta here."

"Billy Go, huh?"

Hiram nodded. "You allus treat me right, Mistah Armand, and I thought you ought to know, but I sure am ascared."

"You ain't got nothin to fear, Hiram."

"They said they'd whip up—"

"Hush now. That colored boy, Dixon, you seen him inside?"

"Yes, sir."

"What about Janie Halloway?"

"She in the kitchen."

"All right, then. You go on and lend a hand. I'll step back there in a minute and have a word with her. And don't you worry none, Odile wouldn't know how to drive that car even if he could get it started, you hear? I'll take care of Odile Halloway. You ain't got nothin to fear from the likes of him."

"Yes, sir." He hesitated.

"What is it?"

"Odile, he say there's a whole world full a them automobiles outside the bayou, Mistah Armand. Say all kinds of colored folk drive em and ain't nobody to say a word about it."

For some reason, the words moved me. It was nothin I could put into words, but I felt a little twist inside me all the same. Hiram had been working in the store since he weren't but knee high to a grasshopper, and I guess I'd gotten accustomed to him. I never took a wife and I've brought no children into this world, but I'd taken a shine to Hiram, even if he were just a colored boy. I wanted to say something to comfort him, but I couldn't seem to find the words. Finally, I just reached out and touched him on the shoulder. "Don't you put no stock in Odile Halloway," I said. "He ain't nothin but swamp gas and bother, that one. Now run along."

Hiram stared at me a moment longer, and then he melted back into the darkness. Inside, the music quickened, Louis's voice rising to a doleful wail. *Quel espoir, quel espoir*, he sang as the song climaxed in a flurry of whoops and claps. In the silence that followed, I felt that presence at my shoulder once again. This time, though, I didn't say a word. I just spat into the dirt, and as the music started up again, I trudged back around the house.

Out front, the old-timers were still at it. Stelly fixed me with his gaze and let his chair legs thump to the floor as I mounted the stairs. A couple of the card-players glanced up, too, men I'd known all my life. And now I saw something in their eyes I hadn't noticed before: a feral sheen of expectation. Stelly's words came back to me—

—*you ain't willin to see it through, there's some who will*—

—as I brushed past them and yanked the screen open. The dance floor was crowded like it always was, but everything seemed slightly off-kilter, the music a hair more frantic than usual, the dancers somehow reckless, as if they couldn't move fast enough —as if they were dancing with the devil hindmost and hell before em. A smell of whiskey and chicken gumbo hung in the air, and the sticky press of too many bodies in too small a space. I nodded at folks as I slipped by, aiming for the kitchen and Janie Halloway.

"Mr. Decoteau!"

Somebody tugged at my sleeve. I turned and there was Lucas Dixon, still cradling that battered leather case. He hovered at the edge of the dance floor. Folks veered about him to the left and right. They studied him askance, never quite meeting his eyes. He seized my hand. If he was aware of the stir he was causing, he didn't show it.

"Mr. Decoteau," he said, his voice pitched so I could hear him above the music. "Mr. Verrett—Avery?—he told me you're the one I needed to talk to."

"Me?"

"Are you the mayor of Sulphur Creek, Mr. Decoteau?"

"Mayor? No, I'm—" I paused, thinking how to put it into words. A place like Sulphur Creek, the store is more than just a store. Day after day, year after year, women gossip across its counters, children crowd its aisles, old men gather to whittle on the porch. A man stands behind that counter long enough, he becomes . . . well, more than just another man. Folks look to him, somehow. It had been true of my father and it was true of me, too. It weren't nothing official. It just *was*, because that's the way it always had been. But there didn't seem to be any way to make Dixon understand any of that. I sighed. "I'm just the storekeep, that's all, Mr. Dixon."

Dixon nodded as if maybe he understood. "Well Mr. Verrett said I was to talk to you."

"What was it you wanted to ask me about?"

"I was thinking if you put in a word for me, maybe people would loosen up a little. Most of them, they don't want to answer my questions at all."

"We're private folk, I told you that."

"The questions aren't intrusive. How many people in your household, stuff like that, nothing personal at all." He stepped closer, leaning toward me and lowering his voice. "And that's not all. It's the black people, especially. I saw them here and there today, but I never got a chance to ask them any questions. When I got here, I stepped back into the kitchen—I've just got a few questions, it wouldn't take a minute—and they wouldn't even acknowledge me."

I stared at him for a moment, knowing now that I'd made a mistake, that I should have sent him packing right away, knowing too that that wouldn't have been a solution. There was no solution. Or there was one, and Stelly Broussard was right: I couldn't stomach it.

"Mr. Decoteau?"

"I'll say a word to them," I said. I turned to go, but he tugged at my shoulder.

His face was solemn. "This is a fascinating place, Mr. Decoteau."

"How's that?"

"No cars, no power-lines, no televisions. Not even a radio. I haven't seen a radio all day. People act like they barely know what I'm talking about. The ones who would even talk to me at all, that is, and not many of them did." Dixon stared at the dance floor. Then he turned his gaze back to mine. "Do you think it's because I'm black, Mr. Decoteau?"

"I shouldn't like to say that, Mr. Dixon."

"Well, I wouldn't either, but this place . . ."

The music wound itself to a crescendo and died away amid scattered applause. In the silence, there was a metallic clatter in the kitchen. I felt the weight of the room's attention swing past, two dozen pairs of eyes skating across my back without ever quite coming to rest. Ernest Fortier ran his bow across his strings, Louis counted out the time, "*Un, deux, trois,*" and the band swung into something new.

Dixon said, "I saw what looked like a little jail today, just one room in the woods behind your store."

I stiffened. "Avery didn't take you down there, did he?"

"No. Nor would he answer my questions when I asked about it. Why is that, Mr. Decoteau?"

I felt a sick smile plaster itself across my face. "Well, we wouldn't want to expose you to the criminal element here in Sulphur Creek, Mr. Dixon. It wouldn't be hospitable, now would it?"

"Maybe not, but it made me think, anyway."

He had my attention now. "Think of what?"

"Just how isolated you folks are. This place is like a whole different world." Dixon licked his lips. "I hope you don't take offense, Mr. Decoteau, but Sulphur Creek is a fine opportunity for field work."

"Field work?"

"Data gathering. Historical studies, anthropology, you name it. When I get back with the census data, you're going to get some attention. I've never heard of an entire town being forgotten like this." He smiled, a chastened smile that reminded me somehow of Hiram, shyly inquiring about the possibility of another world. "But I'm not fooling you, am I? I guess you know I'm really thinking in selfish terms. Of my dissertation. This place is a real opportunity. It's like stepping back in history."

I felt stiff and cold suddenly, like it was mid-January and I'd missed a step in the swamp, plunging deep into the dank chill waters of the Atchafalaya. His words buzzed around in my head like bees, alighting now and then to dip their stingers in my brain. I kept thinking of Hiram. Hiram and Billy Go and Odile Halloway.

"There's some parts of history you don't want to step into," I said when I could get my works unfroze.

"What do you mean?"

I shook my head. "Forget it. I don't mean nothin. Nothin at all."

The words came out harsher than I'd intended them, and something stirred in Lucas Dixon's face, a kind of comprehension. I saw it happen. I saw his gaze slide away and come to rest at a point just over my left shoulder, a point where he could take in the room at a single glance, conscious for the first time maybe of the dearth of black faces on the dance floor, of the way the ones who *were* there hugged the edges of the room, carrying drinks to the folks who sprawled across Ruby Lafitte's sagging furniture. He stepped back, his face puzzled, and all at once it was too much for me, Lucas Dixon and Stelly Broussard and the ghost of my daddy always at my shoulder. The music buffeted me. My head throbbed. I needed to step back a minute, I needed a little time to regroup.

I lifted a hand. "There's someone I need to see," I said. "Just give me a minute, I'll be right back."

I turned away before he could answer, ducking into the kitchen. The heat from the stove enveloped me, sweltering, and the spicy fragrance of the gumbo grew abruptly stronger. My gut twisted. I propped myself against the wall, tipped my head back, and shut my eyes, waiting for the nausea to pass. I found myself longing for my store. I pictured it in my head, the fan turning and turning in the dark above me, breathing winter down into my upturned face. I took a deep breath, felt the world settle into place around me.

I opened my eyes. The kitchen bustled with activity. Colored women worked at the counters or hurried back and forth through the door into the main room, their hands full. Hiram stirred a simmering pot of gumbo at the stove. A baby was crying in the adjoining *parc aux petits*. I glimpsed its nanny through the open door, cradling a squirming bundle against her bosom, her dark face gentle as she walked it patiently back and forth among the sleeping children.

A clatter drew my attention. Janie Halloway turned from capping a big pot of rice on the stove, and from the way her face wrinkled when she saw me, I knew Hiram had been carrying tales out of school. Normally, I'd have scolded him, but I didn't have the heart for it just now. His face kept getting mixed up inside my head with Lucas Dixon's face, and for some reason I found myself thinking of the son I'd never had, how disappointed my father would have been, and how he would have asked me who was going to take over the store when I was gone? Who was going to make the runs to Morgan City then? I didn't know, but I didn't care much either, so long as I never had to tell a son of mine that he'd have to do things he didn't have the stomach for, because that was the price of being a man.

Janie Halloway stood before me, stout and tall, her broad face unlined even as she closed in on fifty. "He's jest a boy, Mistah Armand, that's all he ever was."

"Janie," I said. "You and I both know that Odile has to learn—"

"And if he don't?" She looked up, suddenly fierce, her voice a desperate whisper. "You gonna do to Odile what you did to Billy, Mistah Armand? Is that what you gonna do? Cause I got to tell you, Mistah Armand, I couldn't take it. I couldn't take losin Odile, too."

"Now, Janie—" I said, and then the tears welling up in her eyes spilled over, tracking slowly down her face. Just like that, I felt all the fight go out of me. I clasped her by the shoulders and tried to draw her close, but she stiffened, holding herself away, and the words came unbidden, rising to my lips the way words rise up when you cradle a weeping child, the way they surface out of some lost well of ages, these words of comfort that the first mother used maybe and which you too use, in this hour of need when only words can salve the ache inside you, though you've never so much as held a child before. "Don't you take on, now, Janie, we're gonna find us a way to take care of Odile. Ain't nothin gonna happen to Odile."

"You swear, Mistah Armand?"

"I swear," I said, and I felt it close around us, that promise, like a knot that's been soaked in icy water, the fibers shrinking down and binding us together there in the stifling kitchen. I felt it close around us like a noose.

I stood there a moment longer, gathering my strength, and then I released her. When I stepped back into the main room, Lucas Dixon was gone.

I pushed through the crowded dance floor to the door, the music dying into silence as people turned to stare after me. He wasn't on the porch either. A sick premonition had seized me, and I stumbled down the steps toward the street, ignoring the confused snippets of talk—

"—steady there, Armand—"

"—what's the matter now—"

—that floated after me. And then I was running, though I was far too old to run. An enormous swollen moon had hove halfway above the horizon, pouring through the trees a deluge of orange light like the swamp itself had caught fire. The breeze-combed cypress and live oak screening the far end of town hurled down twisty spokes of shadow, and strange phantoms capered along the weed-clotted ruts of the street, as though hellmouth itself had gaped open, releasing the souls of demons and sinners alike for a midnight frolic. My store loomed against the night sky, throwing its queer elongated shadow across the gleaming hulk of Dixon's car. In the distance, on the other side of a patch of marshy scrub, I could glimpse the little bunker we used as a jail house.

By the time I saw the thing that tripped me up—Lucas Dixon's leather satchel, spilling a sheaf of loose census forms into the street —it was too late. I went tumbling head over tea kettle into the shadows by the porch, the wire grass reaching up to poke at me with a thousand prickly fingers. As I stumbled to my knees, aching from the fall, the wind picked up, whipping Dixon's papers into a narrow funnel. It held its shape for a split second before it came apart. One of the forms plastered itself flapping across my face, momentarily blinding me. Strong hands lifted me to my feet. The wind snatched the paper loose, whirling it away into the dark.

It was Billy Go that held my shoulders. Billy Go, a great hulking man with skin the color of night and handsome negroid features and big mournful eyes that held me fixed for a moment. Only his name wasn't Billy Go, was it? No, and it never had been, though we'd all taken to calling him that these last few years, because Billy, he wouldn't stay. But the name he'd been born to was Billy Halloway, and he had his mother's eyes, and his mother's round, smooth face, and the beads of perspiration glistening on his cheeks might have been his mother's tears. He must have been thirty years old by then, but looking at him there, bare-torsoed in the moonlight with a pair of canvas trousers cinched around his waist, I saw only the boy I'd known so many years ago, when he used to help out around the store, before all his troubles beset him, and Hiram came in to spell him for awhile and somehow just never left.

"Billy," I whispered.

"Mistah Armand," he said.

In the silence, a group of boys emerged from the shadows. Odile Halloway stood in front, looking like a slimmed-down version of his older brother. The De Soto boys trailed along behind him: Marcus, a willowy young nigger who never said much, and Clifton, a rangy caramel-colored boy with one eye normal and the other like an island, stranded in a sea of purple birthmark that spilled out across one cheek to lap at the corner of his mouth. The census taker stumbled between them, dragging his feet as Marcus and Clifton yanked him forward.

A savage anger boiled up inside me at the sight of him. "You just had to go off and have a look at the jail, didn't you?" I snarled. "You and your damned questions, can't leave people well enough alone."

"Now, hush up, Mistah Armand," Billy said gently, drawing me closer, and he kind of winced when he did it. A scab cracked open under his arm, spilling a little rivulet of blood down his side, and Stelly's words—

—*you let it be done, you didn't have the stomach to do it yourself*—

—came back to me in a rush. A taste as bitter as day-old coffee grounds filled my mouth. I looked away, the anger sieving through me as suddenly as it had filled me up, leaving nothing behind but a sour residue of shame.

"You know how I always hated to see em hurt you, Billy," I whispered.

"But they always end up hurtin me jest the same, don't they? I run off and you white mens fetch me back and there you stand noddin your head all mournful like and sayin I sure hate to see em hurt you, Billy, I surely do, but somehow it never make no difference in the end."

"You stop runnin off, that'd make a difference. You could have a good life here. Your mama has a good life."

"My mama ain't free, Mistah Armand. Ain't none of us free."

"That what you want, Billy, no matter what it takes?"

"Thass right, Mistah Armand. No matter what it take."

Odile stepped forward, then, laying a hand across Billy's shoulder. Billy winced again, and when he winced, time slipped around me for a moment. I saw the lash spiral out against the morning sky, like a black snake thrashing in the sun. I saw him flinch away from the whipping post as it descended. I saw the blood, red as any white man's blood.

"Time we be goin, Billy," Odile said. "That strange nigger gonna drive us right on outta here." He jerked his chin over his shoulder. Marcus and Clifton moved toward the car, leading the census taker between them. Odile's gaze settled on my face. "We fixin to leave now, Mistah Armand, and you want to be real quiet. I would hate to have to hurt you, but I will do it. You make me, I will do it. You understand me?"

His eyes were as cold and black as the eyes of a gar, and I saw that he meant it. I nodded.

"Billy," Odile said.

Billy turned me loose, smoothing my shirt where he had gripped it. He held my gaze for the space of a heartbeat, letting me remember the polite young man I'd taken into the store all those years ago, letting me see that nothing had happened to that boy despite all the scars men like Stelly Broussard had carved into his flesh since then. He was still right there, that boy, and I wondered that I hadn't noticed him before, knowing with a kind of looming sickness that I hadn't let myself. He nodded, and turned away. Odile stared at me a moment longer, his face expressionless, and then he followed his brother.

The other boys had slipped into the car by then, easing shut the doors as silently as ghosts. Lucas Dixon stared out at me through the driver's side window, his face slack with shock. Odile and Billy Go were halfway to the car when it happened. "Start it up, now," Odile hissed, and Dixon twisted the key. As the engine coughed to life, Booger tore out from under the porch, barking like his feet were on fire and his tail was catching. Odile lunged toward me, his face twisting. "Shut up that dog, Mistah A—"

He never finished the sentence. Instead a startled look stole across his moonlit features. He hung there, seeming to defy gravity for a moment, and then he pitched forward, thrashing like a man in a fit. In the same instant I heard the shot echoing away into the swamp. By the time it died, Odile Halloway had fallen still.

Billy Go sobbed and hunkered down beside his brother, his hands outstretched.

I twisted my head toward Ruby's place.

The whole town had drifted into the street in my wake, black and white alike, sixty or seventy people I suppose there must have been. Stelly Broussard stood at their head, a dark shape, faceless, like a paper doll hewn out of night and propped up against the blood-red ovoid of that colossal moon. As he lowered the rifle, a little ribbon of blue smoke curled away from the barrel.

"We thought he was goin for you, Armand," Stelly said.

"I reckon you did," I said.

After that, we just stood in silence because there was nothing else to say. The swamp rose up around us and drew us in, clamoring with noise and beauty and the ripe rich stink of death, and the world rolled on beyond it, worlds upon worlds, every one of them wheeling around on the axis of this moment.

Janie Halloway stumbled out of the crowd and went to her knees beside Billy Go, sobbing helplessly over his brother's body. She cradled the dead boy's head and lifted her face to the sky. "Odile!" she screamed. "Odile!"

Something twisted deep inside my guts.

And then the census taker's automobile lurched into gear.

The engine shrieked as the car backed swiftly away, throwing up chunks of sod and wire grass. I caught a glimpse of the interior as it flew past. The two Sulphur Creek boys in the back seat stared out at me, their eyes wide, their mouths gaping in astonishment. But Lucas Dixon never spared me a glance. His knuckles whitened as he fought the wildly spinning wheel. His face was a mask of shock and terror.

And then he was gone, whipping the car around backwards in a long arc, leaving me to stare after him through a cloud of exhaust. "Wait!" I hollered, waving my arms, and for half a second, as I watched the car shudder to a halt, I thought he'd heard me. I thought he was listening. Then lights flickered on the rear end and gears clashed. The car surged forward, weaving like a man with a skinful of liquor. Its headlights carved the dark as it picked up speed. I suppose Lucas Dixon must have seen it at the same time I did: the gravel road he had come in on was gone.

It had just flat disappeared.

The swamp surrounded us, closing the town in the way it always had. Water glimmered in the moonlight, and the cypress trees hunkered on their knees and lifted their arms to the sky. Lucas Dixon screamed. The car veered suddenly, the engine roaring. It went over the bank at full speed. Water foamed up around it like the froth on a bucket of fresh-churned milk. It had risen to the door handles by the time I drew close, the breath heaving in my lungs.

The back doors opened and the De Soto brothers came wading out, looking scared and remorseful. But Lucas Dixon never moved. He just sat there, staring out through the windshield, his hands still clenching the wheel. Even after I splashed out after him, he didn't look at me for a long time. He was sobbing quietly. Big fat tears rolled down his cheeks. His lips trembled as he turned his face to mine.

"Come on, now," I said. "Don't you fret."

It took me a minute to pry the door open and haul him out, dead-weight. Mud sucked at my boots. My pants clung to me like a second skin. Stelly Broussard was waiting on the shore like a man carved of ice. The moonlight shone on everything, gilding the leaves and the faces of the throng that stood behind him and the blued steel barrel of his rifle, which I'd hauled back myself one night on the long, strange run from Morgan City.

"You let him go, he'll bring folks back from outside," Stelly said. "And then where we gonna be, Armand, you thought of that?"

"And how they ever find their way? The swamp, it's always changing, you can't never come the same way twice."

I started to shrug past him, but he stepped in front of me. He lifted the gun. I stared down into it, the machined bore spiraling down into a blackness just the color of death.

"*You* always find a way, don't you?" he said. "You let that boy go where he can talk, them nigger-lovin sons a bitches'll find it, too. They won't rest until they do, and you know it's true, Armand, just like your daddy knew it before you."

"You gonna shoot me, Stelly?"

He stared at me for a long time. Then I reached out and pushed the barrel of the rifle toward the ground.

"I'm takin this boy out of here," I said.

I gathered Lucas Dixon's weight on my shoulder and started limping back toward town. The crowd parted before me silently, leaving a long path at my rear, and it was down that path that Stelly Broussard called out to me.

"What the hell am I supposed to do, Armand? Why don't you tell me that?"

I didn't look back.

"You figure it out yourself, Stelly. You been doin all right so far."

God help me, I took him into the swamp.

I untied my daddy's boat and I poled him deep into the night water, same as my daddy had done with me, all those years before. Just looking at him, hunkered shivering and silent in the bow, brought it all back, the night and the swamp and my daddy strong and silent in the stern. The deck groaned under a load of nutria and muskrat pelts for the Morgan City trade, and the dark sang out mysteriously around me. I was twelve years old, and as I watched the moon rise orange and bloated through the cypress and tupelo-gum, my mind drifted to the stories I'd heard at my nanny's knee, tales of ha'nts and spirits, of the cursed souls called *loup-garous*, and of the

Alligator King, a hundred-foot behemoth that could rise unseen from his watery lair and reduce a pirogue to kindling with a single snap of his great jaws. An obscure terror seized me, and even now, all these years later, that terror hasn't fully passed.

For the bayou is different in the night than it is in the day. The heat dies back, and the smell of the place grows stronger, a rank wild musk of vigor and decay, of yellow-blooming rushes and purple hyacinth and black mangrove striving up and dying back into the mire that nourished it. The night chorus begins to sing, frogs and lubbers and crickets, and occasionally you'll catch a glimpse of the rarest creatures of the Atchafalaya—a bear or a bobcat or the great white flag of a snowy egret hurling itself into the velvet dark with a thunder of mighty wings.

Time slows and the night stretches out forever. The water never takes the same path twice, and your mind turns funny on you, and maybe it's more than your mind. Maybe the whole world turns strange in the long black reach between midnight and dawn, when a stillness moves over the face of the waters and you hear the distant shriek of a loon, like a woman screaming, or the current parting as a gator glides from a rotten log to hunt the moonspun dark.

I was twelve years old, and I hunkered shivering under a blanket, knowing that my time too was drawing near. Knowing for the first time maybe how brief a life was, like a struck match flaring up for a fitful instant in the black well of eternity, and dying back in the same long breath of air. Knowing that my daddy would pass like his daddy had before him, and a time would come that it would fall to me and me alone, this long night passage to Morgan City.

Something huge lumbered off through the undergrowth, and a thin high cry drifted out of the void, a cry older than time. I lifted my face to the sky, and saw that we had left the world I'd known behind.

Two moons hung like Christmas bulbs in the endless deep, and a vast leathery shadow passed far overhead, cruising the night sky on enormous outstretched wings. Its great beak clacked open and once again that unearthly voice rang down the heavens. I felt the terror strong upon me then. I turned to face my father, throwing back the blanket he had draped across my shoulders. "Where are we?" I asked.

It was that same question that Lucas Dixon put to me now. His face was bleached out and he was shaking, the way a man does when the fever's on him. I saw that he'd been in a kind of shock for all this time, brooding on what he'd seen, and now he'd come to some resolve. He'd decided to face the thing. I felt another little surge of respect for him, for the courage that had driven him suddenly to turn and face me there from the front of the boat.

"That road," he said. "It just disappeared." He shivered and stared off into the night for a while, and when he turned back to me, his face had a haunted, hunted look. "What kind of place *is* this, Mr. Decoteau?"

I'd spent years pondering that question. But it was my father's answer that I gave him, for it's the only answer I could ever come to in all those sleepless nights. Swamp is older than any man, I said, and powerful, the most powerful place there is maybe. It is sky and land, it is dry and wet, it is earth and air and water and a powerful strong *hoodoo* bound deep in the place where they all three come together. The swamp is many rivers, I said, all flowing and mingling together and changing, always changing.

My father believed the same was true of all times and all worlds and all places that have ever been or might be yet. There are many worlds, he told me, many lines of possibility, more than any man can comprehend maybe, and they mingle in the swamp like rivers, always flowing, always changing, with Sulphur Creek at the center, alone unchanged in all the years since the first Decoteau settled here, striding deliberately out of the same world that Lucas Dixon had stumbled out of, in a time two centuries before Lucas Dixon's birth. It happens: some poor fool gets swept all unawares into a river of possibility and winds up in a place he could never imagine. And there are those few, the Decoteaus among them when our blood breeds true, who can sense those shifting currents of force in their bones, and navigate them.

"You took a wrong turn and drove down a road into the heart of everything," I told him. "And when you went to drive back out again, that road was gone. The swamp had swallowed it up. You can't ever come the same way twice."

Lucas Dixon stared up at me, his face washed clean with a wonder and terror so pure and dumb that I could hardly plumb it. Moonlight glinted in his spectacles, silvering over his eyes. "Am I lost forever then?"

I didn't answer for a long time. I just stared down into his face, thinking of him in that first moment in my store, pivoting to take it all in, unable to believe the dumb luck that had brought him to my door. *I do love history, Mr. Decoteau*, he'd said, and in that moment he'd seemed so young, so fresh and overflowing with enthusiasm. It put me in mind of Hiram somehow, hungry for things he didn't even know were out there. My mind filled up with faces, with Odile Halloway and Billy Go and Stelly Broussard, his voice tightening like a drum as he said *You let it be done, you didn't have the stomach to do it yourself.* I thought of Janie Halloway, then, and the price you sometimes had to pay to be a man.

"Mr. Decoteau?"

I felt my daddy's presence at my shoulder. I thought I might weep.

"We're all lost," I said.

Dawn hung in the trees like gauze by the time I got back to Sulphur Creek, pushing my way steadily along the channel, feeling the ache of muscle in my shoulders. Stelly Broussard waited on the landing behind my store. When I got close, he leaned out and hauled me in. He looped the stays around their posts and steadied the boat as I stepped out.

I brushed past him, moving toward the store.

He stopped me at the door.

"Armand," he said.

I turned to look at him, thinking of the way this place had shaped us both over the long decades since we were boys. He was big and grizzled and there were crow's feet around his eyes from staring long hours into the swamp and squinting at the sun flashing off the water. It was like looking in a mirror.

"Armand, I just wanted—" He hesitated. "I just—"

"I know," I said. I touched his shoulder and turned away. I went inside then, through the dark storage room and into the front, my feet finding the grooves laid down in the wood by all the Decoteaus who had come before me. I lowered myself into my rocker and lifted my face to the ceiling. The fan still turned patiently up there. I felt the cool air against my cheeks, gentle as a benediction.

Hiram woke me from a dream-haunted sleep when he came in after nine. "Miz Halloway been askin for you," he told me.

"I reckon she has been," I said.

I pushed myself wearily out of my seat. Booger looked up yawning from the porch, and I reached down to pat him before I started up the street. The Halloways lived in an old cabin behind Ruby's place. The door opened as I mounted the steps.

Inside it smelled of flowers and the press of negroes thronging the little room and the kerosene lanterns burning behind the closed shades. I heard the story from Janie Halloway herself, there in the crowded parlor: how she'd run up to Ruby's for some thread to mend Odile's Sunday shirt, and how they'd got to talking and crying as women will, how when she'd started back at last she'd seen the chair overturned on the porch as she came through the trees. For a moment she hadn't understood. It was nothing special, after all, just a plain old kitchen chair, but she couldn't figure how it had come to be there, or why it filled her so with dread to see it lying on its side like that. And then she understood at last, and knowing already what Billy Go had done and why he had done it, she lifted her face to look at him, swinging slowly from the rafters.

She had laid them out in their finest things, both her boys. I stood looking down into Billy Go's swollen face for a long time, thinking back on the days when he used to help out around the store. At last, I reached down and touched his cold hand with my own. Then I turned away, hoping that he'd found some peace at last, now that he was finally free.

There isn't much left to tell.

We go on the same as we've always done here in Sulphur Creek, trapping and hunting and dancing on Saturday nights. Seven or eight times a year, I load up my daddy's boat and set out for Morgan City, trading nutria and muskrat pelts for the few things we can't make on our own.

Most days I get through just fine without ever sparing the census taker a thought. Other days are harder, though, and on those days I walk out toward the edge of town where for the space of a single afternoon a gravel road found its way to the heart of everything, here in Sulphur Creek.

The car's still there, sunk to its windows in water. I stand on the bank, staring out at it and thinking of Lucas Dixon and our night in the Atchafalaya and the price you have to pay to call yourself a man. The car's seen better days. Great patches of rust have started eating away at the hood, and kids throwing rocks have busted out most of the glass. Someday, I guess, it'll disappear altogether. Daddy was right about that too, like he was right about so many things. Give it time enough, the swamp eats anything. Anything at all.

Exodus

RUTH HADN'T BEEN SLEEPING THE NIGHT through for decades, and on this morning—this special morning which she had been looking forward to for days and weeks and endless dragging months—she woke up even earlier than usual: in the cool silence of a May morning at precisely 3:57 according to the clock in her retinal implant. She lay still, inhaling the fresh lilac smell that drifted through the window from the commons while she decided whether she was still tired. She had noticed that as you got older, you craved sleep more but needed it less. Her practical solution to this paradox was to ignore the craving. Her body urged her to remain in her pleasant nest of sheets for another hour or two, but her good sense won out. Nothing could be more depressing than two sleepless hours in bed—especially on your 145th birthday.

So she stood and belted on the new robe Martha had sent her yesterday. Martha, her great-granddaughter, had mailed the robe from some eastern nation—Vietnam? Laos? Ruth had noticed the postmark and had carefully cut it out and put it on the refrigerator. A horrid colorful design like a viral culture infected the robe itself, but Ruth wore it anyway. She had not seen Martha in six years, had not spoken to her in three, had no idea what she was doing in Thailand. But it was nice to be remembered, wasn't it?

In the kitchen, she made coffee the old-fashioned way, ignoring the house's quiet offers of help. She had tried to convince maintenance to disable the whispery little voice, but she hadn't had any luck.

"We can't disconnect the house brain," the maintenance man had told her. "It's against regulations."

"I don't want you to disconnect the brain," Ruth had replied. "Just the voice."

The maintenance man shook his head. No doubt he nursed a grudge against seniors like herself. That would change when he came into his pensions—but it didn't solve her immediate problem.

He shook his head again. "The house brain has to be active in case there's an emergency," he told her. "What if you were to fall?"

Would that be so bad? Ruth thought.

She didn't say it aloud. Instead she submitted—and did her best to ignore the house's attempts to minister to her every whim. She knew some seniors who had fallen into that trap. She would do for herself, or she wouldn't do at all.

She turned on the wall as she sipped her coffee. The nets were all leading with the same stories: another bomb attack by the true-agers, this one in Houston; continued orbital prep for the upcoming launch of the *Exodus*. Nothing she wanted to watch. She put on the rain forest scene instead and finished her coffee to images of bright extinct birds and foliage.

Ruth turned off the wall. She went back to the bedroom to make the bed, but she had forgotten to disable the housekeeping routine again; the house had already taken care of it. The tears started suddenly, the way they did sometimes, and Ruth didn't fight them. She let herself have a good cry there on the narrow bed; when the first gleam of gray light appeared at five, she said, "Stop being so foolish, you old woman." She forced a smile as she gazed in the mirror and started to get ready for her big day. Her 145th.

Celia was coming. At last, at last, Celia was coming. The thought cheered her.

Celia arrived just after eleven. Ruth watched from the window as the car pulled up, a red-and-yellow one-day pass stuck under the windshield wiper, and then she turned for one last quick inspection of the house. She had left her coffee cup on an end table and she hurried it away into the kitchen, but otherwise everything looked spic and span. The chintz covers lay freshly ironed over the chairs, and the house had vacuumed itself. Tantalizing smells perfumed the air. The doorbell rang and rang and rang, but Ruth just stood in the living room and listened to it. It had been so long since she had seen Celia; she wanted to savor it a little.

"The doorbell is ringing," the house whispered, as if she couldn't hear it for herself.

"Well, open it." Ruth stepped forward, half-wanting to open the door herself—to be there waiting—but a sudden fit of shyness possessed her. What should she say? she wondered, but before she could decide, the house opened the door on its noiseless hinges, and there she was. Celia.

"Meemy!" Celia said, and Ruth said, "Celia! Honey, it's been too long!" Celia swept into the room in a gale of sound and motion. Packages and shopping bags fountained out of her arms—how could she carry so much?—and then they embraced, a long fierce embrace, simultaneously laughing and chattering like birds, without pause to listen. A thin, bearded man came in behind her and closed the door gently.

"Gosh, it smells so good," Celia said.

"I've got homemade cobbler cooling in the kitchen. And Florence—next door?—she let me pick some flowers from her garden, so it would be nice for you. Wasn't that generous?"

Ruth took a deep breath and smiled. There was a brief, uncomfortable silence as they all looked at one another and smiled. The man, whoever he was—Celia hadn't asked to bring someone—stooped to gather the fallen shopping bags.

"Well," said Ruth, and she held Celia at arm's length. "Let me get a look at you."

"Let me get a look at *you*!" Celia laughed and turned to grin at the young man. "This is Ben," she said. "And this is Meemy—Ruth."

Ben said something, but Ruth didn't hear him. Celia riveted her attention. Celia! she thought, and tears started up in her eyes again. She blinked them away so she could see Celia, who looked fine, better than fine. Celia looked terrific: tall and slim and draped in some shimmering black garb that seemed almost to float around her, defying gravity; her long face flush with excitement and her dark, angular eyes ashine. Celia, her great-great-granddaughter! Her dark hair, black as her clothes or blacker, and just shot through with a streak of gray, fell in a mass about her shoulders. And that smile. That hadn't changed even if everything else had, if Celia had at last, at last, grown up. How old was Celia exactly? Thirty-five? Forty?

She said, "Oh, Celia, you look wonderful."

"Meemy! I'm trying to introduce you to someone!"

"Ben. Of course, Ben." Ruth smiled.

Ben took her hand. "It's a pleasure, Mrs.—"

"Ruth," Ruth said.

"It's a pleasure, Ruth. I've heard so much about you."

"Well, I haven't heard a thing about you."

"Oh, Meemy," Celia said.

"Sit down," Ruth told them. "I want to hear all about everything. Gosh it's been so long, hasn't it? Seven years! You know," she said to Ben, "I practically raised Celia myself. Her mother—"

"Do we have to talk about Mother?" Celia said. She sat down beside her young man—her Ben—in the loveseat by the window. Ruth stood at the door into the kitchen and gazed back at them, this slim, bearded young man with the intense eyes and her great-great-granddaughter, more like a daughter, like her very own child. Celia had draped her hand casually over Ben's shoulder, and she was staring at Ruth with an expectant expression on her face. But Ruth didn't know what to say. She could hardly think. Spring sunlight, bright against the grassy commons, dazzled her. Maybe the implants had malfunctioned, she thought, and then she blinked and felt tears. My, but she cried easily today. She turned her head before Celia noticed, vowing not to cry. How absurd.

She said, "Let me get you something to drink. I have coffee and soda and I think there may be some tea—"

"Sit down, Meemy. We're not thirsty."

"No, let me," Ruth said. "Coffee, Ben?"

"That would be fine," he said. "Sugar if you have it."

"Meemy—"

Ruth disappeared into the kitchen. She paused, looking out through the kitchen window into Florence's garden as she blinked away the last of the tears. The flowers had erupted into riotous bloom, and it was nice just to stand there and inhale the heady scent of them through the open window while she calmed herself.

"Meemy, what's wrong?"

Ruth switched on the water and made as though she were washing the mug in the sink. "Nothing, dear. I just needed a clean cup."

"Nonsense." Celia lit a cigarette and moved past Ruth to peer out the window. "Someone sure has a way with flowers," she said. And then, almost as an afterthought: "I'm going to miss them."

"It's a nasty habit, smoking."

"It's just a style, Meemy. It doesn't hurt you."

"Cigarettes make your clothes stink."

"Maybe I'll quit."

"Who's talking nonsense? You've smoked since you were sixteen. What's that—twenty-five years now?"

"Twenty-two." Celia ran water over her cigarette. The sunlight loved her. It made her skin almost translucent. It made her hair darker and turned the gray streak blonde.

"You shouldn't leave your friend out there," Ruth said. "It's not polite."

"Who's not being polite?" She watched Ruth fumble with the coffee pot. "Let the house make the coffee," she said. "We don't get to see each other often. Let's take advantage of it."

"I'm done." Ruth placed sugar, mugs, and the warming pot on a silver serving tray, hastily arranged a box of cakes in a semi-circle around one edge, and walked into the living room. Celia followed.

"You have to tell me all about yourself," Ruth said to Ben. "I want to know everything." She saw a quick glance pass between them.

Ben stirred sugar into his coffee. A breeze billowed the filmy curtains and brought the smell of the coffee to her nostrils. "Celia and I met at CelTech," Ben said.

"CelTech," Ruth said. "Such a big company. I wish I could understand what you do, Celia." She said to Ben, "It's so technical, you know."

"We worked together on a project there," Ben said. "I'm a mechanical engineer."

"You don't say! Perhaps you could help me. I've been trying to get maintenance to turn off the house voice, and they refuse to do it. Could you do something like that?"

"Meemy, please."

"It wouldn't be a good idea to disable the house brain," Ben said. "What if you fell?"

"Not the brain. Only the voice."

"Please, Meemy. This is a visit. It's your birthday. Don't you want to see your presents? We have lots of them."

Ben placed his hand on Celia's thigh. "I could do that," he said. "Maybe that's a good idea. It would give you two some time to talk."

"Yes," said Ruth, "Let's go for a walk, Celia."

They walked, sunlight warm against their shoulders. A robin twittered in the big oak, and the scents of fecund, growing things hung resonant in the air. It was possible, if you didn't look hard enough, to imagine that you had stepped out of this day and year into the simple bucolic world Ruth had known as a girl. But then something always happened to shatter the illusion. You saw a needle plane slide silently across the skyline, or you noticed that the park was full of seniors—seniors digging in the little gardens that bordered the commons, seniors walking arm in arm across the grass, seniors chatting on the porches of the whitewashed cottages under the trees.

Ruth took Celia's arm proudly. She guided her on a circuitous route among the cottages and introduced her to everyone she knew, which was everyone.

Celia smoked and didn't talk. After a while, she said, "Let's take a look at the wall."

Ruth sighed. "Tell me about your young man. Ben."

"He's nice isn't he? I like him."

"Well, he's handsome I suppose. How long have you known each other?"

"Oh, I don't know. Six months? Seven?"

"I would know that if you called once in a while. You haven't called in almost a year, Celia."

"I'm sorry," Celia said. "I—I don't know, Meemy. Just busy you know."

"Too busy to return my calls?"

"Busy." Celia knelt to grind out her cigarette against a stone. She slid the butt into a pocket of the black wrap. "It wasn't intentional, you know."

Ruth didn't say anything. They had gone past the last of the cottages and the shopping center that bordered one edge of the commons. They walked down a paved lane overhung with trees.

"I'm glad I wrote and asked you to come today," Ruth said. "I'm glad you decided to come. I've missed you. I was afraid you were going to abandon me, like Martha."

"Mother hasn't turned out so bad. You don't really know her, Meemy."

"And you do?"

"Yes, I do," said Celia icily.

They had reached the wall, thirteen feet of granite so overgrown with ivy that it was virtually invisible. "We'd like to look out," Ruth told the guard at the gate, and he waved them on. They mounted a stone staircase with a black iron railing, and stood atop the wall, looking out over the gray city.

"Did she remember your birthday this year?" Celia asked.

"She sent me a robe. From Laos. What's she doing there?"

"Thailand," Celia said. "She's in Thailand, working on land reclamation. It's good work. Important work."

"Does it pay well?"

"Nothing pays well, Meemy. Not these days."

They were silent for a moment. The breeze started up and came

over the wall in a soft, pleasant wave. It lifted Celia's hair. Ruth
wanted to touch her again. Ruth wanted to embrace her, but Celia
stood aloof, her hands tucked in the folds of her wrap, locked inside
herself.

"Mother didn't abandon you," Celia said.

"Well, I don't know what else you would call it."

"She doesn't approve of you."

"Approve of me?"

"This life," Celia said. "The way you live here."

"Well, I've earned it. I've worked hard all my life. I deserve this.
Your mother's pensions will come, too."

Celia turned away, mumbling.

"What did you say?" Ruth asked. "I didn't hear you."

"Nothing."

They were quiet for a time.

"I'm glad you got to know your mother," Ruth said at last. It was
hard for her to say.

Celia smiled. "Me too."

They turned and went down the stairs, and started back along
the road to the commons. The guard nodded at them, but didn't
speak. The sky looked clear blue and faraway with warmth, and the
trees whispered among themselves in foreign voices. Ruth hardly
noticed. It wasn't supposed to be this way, she thought, this reunion
with Celia. She longed for that special bond they had shared when
Celia was a girl, before Ruth came into her pensions and moved to
the compound. It wasn't supposed to be this way.

"I'm sorry I'm being such a bitch," Celia said.

Ruth didn't answer. What could she say?

During supper Celia acted like her old self, chattering about nothing and everything, her angular features animated with delight. She
drew Ben into the conversation and the awkwardness among them
seemed to evaporate. Ruth thought he seemed like a nice young
man; she didn't mind that Celia had brought him. It was pleasant
to have young people in the house, to have Celia home at last after
she had been gone so many years. What happened to the years?

After they finished the cobbler, Celia brought out the presents.
The bags seemed bottomless. Celia plucked out box after colorfully
wrapped box, and Ruth opened them with nervous fingers, saying,
"You shouldn't have, honey. How are you going to pay for all this?"

"Don't worry," Celia said.

So Ruth didn't. Just once, she thought, I will allow myself to

enjoy. And she did. It was her best birthday in years—in decades—
and by the time they finished with the packages and took their
coffee to the porch, it had begun to turn dark.

They sat quiet for a time. Ruth found it a comfortable kind of
silence; she was glad they had come.

"Beautiful night," Ben said.

"Mmmm," said Celia. "I'll miss this." She tilted her head against
Ben's shoulder. The porch swing drifted with her movement, the
springs whining softly, and Ruth, sitting in the rocker, felt a touch
of envy. Just children, really.

A sprinkle of stars glimmered above them. The crickets started
up. The sound of them soothed her, and her girlhood in Kentucky
came flying back to her: she remembered sitting on the porch of her
father's house, her head tilted against some boy's shoulder just like
Celia's was, wishing on a star. There had been such places, then.
Front porches and lots of open country.

Ben said, "See that red star?" He pointed through the net of lilac
branches at the sky.

"I see it," Celia said.

Ruth gazed up. Her vision blurred for a moment as the retinal
implant drew its focus, and then she saw it: a red star in the sky a
million years away.

"That's not a star," Ben said.

"Mars?" Ruth said.

"That's the jumpship," he said. "The *Exodus*."

Silence, then, the three of them rocking.

"People going a long, long way from here," Ruth said. "I don't
know that I approve."

"People have to have room to live," Ben said. "People have to
live for themselves. They can't always be working to pay some
senior's way."

"That kind of talk sounds like true-ager nonsense to me," Ruth
said. "That kind of talk leads to these bombings you hear about. I
saw one just this morning. Some crazy folks bombed a senior compound in Houston. People need to be patient, their pensions will
come."

"Yes," said Ben, "and who will pay for them?"

Ruth glared up at the red light as if she could wipe it from the
heavens by sheer force of will. "There are always more young folks,"
she said.

"Not as many as there are seniors. Fewer young people all the
time, and more and more seniors every day."

"Well, what should we do? Just die?"

Ben started to speak, but Celia said, "Ben," and he fell silent. Ruth could just see the shape of him in the dark, but she didn't have to see more. She knew what kind of man he was; she had heard such arguments before, and she resented them. She had worked hard all her life without complaint and this was her reward. This place, with its flowers and its trees like you could find nowhere else in the world anymore. She had earned this. She deserved it. She would not listen to someone who wanted to take it away from her.

Then a chill little wave of anxiety crested within her. She thought of how she had been looking forward to this day. This is Celia's friend, she told herself. This is the man Celia loves. And partly to make amends, but mostly because she liked the sound of them, their presence here in her home, she said, "Why don't you stay the night? I could call the gate and have them issue you a night pass."

"You haven't told her, have you?" said Ben.

Ruth stopped rocking. She sat very still. "Told me what?" she said. "What haven't you told me, Celia? I want to know."

"We can't stay, Meemy," she said. "We have to be at the suborbital in Denver in the morning."

"The suborbital? I don't understand."

"We're going away," Celia said.

"Going away?"

Celia started to speak and fell silent. Ben shifted in the swing, ill at ease. After a moment, Ruth said, "You mean a vacation, right?"

"No," said Celia. "It's—"

"The jumpship," Ben said. "We made the final cut for the *Exodus*. We check in tomorrow at the LaGrange Station for some final tests, but . . ." He shrugged.

"But why?" Ruth asked, and she could hear the note of desperation in her voice. She didn't want it to be there, but she couldn't help it. She could feel it bubbling up inside her, the loneliness and the desperation. She could not stop it, she could not keep it from her voice. It kept her up at night.

"Don't be upset, Meemy—"

"Don't be upset! When you just show up here to tell me that you're leaving forever? How could I not be upset?"

"You have to understand," Celia said. "There's no room for us here. You slave all your life to make pensions, just so you can have a few decades of pleasure at the end. We won't be able to afford pensions forever, Meemy, not at this rate. We have to get away, build a new life."

"It's no way to live, the way we have to live," Ben said.

"I didn't want to have to tell you," Celia said. "But I couldn't do that, Meemy. I had to say goodbye."

"But that ship—it won't arrive for a hundred years or more. They don't even know where they're going. They're just . . . going. What kind of life is that?"

"A better life," Ben said. "A better life for our children if we're lucky."

"It's a grand adventure," Celia said.

"And you came here to tell me this? On my birthday?"

Now it all made sense to her. The way Celia had been behaving all day, the little things she had said. *I'm going to miss them*, she had said of the flowers that blazed in Florence's garden. She had said it again just now, hadn't she? And the presents.

"So you're leaving me? Like your mother, is that it?"

"No, Meemy—"

"And you think you can buy my forgiveness with all your presents? Like I'm too dumb or too old to even understand?"

"No—"

"Well, it won't work," Ruth said, standing. "You've ruined everything, do you hear? Everything. And I won't forgive you that."

She turned and went inside and closed the door behind her. "Lock the door," she said to the house, and she heard the mechanism slide into place behind her.

She was crying. She hadn't meant to cry.

"Meemy?" Celia said through the door. "Please don't let it end this way. Please let us say goodbye."

"Open up, Ruth," Ben said. "Be reasonable."

"Go away, I don't care if I ever speak to you again."

"Meemy, please—"

But she wouldn't answer. They could call all night and she wouldn't answer. All of them, all of them had abandoned her. First her sons. And then Martha. And Celia last of all. It wasn't her fault. She wouldn't answer. She would not answer.

"Meemy, please, you have to listen."

But she didn't. She sat in the dark house and wept. They called for a long time before she heard the car start. She went to the window and watched the red tail-lights dwindle through the trees, like the red light in the sky which Ben had pointed out. Like the jumpship, the *Exodus*. Then she went back to the sofa and sat down. No one said a word, not even the house.

The call came through after midnight, coded emergency, but Ruth had silenced the wall and didn't hear it. She woke at 3:07, the bedroom wall pulsing with the pink hue of the emergency beacon. The house brain was programmed to override the silence order in an emergency, but it had failed.

"Why didn't you wake me?" she said to the house.

The house didn't answer, and then Ruth remembered: she had asked Ben to disable the voice.

She felt sluggish, entombed in silence.

"Play the message," she said. The wall dissolved into static. When it cleared, Celia became visible, her face pale and drawn and abnormally elongated by the transmission. "You have a connection," a neutral machine voice said, and Celia looked up.

"Meemy?" she said. She waited a moment and Ruth studied the image. Crowds drifted along a concourse behind Celia. "Meemy, if you're there, please pick up."

She waited a moment longer, her expression hopeful, and then she said, "I don't know what to say to you, but I can't leave it like this. I love you, Meemy, and I understand that you're upset. But you have to understand as well."

Celia paused, and fumbled in her wrap for a cigarette. She exhaled and listened to someone offscreen.

"That's Ben," she said. "We have to hurry. He really liked you, you know. I wanted you to know that. Listen, you have to understand, it's important that you do." She smoked for a moment, and then she said, "We're hungry for something Earth can't give us, Ben and me, lots of people. We're tired of working all the time and seeing everything we've worked for drained away for other people. I suppose it's hard to understand for you—you have everything there in your little world—but people are suffering and starving. There are too many of us, and too many of us are old. But that doesn't mean I don't love you. That doesn't mean I won't be thinking of you. Because I will be."

She glanced offscreen again. "We've got to go," she said. "Remember me, Meemy." She reached out to the screen and the image dissolved into static once again.

"Save message," Ruth said to the house.

The wall went dark.

Ruth could not get back to sleep. After a while, she got up and wrapped herself in Martha's robe and went into the kitchen for coffee. When the horizon began to turn gray, she found herself gazing at Florence's garden. *I'm going to miss them*, Celia had said, speaking of flowers. Ruth tried to imagine a world so devoid of hope that you could willingly leave flowers behind. That was the world Celia lived in, she thought. The world most people lived in.

It was the world she lived in, too, but she had been too blind to see it.

Now she did. Fifteen years she had lived here—fifteen years of chatting with Florence over the flowers, fifteen years of evening walks through the commons, fifteen years of bridge and checkers and Thursday night dances. Fifteen years of sudden tears for no reason she could understand. Fifteen endless years.

She might have two decades more.

She turned on the wall and watched the news nets for a while. Still another attack by the true-agers; grim footage of slums in Bangladesh; more currency troubles in Brazil.

People are suffering, Celia had said. And it was true.

But not the seniors; they had the best of everything.

We paid for it, she thought. We worked long and hard without complaint, and this is our reward.

But now such reasoning sounded hollow even to her. This is our reward: puttering amongst flowers, bridge, sudden inexplicable fits of tears. Fifteen years of selfish, ugly bliss while our children and children's children suffer.

She asked the wall to find Martha's number. Martha hadn't called in three years, she thought. But neither had she called Martha.

Three nights later she tried to get through to Celia at the LaGrange Station. After almost an hour, she found a station receptionist who could spare her a moment

"I'm sorry, ma'am," he said, when she had explained what she wanted to do. He was very young. "The last of the group boarded this morning."

"Can I reach them on the *Exodus?*"

"No, ma'am, that's impossible. I'm sorry." He reached out to cut the connection.

"Just a minute, please," she said.

He blinked at her.

"Can you get them a message?"

"I don't think so, ma'am. There are nearly a thousand people on that ship. Things are pretty hectic over there. The departure window opens in twelve hours—"

"Please," she said.

He paused, and gazed at her quizzically for a moment.

"It's important," she said. "I didn't get a chance to say goodbye."

"Fine, then." He reached for a keypad. "Names?"

"Celia, Celia Fisher. And Ben. Ben someone."

"And your message?"

"Tell them—tell them, I'm sorry. I understand now. Tell them I wish them the best."

"Fine."

"It's important," she said.

"I'll do what I can."

The wall went dark. Ruth ordered up the rain forest, but after a moment she switched it off. You couldn't tell the bright extinct birds and trees from the real thing, the animation was so accomplished, but you knew anyway. That was bad enough.

One last time she walked through the house. Most of her possessions had been boxed up for auction. She went out to the porch where her single suitcase waited. She searched the skies for the red glimmer, and when she found it, she gazed up at it and thought: That's one solution. There must be others.

The cab pulled up outside. Ruth had imagined that the car would be automated, but to her surprise the door opened and a human driver stepped out. Then it came to her. There are too many of us, she thought. People have to work. People have to have something to do.

The driver loaded her suitcase in the trunk and opened the back door for her.

"I think I'll sit in the front with you," she said.

"Whatever you say. The suborbital in Denver?"

"That's right."

They drove down the wooded lane to the gate. Outside, beneath the street lights, the city sprawled barren and ugly. Here and there a blade of grass poked through a crack in the pavement. A few young people moved along the sidewalks, but mostly it was deserted.

"Not often one of you folks leave the compound," he said.

Ruth smiled.

"Where are you going?"

"Thailand, of all places. Isn't that absurd?" She laughed. "I have work to do there."

"Work?"

"That's right."

The driver shook his head. "Not me. When I come into my pensions, I'm going to sit back and enjoy them, you know?"

"I suppose," said Ruth. She leaned forward and gazed for a long moment at the red beacon of the *Exodus*, glimmering there among all the thousand stars. Goodbye, Celia, she thought. Goodbye, Ben. Good luck. And then she turned to her driver. She said, "But you never know, do you?"

Cockroach

AFTER THE EXAMINATION, THEY GATHERED in the office of the physician, an obstetrician named Exavious that a friend of Sara's had recommended. Dr. Exavious specialized in what Sara termed "high-risk pregnancies," which Gerald Hartshorn took to mean that his wife, at thirty-seven, was too old to be having babies. Secretly, Gerald thought of his wife's . . . condition . . . not as a natural biological process, but as a disease: as fearsome and intractable, and perhaps—though he didn't wish to think of it—as fatal.

During the last weeks, a seed of fear Gerald had buried almost ten years ago—buried and *forgotten*, he had believed—had at last begun to germinate, to spread hungry tendrils in the rich loam of his heart, to feed.

And now such thoughts so preoccupied him that Gerald only half-listened as Dr. Exavious reassured Sara. "We have made great strides in bringing to term women of your age," he was saying, "especially women in such superb condition as I have found you to be . . ."

These words, spoken in the obscurely accented English which communicated an aura of medical expertise to men of Gerald's class (white, affluent, conservative, and, above all, coddled by a network of expensive specialists)—these words should have comforted him.

They did not. Specialist or not, the fact remained that Gerald didn't like Exavious, slim and Arabic, with febrile eyes and a mustache like a narrow charcoal slash in his hazel flesh. In fact, Gerald didn't like much of anything about this . . . situation. Most of all, he didn't like being left alone with the doctor when Sara excused herself at the end of the meeting. He laced his fingers in his lap and gazed off into a corner, uncertain how to proceed.

"These times can be difficult for a woman," Exavious said. "There are many pressures, you understand, not least on the kidneys."

Gerald allowed himself a polite smile: recognition of the intended humor, nothing more. He studied the office—immaculate carpet, desk of dark expensive wood, diplomas mounted neatly on one wall—but saw no clock. Beyond tinted windows, the parking light shimmered with midsummer heat. Julian would be nuts at the office. But he didn't see how he could steal a glance at his watch without being rude.

Exavious leaned forward and said, "So you are to be a father. You must be very happy, Mr. Hartshorn."

Gerald folded and unfolded his arms. "Oh . . . I guess. Sure."

"If you have further questions, questions I haven't answered, I'd be happy to . . ." He let the rest of the sentence hang, unspoken, in the air. "I know this can be a trying experience for some men."

"I'm just a bit nervous, that's all."

"Ah. And why is that?"

"Well, her history, you know."

Exavious smiled. He waved a hand dismissively. "Such incidents are not uncommon, Mr. Hartshorn, as I'm sure you know. Your wife is quite healthy. Physiologically, she is twenty-five. You have nothing to fear."

Exavious sighed; he toyed with a lucite pyramid in which a vaguely alien-looking model of a fetus had been embedded. The name of a drug company had been imprinted in black around its base. "There is one thing, however."

Gerald swallowed. A slight pressure constricted his lungs. "What's that?"

"Your wife has her own fears and anxieties because of the history you mentioned. She indicated these during the examination—that's why she came to me in the first place. Emotional states can have unforeseen physiological effects. They can heighten the difficulty of a pregnancy. Most doctors don't like to admit it, but the fact is we understand very little about the mind-body relationship. However, one thing is clear: your wife's emotional condition is every bit as important as her physical state." Exavious paused. Some vagary of the air conditioning swirled to Gerald's nostrils a hint of his aftershave lotion.

"I guess I don't really understand," Gerald said.

"I'm just trying to emphasize that your wife will need your support, Mr. Hartshorn. That's all."

"Are you suggesting that I wouldn't be supportive?"

"Of course not. I merely noticed that—"

"I don't know what you noticed, but it sounds to me—"

"Mr. Hartshorn, please."

"—like you think I'm going to make things difficult for her. You bet I'm nervous. Anyone in my circumstances would be. But that doesn't mean I won't be supportive." In the midst of this speech, Gerald found himself on his feet, a hot blush rising under his collar. "I don't know what you're suggesting—" he continued, and then, when Exavious winced and lifted his hands palms outward, he consciously lowered his voice. "I don't know what you're suggesting—"

"Mr. Hartshorn, please. My intent was not to offend. I understand that you are fearful for your wife. I am simply trying to tell you that she must not be allowed to perceive that you too are afraid."

Gerald drew in a long breath. He sat, feeling sheepish. "I'm sorry, it's . . . I've been under a lot of pressure at work lately. I don't know what came over me."

Exavious inclined his head. "Mr. Hartshorn, I know you are busy. But might I ask you a small favor—for your sake and for your wife's?"

"Sure, please."

"Just this: take some time, Mr. Hartshorn, take some time and think. Are you fearful for your wife's welfare, or are you fearful for your own?"

Just then, before Gerald could reply, the door from the corridor opened and Sara came in, her long body as yet unblemished by the child within. She brushed back a wisp of blonde hair as Gerald turned to face her. "Gerald, are you okay? I thought I heard your—"

"Please, Mrs. Hartshorn, there was nothing," the doctor said warmly. "Is that not correct, Mr. Hartshorn? Nothing, nothing at all."

And somehow Gerald recovered himself enough to accede to this simple deception as the doctor ushered them into the corridor. Outside, while Sara spoke with the receptionist, he turned at a feathery touch on his shoulder. Dr. Exavious enveloped his hand and gazed into his eyes for a long and obscurely terrible moment; and then Gerald wrenched himself away, feeling naked and exposed, as if those febrile eyes had illuminated the hollows of his soul, as if he too had been subjected to an examination and had been found wanting.

"I don't know," Gerald said as he guided the Lexus out of the clinic lot. "I don't like him much. I liked Schwartz better."

He glanced over at Sara, her long hand curved beneath her chin, but she wouldn't meet his eyes.

Rush hour traffic thickened around them. He should call Julian; there wasn't much point in trying to make it back to the office now. He had started to reach for the phone when Sara said, "He's a specialist."

"You heard him: you're in great shape. You don't need a specialist."

"I'd feel more comfortable with him."

Gerald shrugged. "I just didn't think he was very personable, that's all."

"Since when do we choose our doctors because they're personable, Gerald?" She drummed her fingers against the dash. "Besides, Schwartz wasn't especially charming." She paused; then, with a chill hint of emotion, she added, "Not to mention competent."

Like stepping suddenly into icy water, this—was it grief, after all these years? Or was it anger?

He extended a hand to her, saying, "Now come on, Sara—"

"Drop it, Gerald."

"Fine."

An oppressive silence filled the car. No noise from without penetrated the interior, and the concentrated purr of the engine was so muted that it seemed rather a negation of sound. A disquieting notion possessed him: perhaps there never had been sound in the world.

A fractured series of images pierced him: rain-slicked barren trees, black trunks whipped to frenzy by a voiceless wind; lane upon lane of stalled, silent cars, pouring fumes into the leaden sky; and Sara—Sara, her lips moving like the lips of a silent movie heroine, shaping words that could not reach him through the changeless air.

Gerald shook his head.

"Are you ready to go home or do you need to stop by the library?" he asked.

"Home. We need to talk about the library."

"Oh?"

"I'm thinking of quitting," she said.

"Quitting?"

"I need some time, Gerald. We have to be careful. I don't want to lose this baby."

"Well, sure," he said. "But quitting."

Sara swallowed. "Besides, I think the baby should be raised at home, don't you?"

Gerald slowed for a two-way stop, glanced into the intersection, and plunged recklessly into traffic, slotting the Lexus into a narrow space before a looming brown UPS truck. Sara uttered a brief, piercing shriek.

"I hadn't really thought about it," Gerald said.

And in fact he hadn't—hadn't thought about that, or dirty diapers, or pediatricians, or car seats, or teething, or a thousand other things, all of which now pressed in upon him in an insensate rush. For the first time he thought of the baby not as a spectral possibility, but as an imminent presence, palpable, new, central to their lives. He was too old for this.

But all he said was: "Quitting seems a little drastic. After all, it's only part time."

Sara didn't answer.

"Why don't we think about it?"

"Too late," Sara said quietly.

"You quit?"

Gerald glanced over at her, saw a wry smile touch her lips, saw in her eyes that she didn't really think it funny.

"You quit?"

"Oh, Gerald," she said. "I'm sorry, I really am."

But he didn't know why she was apologizing, and he had a feeling that she didn't know why either. He reached out and touched her hand, and then they were at a stoplight. Gerald reached for the phone. "I've got to call Julian," he said.

The instrument of Gerald Hartshorn's ascension at the advertising firm of MacGregor, MacGregor, & Turn had been a six-foot-tall cockroach named Fenton, whom Gerald had caused to be variously flayed, decapitated, delimbed, and otherwise dispatched in a series of TV spots for a local exterminator who thereafter had surpassed even his nationally advertised competitors in a tight market. Now, a decade later, Gerald could recall with absolute clarity the moment of this singular inspiration: an early morning trip to the kitchen to get Sara a glass of grapefruit juice.

That had been shortly after Sara's first pregnancy, the abrupt, unforgettable miscarriage that for months afterwards had haunted her dreams. Waking in moans or screams or a cold accusatory silence that for Gerald had been unutterably more terrible, she would weep inconsolably as he tried to comfort her, and afterwards through the broken, weary house they had leased in those impoverished days, she would send him for a bowl of ice cream or a cup of warm milk or, in this case, a glass of grapefruit juice. Without complaint, he had gone, flipping on lights and rubbing at his bleary eyes and lugging the heavy burden of his heart like a stone in the center of his breast.

He remembered very little of those days besides the black funnel of conflicting emotion which had swept him up: a storm of anger more dilatory than any he had ever known; a fierce blast of grief for a child he had not and could not ever know; and, sweeping all before it, a tempest of relief still more fierce, relief that he had not lost Sara. There had been a close moment, but she at least remained for him.

And, of course, he remembered the genesis of Fenton the cockroach.

Remembered how, that night, as his finger brushed the switch that flooded the cramped kitchen with a pitiless glare, he had chanced to glimpse a dark anomaly flee pell-mell to safety across the stained counter. Remembered the inspiration that rained down on him like a gift as he watched the loathsome creature wedge its narrow body into a crevice and disappear.

The Porter account, he had thought. Imagine:

Fade in with thunder on a screaming housewife, her hands clasped to her face, her expression stricken. Pan recklessly about the darkened kitchen, fulgurate with lightning beyond a rain-streaked window. Jumpcut through a series of angles on a form menacing and enormous, insectoid features more hidden than revealed by the storm's fury. Music as the tension builds. At last the armored figure of the exterminator to the rescue. Fade to red letters on a black background:

Porter Exterminators. Depend On Us.

But the piece had to be done straight. It could not be played for laughs. It had to be terrifying.

And though the ads had gradually softened during the decade since—though the cockroach had acquired a name and had been reduced to a cartoon spokesman who died comically at the end of every spot (*Please, please don't call Porter!*)—that first commercial had turned out very much as Gerald had imagined it: terrifying. And effective.

And that was the way Gerald thought of Fenton the giant cockroach even now. Not in his present animated incarnation, but in his original form, blackly horrifying, looming enraged from some shadowy corner, and always, always obscurely linked in his mind to the dark episode of his lost child and the wife he also had nearly lost.

But despite these connections, the Porter account had remained Gerald's single greatest success. Other accounts had been granted him; and though Fenton was now years in the past, promotions followed. So he drove a Lexus, lived in one of the better neighborhoods, and his wife worked part time as an aide in the children's library not because she had to but because she wanted to.

All things considered, he should have been content. So why, when he picked up the phone to call Julian MacGregor, should the conversation which followed so dishearten him?

"I can't make it back in today," he said. "Can the Dainty Wipe thing wait until Monday?"

And Julian, his boss for twelve years, replied with just a touch of . . . what? Exasperation?

Julian said: "Don't worry about that, I'm going to put Lake Conley on it instead."

Lake Conley, who was a friend.

Why should that bother him?

Gerald came to think of the pregnancy as a long, arduous ordeal: a military campaign, perhaps, conducted in bleak territory, beneath a bitter sky. He thought of Napoleon, bogged down in the snow outside of Moscow, and he despaired.

Not that the pregnancy was without beneficial effects. In the weeks after that first visit to Dr. Exavious—at two months—Gerald saw his Sara's few wrinkles begin to soften, her breasts to grow fuller. But mostly the changes were less pleasant. Nausea continued to plague her, in defiance of Exavious's predictions. They argued over names and made love with distressing infrequency.

Just when Gerald grudgingly acquiesced in repainting a bedroom (a neutral blue, Sara had decided, neither masculine nor feminine), he was granted a momentary reprieve. Sara decided to visit her mother, two hours away.

"I'll see you tomorrow," she told him in the flat heat promised by the August dawn.

Gerald stepped close to her with sudden violent longing; he inhaled her warm powdered odor. "Love you."

"Me too." She flung an arm around him in a perfunctory embrace, and then the small mound of her abdomen interposed itself between them.

And then she was gone.

Work that day dragged through a series of ponderous crises that defied resolution, and it was with relief that Gerald looked up to see Lake Conley standing in the door.

"So Sara's out of town," Lake said.

"That's right."

"Let's have a drink. We should talk."

They found a quiet bar on Magnolia. There, in the cool dim, with the windows on the street like bright hot panes of molten light, Gerald studied Lake Conley, eleven years his junior and handsome seemingly by force of will. Lake combed his long hair with calculated informality, and his suit, half as expensive as Gerald's, fit him with unnatural elegance.

"Then Julian said, 'Frankly, Sue, I don't see the humor in this.' I swear, she nearly died." Lake laughed. "You should have seen it, Gerald."

Gerald chuckled politely and watched as Lake took a pull at his Dos Equis. He watched him place the beer on the bar and dig with slender fingers in a basket of peanuts. Weekly sessions in the gym had shown Gerald that the other man's slight frame was deceptive. Lake was savagely competitive in racquetball, and while it did not bother Gerald that he usually lost, it *did* bother him that when he won, he felt that Lake had permitted him to do so. It bothered him still more that he preferred these soulless victories to an endless series of humiliations.

Often he felt bearish and graceless beside the younger man. Today he just felt tired.

"Just as well I wasn't there," he said. "I'm sure Julian would have lit into me, too."

"Julian giving you a rough time?"

Gerald shrugged.

Lake gazed thoughtfully at him for a moment, then turned to the flickering television that played soundlessly over the bar. "Well," he said with forced cheer. "Sara doing okay? She big as a house yet?"

"Not yet." Gerald finished his drink and signaled for another. "Thank God for gin," he said.

"There's a good sign."

Gerald sipped at the new drink. "Been a while. We're not drinking much at home lately."

"What's the problem, Gerald?"

"She could have told me she stopped taking the pill."

"Sure."

"Or that she was quitting her job."

"Absolutely."

Gerald didn't say anything. A waitress backed through a swinging door by the bar, and tinny rock music blasted out of the kitchen. The sour odor of grease came to him, and then the door swung shut, and into the silence, Lake Conley said:

"You're not too happy about this."

"It's not just that she hasn't been telling me things. She's always been a little self-contained. And she's sorry, I know that."

"Then what is it?"

Gerald sighed. He dipped a finger in his drink and began to trace desultory patterns on the bar. "Our first baby," he said at last. "The miscarriage. It was a close call for Sara. It was scary then and it's even scarier now. She's all I have." Bitter laughter escaped him. "Her and Julian MacGregor."

"Don't forget Fenton."

"Ah yes, the cockroach." Gerald finished his drink, and this time the bartender had another waiting.

"Is that it?"

"No." He paused. "Let me ask you this: you ever feel . . . I don't know . . . weird about anything when Kaye was pregnant?"

Lake laughed. "Let me guess. You're afraid the baby's not yours." And then, when Gerald shook his head, he continued, "How about this? You're afraid the baby is going to be retarded or horrifically deformed, some kind of freak."

"I take it you did."

Lake scooped a handful of peanuts onto the bar and began to arrange them in a neat circle. Gerald looked on in bleary fascination.

Another drink had been placed before him. He tilted the glass to his lips.

"It's entirely normal," Lake was saying. "Listen, I was so freaked out that I talked to Kaye's obstetrician about it. You know what she said? It's a normal by-product of your anxiety, that's all. That's the first baby. Second baby? It's a breeze."

"That so?"

"Sure. Trust me, this is the best thing that's ever happened to you. This is going to be the best experience of your life."

Gerald slouched in his stool, vastly—
—*and illogically*, some fragment of his mind insisted—
—relieved.

"Another drink?" Lake asked.

Gerald nodded. The conversation strayed listlessly for a while, and then he looked up to see that daylight had faded beyond the large windows facing the street. A steady buzz of conversation filled the room. He had a sense of pressure created by many people, hovering just beyond the limits of his peripheral vision. He felt ill, and thrust half an ice-melted drink away from him.

Lake's face drifted in front of him, his voice came from far away: "Listen, Gerald, I'm driving you home, okay?"

Opening his eyes in Lake's car, he saw the shimmering constellation of the city beyond a breath-frosted window, cool against his cheek. Lake was saying something. What?

"You okay? You're not going to be sick are you?"

Gerald lifted a hand weakly. Fine, fine.

They were parked in the street outside Gerald's darkened house. Black dread seized him. The house, empty, Sara away. A thin, ugly voice spoke in his mind—the voice of the cockroach, he thought with sudden lucidity. And it said:

This is how it will look when she's gone. This is how it will look when she's dead.

She won't die. She won't die.

Lake was saying, "Gerald, you have to listen to me."

Clarity gripped him. "Okay. What is it?"

A passing car chased shadow across Lake's handsome features. "I asked you out tonight for a reason, Gerald."

"What's that?"

Lake wrapped his fingers around the steering wheel, took in a slow breath. "Julian talked to me today. He's giving me the Heather Drug campaign. I wanted to tell you. I told him you were depending on it, but . . ." Lake shrugged.

Gerald thought: *You son of a bitch. I ought to puke in your car.*

But he said: "Not your fault." He opened the door and stood up. Night air, leavened with the day's heat, embraced him. "Later."

And then somehow up the drive to the porch, where he spent long moments fitting the key into the door. Success at last, the door swinging open. Interior darkness leaked into the night.

He stumbled to the stairs, paused there to knot his tie around the newel post, which for some reason struck him as enormously funny. And then the long haul up the flight, abandoning one shoe halfway up and another on the landing, where the risers twisted to

meet the gallery which opened over shining banisters into the foyer
below.

Cathedral ceilings, he thought. The legacy of Fenton the cockroach. And with a twist like steel in his guts, the memory of that
nasty internal voice came back to him. Not his voice. The voice of
the cockroach:

This is how it will be when she's dead.

And then the bedroom. The sheets, and Sara's smell upon them.
The long fall into oblivion.

He woke abruptly, clawing away a web of nightmare. He had been
trapped in suffocating dark, while something—

—the cockroach—

—gnawed hungrily at his guts.

He sat up, breathing hard.

Sara stood at the foot of the bed, his shoes dangling in her
upraised hand. She said, "You son of a bitch."

Gerald squinted at the clock radio. Dull red numbers transformed themselves as he watched. 11:03. Sunlight lashed through
the blinds. The room swam with the stink of sleep and alcohol.

"Sara . . ." He dug at his eyes.

"You son of a bitch," she said.

She flung the shoes hard into his stomach as, gasping, he stumbled from the bed. "Sara—"

But she had turned away. He glimpsed her in profile at the door,
her stomach slightly domed beneath her drop-waist dress, and then
she was gone.

Gerald, swallowing—how dry his throat was!—followed. He
caught her at the steps, and took her elbow.

"Sara, it was only a few drinks. Lake and I—"

She turned on him, a fierce light in her eyes. Her fury propelled
him back a step. She reminded him of a feral dog, driving an
intruder from her pups.

"It's not that, Gerald," she said.

And then—

—Goddamn it, I won't be treated like that!—

—he stepped toward her, clasping her elbows. Wrenching her
arm loose, she drew back her hand. The slap took them both by
surprise; he could see the shock of it in her eyes, softening the
anger.

His anger, too, dissipated, subsumed in a rising tide of grief and
memory.

An uneasy stillness descended. She exhaled and turned away, stared over the railing into the void below, where the sun fell in bright patches against the parquet. Gerald lifted a hand to his cheek, and Sara turned now to face him, her eyes lifted to him, her hand following his to his face. He felt her touch him through the burning.

"I'm sorry," they said simultaneously.

Bright sheepish laughter at this synchronicity convulsed them, and Gerald, embracing her, saw with horror how close she stood to the stairs. Unbidden, an image possessed him: Sara, teetering on the edge of balance. In a series of strobic flashes, he saw it as it might have been. Saw her fall away from him, her arms outstretched for his grasping fingers. Saw her crash backwards to the landing, tumble down the long flight to the foyer. Saw the blood—

—so little blood. My God, who would have thought? So little blood!

"I'm sorry," he said again.

She dug her fingers into his back. "It's not that."

"Then what?"

She pulled away and fixed him with her stare. "Your shoes, Gerald. You left them on the stairs." Her hand stole over the tiny mound of her stomach. "I could have fallen."

"I'm sorry," he said, and drew her to him.

Her voice tight with controlled emotion, she spoke again, barely perceptible, punctuating her words with small blows against his shoulder. "Not again," she whispered.

Clasping her even tighter, Gerald drew in a faint breath of her floral-scented shampoo and gazed over her head at the stairs which fell infinitely away behind her.

"Not again," he said.

Gerald watched apprehensively as Dr. Exavious dragged the ultrasound transducer over Sara's belly, round as a small pumpkin and glistening with clear, odorless gel. The small screen flickered with a shifting pattern of gray and black, grainy and irresolute as the swirling path of a thunderstorm on a television meteorologist's radar.

Sara looked on with a clear light in her face. It was an expression Gerald saw with increasing frequency these days. A sort of tranquil beauty had come into her features, a still internal repose not unlike that he sometimes glimpsed when she moved over him in private rhythm, outward token of a concentration even then wholly private and remote.

But never, never so lost to him as now.

"There now," Exavious said softly. He pointed at the screen. "There is the heart, do you see it?"

Gerald leaned forward, staring. The room, cool, faintly redolent of antiseptic, was silent but for Sara's small coos of delight, and the muted whir of the VCR racked below the ultrasound scanner. Gerald drew a slow breath as the grayish knot Exavious had indicated drew in upon itself and expanded in a pulse of ceaseless, mindless syncopation.

"Good strong heart," Exavious said.

Slowly then, he began to move the transducer again. A feeling of unreality possessed Gerald as he watched the structure of his child unfold across the screen in changeable swaths of light. Here the kidneys—"Good, very good," Exavious commented—and there the spine, knotted, serpentine. The budding arms and legs—Exavious pausing here to trace lambent measurements on the screen with a wand, nodding to himself. And something else, which Exavious didn't comment on, but which Gerald thought to be the hint of a vestigial tail curling between the crooked lines of the legs. He had heard of children born with tails, anomalous throwbacks from the long evolutionary rise out of the jungle.

Sara said, "Can you get an image of the whole baby?"

Exavious adjusted the transducer once more. The screen flickered, settled, grew still at the touch of a button. "Not the whole baby. The beam is too narrow, but this is close."

Gerald studied the image, the thing hunched upon itself in a swirl of viscous fluid, spine twisted, misshapen head fractured by atavistic features: blind pits he took for eyes, black slits for nostrils, the thin slash of the mouth, like a snake's mouth, as lipless and implacable. He saw at the end of an out-flung limb the curled talon of a hand. Gerald could not quell the feeling of revulsion which welled up inside him. It looked not like a child, he thought, but like some primitive reptile, a throwback to the numb, idiot fecundity of the primordial slime.

He and Sara spoke at the same time:

"It's beautiful."

"My God, it doesn't even look human."

He said this without thought, and only in the shocked silence that followed did he see how it must have sounded.

"I mean—" he said, but it was pointless. Sara would not meet his eyes.

Dr. Exavious said, "In fact, you are both correct. It is beautiful indeed, but it hardly looks human. Not yet. It will, though." He patted Sara's hand. "Mr. Hartshorn's reaction is not atypical."

"But not typical either, I'm guessing."

Exavious shrugged. "Perhaps." He touched a button and the image on the screen disappeared. He cleaned and racked the transducer, halted the VCR.

"I was just thinking it looks . . . like something very ancient," Gerald said. "Evolution, you know."

"Haeckel's law. Ontogeny recapitulates phylogeny."

"I'm sorry?"

"A very old idea, Mr. Hartshorn. The development of the individual recapitulates the development of the species."

"Is that true?" Sara asked.

"Not literally. In some metaphorical sense, I suppose." Bending, the doctor ejected the tape from the VCR and handed it to Gerald. "But let me assure you, your baby is fine. It is going to be a beautiful child."

At this, Gerald caught Sara's eye: I'm sorry, this look was meant to say, but she would not yield. Later though, in the car, she forgave him, saying: "Did you hear what he said, Gerald? A beautiful child." She laughed and squeezed his hand and said it again: "Our beautiful, beautiful baby."

Gerald forced a smile. "That's right," he told her.

But in his heart another voice was speaking, a thin ugly voice he knew. *Ontogeny recapitulates phylogeny*, it said, and Gerald gripped the steering wheel until the flesh at his knuckles went bloodless; he smiled at Sara, and tried to wall that voice away, and perhaps he thought he succeeded. But in the secret chambers of his heart it resonated still. And he could not help but listen.

Three weeks later, Indian summer began to die away into fall, and Sara reported that the baby had begun moving within her. Time and again over the next few weeks, Gerald cupped his hand over the growing mound of her belly, alert to even the tiniest shift, but he could feel nothing, nothing at all.

"There," Sara said. Breathlessly: "Can you feel it?"

Gerald shook his head, feeling, for no reason he could quite articulate, vaguely relieved.

Sara continued to put on weight, complaining gamely as her abdomen expanded and her breasts grew sensitive. Gerald sometimes came upon her unawares in the bedroom, standing in her robe and gazing ruefully at the mirror, or sitting on the bed, staring thoughtfully into a closet crowded with unworn clothes and shoes that cramped her swollen feet. A thin dark line extended to her naval (the rectus muscle, Exavious told them, never fear); she claimed she could do nothing with her hair. At night, waking beside her in the darkness, Gerald found his hands stealing over her in numb bewilderment. What had happened to Sara, long known, much loved? The clean, angular lines he had known for years vanished, her long bones hidden in this figure gently rounded and soft. Who was this strange woman sleeping in his bed?

And yet, despite all, her beauty seemed to Gerald only more pronounced. She moved easy in this new body, at home and graceful. That clear light he had glimpsed sporadically in her face gradually grew brighter, omnipresent, radiating out of her with a chill calm. For the first time in his life, Gerald believed that old description he had so often read: Sara's eyes indeed *did* sparkle. They danced, they *shone* with a brilliance that reflected his stare—hermetic, enigmatic, defying interpretation. Her gaze pierced through him, into a world or future he could not see or share. Her hands seemed unconsciously to be drawn to her swollen belly; they crept over it constantly, they caressed it.

Her gums swelled. She complained of heartburn, but she would not use the antacid tablets Exavious prescribed, would not touch aspirin or Ibuprofen. In October, she could no longer sleep eight hours undisturbed. Once, twice, three times a night, Gerald woke to feel the mattress relinquish her weight with a long sigh. He listened as she moved through the heavy dark to the bathroom, no lights, ever considerate. He listened to the secret flow of urine, the flushing toilet's throaty rush. He woke up sore eyed, yawning, and Dr. Exavious's words—*there are many pressures, you understand, not least on the kidneys*—began to seem less like a joke, more like a curse.

In November, they began attending the childbirth classes the doctor had recommended. Twice a week, on Tuesday and Thursday afternoons, Gerald crept out of the office early, uncomfortably aware of Julian MacGregor's baleful gaze; at such moments, he could not help but think of Lake Conley and the Heather Drug campaign. As he retrieved the Lexus from the garage under the building and drove to the rambling old Baptist church where the classes met, his thoughts turned to his exhaustion-stitched eyes and his increasingly tardy appearances at the office every morning. Uneasy snakes of anxiety coiled through his guts.

One afternoon, he sneaked away half an hour early and stopped by the bar on Magnolia for two quick drinks. Calmer then, he drove to the church and parked, letting himself in through the side door of the classroom a few minutes early. Pregnant women thronged the room, luminous and beautiful and infinitely remote; those few men like himself already present stood removed, on the fringes, banished from this mysterious communion.

For a long terrible moment, he stood in the doorway and searched for Sara, nowhere visible. Just the room crowded with these women, their bellies stirring with a biological imperative neither he nor any man could know or comprehend, that same strange light shining in their inscrutable eyes. *They are in league against us,* whispered a voice unbidden in his mind. *They are in league against us.*

Was that the cockroach's voice? Or was it his own?

Then the crowd shifted, Sara slipped into sight. She came toward him, smiling, and he stepped forward to meet her, this question unresolved.

But the incident—and the question it inspired—lingered in his mind. When he woke from restless dreams, it attended him, nagging, resonant: that intimate communion of women he had seen, linked by fleshly sympathies he could not hope to understand. Their eyes shining with a passion that surpassed any passion he had known. The way they had—that Sara had—of cradling their swollen bellies, as if to caress the—

—*Christ, was it monstrous that came to mind?*—

—growths within.

He sat up sweating, sheets pooled in his lap. Far down in the depths of the house the furnace kicked on; overheated air, smelling musty and dry, wafted by his face. Winter folded the house in chill intimacy, but in here . . . hot, hot. His heart pounded. He wiped a hand over his forehead, dragged in a long breath.

Some watchful quality to the silence, the uneven note of her respiration, told him that Sara, too, was awake. In the darkness. Thinking.

She said, "You okay?"

"I don't know," he said. "I don't know."

And this was sufficient for her. She asked nothing more of him than this simple admission of weakness, she never had. She touched him now, her long hand cool against his back. She drew him to the softness at her breast, where he rested his head now, breath ragged, a panic he could not contain rising like wind in the desert places inside him. Heavy dry sobs wracked him.

"Shhh, now," she said, not asking, just rocking him gently. Her hands moved through his hair.

"Shhh," she whispered.

And slowly, by degrees imperceptible, the agony that had possessed him, she soothed away. Nothing, he thought. Of course, it had been nothing—anxieties, Lake Conley had said.

"You okay?" she asked again.

"I'm fine."

She pulled him closer. His hand came to her thigh, and without conscious intention, he found himself opening her gown, kissing her, her breasts, fuller now than he had ever known them. Her back arched. Her fingers were in his hair.

She whispered, "Gerald, that feels nice."

He continued to kiss her, his interest rising. The room was dark, but he could see her very clearly in his mind: the Sara he had known, lithe and supple; this new Sara, this strange woman who shared his bed, her beauty rising out of some deep reservoir of calm and peace. He traced the slope of her breasts and belly. Here. And here. He guided her, rolling her to her side, her back to him, rump out-thrust as Exavious had recommended during a particularly awkward and unforgettable consultation—

"No, Gerald," she said. She said, "No."

Gerald paused, breathing heavily. Below, in the depths of the darkened house, the furnace shut off, and into the immense silence that followed, he said, "Sara—"

"No," she said. "No, no."

Gerald rolled over on his back. He tried to throttle back the frustration rising once more within him, not gone after all, not dissipated, merely . . . pushed away.

Sara turned to him, she came against him. He could feel the bulk of her belly interposed between them.

"I'm afraid, Gerald. I'm afraid it'll hurt the baby."

Her fingers were on his thigh.

"It won't hurt the baby. Exavious said it won't hurt the baby. The books said it won't hurt the baby. Everyone says it won't hurt the baby."

Her voice in the darkness: "But what if it does? I'm afraid, Gerald."

Gerald took a deep breath. He forced himself to speak calmly. "Sara, it won't hurt the baby. Please."

She kissed him, her breath hot in his ear. Her fingers worked at him. She whispered, "See? We can do something else." Pleading now. "We can be close, I want that."

But Gerald, the anger and frustration boiling out of him in a way he didn't like, a way he couldn't control—it scared him—threw back the covers. Stood, and reached for his robe, thinking: *Hot. It's too hot. I've got to get out of here.* But he could not contain himself. He paused, fingers shaking as he belted the robe, to fling back these words: "I'm not so sure I want to be close, Sara. I'm not at all sure *what* I want anymore."

And then, in three quick strides, he was out the door and into the hall, hearing the words she cried after him— "Gerald, *please*"— but not pausing to listen.

The flagstone floor in the den, chill against his bare feet, cooled him. Standing behind the bar in the airy many-windowed room, he mixed himself a gin and tonic with more gin than tonic and savored the almost physical sense of heat, real and emotional, draining along his tension-knotted spine, through the tight muscles of his legs and feet, into the placid stones beneath.

He took a calming swallow of gin and touched the remote on the bar. The television blared to life in a far corner and he cycled through the channels as he finished his drink. Disjointed, half-glimpsed images flooded the darkened room: thuggish young men entranced by the sinister beat of the city, tanks jolting over desert landscape, the gang at *Cheers* laughing it up at Cliff's expense. Poor Cliff. You weren't supposed to identify with him, but Gerald couldn't help it. Poor Cliff was just muddling through like anyone—

—*Like you*, whispered that nasty voice, the voice he could not help but think of as the cockroach.

Gerald shuddered.

On principle, he hated the remote—the worst thing ever to happen to advertising—but now he fingered it again, moved past Letterman's arrogant smirk. He fished more ice from the freezer, splashed clean-smelling gin in his glass, chased it with tonic. Then, half-empty bottle of liquor and a jug of tonic clutched in one hand, drink and television remote in the other, Gerald crossed the room and lowered himself into the recliner.

His anger had evaporated—quick to come, quick to go, it always had been—but an uneasy tension lingered in its wake. He should go upstairs, apologize—he owed it to Sara—but he could not bring himself to move. A terrific inertia shackled him. He had no desire except to drink gin and thumb through the channels, pausing now and again when something caught his eye, half-clad dancers on MTV, a news story about the unknown cannibal killer in L.A., once the tail end of a commercial featuring none other than Fenton the giant cockroach himself.

Christ.

Three or four drinks thereafter he must have dozed, for he came to himself suddenly and unpleasantly when a nightmare jolted him awake. He sat up abruptly, his empty glass crashing to the floor. He had a blurred impression of it as it shattered, sending sharp scintillas of brilliance skating across the flagstones as he doubled over, sharp ghosts of pain shooting through him, as something, Christ—

—*the cockroach*—

—gnawed ravenously at his swollen guts.

He gasped, head reeling with gin. The house brooded over him. Then he felt nothing, the dream pain gone, and when, with reluctant horror, he lifted his clutching hands from his belly, he saw only pale skin between the loosely belted flaps of robe, not the gory mess he had irrationally expected, not the blood—

—*so little blood, who would have thought? So little blood and such a little*—

No. He wouldn't think of that now, he wouldn't think of that at all.

He touched the lever on the recliner, lifting his feet, and reached for the bottle of gin beside the chair. He gazed at the shattered glass and then studied the finger or two of liquor remaining in the bottle; after a moment, he spun loose the cap and tilted the bottle to his lips. Gasoline-harsh gin flooded his mouth. Drunk now, dead drunk, he could feel it and he didn't care, Gerald stared at the television.

A nature program flickered by, the camera closing on a brown grasshopper making its way through lush undergrowth. He sipped at the gin, searched densely for the remote. Must have slipped into the cushions. He felt around for it, but it became too much of an effort. The hell with it.

The grasshopper continued to progress in disjointed leaps, the camera tracking expertly, and this alone exerted over him a bizarre fascination. How the hell did they film these things anyway? He had a quick amusing image: a near-sighted entomologist and his cameraman tramping through some benighted wilderness, slapping away insects and suffering the indignities of crotch-rot. Ha-ha. He touched the lever again, dropping the footrest, and placed his bare feet on the cool flagstones, mindful in a meticulously drunken way of the broken glass.

Through a background of exotic bird calls, and the swish of antediluvian vegetation, a cultured masculine voice began to speak: "Biological mimicry, developed by predators and prey through millennia of natural selection is still . . ."

Gerald leaned forward, propping his elbows on his knees. A faraway voice whispered in his mind. Natural selection. Sophomore biology had been long ago, but he recognized the term as an element of evolutionary theory. What had Exavious said?

That nasty voice whispering away . . .

He had a brief flash of the ultrasound video, which Sara had watched again only that evening: the fetus, reptilian, primitive, an eerie wakeful quality to its amniotic slumber.

On the screen, the grasshopper took another leap. Music came up on the soundtrack, slow, minatory, almost subliminal. " . . . less commonly used by predators," the voice-over said, "biological mimicry can be dramatically effective when it is . . ." The grasshopper took another leap and plummeted toward a clump of yellow and white flowers. Too fast for Gerald really to see, the flowers exploded into motion. He sat abruptly upright, his heart racing, as prehensile claws flashed out, grasped the stunned insect, and dragged it down. "Take the orchid mantis of the Malaysian rain forest," the voice-over continued. "Evolution has disguised few predators so completely. Watch again as . . ." And now the image began to replay, this time in slow motion, so that Gerald could see in agonizing detail the grasshopper's slow descent, the flower-colored mantis unfolding with deadly and inevitable grace from the heart of the blossom, grasping claws extended. Again. And again. Each time the camera moved in tighter, tighter, until the mantis seemed to fill the screen with an urgency dreadful and inexorable and wholly merciless.

Gerald grasped the bottle of gin and sat back as the narrator continued, speaking now of aphid-farming ants and the lacewing larva. But he had ceased to listen. He tilted the bottle to his lips, thinking again of that reptilian fetus, awash in the womb of the woman he loved and did not want to lose. And now that faraway voice in his mind sounded closer, more distinct. It was the voice of the cockroach, but the words it spoke were those of Dr. Exavious.

Ontogeny recapitulates phylogeny.

Gerald took a last pull off the bottle of gin. Now what exactly did that mean?

The ball whizzed past in a blur as Gerald stepped up to meet it, his racquet sweeping around too late. He spun and lunged past Lake

Conley to catch the ricochet off the back wall, but the ball slipped past, bouncing twice, and slowed to a momentum-draining roll.

"Goddamn it!" Gerald flung his racquet hard after the ball and collapsed against the back wall. He drew up his legs and draped his forearms over his knees.

"Game," Lake said.

"Go to hell." Gerald closed his eyes, tilted his head against the wall and tried to catch his breath. He could smell his own sweat, tinged with the sour odor of gin. He didn't open his eyes when Lake slid down beside him.

"Kind of an excessive reaction even for you," Lake said.

"Stress."

"Work?"

"That, too." Gerald gazed at Lake through slitted eyes. "Ahh."

They sat quietly, listening to a distant radio blare from the weight-room. From adjoining courts, the squeak of rubber-soled shoes and the intermittent smack of balls came to them, barely audible. Gerald watched, exhaustion settling over him like a gray blanket, while Lake traced invisible patterns on the floor with the edge of his racquet.

"Least I don't have to worry about the Heather Drug campaign," Gerald said. Almost immediately, he wished he could pull the words back. Unsay them.

For a long time, Lake didn't answer. When he did, he said only, "You have a right to be pissed off about that."

"Not really. Long time since I put a decent campaign together. Julian knows what he's doing."

Lake shrugged.

Again, Gerald tilted his head against the wall, closing his eyes. There it was, there it always was anymore, that image swimming in his internal darkness: the baby, blind and primitive and preternaturally aware. He saw it in his dreams; sometimes when he woke he had vague memories of a red fury clawing free of his guts. And sometimes it wasn't this dream he remembered, but another: looking on, helpless, horrified, while something terrible exploded out of Sara's smoothly rounded belly.

That one was worse.

That one spoke with the voice of the cockroach. That one said: *You're going to lose her.*

Lake was saying, "Not to put too fine a point on it, Gerald, but you look like hell. You come to work smelling like booze half the time, I don't know what you expect."

Expect? What did he expect exactly? And what would Lake say if he told him?

Instead, he said, "I'm not sleeping much. Sara doesn't sleep well. She gets up two, three times a night."

"So you're just sucking down a few drinks so you can sleep at night, that right?"

Gerald didn't answer.

"What's up with you anyway, Gerald?"

Gerald stared into the darkness behind his closed eyes, the world around him wheeling and vertiginous. He flattened his palms against the cool wooden floor, seeking a tangible link to the world he had known before, the world he had known and lost, he did not know where or how. Seeking to anchor himself to an Earth that seemed to be sliding away beneath him. Seeking solace.

"Gerald?"

In his mind, he saw the mantis orchid; on the screen of his eyelids, he watched it unfold with deadly grace and drag down the hapless grasshopper.

He said: "I watch the sonogram tape, you know? I watch it at night when Sara's sleeping. It doesn't look like a baby, Lake. It doesn't look like anything human at all. And I think I'm going to lose her. I think I'm going to lose her, it's killing her, it's some kind of . . . something . . . I don't know . . . it's going to take her away."

"Gerald—"

"No. Listen. When I first met Sara, I remember the thing I liked about her—one of the things I liked about her anyway, I liked so much about her, everything—but the thing I remember most was this day when I first met her family. I went home with her from school for a weekend and her whole family—her little sister, her mom, her dad—they were all waiting. They had prepared this elaborate meal and we ate in the dining room, and you knew that they were a family. It was just this quality they had, and it didn't mean they even liked each other all the time, but they were there for each other. You could feel it, you could breathe it in, like oxygen. That's what I wanted. That's what we have together, that's what I'm afraid of losing. I'm afraid of losing her."

He was afraid to open his eyes. He could feel tears there. He was afraid to look at Lake, to share his weakness, which he had never shared with anyone but Sara.

Lake said, "But don't you see, the baby will just draw you closer. Make you even more of a family than you ever were. You're afraid, Gerald, but it's just normal anxiety."

"I don't think so."

"The sonogram?" Lake said. "Your crazy thoughts about the sonogram? Everybody thinks that. But everything changes when the baby comes, Gerald. Everything."

"That's what I'm afraid of," Gerald said.

After the gym, Gerald drove for hours without conscious purpose, trusting mindless reflexes to take him where they would. Around him sprawled the city, senseless, stunned like a patient on a table, etherized by winter.

By the time he pulled the Lexus to the broken curb in a residential neighborhood that had been poor two decades past, a few flakes of snow had begun to swirl through the expanding cones of his headlights. Dusk fell out of the December sky. Gerald cracked his window, inhaled cold smoke-stained air, and gazed diagonally across the abandoned street.

Still there. My God, still there after these ten years. A thought recurred to him, an image he had not thought of in all the long months—ages, they felt like—since that first visit to Dr. Exavious: like stepping into icy water, this stepping into the past.

No one lived there anymore. He could see that from the dilapidated state of the house, yard gone to seed, windows broken, paint that had been robin's egg blue a decade ago weathered now to the dingy shade of mop water. Out front, the wind creaked a realtor's sign long since scabbed over with rust. The skeletal swing-set remained in the barren yard, and it occurred to him now that his child—his and Sara's child—might have played there if only . . .

If only.

Always and forever if only.

The sidewalk, broken and weedy, still wound lazily from the street. The concrete stoop still extruded from the front door like a grotesquely foreshortened tongue. Three stairs still mounted to the door, the railing—Dear God—shattered and dragged away years since.

So short. Three short stairs. So little blood. Who could have known?

He thought of the gym, Lake Conley, the story he had wanted to tell but had not. He had not told anyone. And why should he? No great trauma, there; no abuse or hatred, no fodder for the morning talk shows; just the subtle cruelties, the little twists of steel that made up life.

But always there somehow. Never forgotten. Memories not of

this house, though this house had its share God knows, but of a house very much like this one, in a neighborhood pretty much the same, in another city, in another state, a hundred years in the past or so it seemed. Another lifetime.

But unforgettable all the same.

Gerald had never known his father, had never seen him except in a single photograph: a merchant mariner, broad-shouldered and handsome, his wind-burned face creased by a broad incongruous smile. Gerald had been born in a different age, before such children became common, in a different world where little boys without fathers were never allowed to forget their absences and loss. His mother, he supposed, had been a good woman in her way—had tried, he knew, and now, looking back with the discerning eye of an adult, he could see how it must have been for her: the thousand slights she had endured, the cruelties visited upon a small-town girl and the bastard son she had gotten in what her innocence mistook for love. Yes. He understood her flight to the city and its anonymity; he understood the countless lovers; now, at last, he understood the drinking when it began in earnest, when her looks had begun to go. Now he saw what she had been seeking. Solace. Only solace.

But forgive?

Now, sitting in his car across the street from the house where his first child had been miscarried, where he had almost lost forever the one woman who had thought him worthy of her love, Gerald remembered.

The little twists of steel, spoken without thought or heat, that made up life.

How old had he been then? Twelve? Thirteen?

Old enough to know, anyway. Old enough to creep into the living room and crouch over his mother as she lay there sobbing, drunken, bruised, a cold wind blowing through the open house where the man, whoever he had been, had left the door to swing open on its hinges after he had beaten her. Old enough to scream into his mother's whiskey-shattered face: *I hate you! I hate you! I hate you!*

Old enough to remember her reply: *If it wasn't for you, you little bastard, he never would have left. If it wasn't for you, he never would have left me.*

Old enough to remember, sure.

But old enough to forgive? Not then, Gerald knew. Not now. And maybe never.

✳   ✳   ✳

They did not go to bed together. Sara came to him in the den, where he sat in the recliner, drinking gin and numbly watching television. He saw her in the doorway that framed the formal living room they never used, and beyond that, in diminishing perspective, the broad open foyer: but Sara foremost, foregrounded and unavoidable.

She said, "I'm going to bed. Are you coming?"

"I thought I'd stay up for a bit."

She crossed the flagstone floor to him in stocking feet, soundlessly, like a grotesquely misshapen apparition—her belly preceding her. He wondered if the long lines of the body he used to know were in there somewhere. She was still beautiful, still graceful, to be sure. But she possessed now a grace and beauty unlike any he had known, ponderous and alien, wholly different from that she had possessed the first time he had seen her all those years ago—ghostlike then as well, an apparition from a world stable and dependable, a world of family, glimpsed in heart-wrenching profile through the clamorous throng of the University Center cafeteria.

She knelt by him. "Please come to bed."

He swished his drink. Ice bobbed and clinked. "I need to unwind."

"Gerald . . ."

"No really, I'm not sleepy, okay?" He smiled, and he could feel the falseness of the smile, but it satisfied her.

She leaned toward him, her lips brushed his cheek with a pressure barely present—the merest papery rush of moth wings in a darkened room. And then she was gone.

Gerald drank: stared into the television's poison glow and drank gin and tonic, nectar and ambrosia. *Tastes like a Christmas tree,* Sara had told him the first night they were together, really together. He had loved her, he thought. He touched the remote, cycled past a fragmentary highlight of an NFL football game; past the dependable hysteria over the L.A. cannibal killer, identity unknown; past the long face of Mr. Ed. Drank gin and cycled through and through the channels, fragmentary windows on a broken world. Oh, he had loved her.

Later, how much later he didn't know and didn't care, Gerald found his way to the bedroom. Without undressing, he lay supine on the bed and stared sightlessly at the ceiling, Sara beside him, sleeping the hard sleep of exhaustion for now, though Gerald knew it would not last. Before the night was out, the relentless demands of the child within her would prod her into wakefulness. Lying there, his eyes gradually adjusting to the dark until the features of the room appeared to stand out, blacker still against the blackness, something, some whim, some impulse he could not contain, compelled him to steal his hand beneath the covers: stealthy now, through the folds of the sheet; past the hem of her gown, rucked up below her breasts; at last flattening his palm along the arc of her distended belly. Sara took in a heavy breath, kicked at the covers restlessly, subsided.

Silence all through the house, even the furnace silent in its basement lair: just Sara's steady respiration, and Gerald with her in the weighty dark, daring hardly to breathe, aware now of a cold sobriety in the pressure of the air.

The child moved.

For the first time, he felt it. He felt it move. An icy needle of emotion pierced him. It moved, moved again, the faintest shift in its embryonic slumber, bare adjustment of some internal gravity.

Just a month, he thought. *Only a month.*

The child moved, *really* moved now, palpable against his outstretched palm. Gerald threw back the covers, sitting upright, the room wheeling about him so swiftly that he had to swallow hard against an obstruction rising in his throat. Sara kicked in her sleep, and then was still.

Gerald looked down at her, supine, one long hand curled at her chin, eyes closed, mouth parted, great mound of belly half-visible below the hem of her upturned gown. Now again, slowly, he lay a hand against her warm stomach, and yes, just as he had feared, it happened again: the baby moved, a long slow pressure against his palm.

Ontogeny recapitulates phylogeny, hissed the thin nasty voice of the cockroach. But what exactly did that mean?

He moved his palm along her taut belly, pausing as Sara sighed in her sleep, and here too, like the slow pressure of some creature of the unknown deep, boiling through the placid waters, came that patient and insistent pressure. And then something more, not mere pressure, not gentle: a sudden, powerful blow. Sara moaned and arched her back, but the blow came again, as though the creature within her had hurled itself against the wall of the imprisoning womb. *Why didn't she wake up?* Gerald drew his hand away. Blow wasn't really the right word, was it?

What was?

His heart hammered at his ribcage; transfixed, Gerald moved his hand back toward Sara's belly. No longer daring to touch her, he skated his hand over the long curve on an inch-thin cushion of air. My God, he thought. My God. For he could see it now, he could *see* it: an outward bulge of the taut flesh with each repeated blow, as though a fist had punched her from within. He moved his hand, paused, and it happened again, sudden and sure, an outward protrusion that swelled and sank and swelled again. In a kind of panic—

—what the hell was going on here—

—Gerald moved his hand, paused, moved it again, tracing the curve of Sara's belly in a series of jerks and starts. And it *followed* him. Even though he was no longer touching her, it followed him, that sudden outward protrusion, the thing within somehow aware of his presence and trying to get at him. The blows quickened even as he watched, until they began to appear and disappear with savage, violent speed.

And still she did not wake up.

Not a blow, he thought. A strike.

Like the swift, certain strike of a cobra. An image unfolded with deadly urgency in Gerald's mind: the image of the orchid-colored mantis exploding outward from its flowery hole to drag down the helpless grasshopper and devour it.

Gerald jerked his hand away as if stung.

Sara's abdomen was still and pale as a tract of mountain snow. Nothing moved there. He reached the covers across her and lay back. A terrific weight settled over him; his chest constricted with panic; he could barely draw breath.

The terrible logic of the thing revealed itself to him at last. Ontogeny recapitulates phylogeny, Exavious had told him. And what if it was true? What if each child reflected in its own development the evolutionary history of the entire species?

Imagine:

Somewhere, far far back in the evolutionary past—who could say how far?—but somewhere, it began. A mutation that should have died, but didn't, a creature born of man and woman that survived to feed . . . and reproduce. Imagine a recessive gene so rare that it appeared in only one of every ten thousand individuals—one of every hundred thousand even. For that would be sufficient, wouldn't it? Gerald couldn't calculate the odds, but he knew that it would be sufficient, that occasionally, three or four times in a generation, two carriers of such a gene would come together and produce . . . What? A child that was not what it appeared to be. A child that was not human. A monster clothed in human flesh.

Beside him, Sara moaned in her sleep. Gerald did not move.

He shut his eyes and saw against the dark screens of his eyelids the flower-colored mantis, hidden in its perfumed lair; saw its deadly graceful assault, its pincers as they closed around the helpless grasshopper and dragged it down. The words of the narrator came back to him as well: natural selection favors the most efficient predator. And the most efficient predator is the monster that walks unseen among its chosen prey.

Terror gripped him as at last he understood how it must have been through all the long span of human history: Jack the Ripper, the Zodiac, the cannibal killer loose even now in the diseased bowels of Los Angeles.

We are hunted, he thought. We are hunted.

He stumbled clumsily from the bed and made his way into the adjoining bathroom, where for a long time he knelt over the toilet and was violently, violently sick.

Sanity returned to him in perceptual shards: watery light through the slatted blinds, the mattress rolling under him like a ship in rough waters, a jagged sob of fear and pain that pierced him through. Sara.

Gerald sat upright, swallowing bile. He took in the room with a wild glance.

Sara: in the doorway to the bathroom, long legs twisted beneath her, hands clutched in agony at her bloated abdomen. And blood—

—*my God, how could you have*—

—so much blood, a crimson gout against the pale carpet, a pool spreading over the tiled floor of the bathroom.

Gerald reached for the phone, dialed 911. And then he went to her, took her in his arms, comforted her.

Swarming masses of interns and nurses in white smocks swept her away from him at the hospital. Later, during the long gray hours in the waiting room—hours spent staring at the mindless flicker of television or gazing through dirty windows that commanded a view of the parking lot, cup after cup of sour vending machine coffee clutched in hands that would not warm—Gerald could not recall how they had spirited her away. In his last clear memory he saw himself step out of the ambulance into an icy blood-washed dawn, walking fast beside the gurney, Sara's cold hand clutched in his as the automatic doors slipped open on the chill impersonal reaches of the emergency room.

Somehow he had been shunted aside, diverted without the solace of a last endearment, without even a backward glance. Instead he found himself wrestling with a severe gray-headed woman about insurance policies and admission requirements, a kind of low-wattage bureaucratic hell he hated every minute of, but missed immediately when it ended and left him to his thoughts.

Occasionally he gazed at the pay phones along the far wall, knowing he should call Sara's mother but somehow unable to gather sufficient strength to do so. Later, he glimpsed Exavious in an adjacent corridor, but the doctor barely broke stride. He merely cast at Gerald a speculative glance—

—*he knows, he knows*—

—and passed on, uttering over his shoulder these words in his obscurely accented English: "We are doing everything in our power, Mr. Hartshorn. I will let you know as soon as I have news."

Alone again. Alone with bitter coffee, recriminations, the voice of the cockroach.

An hour passed. At eleven o'clock, Exavious returned. "It is not good, I'm afraid," he said. "We need to perform a Cesarean section, risky under the circumstances, but we have little choice if the baby is to survive."

"And Sara?"

"We cannot know, Mr. Hartshorn." Exavious licked his lips, met Gerald's gaze. "Guarded optimism, shall we say. The fall . . ." He lifted his hand. "Your wife is feverish, irrational. We need you to sign some forms."

And afterwards, after the forms were signed, he fixed Gerald for a long moment with that same speculative stare and then he turned away. "I'll be in touch."

Gerald glared at the clock as if he could by force of will speed time's passage. At last he stood, crossed once more to the vending machines, and for the first time in seven years purchased a pack of cigarettes and a lighter. After a word with the receptionist, he stepped into the bitterly cold December morning to smoke.

A few flakes of snow had begun to drift aimlessly about in the wind. Gerald stood under the E.R. awning, beneath the bruised and sullen sky, the familiar stink of cigarette smoke somehow comforting in his nostrils. He gazed out over the crowded parking lot, his eyes watering. Like stepping into icy water, he thought, this stepping into the past: for what he saw was not the endless rows of cars, but the house he had visited for the first time in a decade only a day ago. And the voice he heard in his head was neither the voice of the hospital P.A. system or the voice of the wind. It was the voice of the cockroach, saying words he did not want to hear.

You, the cockroach told him. *You are responsible.*

Gerald flipped his cigarette, still burning, into the gutter and wrapped his arms close about his shoulders. But the cold he felt was colder than mere weather.

Responsible.

He supposed he had been. Even now, he could not forget the isolation they had endured during the first years of their marriage. The fear. It hadn't been easy for either of them—not for Gerald, sharing for the first time the bitter legacy of a life he had still to come to terms with; not for Sara, smiling patrician Sara, banished from a family who would not accept the impoverished marriage she had made. To this day Gerald had not forgiven his in-laws for the wedding: the thin-lipped grimace that passed for his mother-in-law's smile; the encounter with his father-in-law in the spotless restroom of the Mariott, when the stout old dentist turned from a urinal to wag a finger in Gerald's face. "Don't ever ask me for a dime, Gerald," he had said. "Sara's made her choice and she'll have to abide by it."

No wonder we were proud, he thought. Sara had taken an evening job as a cashier at a supermarket. Gerald continued at the ad agency, a poorly paid associate, returning nightly to the abandoned rental house where he sat blankly in front of the television and awaited the sound of Sara's key in the lock. God knows they hadn't needed a baby.

But there it was. There it was.

And so the pressure began to tell, the endless pressure to stretch each check just a little further. Gerald could not remember when or why—money he supposed—but gradually the arguments had begun. And he had started drinking. And one night . . .

One night. Well.

Gerald slipped another cigarette free of the pack and brought it to his lips. Cupping his hands against the wind, he set the cigarette alight, and drew deeply.

One night, she was late from work and, worried, Gerald met her at the door. He stepped out onto the concrete stoop to greet her, his hand curled about the graying wooden rail. When Sara looked up at him, her features taut with worry in the jaundiced corona of the porch light, he had just for a moment glimpsed a vision of himself as she must have seen him: bearish, slovenly, stinking of drink. And poor. Just another poor fucking bastard, only she had married this one.

He opened his arms to her, needing her to deny the truth he had seen reflected in her eyes. But she fended him off, a tight-lipped little moue of distaste crossing her features—he knew that expression, he had seen it on her mother's face.

Her voice was weary when she spoke. Her words stung him like a lash. "Drinking again, Gerald?" And then, as she started to push her way past him: "Christ, sometimes I think Mom was right about you."

And he had struck her.

For the first and only time in all the years they had been married, he had struck her—without thought or even heat, the impulse arising out of some deep poisoned wellspring of his being, regretted even as he lifted his hand.

Sara stumbled. Gerald moved forward to steady her, his heart racing. She fell away from him forever, and in that timeless interval Gerald had a grotesquely heightened sense of his surroundings: the walk, broken and weedy; the dim shadow of a moth battering itself tirelessly against the porch light; in the sky a thousand thousand stars. Abruptly, the world shifted into motion again; in confusion, Gerald watched an almost comically broad expression of relief spread over Sara's face. The railing. The railing had caught her.

"Jesus, Sara, I'm sorr—" he began to say, but a wild gale of hilarity had risen up inside her.

She hadn't begun to realize the consequences of this simple action, Gerald saw. She did not yet see that with a single blow he had altered forever the tenor of their relationship. But the laughter was catching, and he stepped down now, laughing himself, laughing hysterically in a way that was not funny, to soothe away her fears before she saw the damage he had done. Maybe she would never see it.

But just at that moment, the railing snapped with a sound like a gunshot. Sara fell hard, three steps to the ground, breath exploding from her lungs.

But again, she was okay. Just shaken up.

Only later, in the night, would Gerald realize what he had done. Only when the contractions took her would he begin to fear. Only when he tore back the blankets of the bed and saw the blood—

—so *little blood*—

—would he understand.

Gerald snapped away his cigarette in disgust. They had lost the child. Sara, too, had almost died. And yet she had forgiven him. She had forgiven him.

He shivered and looked back through the cold-fogged windows at the waiting room, but he couldn't tolerate the idea of another moment in there. He turned back to the parking lot, exhaled into his cupped hands. He thought of Dr. Exavious, those febrile eyes, the way he had of seeming to gaze into the secret regions of your heart. Probing you. Judging you. Finding you wanting.

There was something else.

Last night.

With this thought, Gerald experienced bleak depths of self-knowledge he had never plumbed before. He saw again the smooth expanse of his wife's belly as he had seen it last night, hideously aswarm with the vicious assaults of the creature within. Now he recognized this vision as a fevered hallucination, nothing more. But last night, last night he had believed. And after his feverish dream, after he had been sick, he had done something else, hadn't he? Something so monstrous and so simple that until this moment he had successfully avoided thinking of it.

He had stood up from the toilet, and there, in the doorway between the bedroom and the bathroom, he had kicked off his shoes, deliberately arranging them heel up on the floor. Knowing she would wake to go to the john two, maybe three times in the night. Knowing she would not turn on the light. Knowing she might fall.

Hoping.

You are responsible.

Oh yes, he thought, you are responsible, my friend. You are guilty.

Just at that moment, Gerald felt a hand on his shoulder. Startled, he turned too fast, feeling the horror rise into his face and announce his guilt to anyone who cared to see. Exavious stood behind him. "Mr. Hartshorn," he said.

Gerald followed the doctor through the waiting room and down a crowded corridor that smelled of ammonia. Exavious did not speak; his lips pressed into a narrow line beneath his mustache. He led Gerald through a set of swinging doors into a cavernous chamber lined with pallets of supplies and soiled linen heaped in laundry baskets. Dusty light bulbs in metal cages cast a fitful glow over the concrete floor.

"What's going on?" Gerald asked. "How's Sara?"

Exavious did not reply. He stopped by a broad door of corrugated metal that opened on a loading dock, and thumbed the button of the freight elevator.

"One moment, please, Mr. Hartshorn," he said.

They waited silently as the doors slid aside. Exavious gestured Gerald in, and pressed the button for six. With a metallic clunk of gears, they lurched into motion. Gerald stared impassively at the numbers over the door, trying to conceal the panic that had begun to hammer against his ribs. The noisy progress of the elevator seemed almost to speak to him; if he listened closely, he could hear the voice of the cockroach, half-hidden in the rattle of machinery:

She's dead, Gerald. She's dead and you're responsible.

Exavious knew. Gerald could see that clearly now. He wasn't even surprised when Exavious reached out and stopped the lift between the fifth and sixth floors. Just sickened, physically sickened by a sour twist of nausea that doubled him over as the elevator ground to a halt with a screech of overtaxed metal. Gerald sagged against the wall as a wave of vertigo passed through him. Sara. Lost. Irrevocably lost. He swallowed hard against the metallic taste in his mouth and closed his eyes.

They hung suspended in the shaft, in the center of an enormous void that seemed to pour in at Gerald's eyes and ears, at every aperture of his body. He drew it in with his breath, he was drowning in it.

Exavious said: "This conversation never occurred, Mr. Hartshorn. I will deny it if you say it did."

Gerald said nothing. He opened his eyes, but he could see only the dull sheen of the elevator car's walls, scarred here and there by careless employees. Only the walls, like the walls of a prison. He saw now that he would not ever really leave this prison he had made for himself. Everything that had ever been important to him he had destroyed—his dignity, his self-respect, his honor and his love. And Sara. Sara most of all.

Exavious said: "I have spoken with Dr. Schwartz. I should have done so sooner." He licked his lips. "When I examined your wife I found no evidence to suggest that she could not carry a child to term. Even late-term miscarriages are not uncommon in first pregnancies. I saw no reason to delve into her history."

He said all this without looking at Gerald. He did not raise his voice or otherwise modify his tone. He stared forward with utter concentration, his eyes like pebbles.

"I should have seen the signs. They were present even in your first office visit. I was looking at your wife, Mr. Hartshorn. I should have been looking at you."

Gerald's voice cracked when he spoke. "Schwartz—what did Schwartz say?"

"Dr. Schwartz was hesitant to say anything at all. He is quite generous: he wished to give you the benefit of the doubt. When pressed, however, he admitted that there had been evidence—a bruise on your wife's face, certain statements she made under anesthesia—that the miscarriage had resulted from an altercation, a physical blow. But you both seemed very sorrowful, so he did not pursue the matter."

Exavious turned to look at Gerald, turned on him the terrific illumination of his gaze, his darkly refulgent eyes exposing everything that Gerald had sought so long to hide. "A woman in your wife's superb physical condition does not often have two late-term miscarriages, Mr. Hartshorn. Yet Mrs. Hartshorn claims that her fall was accidental, that she tripped over a pair of shoes. Needless to say, I do not believe her, though I am powerless to act on my belief. But I had to speak, Mr. Hartshorn—not for you, but for myself."

He punched a button. The elevator jerked into motion once more.

"You are a very lucky man, Mr. Hartshorn. Your wife is awake and doing well." He turned once more and fixed Gerald in his gaze. "The baby survived. A boy. You are the father of a healthy baby boy."

The elevator stopped and the doors opened onto a busy floor. "It is more than you deserve."

Sara, then.

Sara at last, flat on her back in a private room on the sixth floor. At the sight of her through the wire-reinforced window in the door, Gerald felt a bottomless relief well up within him.

He brushed past Dr. Exavious without speaking. The door opened so silently on its oiled hinges that she did not hear him enter. For a long moment, he stood there in the doorway, just looking at her—allowing the simple vision of her beauty and her joy to flow through him, to fill up the void that had opened in his heart.

He moved forward, his step a whisper against the tile. Sara turned to look at him. She smiled, lifted a silencing finger to her lips, and then nodded, her eyes returning to her breast and the child that nursed there, wizened and red and patiently sucking.

Just a baby. A child like any other. But different, Gerald knew, different and special in no way he could ever explain, for this child was his own. A feeling like none he had ever experienced—an outpouring of warmth and affection so strong that it was almost frightening—swept over him as he came to the bedside.

Everything Lake Conley had told him was true.

What happened next happened so quickly that Gerald for a moment believed it to be a hallucination. The baby, not yet twelve hours old, pulled away from Sara's breast, pulled away and turned, turned to look at him. For a single terrifying moment Gerald glimpsed not the wrinkled child he had beheld when first he entered the room, but . . . something else.

Something quicksilver and deadly, rippling with the sleek, purposeful musculature of a predator. A fleeting impression of oily hide possessed him—of a bullet-shaped skull from which glared narrow-pupilled eyes ashine with chill intelligence. Eyes like a snake's eyes, as implacable and smugly knowing.

Mocking me, Gerald thought. Showing itself not because it has to, but because it wants to. Because it can.

And then his old friend the cockroach: *Your child. Yours.*

Gerald extended his hands to Sara. "Can I?" he asked.

And then he drew it to his breast, blood of his blood, flesh of his flesh, this creature that was undeniably and irrevocably his own child.

❖   ❖   ❖

Sheep's Clothing

I HAVE NEVER MUCH ADMIRED ASSASSINS.
Their methods—subterfuge and unexpected violence—possess
little appeal for me; in those rare situations when action is necessary, I have always favored direct confrontation. Anything less seems
unethical.

Certainly I never aspired to be one.

I saw some of that kind—or so I have always imagined—in the
Brazilian Conflict. The steambox, we called the place, and on a still
night you could lie wakeful in the equatorial heat of the Cuiabá bar-
racks and listen to the detonations of sniper fire bat away through
the dark, humid air. And, of course, there were more than a few of
the type on our side, as well. Types, I should say, for if you have
devoted any thought to the matter at all—and during these last
months I have thought of little else—it is evident that no two assassins are driven by precisely the same motives.

Not that there aren't broad categories.

I can think of three. There is the madman, most common I suppose, fired by the blaze of his own obsessions. He hears the voice of
God or he is anxious for the warrior's paradise. He is the crazed fan,
the car bomber.

There is the killer motivated by greed. He works for the highest
bidder, and takes pride in his skills. He is the mercenary, the hired
gun, the hit man.

Finally, there is the man driven by the genuine belief that he is committing violence for utilitarian purposes—that his small evils are counterbalanced by a greater good. Of the three, he is most rare, most dangerous.

And of course, he always runs the risk that he is one of the other type, and simply hasn't the wisdom to see it.

"Senator Philip Hanson of North Carolina," Napolean Thrale said. He sat behind a polished mahogany desk, impressively barren, refulgent in the luminous halo of the floor-to-ceiling windows that formed the outer wall.

"What do you think of the man, Mr. Stern?"

The question took me by surprise. I'm not sure what I had expected when the creamy invitation had been hand-delivered the previous afternoon to the door of my Annapolis home, but certainly it wasn't this.

I say invitation, but it was a summons really, for what else can you call such a request from one of the most powerful men in the country? Certainly I was in no position to refuse. Every other semester or so, I teach a course at the Naval Academy in virtual remote warfare, but I do it on an adjunct basis. The rest of the time I do not work, and as a result I live with a certain austere economy, nibbling away at my small inheritance and waiting for my military pension. Economic realities, if nothing else, compelled me to attend.

Now, however, I found myself uncertain how to proceed. I glanced at the two people sitting on the couch opposite, an owlish-looking young man in silver-rimmed glasses, and a slim middle-aged woman with graying hair pulled severely away from the angular planes of her face. Neither of them spoke, so I turned to look at Thrale, to look past him.

Thrale's desk, the couch, and the chair where I sat formed an island of furniture in the center of the large, high-ceilinged chamber. The windows beyond Thrale commanded a magnificent view. From my chair, I could see the immaculate grounds of the house drop abruptly to the turbulent rim of the Chesapeake Bay. A gull wheeled through the clear sky, and for a moment I imagined how it would feel to soar through that lofty emptiness. Free, I thought. That's how it must feel. And suddenly I wondered if the man behind the desk ever thought of birds, and if he envied them.

Napolean Thrale did not appear to envy anyone. He sat rigidly erect in a motorized wheelchair, his hands folded on the desk. His upper body was broad and heavily muscled beneath his tailored shirt. Though his legs were hidden beneath the desk, I knew that they were shrunken and useless—his badge of honor from the Brazilian Conflict. Mine is engraved upon my heart.

The owlish-looking fellow cleared his throat, but Thrale spoke first, his voice carrying the tone of quiet authority I have come to associate with men accustomed to unquestioning obedience. "Please, Dr. Truman. Give the man time." Thrale turned the terrific weight of his regard on Truman, and with the movement afternoon sunlight gleamed against his clean-shaven skull.

Truman fell silent.

Out the window, the seagull dived toward the dark water. It rose through spray, a fish clutched in its beak. I suddenly realized that my hands were shaking.

"Senator Hanson." I clenched my hands into hard fists. "Perhaps it would be most diplomatic to say that I am violently opposed to his politics."

Thrale studied me out of eyes as green and depthless as the eyes of a snake. I'd seen that unwavering gaze before—any soldier who's been in combat has. They call it the thousand-yard stare. "The question is, Mr. Stern," Thrale said, "just how violently opposed are you?" He emphasized the word "violently" in a way that I didn't necessarily like.

"Why is that the question?"

Thrale readjusted himself in his chair with a movement suggestive of a deliberate attempt to be casual. Had he been able, I feel certain, he would have pushed his chair back and stretched out his legs. Instead he contented himself with slumping his powerful upper body and tenting his long fingers atop the desk. "My people have looked into you, Mr. Stern. You are a man rife with contradiction, did you know that?"

"So I've been told."

He nodded, almost imperceptibly, and the woman stood. I had the sense that I was at the heart of some elaborately choreographed dance. She crossed the space between us and clasped my hand with a brief masculine intensity. "Dr. Elise Pangborn," she said, and with a gesture at the couch, "Dr. Gregory Truman." The other man dipped his head. Without looking at the Bay, Pangborn circled the desk to stand behind Thrale. She placed her hands atop his broad shoulders with a gesture at once proprietary and maternal.

"You've quite an impressive background, Mr. Stern," she said. "Forty confirmed kills in the Mato Grosso, instructor at the U.S. Naval Academy, a leading expert in virtual remote warfare."

"And yet," said Thrale, "in your published writings an outspoken advocate of disarmament."

This was all true, yet I could not help but agree with Truman when he coughed theatrically and said, "For Christ's sake, the man knows his own resume." He stood and crossed the room to study the giant Picasso affixed to one wall.

"But what do you want with me?" I said.

"That brings us back to Senator Hanson," Pangborn said.

"There's a proposal for a sizable new weapons program that's been locked up in committee for some time," Thrale said. "Hanson has the swing vote on the thing and he's dithering—not out of civic responsibility, you understand, but simply because he wants a larger piece of the action."

"He's about to get it," Pangborn said. "One of the companies that stands to benefit has proposed building a major facility in the senator's district. You see the implications, of course."

"Hanson's going to give it the green light, I suppose," I said. "So what? It's hardly the first weapons initiative, and I'm sure it won't be the last."

Thrale smiled a thin unpleasant smile. "Of course not. However, the proposed facility is not a factory, Mr. Stern. It is a laboratory designed to engineer tailored viruses amongst other things. Just like Brazil, only this time right in the middle of downtown Asheville."

Thrale's words sent an icy blade skating along my spine. No one had known about the biological agents being used along the Xingú—not until too late. It was the biggest scandal in U.S. government since Watergate; heads rolled at every level of the intelligence agencies, but that didn't stop the rot.

It didn't keep my daughter from dying.

"Not that Hanson gives two shits about the danger," said Elise Pangborn, and the profanity was shocking here in this formal room with the Bay, scrubbed and unpolluted, crashing on the rocky shore beyond the windows.

"For him it's essentially pork," Thrale said. "But accidents happen, we can both attest to that, Mr. Stern."

"There's one other thing," Pangborn said. "Our source on the senator's staff has informed us that he intends to introduce new legislation this term." She walked around the desk and sat on the couch, fixing me with an earnest gaze. "Quarantine camps, to keep the rot from spreading. We hoped that if nothing else convinced you, that would."

"Convince me to what?" I said.

But the answer, when it came, was spoken not by Pangborn or by Thrale, but by Truman. I had almost forgotten his presence, but during the course of the conversation he had moved soundlessly across the plush carpeting to stand behind me. I could scarcely believe that he had said the words I thought I'd heard, and when I turned to stare at him, he was standing with his hands shoved in his pockets and a startled expression on his face, as if he too was amazed at the idea for the first time spoken aloud.

I could not see his eyes. The glare from the afternoon sun across the Bay made bright metallic discs of his spectacles, as if his humanity was but a sham, and probing out from the rubber mask of his disguise were the alien beacons of some terrible intelligence.

"What did you say?" I asked him.

And when he repeated the words, they came out just the same. "They want you to kill him," Truman said.

There is an image that I hold always in my mind, an image I will forever associate with my daughter's death.

Even now, of course, no one is certain what causes the rot—no more than they were certain that HIV was responsible for AIDS back in the early 80s. All that can be said for certain is that it was first diagnosed during the Brazilian Conflict, among the soldiers who served in the Mato Grosso. Its spread was random, ugly, and exponential; it continues to this day. You have undoubtedly heard the pathology of the disease described a hundred times. You probably are aware that scientists have isolated any number of pathogens and tailored viruses—most of them deriving in the biological agents released in the jungle—that might be responsible. Certainly, you know there are still no answers.

If you're interested, blood tests have confirmed that I am infected with most of the suspected agents. Nevertheless, I have yet to get sick. Some people never do.

Others aren't so lucky.

After the war, Anna and I remained in her native Brazil. We did not return to the States until several years later, when black pustulant sores began to erupt in our five-year-old daughter's flesh.

I can never forget the stench of the hospital room where she died—a noxious odor compounded of the sterile smell of the hospital corridors and a fulsome reek of decay, like rotting peaches, inside the room itself. At the last, my eyes watered with that smell; Anna could barely bring herself to enter the room. My daughter died alone, walled away from us by the surgical masks we wore over our noses and mouths.

Afterwards, I had to face the reporters.

You may remember that year: the rot beginning to make headlines, Senator Philip Hanson fighting for his political life in a North Carolina senate race. People remembered the AIDS pandemic, and Hanson turned that fear to his advantage, as politicians will. Using my daughter's illness, he transformed his election into a referendum on the tough immigration legislation he had proposed—legislation that denied even infected foreign-born citizens admission into the U.S., never mind the hypocrisy of such a policy. Lisette died in an Annapolis hospital before that proposal became law, but not before she became a *cause celebre* during those last painful weeks.

And not before Senator Philip Hanson won his fourth six-year senate term.

After I talked to the reporters I walked down the long tiled corridors to Lisette's room, and there, despite the terrible stench and the sound of Anna weeping in the hall, I sat with her for one last time. The television was on, post-election coverage of Hanson's celebratory round on the links.

That is the image I can never forget: Hanson, smiling his rugged smile as he teed off on a North Carolina fairway hundreds of miles away, while I sat with the corpse of my daughter and held her small cold hand in mine.

After Truman spoke, he shook his head, turned away, and began to pace.

There was a silence in the room that I can compare only to that of the Mato Grosso following a frenzied exchange of gunfire, when all the birds and insects and jungle creatures are still. No one spoke. I could hear the discreet whisper of air-conditioning, the crash of waves along the shore.

"Oh, Christ," I said.

Truman lowered himself to the couch with a sigh. Elise Pangborn leaned forward and placed her elbows on her knees, directing at me a speculative stare. Without even looking over at Thrale, I could feel the hot points of his attention.

"Can I have a minute?" I asked.

Truman sighed, but Thrale lifted his hands in assent.

I walked to a distant corner of the room and stared out at the Bay. The afternoon sun carved a scintillant path through the swells. Far out, three sailboats bobbed like toys atop the water, and the gull, diminished now to a dark speck, wheeled in the cobalt sky.

I knew something about Napolean Thrale—the basic facts most people know, I guess, for the story has passed into contemporary folklore: how he left school to enlist in the conflict over ecological policy in the Mato Grosso; how he returned a paraplegic; how he built a communications empire that rivaled Time-Warner. Thrale Enterprises owned over seventy broadcast networks, ran countless online and multimedia services, had pioneered applications of virtual reality in the entertainment industry—impressive achievements for a Phys. Ed. major who left College Park in his sophomore year.

Recently, however, he had entrusted the management of his holdings to the bureaucracy that accretes about such institutions. I had seen speculation that he had fallen ill or retreated into self-pity, but I didn't think either was the case.

I thought I knew what had occupied his time. He wasn't the first man who had sought to prevent violence through the use of violence, but I wasn't sure I liked the idea.

I wasn't sure I didn't like it either.

There had been a point in my life—shortly after Parris Island—when I looked to the war as a glorious adventure. I didn't know myself well then. I had never killed a man.

Without looking away from the sea, I asked, "Why me?"

I turned away from the window and walked back across the long expanse of carpet and sat in my chair. "Why not the mob or a professional assassin?" I stared right at Thrale as I spoke, right into his glazed eyes.

"There's a certain symmetry to your involvement that appeals to me," he said.

"It's important that you understand," Pangborn said. "This isn't a vendetta."

"Then what is it?"

"It's the policy."

Momentarily my eyes met those of Truman, round and liquescent behind their silver cages. "Murder a tool of diplomacy?"

"Save us the charade of innocence," said Napolean Thrale. "If it happens that you wish not to sully your hands through the use of such a tool, that is very well, and you may reject our offer. But save us the charade."

"I'm sorry," I said, and then, turning to face Pangborn again, "but it's important that I understand."

Pangborn pressed her thin colorless lips together for an instant. In the slow patient way you might explain something to a child, she said, "Hanson has a daughter—Amanda Hanson Brewer. Same party, same far-right agenda. She's presently serving in the North Carolina senate, but she's certain to be appointed to her father's office in the event of his death. We hope to prevent that if we can. Our goal is not merely to eliminate the senator. It is to eliminate his objectives."

"And that's where Dr. Truman comes in," Thrale said.

Truman shifted uncomfortably and cleared his throat. He would not meet my eyes. "It's really a matter of your experience in the Amazon basin. You were the best with the spiders. No one else even came close."

"Oh?"

"Have you ever been to the virtuals, Mr. Stern?"

"No."

"What do you know of the technique?"

"Not much."

"Essentially," Truman said, "it's a full sensory array that plugs you into a pre-designed cyberspace fantasy. It utilizes a more sophisticated version of the virtual reality technology that allowed you to ride the spiders in Brazil."

"That wasn't fantasy," I said.

"No, no, of course not. I'm not explaining this well, am I?" He rubbed his forehead. "The sophisticated sensory array of the virtuals, together with the use of virtual remote vehicles in the Amazon basin suggested new avenues of research, new applications of virtual reality. What I'm trying to say—"

"What he's trying to say," said Pangborn, her voice dry, "is that we've pioneered a technique to inject nanomachines into the bloodstream of a human being. The machines propel themselves to pre-determined points in the nervous system—the base of the brain, visual and aural centers, other sensory centers—where they lodge and become active. At that point, a broadband transmitter and receiver-array should allow a second individual to access the host's sensory data, and briefly supersede her neural commands."

"Not her consciousness," Truman said. "That's impossible—but her nerve paths and motor functions."

"You see the implications," Pangborn said.

For a moment I could not speak. "I'm not sure," I said, but I thought maybe I was lying.

Truman confirmed my suspicions with his next words. "What you've got is a living, breathing marionette—a human being you can control just as you controlled the spiders in Brazil." He glanced nervously from Pangborn to Thrale. "Of course the applications of such technology are manifold."

Thrale said, "In two months Amanda Brewer will be visiting the senator in his D.C. home. With your help we hope to apply it to framing her for her father's murder."

"We've had some success with experimental interfaces," Pangborn said. "We feel sure we can do even more with an operator of your skill and experience."

"You'll be well compensated for the risk, Mr. Stern," said Thrale.

And that was when I realized that I had no choice in the matter, not immediately anyway. If I refused to go along with them, they would never allow me to leave the estate alive. Or there would be an accident during the limo ride home. Or something equally dramatic.

But that wasn't really the issue. They would never have approached me in the first place if they hadn't been almost certain that I would go along. And even as I listened to Thrale speak, I knew that I would. Not out of any personal antipathy for the way Hanson had used my daughter, though I would be lying to you if I told you no such antipathy existed. And not out of any sense of greed, though I knew I would be well paid. Mainly, I suppose, it was out of some sense of responsibility to all the people who had died—not just Lisette and Anna, and not just the friends I had seen killed in combat, but the thousands who had died as a result of the tailored viruses released in Brazil. All the thousands more who would die before the madness ended.

Still, I could not quite suppress a thrill of excitement at what Thrale said next—for it meant freedom forever from the occasional class at the Naval Academy, from the house in Annapolis where I had lived since returning from Brazil.

"Two million new-American dollars." Thrale touched a button on his desk. A screen rose from a recessed panel, and numbers flitted by. "Placed in numbered Swiss accounts by electronic transfer. The first now, the second afterwards. What do you say, Mr. Stern?"

"You've just bought yourself a wolf," I said.

The next two months passed swiftly. I closed the house in Annapolis and moved to Napolean Thrale's estate, where I slept in a small suite with an ocean view. I took my meals alone, and I did not communicate with anyone but Pangborn and Truman. The only people with whom I might wish to speak were dead. It was almost a relief to spend my time working and studying.

The biggest problem with running a spider was the difficulty of translating human thought-commands into a form that could be assimilated by a host mechanism with a significantly different body shape—for instance, when you command a spider to run, that command must be translated into a sequence comprehensible to a machine with not two legs, but eight. The engineers had essentially solved this problem by sidestepping it altogether. The operator's command does not actually guide a spider; rather, it triggers an autonomous subroutine of pre-programmed movements that sends the machine scurrying in the chosen direction.

Theoretically, with a human-to-human operator/host link, such problems should not exist. In reality, other problems—every bit as complex—cropped up.

"Once the interface is established," Truman told me my first day in the lab, "it will be serviceable only for twenty minutes or so before the nanomachines are metabolized by the host system. And the transmitter is limited to about a kilometer. We'll have to be almost on top of you."

Then there was the problem of muscle-tissue strength. As a thirty-seven-year-old man in better-than-average physical condition, I could conceivably shred Amanda Hanson Brewer's musculature just by walking her across the room.

"In short," said Pangborn, "you must learn to walk again."

I sat naked on an ice-cold steel table, having just undergone an uncomfortably thorough physical examination; neither doctor seemed the least perturbed by my discomfort.

Truman touched a button on his clipboard and a curtain on the far side of the long room swept back to reveal the metallic figure of a vaguely human-shaped hostmech.

Truman crossed the room to stand by the machine. "We've programmed the hostmech to simulate the musculature responses you can expect from Amanda Brewer. It's not going to be perfect—we could only learn so much even by hacking private medical files—but we've recreated it as closely as we can."

"In one respect, anyway," said Pangborn, "you're lucky."

"How's that?"

"She's in good shape. She runs two or three miles a day and works out on the machines twice a week. Good looks don't hurt a political career—her father taught her that."

"The differences between your own muscle responses and those you encounter when you take over the host system shouldn't be prohibitive," Truman said, "but they'll be big enough to be problematic. So we'd better get started."

With the help of the two doctors, I donned a skinsuit hardwired for full tactile sensation and then reclined on the table while Pangborn adjusted the helmet array containing the goggles and 3D speakers that would allow me to share Amanda Brewer's visual and auditory input. In the darkness that followed, I felt a sharp needling pressure at the base of my skull as Pangborn inserted the probes that would re-route my neural impulses to the broadband transmitter. On the day of the assassination attempt, all of this equipment would be packed into a van parked outside Hanson's home—a calculated risk. For the practice sessions, however, we used the more expansive lab.

"Ready?" Pangborn asked.

"I guess."

"You're going to feel some brief discomfort when I give you the injection, and then you'll experience a moment of disorientation as I activate the interface."

I felt the sharp bite of a needle as Pangborn injected the neural buffer that prevented my own body from trying to execute the commands being relayed to the hostmech, and then a wave of dizzying vertigo, as if I had been swept into the maelstrom of a whirlpool.

There is no way to adequately describe the sensation of a virtual remote interface. I have read descriptions of after-death experiences—the ones where the victim finds himself hovering at the ceiling and staring down at his own inert body—and in some ways, I imagine, the experience is not dissimilar. Certainly there is a feeling of disembodiment and momentary disorientation that will only diminish with repeated interfaces.

However, it had been years since I had experienced the virtual link. Not since my last battlefield sessions, just before the Rio Accord, had I experienced anything even slightly similar. When the momentary disorientation passed, the darkness flickered with ghostly telemetry; then the image cleared. With a shock of recognition, I saw my body strapped to the table across the room. My head and face were obscured by the bulky mass of the helmet array, and for a single panicky moment it looked as if some bizarre metallic creature were devouring me from the head down.

Pangborn stood at a nearby console, monitoring the data from the skinsuit's biofeed. Truman glanced quizzically at his clipboard. After a moment, he raised his head to meet the hostmech's gaze.

"Well, good," he said. "Let's try to move, shall we?"

I consciously cleared my mind and directed the hostmech to take a step. It lurched forward, tottered for a long uncertain instant, and collapsed to the floor with a crash.

*   *   *

During the next two months, I saw Napolean Thrale only twice. The house was huge, and both the lab and my suite were—with Truman's—off a single corridor in the west wing. I did not know where Pangborn slept, and I had little opportunity to find out, as I rarely entered another part of the house. I passed long days in the lab, gradually gaining proficiency in the manipulation of the host-mech's weaker musculature. Nights I spent alone in my suite, studying Thrale's extensive dossiers on Hanson and his daughter. And frequently in the cool autumn dusks, I let myself out for long runs along the beach. It was during one such excursion that I finally saw Thrale again.

I was running wind sprints along the rocky shore when I happened to glance up at the house, dark as some Gothic pile against a sky tinged bloody by the westering sun. High up in the central facade, the floor-to-ceiling windows of Thrale's office were glaringly ablaze. Two figures were limned against the light, staring eastward toward the sea: the half-familiar shape of Elise Pangborn, and the unmistakable silhouette of Napolean Thrale, stout and indomitable even in the frame of his wheelchair.

I stood there a moment, arms akimbo, trying to catch my breath in the salt-tinged breeze. The waves broke clamorously against the rocks behind me, and far away in the darkening sky I heard a gull scream. I could not help but remember the day when this had all begun: the gull turning and turning in all that flawless blue, and the thought I'd had then. Did Thrale think of birds and did he envy them?

I suddenly wasn't so sure that he did not.

I waited an instant longer, until finally I could breathe easy again, and then I lifted my arm in some kind of greeting—a salute or an acknowledgment of the man and his pain over all the long shadowy distance between the house and the beach, between his prison and my own.

Thrale did not lift his hand in response, and a moment later the light went out, plunging the house into darkness.

One evening when I returned to my rooms following a run, I found a package waiting for me—an addition to the Brewer dossier, two readerdiscs labeled as further biographical data and a videodisc with a slip of paper affixed to one side. *Thought you might enjoy this,* the note said, and it was signed Elise Pangborn. Swabbing sweat from my forehead with a hand towel, I plugged the unlabeled disc into a viewer and sat down to watch it.

The screen dissolved with static, cleared, and I found myself

looking at a black and white image of a hotel room, obviously pho-
tographed by hidden microcam. At the bottom of the screen, the
time and date of the recording glowed—eleven thirty-seven P.M., two
days previously—but I barely noticed them. I was watching the two
women writhing in the bed. Their intertwined images possessed
none of the self-conscious histrionics I have come to associate with
professional pornography, and the uninhibited spontaneity of the
participants, together with the unaccustomed thrill of voyeurism,
made the whole experience simultaneously disturbing and arousing.
I had watched for some time before a shift in positions revealed the
dark-headed slim woman as Amanda Brewer, her heavy blonde part-
ner as a trusted advisor. I wondered briefly why Pangborn had bothered to send this to me—and then I stood up and turned the thing
off. I had not made love to a woman since Anna's death, and even a
cold shower was not enough to drive those images from my mind.

After I had dressed, I walked across the corridor to the suite of
rooms Truman occupied. He answered the door with a reader in
one hand—some tech journal I imagined—and he did not seem
pleased to see me. I had never been to his suite before, and his few
visits to my rooms had been limited and purposeful in nature.
Nonetheless, he invited me in and waved me to a chair in the sitting room.

"What can I help you with?" he asked.

"Information," I said.

"What do you want to know?"

"I've been looking over the Brewer dossier. It's . . . pretty thorough."

"And?" He studied the reader with one eye.

"And I was wondering how they chose me?"

Truman laughed and set the reader aside. "You're wondering if
they invaded your privacy the way they've invaded hers."

"I guess."

"Rest assured, they did. They invade one's privacy with
impunity."

"I was wondering, too, how you knew I would go along with
this."

"Well, we didn't know, obviously."

"But you had a good idea."

"*They* had a very good idea." Truman propped his legs atop the
coffee table. "Your psych profile was exhaustive and unambiguous,
Stern. They know you better than you know yourself. I remember
two especially pertinent remarks."

"And those are?"

"That you've perfected the art of rationalization. And that you are a very angry man."

I didn't reply. I like to think I know myself, and I was trying to reconcile Truman's description with my own self-image. Truman picked up the reader.

"Why are you involved?" I asked.

He pretended to study the reader. "I'm the brain."

"Pure research?"

"That's right, it's the glorious quest for knowledge. That's why I'm here, at the very center of the scientific universe."

I felt a surge of almost atavistic dislike for this condescending man. I could not help myself. "Have you ever read anything about the scientists who built the bomb?"

He set the reader down to glare at me. "You're hardly in a position to second-guess me."

"I'm not in a position to second-guess anyone," I said, "but neither are you."

Though his features colored, Truman met my gaze squarely for the space of a long heartbeat. When he spoke, his voice was icily cordial. "Well, now that we've clarified that, I think you were just leaving?"

"I want to know where Pangborn stays. How come her rooms aren't on this corridor?"

"I wouldn't get too interested in Pangborn."

"But where does she stay?"

"You have to be kidding."

"No."

"Are you blind, Stern? She stays with Thrale. She sleeps with him, she eats with him, she shoots him up when he needs a fix."

"Thrale struck me as fairly independent."

"I hope you're a touch more observant when it comes to Amanda Brewer. Take a look at the man's eyes. They practically glow." Truman sneered. "There are three things that keep Napolean Thrale going. Morphine, Elise Pangborn, and the precious military discipline that allows him to pretend the first two don't exist. Anything else?"

I stood to go. "No, I think that'll do it."

And then there was the dream.

It began a week or two following that glimpse of Thrale and Pangborn as they looked out over the Bay from the office windows, several nights after I had found the unlabeled videodisc waiting in my room. It had been an especially long and frustrating day in the lab. I seemed to have hit a plateau in my work with the hostmech—I could control the thing, but only with a kind of shambling clumsiness akin to that of a wind-up soldier—and I was growing equally tired of Truman's smug condescension and Pangborn's humorless efficiency. I had been drinking—just three or four rum and cokes, nowhere near what I had been drinking in the days and weeks following Anna's death—but enough. Enough to get that pleasantly numb sensation in the nerves of my face, enough to derive a kind of giddy adolescent excitement from replaying the disc of Amanda Brewer and her blonde girlfriend.

It must have been around midnight when I finally snapped the viewer off and stumbled through the darkness to the bedroom, already dreading the day to follow. During the endless vigilant nights of my stay in Napolean Thrale's home I had mastered a certain technique of staring wakefully out through the bedroom windows at the moonlit surf that crashed against the broken beach beyond. It was not exactly a cure for my insomnia, but it was a relief nonetheless, for after an interval of timeless staring, it seemed as if my consciousness was drawn from my body and cast out over the restless ocean. I can recall very clearly the dark house receding around me until there was only the heaving water, moonlight coruscant along the foaming edges of the waves, and my own consciousness, wheeling free above the swells, like the lone gull I had seen my first day at Thrale's, haunting the vacant sky.

This night, however, there was no need for fantasy. I fell immediately into fathomless drunken sleep, and somewhere in the poisonous hours before dawn, sleeping turned to dream.

It began with physical sensation—the rocking jostle of an ATV as it ripped a path through the lush undergrowth of the jungle. I sat far back in the cramped vehicle with a support technician, the anemic sheen of her complexion sporadically flushed by the ruddy pulse of the emergency beacon. Through the carbonized stink of overtaxed equipment and the intermingled stenches of sweat and mold, the electric tension that preceded combat was palpable. The air rang with the cacophony of the vehicle jolting over rough terrain and the constant chatter of the driver as he relayed position markers to HQ. With a metallic screech of protesting gears, the vehicle ground to a halt.

In the sudden silence, I could hear the distant babble of the radio, the hiss of pressure valves, the surging boom of blood through my temples.

"We're here," said the tech in a somehow familiar voice, dopplered with the agonizing distortion of dream.

The emergency beacon pulsed red through the interior, and in the succeeding gloom, the driver turned to face me, his flesh waxen as that of some cave-dwelling amphibian in the green backwash of his tactical displays.

"It's time," said Napolean Thrale.

Even as I opened my mouth to protest, servos whined, and the helmet array was lowered into place. I felt the needling lance of the probes in the flesh at the base of my skull and then the swift painful jab of the hypo as the tech injected the neural buffer.

In the moment before the tech established the interface, I listened to Napolean Thrale chant maniacally—"*Let's go, let's go, let's go*—"

—and then I was plunged into night and silence, all tactile sensation obliterated. Ghostly telemetry flickered in the darkness; with a *woosh* of hydraulic pressure, a door hissed open in the metallic belly of the ATV.

Jungle.

In my dream, I was riding the spider, chasing the beacon of an intelligence comsat through the labyrinthine jungle. Luminescent tactical data flickered at the periphery of my vision. Antediluvian vegetation blurred by on either side. Small terrified creatures flashed through the tangled scrub. The forest reverberated with the raucous complaints of brightly plumed birds, the thrash of contused undergrowth.

How I loved the hunt.

I had always loved it.

Razored mandibles snapped the humid air as I drove the spider through the shadowy depths, emerging at last through a wall of steaming vegetation into a hotel room, dropped whole into the tangled Mato Grosso.

I stopped the spider short. Servos whirred. High-resolution cameras scanned the area.

The sun penetrated the clearing in luminous shards. The jungle symphony swelled into the stillness. Two women writhed on the bed, oblivious to everything but one another.

"It's time," said the voice of Napolean Thrale.

I urged the spider forward. Whiskered steel legs clawed the moist earth, the bed-sheets. Just as the mandibles closed about their fragile bodies, one of the women turned to look at me, her features contorted in the involuntary rictus of orgasm.

She wore my daughter's face.

I screamed myself awake, sitting upright in the soured sheets, my penis like a stiffened rod against my belly.

*   *   *

On the eve of the assassination, I spoke with Napolean Thrale again. It was night, the room incandescent with light. I could see the four of us in the reflective sheen of the windows, the Bay invisible beyond a mirrored tableau executed on the template of our meeting two long months ago.

Napolean Thrale sat in his wheelchair, his hands flat against his desk. There was a preternatural stillness about him, as if he had been hewn from stone. Only his mouth moved as he directed his attention to Truman, sitting restlessly on the couch by Pangborn. "Is everything in readiness?"

"I suppose."

Thrale shifted in his chair. "Let's hope so. We have a unique window of opportunity. Brewer leaves her father's home to return to North Carolina in three days."

Pangborn glanced at her clipboard. "Our people in D.C. tell us that Brewer usually leaves the grounds to jog between five and five-fifteen A.M. She returns to breakfast with her father at six."

"There won't be anyone else in the house?" I asked.

"Servants. Hanson's wife should be sleeping. As we had expected, Brewer's husband remained in Asheville. He doesn't care for the in-laws."

"Brewer runs the same course every day." Thrale touched a button and a holographic map appeared over the desk. A thin purple line stenciled in Brewer's route; a cursor pulsed over one isolated stretch of road. "A sniper will be waiting here. The hypodermic dart will be less painful than a bee sting. She'll brush it away. As soon as the nanomachines reach their activation points, she's all yours."

The map disappeared.

Truman stood abruptly and crossed the room with the jerky movements of an automaton. Momentarily, I met Thrale's glassy eyes over the expanse of burnished desk, and then Pangborn began to speak again.

"There are some things we should go over if Dr. Truman feels up to it," she said.

Truman turned. He had gone very pale. "For God's sake, we've gone over this. This is hardly necessary—"

"It is quite necessary," Thrale said. "We must be sure that every variable has been considered. Please join us."

Truman returned to the couch and sat down, clasping his hands between his knees.

"Let us consider the technical limitations," Thrale said.

"He knows the technical limitations."

Pangborn sighed in exasperation. "The link will last only twenty minutes at most. It's best if you can time it just before the interface decays," she said. "That way you won't have to deal with the mess."

"After the objective has been accomplished—and make sure that it has been accomplished, Mr. Stern, it will not do to have the man survive—afterwards, you will proceed to the parking garage in Baltimore where the van will be met by a disposal team. Three cars will be waiting there. You are free to go wherever you wish. Do not return here."

"And the money?"

"It will be transferred to your Swiss account." He allowed himself a grim smile. "Is there anything else?"

No one spoke.

"Then perhaps you should get some sleep. You leave well before dawn."

There was no sleep.

Truman appeared at my door not ten minutes after the meeting. I showed him into the sitting room.

"I don't know," he said. "I don't know about this."

"About what?"

"This whole thing." He snatched a floor plan of the Hanson home from the end table and began to turn it in his hands. "I'm having second thoughts."

I thought of that first interview, of the somehow startled expression that had passed over Truman's face when he had finally spoken the words that must have been in his mind, unspoken, for a long time—"They want you to kill him." *They*, he had said.

"It's kind of late now, don't you think?"

"I don't know. Don't you have doubts?"

"Sure, I have doubts."

"We're bound to get caught. There are too many people involved—"

"Most of whom don't know what's going on. Only the four of us know everything."

"People still talk about the Kennedy assassination, even now. They won't let it die."

"But that's not what's really bothering you, is it? Getting caught?"

His fingers trembled as he began to tear the floor plan into long strips. "I read something about the scientists who built the bomb," he said. "After what you said."

"And?"

"Oppenheimer once wrote, *physicists have known sin*, did you know that? He wrote *physicists have known sin; and this is a knowledge which they cannot lose.*"

"I guess we've all known sin," I said.

He continued as if he hadn't heard me, his fingers separating the floor plan into surgically precise lengths. "And Rabi—do you know Rabi?—he said that scientists had abdicated the responsibility that came with knowledge. Do you know what that means?"

He did not even look up, did not want a response. I could sense the frustration building in him the way you can sense a kettle getting ready to boil. His hands flew up in a gesture of futile anger and the strips of paper fluttered to the carpet like wounded doves.

"I know you don't like me, Stern. I haven't devoted much time in my life to making people like me. Maybe that's why I'm here— maybe that's why we're all here. But I'm not saying anything overtly romantic. I'm not saying that there are things we shouldn't delve into."

"What are you saying?"

He leaned forward. "Just that you shouldn't abdicate responsibility. You ought to take some responsibility for the way things are used."

"Maybe that's what we're doing," I said, and that image of Lisette, her cold features disfigured with suppurating lesions while Hanson waved from the links, passed unbidden through my mind. "Have you ever seen someone you love just rot away before your eyes? That's what people like Hanson did before, that's what we have to prevent."

"Is that why you're doing this? Is that really why?"

I didn't have an answer. I just sat there, looking across at him, at his distressed face. "Why are you?" I asked finally, the same question I had asked him before, when he would not or could not answer.

He hesitated. "Nowhere else to go. I was at MIT for a while. There was an incident, an instance of academic dishonesty."

"That's all?"

"I was fascinated I suppose. The technical challenge was intriguing."

"And now you've done it."

"So it would seem." Then, at last, he met my gaze, and his eyes had the look of a hunted animal. "But maybe it's not too late."

"How do you mean?"

"I mean this whole thing is in your hands. Just yours. You can call it off any time—right up to the last moment."

I did not answer. What he had said was true and I had thought of it before and I did not know what to say.

Truman sighed and stood. He paused with his hand on the door-knob. "I just wanted you to think about it," he said, and then he went out and pulled the door closed behind him.

In the night, as I lay restless in the silent bedroom, I heard the door into the corridor open and close gently. I heard the sound of footsteps in the hall.

Pangborn came into my bedroom. In the moonlight her body shone sinewy and lean, almost masculine in its dearth of flesh. When she kissed me her tongue was rough, the sex that followed brusque and fierce, contusive as an act of violence. Afterwards, we were silent for a long time. When at last she spoke, the dry sandpaper rasp of her voice in the gloom was almost shocking. In all the time I had known her, not once had she violated her iron reserve. Not once had she revealed a single vulnerability.

"I was in Brazil," she said now, "I saw my fiancee die."

I did not have to ask her how, for though I had not recognized it, I had seen it a hundred times when I returned her inscrutable gaze. It is astonishing to me how people live through fracturing events, how afterwards they piece together a life from the shards, how those lives are like houses built on unstable foundations, sliding irrevocably into the past.

"Do you think of them often?" Pangborn asked. "Your wife and daughter?"

I thought then of all the times I had lain awake in this very room, staring wakeful at the ceiling, wishing to commune with the dead. "Every day," I said.

She nodded, moved close against me, and sometime in the night I felt her slip away into sleep. But I did not sleep; I could not, for fear of dreaming. I lay wakeful through the night, watching the surf, relentless along the shattered rim of the continent, and at some point it seemed as if Pangborn and the bedroom, the house itself—everything—began to recede slowly into the blackness, and there was only the night and the restless water, and my spirit like a seabird, hunting the endless dark.

At four A.M., two long hours before rush hour began, the Beltway was virtually deserted. The van's headlights sprayed diminishing cones of incandescence across the southbound lanes. Occasionally, eighteen wheelers lumbered out of the fog like the unquiet spirits of prehistoric beasts, and once an ambulance whizzed by, its revolving lights slashing bloody streaks through the darkness.

Pangborn drove, her knuckles blanched around the wheel, and I rode beside her. Truman had been waiting for us when we slipped out to the garage earlier that morning, his eyes red-rimmed and bloodshot. Now he rode in back, silent, secreted with the equipment behind the dark curtains that occluded the van's interior.

Pangborn steered the van from I-495 to a secondary highway. Yellow earth-moving machinery had been abandoned by the exit, and the van jolted over a patch of rough road, reminding me of the dream, the jolting ATV, my daughter. Then we were speeding through residential areas on the outskirts of the city. The sky began to brighten, lights to gleam in the small houses that scrolled by the windows.

"Nervous?" Pangborn asked, her voice low-pitched.

"Absolutely," I said. I thought of Lisette, dead four long years; of Anna, dead two.

Pangborn took us through a series of turns, over a concrete bridge where brown water churned sluggishly through a narrow channel, and onto a broad avenue lined with stores, shuttered behind aluminum security gates.

I thought of Pangborn, of last night, what it might have meant. "The disc," I said. "Why did you send me that disc?"

Her eyes didn't deviate from the quiet streets. "It's going to come in handy. It's going to put her away."

"But why did you send it to me?"

She spared me an annoyed glance. "It was part of the dossier, that's all."

"The note wasn't part of the dossier," I said, sipping coffee from a Styrofoam cup on the dash.

Pangborn braked at a yellow light, signaled left, and gazed impassively into the gray morning as the light cycled through to green. "I don't know why," she said, touching the gas. The van surged through the intersection and her face took on an uncommunicative facade, the mental equivalent of the security gates protecting the stores we had passed.

Once again, I had the feeling of being at the center of some elaborately choreographed dance, each seemingly random move leading into the next series of positions. *Your psych profile was exhaustive and unambiguous,* Truman had said, and now it occurred to me to wonder what else that profile might have said. That they could best approach me with simultaneous appeals—to an ethical rationale, to the poisonous anger I nursed within? That Pangborn's disc and the seduction that followed were both avenues to an unacknowledged need, some fundamental weakness at my core? That I loved the hunt?

That I missed it?

Glancing out the window, I saw that we had entered a neighborhood of tree-lined boulevards littered by drifts of fallen leaves; wide sidewalks; and large houses set well back from the streets, half-hidden beyond screens of shrubbery, beyond walls and verdigris-stained fences. Pangborn pulled the van into the shadow of a brick privacy wall, some fifty meters short of a pair of blackened iron gates, and killed the engine. Truman brushed aside the curtain to peer out between us at the breaking day.

Presently the gates swung open and Amanda Hanson Brewer emerged. She did not even glance at us as she turned away and moved down the street at a slow jog, her breath smoky in the chill air.

This is where it had brought me, that intricately choreographed dance of sorrow, grief, and need that Pangborn and Thrale and even Truman had swept me into. I had come to kill a man, I had one million new-American dollars securely stashed in a numbered foreign account, and I could not get Truman's words out of my head: *This whole thing is in your hands,* he had said. *You can call it off any time, right up to the last moment.*

The interior of the van was dark and still, lit only by the pale glow of the instruments. I lay uncomfortably flat, strapped to the narrow table, Truman's and Pangborn's faces seeming to float over me, pale ovals as alien and disembodied as abandoned Halloween masks.

The radio crackled and a voice I had never before heard and could not identify, said, "Green light."

I heard the hum of machinery as the helmet descended from the shadows above, and it occurred to me suddenly that I was infinitely vulnerable, that it was possible, even likely, that I might never wake up. In the last instant before the helmet cut off my field of vision, Truman leaned forward, his eyes wild and uncertain. "Twenty minutes," he said, and I found myself hoping Amanda Brewer would be wearing a watch.

Then darkness, the faint uncomfortable sting of the neural

probes, a more painful jab in my upper arm followed by the hiss of the hypo.

"Good luck," Pangborn whispered, and in the moment before all feeling departed, I felt her squeeze my hand.

Vertigo.

I fell into a void of night.

Presently, my vision cleared. I was leaning against the bole of a large tree, bark rough against my back, breath fiery in my lungs. Dry leaves drifted over my sneakers. An unusually sharp smell of perspiration tickled my nostrils. I could feel the sting of sweat in my eyes, the tight pleasant pull of taxed muscles in my thighs and buttocks. I could feel the soft weight of breasts, round and unaccustomed, and I had to stifle an urge to touch them.

Time, I thought, time.

I glanced at either arm—thin, downed with light brown hair—to see if Amanda Hanson Brewer wore a watch when she exercised. She did not.

I looked around to get my bearings. I stood on a quiet tree-bordered street about half a mile from the senator's home. I could not see the van. I could not see my body. I could see nothing but this strange street, strange trees and leaves, and lucid morning light, the whole scene tinged with slight distortion, colors subtly wrong, as if I were staring through an imperfect lens of ice.

And I was running out of time.

Telling myself to ignore the panicky syncopation of Amanda Brewer's heart, I took a halting uncertain step. Just like the host-mech, I told myself, and I took another step, almost stumbling. Then I had the rhythm of it, the old rhythm of a well-toned body—anybody's body—in accustomed exercise. The soft beat of feet against the sidewalk, breath coming easy now, pulse steadying down.

What could she be thinking?

But it did not matter. An old lesson from the marines came back to me, a lesson from the hunt: you must never empathize with the enemy. You must kill him without fear or emotion, because if you do not he will certainly kill you. You must believe this, even if it is not true.

I turned a corner and began the final leg of the run, in the shadow of the privacy wall. Muscles pulled and loosened easily. I had the rhythm of it now, though I drove her hard out of fear of time. She would be sore later.

It would be the least of her worries.

I kept her head lowered, her vision on the pavement a few steps ahead of me (her? us?). *She must not see the van*, Pangborn had said, and she did not, though I could sense it as I passed.

Then the gates, and then we were within.

I did not know how long I had stood beneath the tree, confused, exploring the sensations of this new body. I might have ten minutes left, I might have five.

I crossed the manicured lawn at a jog, twisted the knob on the front door, and stopped dead. The door was locked. I paused, panting, and thought back on the run. I could not remember the jingle of keys. The running shorts had no pockets. No key was strung around my neck.

I felt a rising wave of panic—*my* panic this time—surge through Amanda Brewer's body, and I forced myself to take long slow breaths. *Think.*

I glanced at my feet, saw the key knotted into the laces of the left shoe, and sat abruptly on the concrete stoop. The laces were double knotted. The manicured nails got in my way. At last I freed the key. Without bothering to retie the laces, I stood, drove the key into its slot, twisted it, and opened the door.

Flat air-conditioned air, tinged with the lemony scent of furniture polish and the faint flowery odor of potpourri, like the smell of a funeral. There was not a speck of dust. No books lay open on tables, no glasses rimmed with ice-melt stood abandoned from the night before. Morning light lanced through windows in clinical shafts, illuminating buttery patches of furniture and hardwood floor.

No one seemed to live there. The rooms were so perfect that velvet rope might have been strung along brass posts to keep you from entering them.

I paused a moment to recall the floor plan of the house. The kitchen and breakfast nook should be in back along this hallway. I could hear faint sounds, the rattle of crockery. I started back, knowing there could not be much time.

The breakfast table was set for two. Croissants lay heaped in a basket in the middle of the table. I could smell bacon frying.

Hanson was not there.

A slim black woman, very pretty, entered the room, carrying a carafe of orange juice and two crystal glasses on a sterling tray. "Your father's having his coffee in the office, Mrs. Brewer," she told me.

I thought about speaking, decided not to risk it, nodded curtly, and left the room. There could not be more than five minutes remaining, probably less.

The office lay on the eastern side of the house, looking over the gardens. I spent two minutes finding it, rapped at the open door, and went in. It was like stepping from an impossibly perfect magazine layout into a real living space. My cursory survey revealed worn leather appointments; books, scuffed in their leather bindings; plaques and awards affixed to one wall; tastefully unobtrusive photographs of the senator with three Republican presidents. I could smell the rich pleasant aroma of fresh-brewed coffee, faint scents of leather and tobacco.

Senator Hanson had been standing at the picture windows, studying the well-kept lawn beyond. He had turned at my knock, and now he smiled, his steaming mug held aloft in his right hand. The morning light revealed his craggy face, still handsome after decades of circumspect intemperance. For a moment he was still, his face half-limned by golden light in a tableau as subtly magisterial as a campaign photograph.

Then he took a step forward. "Good morning," he said, placing his mug on a desk as resolutely untidy as Napolean Thrale's had been obsessively neat.

I crossed the room soundlessly to stand before the desk.

For years I had imagined this moment, and now that it had come, I experienced a sudden reevaluation of all that I had believed, all that I had intended to do. Had I come to kill a man dangerous in his power, or a man who somehow, in my mind, had gotten tangled up with the touch of Lisette's cold hand, the note I had found scrawled on a sheet of paper by the bathtub where Anna had slit her wrists: *Forgive me?*

The senator was handsome and charismatic, and in the long silent interval following his words an expression of genuine concern crossed his face.

"Amanda," he asked, "are you all right?"

At that moment the interface began to decay. Amanda Brewer's fingers twitched with a movement I had not commanded. I had perhaps a moment more, and all I could think of was Truman, his eyes wild and uncertain behind the silver sheen of his spectacles.

"Dad?" said Amanda Brewer—not me—in a voice halting and fraught with panic.

The senator started around his desk, his expression veering from concern to fear. His hand struck a framed picture I had not noticed, and I saw that it was a photograph of himself, triumphant on the links, and that old rage, corrosive as acid, welled up within me.

With a swift movement I swept up his mug and dashed the

steaming coffee into his face. He screamed, took a quick step backwards, and screamed again when I smashed the mug on the rim of the desk.

And then, even as the interface decayed further and dark spots began to expand across my vision, the senator stopped screaming, for I had twisted a razor-edged shard of the shattered mug into his throat.

His fingers clawed at his neck and an almost comic expression of dismay crossed his face. He staggered and collapsed explosively into the windows. I was on him in a moment, sawing at his throat with a jagged edge of glass, and then there was a bright arterial pulse, warm across my hands.

Amanda Hanson Brewer screamed.

I fell into darkness, began the swift vertiginous plunge into myself.

There are any number of reasons to prefer the Cayman Islands to Switzerland, but the principal ones are the bank privacy laws and the climate. The employees of the three-hundred-plus banks on Grand Cayman, the largest and most populous of the three islands, surpass even the Swiss in their discretion, and in the Caymans, taxes are unknown. The days are hot and clear, the tropical humidity leavened by a breeze that sweeps endlessly from the sapphire waters of the Caribbean. On the whole, it is a very comfortable place to hide two million new-American dollars.

From the cottage where I sit and write this, I can see the lucid waters; the surf eternal on the unsurpassed beach; far overhead, some dark bird, turning, turning.

You almost certainly know the rest of the story. You have seen the disc—leaked to the press within hours of the crime—that police officers discovered on Hanson's desk. It was in an open envelope postmarked the previous morning, but I do not believe Philip Hanson had yet seen it. In the long run, it doesn't matter. Rumor has it that prosecutors intend to introduce it as evidence in Amanda Brewer's upcoming trial, but I don't guess that really matters either. It has suppressed the inevitable conspiracy theories; it has given the investigating agencies the motive they sought.

As for me?

Six months on Grand Cayman have left me dark and trim. For a while it was women, always available when one is wealthy. For a while it was rum and Red Stripe beer.

But I cannot escape the dreams. Frequently, it is that dream of the hunt, begun so long ago in the home of Napolean Thrale—riding the spider through the Mato Grosso, the hotel room, the clearing, my daughter's face as the mandibles close about her.

Sometimes—on the good nights—there is another dream. I walk along a broken strand with the sea restless beside me. In the wind that rushes across the water there are voices. I can hear Lisette and Anna, I can hear them call to me.

In the night I sit on the beach and watch the tide break against the shore, and sometimes it seems as if all the world recedes and there is nothing but the night sky and the waters and my spirit, haunting the dark reaches between. Often, I think of Pangborn and Truman and Napolean Thrale. I think of myself, too, and at such moments I cannot help but believe that our lives are like some swift ocean current, bearing us inexorably toward the shattered continent of the past.

The ocean beckons to me.

In a matter of mere moments I will finish this document, seal it in its envelope, and dispatch it to Amanda Brewer's defense attorneys—my penultimate act, perhaps the only one that Napolean Thrale's psych profile could not foresee. The daughters have suffered enough.

And then I will enter the dark water and strike off toward the horizon, where I can hear the voices of Anna and Lisette, calling to me like the sirens of myth. I will have no fear, no regret. I have never much admired assassins.

In Green's Dominion

Midway along the journey of our life
I woke to find myself in a dark wood,
for I had wandered off from the straight path.
—Dante, *Inferno*

1

Come to me—

The voice arose unbidden, coaxing, earth-succored, barely a voice at all: a whisper of wind and trees, a rustle of greenery driving up through rich loam. She saw a dim figure, a shadow moving in the recess of a tangled wood.

Come to me—

More than fifty years had passed. Sylvia slept restlessly and woke with no memory of what had passed in the night.

Even now, it was the voice she heard in dreams.

2

She fooled herself into believing it had started with the incident in the garden, but of course it began before that. With the want of a word, maybe, and maybe before that, all the way back—

—in England, it began in England—

—on the day when she walked out of a classroom for the last time. The incident in the garden marked a turning point, perhaps *the* turning point—yet even then it was the word that concerned her. She had been a connoisseur of words her entire life, reserving for them an appetite usually lavished on more sensual pleasures. It disturbed her that now, here, in this late stage of her decline, she could find no word to describe the state of her soul.

About her physical state, Sylvia had no illusions. She could think of a plethora of words to describe *that*, ranging from the innocuous (elderly and superannuated) to the hateful (desiccated and obsolete, among others). In the parlance of the day, she was a senior citizen; in the secret language of her heart, she was old.

Just old.

But she had no ready language for her soul.

On a narrow shelf in her study stood two slim volumes, her life's work—her *corpus*, she called it in her grimmer moments. A book of poems published when she was twenty-four, hardly more than a girl back from her post-graduate tour of England; a work of negligible scholarship published much later, during her years at Holman, when the ardor of youth had hardened into austerity and the failure of her muse became intolerable. Yet this was not much consolation after all: her past expressiveness haunted her present, coloring these last days with a sour tincture of desperation that only grew more oppressive.

She fidgeted. She could not concentrate. Words seemed to swarm the very air around her, ghostly, insubstantial. And so it went, until at last her discontent entered a more desperate season.

Afterwards, she remembered the moment only in fragments, bright razor-edged shards of perception. The garden behind the house, where the wood encroached in a wild tangle. The April air bright and dense with moisture. A single lonely birdcall.

Crouching there, her fingers knotted around the spade, Sylvia saw how the flesh of her hands had shrunk from the marbled ridges of her veins. Dizziness overwhelmed her. And then the world blossomed with fierce beauty. A fecund vapor breathed from the ripe soil, root woven and strewn with the regenerative fragments of spade-torn worms. Sunlight bathed her in fragrant waves. Her heart lurched. Involuntarily, half-uncertain how to account for her sudden panic, Sylvia cried out, lifted her hands to her face, and saw that the sharp edge of the spade had slit her ring finger. A single ruby droplet fell away. The thirsty earth drank it in.

*   *   *

3

"Horny," said Daphne the next day at lunch.

"Excuse me?" Sylvia placed her sandwich atop a stack of exam booklets and stared at the woman behind the desk.

Thirty-seven, unmarried, dressed in lime-green pants and a baggy cream sweater, Daphne wore her weight like armor, her beauty—which was genuine if unfashionable, the voluptuous generosity of a Renoir—sheathed in smooth protective fat. "Horny," she said once again. "Maybe that's the word you're looking for." She swallowed a spoonful of yogurt and grinned.

"I'm seventy-four years old."

"You want something fancier? Ennui, maybe? Malaise?"

"All I'm saying—"

"All *I'm* saying is, you're human, you've got needs."

"It's more complicated than that."

"Oh?"

"Something happened yesterday." Sylvia shifted on her chair. Daphne's office smelled of books and chalk dust, but Sylvia found it disconcerting all the same. The books had odd titles: *Geographies of Female Desire, Text(SEX)uality: Eros in Post-Modern Fiction*, others. Sex, that rude biological imperative, glistening and organic, thrusting its way even into this sacrosanct retreat.

"What happened?"

Sylvia sighed and looked out the window. Two stories below, students clustered in groups or strolled across the quad toward the library. "Nothing. I was in the garden. I felt a little dizzy is all."

Daphne pursed her lips. She stirred her yogurt for a moment in silence. Then: "You miss teaching, don't you?"

"My life is very full."

"Are you working on anything? Are you writing?"

"Trying," Sylvia lied. And then, an impulse she could not quite define compelled her to elaborate: "I'm trying to write poetry again, but it's not easy. It's been so long."

"I really think you need someone."

"*You* don't have anyone."

"In case you haven't noticed, I'm not conventionally beautiful," Daphne said breezily. "And anyway, I'm not the issue here."

"Am I? Is that what I've become? An issue?"

In the succeeding silence, they stared across the desk at one another. Daphne skated her spoon around the rim of the yogurt cup. "I have this," she said, waving the spoon in a gesture that took in the office, the campus, everything—the entire life Sylvia had surrendered. "Besides, I don't mean a lover, not really. God save us both from lovers. I was just having some fun with you."

"Then what do you mean?"

"You're not getting any younger, Sylvia. At your age, you have to look at life a little differently."

"I suppose you mean I should stop living altogether."

"Don't be ridiculous. All I'm saying is you should slow down a little. You don't need a garden, for example, and certainly not such a big one."

"And if I want one?"

"Of course you want one. But it's not wise. Anything could happen out there."

The wall clock ticked, dividing the silence into discrete segments of discomfort. A chorus of laughter drifted up from the quad. Sylvia began to pack the remains of her lunch.

"Sylvia, what are you doing?"

A spoon clattered to the floor. Sylvia snatched it up with shaking fingers. "What does it look like I'm doing?"

"That's no way to behave—"

"I'm not a child. I'm capable of deciding when my behavior is inappropriate."

"I'm just concerned, Sylvia. I think it might be a good idea for you to hire someone to stay with you, that's all."

Sylvia picked up her lunch.

Daphne stood, looking stricken; her earrings dazzled the room with bright reflective coins. "Sylvia—"

"You were my student once, Daphne. I won't have you speak to me this way."

"Sylvia, please—"

"Please what? We have been friends for years—*friends!* I am an adult, I have a Ph.D., I have written two books. I am not ready to be packed off to the old folk's home, and I certainly don't need a *baby sitter.* I *need* a friend, but I'm not sure I have any." Standing there, clasping her lunch bag to her fallen breasts, Sylvia felt tears start up—

—but no—

—she would not allow herself that weakness. She drew herself erect. "I will not be patronized," she said, and she let herself out of the office, shutting the door quietly behind her.

Half-blinded by tears, she turned toward the elevators, and ran headlong into a wiry young man in faded blue jeans and a tweed sport coat. "Dr. Woodbine," he said, blinking owlishly at her from under a thicket of unruly brown hair, and for a moment she clutched desperately for his name. Robin something, her replacement. He'd called one day to talk about a syllabus he'd been having some trouble with, but otherwise they'd never spoken. Sylvia had never wanted to be one of those hapless emeriti profs who continued to orbit Holman like the cinders of burnt-out stars—hopeless, pitiful creatures—and so she'd broken with the college—Daphne excepted, of course, but Daphne had always been an exception, from the day Sylvia read her first in-class essay and realized what a bright, bright girl she was, this fat unhappy child at the back of her class.

What *was* his name? And then she had it. "Professor Green. I didn't see you."

"I know. You had a real head of steam up there. Say—" He looked at her closely. "You all right?"

"I'm fine," she said. She waited for him to step aside and let her pass, but he only stood there, fidgeting, his mouth screwed into a thoughtful grimace. After a moment, she said, "Are you settling in here at Holman, then?"

He rubbed his face. "Oh, yeah, yeah I am." He laughed nervously.

"Is your semester going well?"

"Great. I meant to thank you for your notes by the way. The ones on Capellanus?"

She wasn't sure why he had phrased this as a question.

"Daphne—Dr. Maclean—said they'd help," he went on, "and she was right. Dr. Maclean, I mean."

"Yes. Well. Always glad to help. If there's anything else I can do—" She lifted her eyebrows.

"Right. You bet."

He ran a hand through his thatch of hair, started to speak, reconsidered.

"I'll just be going then."

She stepped past him and moved toward the elevators, conscious of his eyes upon her back, conscious also of Daphne's closed door. She was obscurely hurt that Daphne hadn't—

"Dr. Woodbine."

She turned.

"There is one thing actually. You could do to help, I mean." He touched her elbow, drawing her into the alcove by the stairwell. He stood there, bouncing uncertainly on his heels.

"What's that?"

"It's about Daphne? Dr. Maclean?"

"Yes."

"I— Well, I couldn't help noticing that you're friends, the way you come up and have lunch with her every Thursday?"

"Yes. Daphne was my student, here at Holman actually, years and years ago."

"Right, well, what I was wondering, see, was, is she . . . you know, seeing anyone?"

"Daphne?"

"Yeah."

She hesitated, a wave of obscure emotion welling up within her. The alcove seemed oppressive suddenly, crowded with Green's nervous energy. She could smell him, a faint woodsy scent of coffee and something else, something earthy and organic, as if he'd broken a light sweat beneath his clothes. Not unpleasant, but too much somehow. Somehow overpowering.

"No," she said. "Not that I know of."

"Oh great, that's great. You don't think she'd be . . . you know—"

"Really, Professor Green, I can't speak for her."

"Yeah, I know, right." He paused. "Well, if you wouldn't mention this to her—"

"Of course not."

"Thanks, then," he said. He nodded, lifted his arm as though he wanted to shake hands, and then drew it back. A moment later, he was gone. She stood there a moment longer, catching her breath, and then, hearing a door—

—*Daphne's door?*—

—open in the hall, she ducked into the stairwell and started home.

Which was a mistake.

In the dank, cigarette-smelling stairwell, memory hit her dead on, like a truck. Sylvia stumbled, her heart racing. Her lunch sack slipped away, and she clutched at the iron rail as if it could anchor her in the moment. A dizzying bank of vertigo rolled over her.

Then, one hand clenched at her breast, Sylvia settled back into the present. Blood throbbed at her temples. The door eased shut behind her with a pneumatic hiss. She gasped when it clamped into its metal frame with a boom that scaled the risers.

It might have been a prison door.

In the silence that followed, she felt her dry lips—unwilled, unwilling—shape his name. "John." It was the name of a stranger. "John."

Forty-three years. Had it been so long?

4

She had known him before they became friends—she'd met him when she interviewed at Holman, they'd exchanged pleasantries in the mailroom. Once they'd spoken at a party, but only once; Sylvia usually came to parties late and left early, and John Thistle—she noticed—rarely came at all. He was pleasant but aloof, a bit forbidding. An air of old catastrophe clung to him, something too terrible for words.

Their first memorable encounter—unforgettable to her, anyway—had come her second year at Holman, on a Friday night. Returning to campus late to collect a forgotten book, Sylvia had come upon him unawares. He hadn't seen her, and afterwards she'd been grateful, for there had been about him an aura of privacy she was loathe to disturb.

She had been striding down the darkened corridor with the stealthy haste of a woman at night, alone and apprehensive, when she came around a corner into a wedge of golden light. She stopped abruptly, and without pausing to wonder why, stepped back into the shadows.

The light radiated from John Thistle's half-open office door, and that in itself—even on a Friday night—was not entirely unusual. Pulling into the gravel lot, Sylvia had noticed two or three lighted offices in the dark facade of Ayers Hall. What was unusual—so unusual that she could not forget it—was that John Thistle wasn't *doing* anything. Not reading or making notes, not staring pensively into the dark well beyond the window, not even sneaking a flask from an open drawer.

Just nothing. Nothing at all.

Through the open door, Sylvia could see a wall of books, a length of checkered tile, a desk, barren in the glow of the reading lamp. Thistle sat stiffly, his hands splayed on the desk, his tie loosened. His rough-hewn face, thrown half into shadow, was utterly still, but it was the stillness of becalmed waters, where dangerous currents churn the depths. His hair tumbled in untutored rings over his collar, but there was nothing of vanity in it—a want of female attention maybe, or the riotous vitality that radiated from the man even in repose, but nothing of vanity.

From the corridor, Sylvia watched for an instant, afraid to breathe. Still he did not move. He merely sat there, patient and enduring as an oak, with something of an oak's weathered dignity.

A terrible certainty possessed her: he would look up, he would see her standing there in her white dress, ghostly in the shadowy corridor. And though she could not imagine why the idea of such a confrontation might disturb her, it did. It disturbed her very much. She spun silently and fled, her traitorous shoes ringing down the tiled corridor, and then the stairwell, these same torturous stairs, and out, out into an October night chill with rumors of winter.

Now, standing in the same stairwell, breathing in the same odors of smoke and damp concrete, her hand curled about the same cool railing—all things being the same, feeling the same—now, this incident flew back to her, palpable as a pressed rose—

—*a leaf*—

—between the pages of a dusty book.

Forty-three years.

Sylvia knelt to retrieve her lunch sack, but she could not shake the feeling that she had somehow stepped into the past. The recollection had a brittle clarity, a disquieting immediacy she associated with senility. She thought of her grandmother in her dotage, chatting tranquilly to people decades lost.

Shaking her head briskly, Sylvia descended the stairs with a swollen-legged old woman's gait. And though she believed she had quite overcome her confusion by the time she emerged from the stairwell and stepped outside, she was distressed to discover there not the crisp October night she had half-expected, but only April.

5

A hawk circling far overhead, a distant speck against the blue, spring sky, might have observed her: an old woman fleeing from the little cluster of buildings where she had passed her working life (what kind of life? at what price?); an old woman threading the currents of young people who flowed down the shaded walks, their chatter rising to these rare altitudes as a faint faraway cacophony, mere human noise; an old woman passing now the brick clocktower where the hawk had lately roosted, slipping now beneath the vast canopies of the centuries-old oaks, where lovers lazed this bright April noon, careless of their studies; an old woman moving at last into the town itself, Holman, like the college, with its quaint brick sidewalks, its tiny business district (a grocery market and a bookstore and a strip of bars just below Fraternity Row), its winding streets, and (had the hawk known to look) the old woman's rambling Victorian farmhouse, swathed in spring finery at the very edge of the deep wood. Higher still, the hawk might have seen the town entire: a small place fast in its bowl of hills, tethered to the bustling world beyond by a few narrow strands of gray concrete, cracked and weather pitted, rent by the deep-thirsting roots of the great trees, the wild wood, the ancient forest rising up to hem the town in, to surround it, to envelop it with the threat and promise of an older world, the powers and dominions of a world that could be beaten back, cut down, that could be paved over and driven into submission with enough vigilance and determination, but that would ever and again reassert its presence, in the shriek of the hawk itself maybe—

—*come to me*—

—drifting down the wind, or in the first blade of grass to thrust through the frost-heaved macadam of some abandoned parking lot; and, yet higher, reaching now to the very limits of its great wings and peering down through shreds of thin high vapor, might have seen even this disappear, might have seen the very curve of the Earth, might have seen all this and more and still not seen the lie in the old woman's heart.

Lie?

Oh yes, she had lied to Daphne.

Nearly twenty years of friendship in which Sylvia had never been anything less than honest and now, today, she had lied to her twice. She had promised herself all those years ago never to lie to her students—promised to show them the beauty of the world, yes, but to show them the steely truth of it as well, that beauty did not last, and the Earth to its very core was made of iron.

Yet she had lied.

Now, hurrying home, Sylvia passed students lunching under trees or drifting classward, all of them talking, talking, talking. The air swarmed with their prattle and everywhere she looked Sylvia saw girls with careful eyes and voices brassy with false confidence. Girls like Daphne all those years ago—Daphne, alone in the back row, overweight and armored with sarcasm, but bursting with shrewd intellect. Sylvia had vowed to reach her then, had succeeded, and ten years later, when Daphne returned to teach at Holman, Sylvia had vowed to befriend her. She had succeeded there, too. And she had never lied to her.

Until now.

Lie number one: it was just a dizzy spell.

In truth, she could not remember *what* had happened in the garden, could recall only the smell of the air and the slant of sunshine and that strange light which had blossomed in every surface of leaf and earth. And her heart, her heart hurling itself at the cage of her breast like a maddened bird.

Perspiring, suddenly afraid, Sylvia paused in the shadow of an enormous oak arching above the sidewalk. A car slipped by. She swallowed. There were other things she might have said if the conversation with Daphne had gone differently.

The incident in the car, for example. Coming home from the supermarket, at an intersection not two blocks from her house, she had forgotten which way to turn. She had hesitated, frozen with alarm, until the driver behind her touched her horn. Pulling to the curb, Sylvia had watched the other car move past, a station wagon full of kids with a bright red sticker pasted to the bumper: *Choose life.*

Funny how the mind worked. You could forget the most basic facts of your existence, you could forget how to find your way home, but the most insignificant things imprinted themselves on your memory forever. She didn't think she'd ever forget that ridiculous bumper sticker; it seemed in its blind certainty to epitomize the absurdity of her predicament, and she had still been staring at it when she burst into tears. That's when it came to her. A left. A left turn. And just as suddenly the tears had turned to laughter, glassy laughter edged with hysteria, and somehow that had frightened her even more. She might have said *that* to Daphne—but how could she?

So she had hinted only—just a little dizziness—and in the end she had lied.

"I'm writing poetry again," she had said, another lie, except—

—and here, at the very edge of town, Sylvia turned the corner and saw her house, her familiar, orderly house, with flowers, everywhere flowers, tumbling like waterfalls from window boxes, nodding like drowsy old men in planters, bowing in neat rows in bed after glistening bed—

—except maybe that wasn't a lie.

Sylvia paused, mindful of the nagging pain in her joints, and surveyed the house, a hundred years old or older, standing there at the end of its street, encircled on three sides by the forbidding wall of the forest, which she had fought so hard all these years to subjugate, beating it back and back, waging a relentless campaign to establish and preserve the wholesome order of the grounds, their harmony. *Her* house. The yard had caught fire with flowers, the house burned with color.

It was a revelation.

I am still writing poetry, she thought. This house, this garden is my poem.

And once again she thought of Daphne—fat, shy, frightened Daphne who under her guiding hand had blossomed into a woman.

Daphne is my poem.

6

A weed had sprung up in the back garden, there where the wood spilled over into lawn. Had it been there yesterday, when she had knelt in that very spot, turning up the rich earth with her spade?

Sylvia stood in her gardening clothes, rubbing the scab on her ring finger, frightened not so much by the plant itself, though it had a poisonous beauty (she thought of Rappaccini's fabled garden), as by the implications of the memory lapse. Surely she'd have noted the thing if it had been there; surely she'd have uprooted it. She shuddered, recalling the incident in the car, recalling Daphne's words—

—maybe you should hire someone to stay with you—

—bright and hurtful as broken glass.

And if it *hadn't* been there, well, that raised an entirely different issue: how on Earth had it grown so large?

Sylvia stared down at it, erupting from a bed of annuals like a tumor, a thorny hateful thing anchored by medusa coils of encircling runners. Each serrated leaf shimmered blackly, iridescent as the carapace of a fly. A single blossom glistened at its heart: broad petals of midnight purple cradling a greenish black bud already swollen to the size of a man's fist. She could smell it from here, sweet and pervasive as compost, rotting to pulp beneath a humid sky.

7

She dreamed that night of John Thistle.

In the dream, she sat alone in a lecture hall while Thistle stood at the lectern, expounding on Andrew Marvell. She couldn't follow it—something about Marvell's fame as a politician, something about—

But who cared?

There were other things to think about—the sweet breath of wind that blew in through the wide-flung windows (was it a forest that grew out there?); or John Thistle's craggy face (was there another face behind that face?), that wide mouth, those knowing eyes. He leaned forward, gripping the lectern, and she saw the strength rooted in those fingers. Just for a moment she imagined how it might feel to let him touch her, those strong fingers sliding across her flesh . . .

(She felt the forest press close.)

"Miss Woodbine!"

She stretched languorously, knowing how the sweater would cling to her breasts.

"The quotation," he said. "Identify the quotation."

"I don't know. I didn't hear it."

And so he repeated it:

How could such sweet and wholesome hours,
Be reckoned but with herbs and flowers?

Sylvia said, "I don't know. It doesn't matter."

He circled the lectern and paused before her, leaning close. She could taste his breath, a deep woodsy scent, still waters and the shade under old trees. She lifted her fingers to his cheeks (that face, was there another face?) and drew him near, tilting her head to be kissed—

(A green frond brushed the windowsill, listening.)

She woke blushing, and glanced at the clock. It was after four, that dead hour just before dawn.

She threw back the covers and crossed the room. There, in the armchair by her window, wrapped in an Afghan, she gazed out over her garden, toward the thick forest rising beyond it. After a minute, she lifted the sash an inch, just enough to taste the night air, the scent of the wood, a wild earthy odor of leaf rot and hidden pools scummed green with algae.

Memory stirred inside her. She closed her eyes.

She stood at his door as she had stood speechless that October night not so many weeks ago, watching John Thistle as she watched him now, making notes on a legal pad, his face cast in shadow by the reading lamp at his shoulder. At four on Friday afternoon, Ayers Hall stood vacant, redolent of the pine-scented cleanser the janitors used.

She did not know how to begin.

But he saved her the trouble, for abruptly he looked up, sensing her there maybe, poised on the knife-edge of uncertainty. He blanched, his hand trembling as he placed his pen on the blotter.

"Sylvia, you frightened me. For a moment there you reminded me—" He broke off. "Come in, please. How can I help you?"

She sat, smoothing her white dress across her knees. "If you have a minute—"

"Reading for Monday. It can wait."

He closed the book and folded his hands on the desk. She studied them for a moment—the long powerful fingers and the clean nails, the tiny hairs that curled just below the knuckles—and then she looked up. The intensity of his green eyes was ferocious, unnerving. She suddenly understood his reputation: why students notorious for disrespect held him in awe, why colleagues infamous for gossip held their tongues on the subject of John Thistle. Simply put, there was no hiding from those eyes. As he gazed across the desk at her, she felt that for the first time in her life she was being truly and fully seen, as though he could pierce right through whatever disguise she might fling up to protect herself.

"Sylvia?"

"I'm sorry. It's—there was a boy in my office just now, he's not doing well. His papers are—he's practically illiterate—"

"What happened?"

"He *cried*. He wept like a baby, and I tried, I *tried* to show him how he could do better and—" And suddenly she found that *she* was crying, that *she* was weeping like a baby. "I couldn't *help* him. I don't know how to help *any* of them."

She cradled her head in her arms, right there on the desk. Thistle said nothing. He simply touched her, a single hand across her forearm, and not as other men had tried to touch her. It asked nothing of her, that hand. Expected nothing. I'm here, it said. Simple human contact, nothing more.

After a moment, he stood and closed the door. When he sat down again, the hand came back.

"They laugh," she said. "When I turn my back, I can hear them snickering. When I ask a question, all I get is this sullen silence— or something smart. And then they'll laugh again."

He said nothing. The hand went away to peck on the desk. Her skin burned in its absence. Then:

"How long have you been teaching, Sylvia?"

"Two years. I started here."

"Well that's the secret, then. Everybody is bad when they start."

"You?"

"I was the worst. When I started, I prepared for hours. Wrote lectures, rehearsed jokes—*rehearsed* them, can you imagine—and every day I went in and fell flat on my face. I thought about quitting, *would* have, probably, except one day I said, to hell with it. I went into the classroom, I said, 'Are there any questions?' and a moment of shocked silence passed. Then someone—a girl, bless her, I remember her to this day—she raised her hand. From then on it got better. I had bad days, I *still* have bad days, but it got better."

And somehow she found herself laughing—an unpleasant, mocking laugh. "So that's it—I'm supposed to walk in without an ounce of preparation and just wing it?"

He barely raised an eyebrow. "Of course not." He leaned forward, steepling his long hands. "But you *do* have to surrender some control—let the class follow its own course, and learn that it's okay if a question arises and you don't have the answer. It's okay to say, 'I don't know.'"

He was silent for a moment and then he turned in his chair to gaze out the window into the barren November quad. When he turned to face her, Sylvia had the sense that his thoughts had drifted away from her, that when he spoke again he wasn't talking entirely about teaching anymore.

He said, "The secret is not to be afraid."

Not to be afraid.

Yet she had been, hadn't she? Afraid when that first talk led to another ("How are things going, Sylvia?" he'd said in the hall the following Tuesday) and then another, and then, somehow, to lunch, once, twice, three times a week. Afraid when one Friday afternoon he took her walking down the paths that dipped into the deep wood beyond the campus, afraid when somehow, as they dallied beneath the sun-dappled canopy of the forest, her small hand found its way into his large one, his long fingers every bit as strong as she had imagined. Afraid of the way her colleagues wouldn't meet her eyes after they glimpsed the two of them together in the halls. Afraid of what her parents would say (he's old enough to be your father, they would say).

She had come to Holman to get away from all that, just as she had fled to England the summer after she had finished her undergraduate degree—three summers waiting tables and she had blown it all on that vast romantic gesture of defiance. A child's gesture, her father had called it (it's time to put aside this literary nonsense, he'd said, time to take that position in policy adjustment he'd been holding for her). And she supposed he had been right. But it had been necessary all the same. Necessary if she were ever to shrug off the woolen shroud of their expectations. But her parents had followed her even to England, and now she discovered that they had followed her here as well. They were in her head. She knew what they would say without ever having to ask. And in that thirty-first year of her life, her second at Holman, she had feared that, too: feared that she wouldn't ever stop hearing their voices in her head.

Most of all, she was afraid of John Thistle. She feared the feelings he engendered within her. She hadn't wanted him to relinquish her hand that day in the wood. She hadn't wanted him to stop at the hand. And one day—this was at the end of the semester, during the waning days of the year, with Christmas on the horizon and the threat of snow perpetually in the sky—one day he didn't.

She hadn't known he was on campus, hadn't expected him to be. Exams were over. Most of her colleagues had already finished up. But Sylvia took her time about grades, she always did. She relished the process, following the neat lines of numbers as they trundled across the ruled pages of her record book, toting up the passes and failures, the triumphs and the disappointments; most of all, the fact that here, finally, at the close of the year, the turmoil of another semester resolved itself into a kind of order. So there she was, summing it all up, when a shadow fell across her.

John Thistle leaned in her doorway, his great thicket of hair in its usual disarray.

She stood, smoothing her dress.

"Nearly done?" he said.

"Almost," she said, flustered, the memory of their walk in the woods rising up inside her, the memory of her small hand in his.

He came all the way in, brushing the door half closed behind him. "So you're going away for the holidays?"

"I'm not sure yet actually. And you?"

"No, I'll be here. I'll be right here in Holman."

An uncomfortable silence stretched between them.

"Well, I just wanted to say goodbye," he told her. "Happy holidays and all that."

"Yes. Merry Christmas."

He turned to go, his hand gripping the door knob. And then, without really intending to move, she found herself on the other side of the desk, an arm's length away, the pile of final exams forgotten behind her. She could smell him, a faint smoky odor of tobacco, and beyond that, or under it, his own smell: the smell of his flesh, an earthy virile scent, unwashed, but not unclean.

"John?" Her face felt heated.

"Yes?"

"Will you be spending the holidays with family?"

He hesitated. He *always* hesitated when she made some personal inquiry, and in that moment of hesitation, her courage always failed her; *she* always waded in with some other statement. The truth was, she didn't *want* to know about his family, didn't want to know if he even had one, and to forestall his response, she said, "The holidays can be so hard, can't they?"

"Yes, they can be difficult."

"I just wanted you to know how much I appreciate your help this semester. It's made all the difference."

"Yes. I've enjoyed it. In fact—" He hesitated, looking down at her, and she had for the first time that odd sense that another face, a true face, lay concealed beyond the familiar lineaments of this visage which had lately grown so familiar to her: those startling green eyes, that remote and slightly self-mocking smile. "In fact," he said, "you've become quite important to me."

She swallowed, at a loss for words.

Thistle moved toward her, hesitated, and then his hands came to her cheeks. *No*, she started to say, but the word died on her lips. She didn't in that moment need words, didn't for once in her life *want* them. What she wanted, what she *needed*, was this, only this: John Thistle's intense green eyes, his weathered face, his hands against her skin. *No*, she did not say, and lifted her face to kiss him, gently at first, and then with growing hunger, a kind of fierce gnawing privation she hadn't known was in her. She let him embrace her, there in her office with the door half open at his back, let him kiss her, let him bear her back until her hips crashed into the edge of the desk. A stack of exams slid to the floor, and still he kissed her. Unbidden, her arms drew him closer. She could feel the length of his body, sinewy and hard, she could feel one strong hand kneading her breast, the other sliding down across her stomach—

"No," she whispered.

A bright wire drew tight within her. She tilted her hips to meet his touch.

And now, stronger, she said, "No. No, John, no—"

He stepped away, breathing hard. In the next moment she heard it, they both heard it: the clatter of footsteps receding down the hall.

He drew the back of his hand across his mouth. "I'm sorry," he said, but there was nothing sorry in his green eyes.

"Did someone—"

"No."

"Someone *did*, I heard them, *you* heard them—"

"Listen—"

"*You* listen." A fit of trembling possessed her. "You've got nothing to lose here, you've got tenure—"

He stepped forward, enfolding her in his arms again. She didn't know how long they stood like that. Her heart pounded. Her lips felt bruised. She hated him. She wanted him to kiss her again. The trembling passed.

He stepped away. "I'll go."

She nodded. She didn't trust herself to speak.

At the door, he turned back. "Sylvia," he said, "there's nothing to be afraid of." He held her gaze a moment longer. Then he was gone.

And yet she was afraid.

Now, remembering, Sylvia thought, perhaps *that's* the word. Afraid.

She leaned closer to the window and gazed past her ghostly reflection into the night. The garden was a well of shadows, the trees black against the opalescent sky. In the distance, Holman's clocktower sounded out the hour—five musical chimes borne to her through the still April air. Dawn was breaking, and it was easy enough to imagine the town bestirring itself for the day, kids waking and dogs pawing at back doors while their owners sat yawning in sleep-churned sheets. Soon newspapers would be thumping against porches; soon the first birds would test the dew-sodden air.

But nothing stirred here, not in this narrow crepuscular bedroom.

Sylvia leaned her head against the glass as dawn poured slowly across the lawn, drenching in nacreous gray the ranks of flowers, the careful symmetry of the garden paths, the sundial in the grotto where she sat most evenings, there on the moss-grown bench, where the little fountain chattered and danced. The garden comforted her somehow, its harmony, its simple human order.

But this too would pass. That was the bitter truth of the thing: *everything* passed, even this simple garden. She could see how it would happen, how the forest would creep in, gradually at first—here a questing vine, there a stray sapling—and then faster, until it reasserted its dominion at last. A season, that's all it would take. Weeds would crowd out the delicate annuals. Vines would shatter the stone pedestal of the birdbath. In the end it would swallow even the house. Maybe some wanderer would stumble across the site centuries hence. Catching a flash of sunlight in the weeds, he would hunker down and fish from the tangled undergrowth the brass compass of the sundial. He would scrape away the crusted residue of years and hold the tarnished face to the sky, wondering how such a relic had come to be here, in this wild place.

It had begun already, she saw. There at the back of the lot, where the woods had encroached upon her handiwork, where the vile weed lifted its face to the morning sun. She could see it. She could see the thing from here, visibly larger, impossibly larger, squatting like a toad amid her drowsy banks of annuals: the bowl of midnight purple petals and the great greenish-black bud at its heart, a strangely beautiful seedpod the size of a severed head.

Her heart stuttered as she stared out at the thing, transfixed by horror. A scrap of some old nursery rhyme lodged in her mind—

—*Mary, Mary, quite contrary, how does your garden grow*—

—and in short, she was afraid.

8

Work was the thing for it. She had that much from her parents anyway, the old Puritan legacy of labor. *Idle hands are the devil's tools*, her father had been fond of saying, and Sylvia had never escaped that principle, not even during her wild flight to England, when she had vowed in defiance to do no work at all and had instead found herself scratching her first poems in a dog-eared notebook, laboring to order and define the rugged Yorkshire landscape, the stone fences hemming in the sheep-mown hills, the stark green line where the heath met the English sky.

It had paid off, that work—paid off when she first held in her hands the slim published volume, and paid off again by landing her the position at Holman when otherwise she might have been forced to declare it all a failure and take a job in her father's agency. And it would pay off, now, too. She could lose herself in gardening and forget everything else—forget John Thistle and the trouble with Daphne and this strange sense she had of being ill at ease in her own skin, at a loss for any word to describe her lot here in this late day, when she should have been well content with the life she had chosen. Work was the answer for it. Through work she would escape it all, even the strange vile weed growing there at the edge of the lot, where the forest began.

Over breakfast she had decided to destroy the thing, to uproot it and hurl it back under the trees, where it couldn't do any damage if it went to seed. But when she stepped out on the back porch just after eight, she saw that the weed had, impossibly, grown larger still. The great purple blossom had turned black, the petals slowly deliquescing. The seedpod glistened in its bed of serrated green-black leaves, a bulging cocoon the size of a watermelon, covered with faint, shiny down. She would have to get the shovel from the garage. She'd have to dig the thing up, she'd do it first thing—

But the strength seemed to have gone from her legs. Sylvia lowered herself heavily to the porch step and sat there a long time, staring at the thing. A fly buzzed in the morning stillness. In the dim reaches of the wood a bird whistled tentatively. The sun crept imperceptibly higher. It must be nearly nine by now, she realized with a sudden pang of longing. She had given it up, she had given it all up: the desks in their sensible rows, the busy hum outside her office door, the security of her nine o'clock Chaucer, predictable as clockwork for more than four decades. Daphne was right: she missed it. How she missed it—

Inside, the phone rang. Sylvia climbed to her feet, gripping the baluster for support, and slipped back through the screen to lift the receiver. The phone brayed once again as she searched for the right button. It had been a gift from Daphne, one of those sleek ultramodern devices with a rubberized antenna (*so you can carry it in the garden*, Daphne had said), and Sylvia had never really gotten accustomed to the thing—

There. She punched the button, silencing it mid-ring.

"Sylvia?" Daphne said.

"Shouldn't you be in class?"

"I've got a minute, I just wanted to call. Listen, about yesterday—"

"I don't have anything to say about yesterday."

"We have to talk about it—"

"I *said* I don't have anything to say."

"Sylvia—"

Sylvia broke the connection. Sliding the phone into the pocket of her gardening apron, she stepped back out onto the porch. The weed awaited her, but she suddenly didn't have the heart to deal with it.

Besides, there was plenty else to do. The bed on the north end of the house needed weeding and she'd been meaning to stake the tomato plants she'd planted in the little vegetable garden at the end of March. Work was the thing for it. And when the phone rang again, just after ten, spilling shrill vibrations through her, she was fertilizing the forsythia that bordered the porch. She jumped, reaching toward her pocket to silence the thing, but then, mindful of Daphne's Friday schedule (Shakespeare at nine, World Lit at eleven), she drew her hand away. She simply stood there, her knuckles white on her clippers, counting the rings. Eleven, twelve, thirteen—

And then it was still.

She sighed, gathered her strength, and went back to her trimming.

She wouldn't think about it. Not Daphne, not John Thistle. Not the bizarre weed. She focused on the tasks at hand, the simple rhythm of trimming and weeding and crushing underfoot the black slugs which feasted on the flowers. At ten-thirty, the phone rang again. Twelve rings. She wouldn't think of that either.

It rang again at ten-forty-five. Again she ignored it.

Yet perhaps they *had* upset her, all those phone calls. Normally, she'd have taken a break around eleven—a glass of iced tea on the porch, a slice of cantaloupe. But today, despite a faint unsteadiness in her legs, she continued to work, obstinately lugging the tomato stakes to the vegetable patch at the south end of the lawn. She dumped them at the garden's edge and began driving them one by one, using the flat of her hammer to pound them deep into the soft earth. Each blow throbbed in the taut muscles of her arm, the tense column of her spine. She paused, panting, and glanced back down the row, each plant bound neatly upright with ribbons of white cloth. The black soil glistened, weedless and moist. Sweat stung her eyes. The sun beat down upon her.

When had it gotten so hot?

She knelt for another stake. A wave of dizziness rolled through her. She levered herself erect, using the stake as a crutch. The world reeled around her, the air suddenly ablaze. The earthy fragrance of the vegetable patch flooded her nostrils: the scent of rich soil and bagged manure, of sun-stroked greenery ripening inexorably toward decay. Her heart slammed against her ribs. The woods loomed against the sky, a green hieroglyph—

—*come to me*—

—pulsing with enigmatic significance. The hammer slipped from her nerveless fingers. She watched it tumble away in slow motion, end over end, and then, somehow, she too was falling, the stake slipping away as the ground lifted itself to meet her. She tried to cry out, but there was no sound, only the rustle of her own body settling painlessly to earth, and then a deep pervasive stillness.

Damp soil buoyed her up. She lay still, staring through a tangle of greenery at one outflung hand. The telephone had tumbled from her apron, a slim white lozenge half hidden by drooping fronds. She would just lie here for a moment, and then she would reach out and pick it up. She would climb to her feet and go inside and pour herself a glass of ice tea. She would make herself a cucumber sandwich, and eat it in the cool shadows of the back porch . . .

An ant trundled up the curving slope of her ring finger, pausing to investigate the scabbed-over wound.

Sylvia took a deep breath. She just needed a minute to gather her strength.

Any time now.

The telephone started to ring. Sylvia closed her eyes.

9

Words had been her true passion, her Avalon, her *axis mundi*.

In her wildest flights of fancy, it was words that snatched her home and centered her, words her compass and her core, her ballast and her anchor (it was words that weighed her down). In the midst of tempests, it was words she clung to; in the whirlwind, it was words; it was *always* words, ordering, imposing, and clarifying words, first orison of creation—

—*in the beginning was the word*—

—and final supplication, the world (the word) itself a kind of poem maybe, endlessly dying, endlessly renewed. Now, groping blindly in the dark, she sought the solace of a word, and they enveloped her, a pathless wood of words, a wild thicket of them, a briar-patch, a thorny labyrinth of thistle and bramble—

—*bramble?*—

—where a clutch of sweet berries grew.

Earth welled up between her toes. She opened her eyes.

She stood before the book shelf in her study. She stood in an abandoned lecture hall, gazing through an open window. (Was it a forest that grew out there?) She stood in the nave of a vast cathedral, in a green and silent space, a canopy of interwoven branches (branches?) arching high above her. A carven figure leered down from a high cornice, a daemonic man with fierce eyes and a face made all of leaves. The thing's mouth opened—

—*come to me*—

—and a plume of greenery spewed forth to wind around her, to enfold and penetrate her. A wild hunger blossomed in her as the branches swept her up, and she cried aloud in ecstasy and terror. The cathedral fell. Roots plunged deep, stone cracked and shattered, the altar fell to ruin. A shaft of moted sunlight pierced the green shade and all the world was forest.

Sylvia pulled down a book and let it fall open in her hands.

(A leaf eddied slowly to the earth.)

She plucked the berries and crushed them to her lips.

10

She woke to flowers, green jacketed and headily aromatic. For a moment the dream—had it been a dream?—lingered: a leaf drifting slowly earthward, the taste of berries on her lips, wild and sweet as wine. A fragment of some old poem—

—*all in green came my love riding*—

—spilled through her thoughts, and then the illusion dissolved.

The flowers stood in a cut crystal vase. When she moved, an IV needle tugged at her arm. Her last moments in the garden came back to her: the cool soil against her cheek, the ant trundling up the curving thoroughfare of her index finger.

She took in the room at a glance, a silent white room with the dead eye of a television peering down from one wall. A faint antiseptic odor hung in the air. It was the kind of room where they brought old people to die, Sylvia thought, and the presence of a roommate—*another* old woman, shrunken and still beneath her covers—seemed to confirm the notion.

She swallowed and turned her head. Daphne stood at the window, gazing out into a dusk-shrouded parking lot. A hard rain slanted past the glass, a root-stretching, flower-budding rain.

She closed her eyes, opened them, and spoke, her voice a dry croak. "Daphne?"

Daphne turned. Her cheeks were flushed, her mascara smeared. "You're awake."

Sylvia swallowed. "Something to drink."

Daphne poured water from a plastic pitcher and held the cup to her lips. Sylvia sipped at it for a moment, and then, feeling stronger, tilted it sharply, drinking greedily. When she finished, she said, "What happened?"

"I found you in the garden. I got worried. You hadn't answered the phone."

"Yes, but— What happened? What caused it?"

"Well, that's kind of a mystery right now."

The breathing of the old woman in the next bed filled the silence. Rain ticked against the window.

Daphne swiped at her eyes angrily. She reached down to take Sylvia's hand. "You scared me, Sylvia. You scared the hell out of me."

"I'm sorry."

"Why did you have to hang up like that?"

"I'm sorry. I was angry."

Daphne squeezed her hand.

They said nothing for a long time.

"That goddamn garden," Daphne said. She said, "Don't you know you're all I have?"

Sylvia couldn't sleep.

The IV line tangled. Rain hammered the window with the steady cadence of a metronome. When at last she dozed, a nurse jarred her awake. Sylvia endured in silence the awkward business of the blood-pressure cuff, the icy disk of the stethoscope in the fold of her elbow.

"The woman in the next bed," she said when the nurse finished. "She hasn't moved."

"I shouldn't think so."

"What's the matter with her?"

"Alzheimer's. It's end stage now. She won't be much company to you, I'm afraid."

"I won't be here long."

The nurse smiled over her clipboard. She made a note on Sylvia's chart.

"Do you know her name?"

"Philbrick, I think. Louise Philbrick." The nurse hung the chart over the foot of the bed. "She won't disturb you, anyway."

"No, I suppose not."

"Can I get you anything?"

"No."

The nurse nodded and stepped out. When the door swung closed, a forest of shadows sprang up. Sylvia adjusted her pillow. The noises of the hospital weighed upon her: the drumming rain and the cool hum of monitors, the moist, steady clamor of her roommate's respiration. Turning, Sylvia gazed at the next bed. The woman lay still, her mouth slack. *She won't disturb you anyway*, the nurse had said, but in fact she disturbed Sylvia plenty, the name most of all.

Louise Philbrick.

Not because she recognized it, either. No, it disturbed her simply for the human face it cast over the shriveled husk beneath the sheets. Louise Philbrick's first kiss, the taste of wine against her parched lips: these things had happened in some irretrievable past. There might have been a Mr. Philbrick once—lovers, children, the thousand trivial events of a human life. And now the name alone survived—Louise Philbrick—sole relic of a history otherwise forgotten, erased as surely as Sylvia had herself erased her chalked notes after a lecture, restoring the slate to a blank and perfect void. *Tabula rasa.* In the end as in the beginning.

Everything perished.

Sylvia closed her eyes. She summoned the steady pulse at her temples, the rhythm of her heart still beating in her chest; she let them lull her into uneasy sleep. She dreamed of the green nave, of John Thistle at her back, his hands upon her breasts. She cried aloud, she turned to embrace him, to pierce the veil at last, to see the face behind his face—

Don't you know you're all I have? Daphne said.

What kind of life? What kind of life?

A leaf drifted from the pages of an open book.

In the shadows, a foliate face peered down at her.

She dreamed of England.

"I want to go home," she told the doctor, Schaper, the next morning.

Schaper was a thin woman, small, aging gracefully into handsome middle age. She gazed steadily at Sylvia, her gray eyes piercing and attentive.

"One thing at a time," she said. "Why don't you try telling me what happened in the garden?"

"I got dizzy, that's all. I woke up here."

"What did you feel beforehand? Do you remember?"

"I remember thinking how hot it was. The heat made me dizzy."

"Nothing like this has happened before? Episodes of vertigo? Forgetfulness?"

Had Schaper been talking to Daphne?

Sylvia hesitated, thankful she'd said nothing about the incident in the car. Her gaze fell on the shrunken frame of Louise Philbrick. "Nothing I can think of," she said.

"What about after you fell? Do you remember anything at all about that?"

"No."

"Paralysis? Aphasia?"

Sylvia pictured the ant ascending the crook of her index finger. She could feel the moist earth against her face. "Are you suggesting I had a stroke?"

"Nothing quite so serious, I hope. Maybe a mini-stroke. Or something called TIA—transient ischemic attacks. The blood vessels spasm in the brain, producing temporary stroke-like symptoms. Or maybe you're right. Maybe it *was* just the heat. We'll have to look into it."

"I want to go home."

"Let's do some tests first. Four or five days, that's all."

Sylvia crossed her arms sullenly. "I want to go home."

Schaper merely smiled.

In the end, it was six days, six interminable days. Orderlies hurried her down echoing corridors and abandoned her to hateful anterooms, with vast engines thundering in the wings. She navigated a bewildering maze of abbreviations and medical jargon (CTs and MRIs and carotid sonograms). She endured a battery of psychological and neurological tests—word analogies, at her age! *Good God*, she wanted to scream at the hapless proctor, *I've written books!* She stared blindly into the pages of a monograph on the Gawain poet (Daphne had brought it). She chafed in the prickly hospital linen.

There was something subtly infantilizing about the experience, as if the entire hospital staff had pooled their resources in a covert campaign of diminishment, a vast, well-intentioned conspiracy to strip her of every token of maturity. One nurse scolded her for getting up to empty her bladder without assistance. Another prodded her to eat her vegetables. And everyone called her by her first name. *You must be Sylvia*, they would say, or, barging cheerily into her room without knocking, *Good morning, Sylvia!*, thus neatly divesting her of two graduate degrees, more than forty years in the classroom, her very status as an adult—of, in short, everything.

Daphne was her consolation. She came every night, lingering until visiting hours closed and the nurses harried her to the elevators. Even then her words seemed to hang in the air, somehow disquieting. *Don't you know you're all I have?*

"I don't want to be a burden," Sylvia told her.

It was evening. Clouds hung like smoke in the square of sky beyond the window, and a gray drizzle fogged the air. It had rained for five days running, one shower after another interspersed with heartbreaking intervals of sunshine. It would be good for the garden, anyway, Sylvia told herself. At least it had saved Daphne the trouble of watering—Daphne, who looked up from the set of quizzes she'd been marking, her soft features puzzled.

"A burden? Whatever gave you that idea?"

"Well, you're here every night, like clockwork."

"I want to be here, I *like* being here."

"Don't you have something else to do?"

There was a brittle edge to Daphne's laugh. She waved the sheaf of quizzes. "I'm doing it *here*," she said. "*This* is what I do."

Sylvia said nothing. She stared at the rain, pattering softly against the glass, in counterpoint to Louise Philbrick's sonorous breathing. Sylvia had tried pulling the privacy curtains around her bed, but that was worse somehow. They obstructed any view of the corridor, entombing her in diaphanous white—and they did nothing to stop the sound. So she endured the other woman instead: the steady cadence of her respiration, the faint moans she emitted when white-jacketed orderlies came to turn her in her bed. The turning didn't stop the bedsores. Sylvia could smell them: a faint rotten odor lurking just beneath the omnipresent scent of antiseptics and industrial detergent. She had glimpsed them once, oozing pits in the woman's untoned flesh—glimpsed them, and turned away.

When she judged a decent interval had passed, Sylvia said, "I saw Robin Green the other day."

"Thursday?" Daphne chewed her pen.

"After lunch."

Daphne arched one eyebrow. "Umm."

"Is he settling in at Holman all right?"

"I guess. Students seem to like him okay." She looked up. "He said your notes were a lifesaver."

Sylvia smiled.

"He's kind of . . ." Daphne hesitated. "Bothersome. He's harmless enough—he's actually kind of nice—but he's always hanging around. He pokes his head inside my office half a dozen times a day."

"Maybe he's interested."

"Yeah, I get that a lot," Daphne said drily. "Interest, you know. From men."

"You needn't be sarcastic."

"Well, come on, Sylvia. He's not a bad-looking man."

"I never said he was."

"He can do better. Trust me. He wants me to be his girl Friday or something, that's all. Or his best friend. You know, the cheerful fat chick who helps him win the movie-star blonde."

"Don't be so hard on yourself."

"I'm not being hard on myself. I'm being realistic."

"You don't have to be alone."

"Do we have to talk about this right now?"

"We don't have to talk about it at all."

Daphne capped her pen and stuffed the quizzes into her briefcase. "Maybe I *choose* to be alone," she said abruptly. "*You* did." She held Sylvia's gaze for a moment, and then turned away, biting her lip.

A minute passed in silence. Sylvia looked out the window. Night spilled through the sky, an inky backdrop to the clouds. She should have known better. It wasn't her place. "Daphne—" she said. And when the other woman turned to look at her, her eyes bright: "I'm sorry, really I am."

Daphne sighed. "No, I am." She stood, adjusting the strap of her briefcase. "Look, we're both a little stir crazy. Let's start fresh tomorrow, what do you say?"

"I'd like that."

Daphne bent to embrace her, and for a moment it was enough: this simple human contact. Sylvia hadn't known how much she'd missed it. And then Daphne withdrew, letting her lips brush Sylvia's cheek before she strode resolutely into the corridor. Her words seemed to echo inside the room.

Maybe I choose *to be alone. You* did.

Sylvia touched a button, lowering the bed, and turned out the light. She stared into the shadows until patterns began to coalesce before her, faces, enigmatic constellations of meaning, a print of leaves against a harvest moon.

Did I? she wondered. Is that what I chose?

11

Christmas had been hard that year. Her father had called, entreating her to come home. "We're not getting any younger, Sylvia," he'd said, and she could picture him in her mind as he said it, cradling the phone against his shoulder as he paced the length of its cord, the desk at his back covered with reports, half-written policies, the actuarial tables he had stared at for so many years he hardly needed them anymore. Thirty-five, male, a smoker? He didn't have to look it up, he knew your odds in his bones. He knew plenty about mortality, her father did, and *she* knew that he was right—none of them were getting any younger. She was thirty-one years old, unmarried, alone. She knew everything she ever wanted to know about not getting any younger.

But all she said was, "Not this year, Dad."

She stayed in Holman and worked—or tried to. She was still trying to write poetry then, knowing with a kind of inarticulate certainty that her muse had died, hopeful that praying over the corpse might somehow resurrect it. She hunched over her desk for hours at a time, tore pages from her notebook by the handful, paced the still unfurnished floors of her old farmhouse until the dark behind the windows deepened to black, when the only sounds were the college clocktower measuring out the hours and the occasional shriek of some small hunted thing as an owl swooped down from the surrounding wood.

One night, desperate to discover the source of that one great flood of words, she plucked her slim volume of verse from the shelf. When she opened the book, a leaf had slipped from between the pages. (It had! She remembered; an old woman in a narrow hospital bed, she remembered at last.) She picked up the leaf—she hardly glanced at it—and tucked it back in place, staring with incomprehension at the poems. She read until the print blurred before her eyes, until the words dissolved into green chaos. And then she closed the book and collapsed into her spinster's bed, where she dreamed a long involved dream. In the dream, a green shade pursued her through emerald depths of forest. She fled before him until the breath burned in her lungs, until her legs ached, until she could taste her own sweat, salty against her lips—until finally she collapsed, exhausted, in a sunshot glade at the very center of the world, in the heartwood itself. Her pursuer appeared beneath the trees, clad all in green, and she stood to embrace him. The face he wore was John Thistle's face, but as she tilted her head to meet his kiss, she saw that there was another face behind his face—

The dream haunted her all the next day—the day the letter came, an unassuming envelope without return address, tucked among the Christmas cards and catalogs. It had been postmarked at the college, and her name and address had been typed neatly, anonymously, on the outside. Curious, she unfolded the single page of white paper within. Two words had been typed at the center of the page: *He's married*. Nothing more. Yet the two words shook her to her very core. Married? In a kind of horror she recalled that moment in her office: the exam booklets sliding unheeded to the floor, his mouth hot against her own, the clatter of footsteps in the hall.

Married?

She crumpled the letter and threw it away—nasty thing (*you're the nasty thing*, she heard her father say)—only to find herself standing over the trash basket not ten minutes later, drawn back to the thing as inexorably as the needle of a compass, spinning and spinning until it settled at last on its own true north, this lodestone lodged like a weight in the center of her breast. She fished it out and unfolded it, smoothing the wrinkles in the paper. She had misread it, surely she had misread it. But the same words—

—*he's married*—

—stared up at her, stark and accusatory. Married. Married. Married. How long did she stand there, clutching the letter, listening to the funereal toll of that word inside her mind? For of course she had known it, hadn't she? She had suspected it all along. She had seen it in the averted eyes of her colleagues. Wasn't that why she'd avoided asking him any personal questions? *Wasn't it?*

Anger boiled up inside her—at herself, at John Thistle. Anger drove her out of the house, and into the twilit streets, coatless and bareheaded, clutching the letter before her like a talisman, impervious to the cold and the strange hard beauty of the night as a horned moon climbed the rungs of heaven. A few crystal flakes of snow began to spin down out of the dark, and as she hurled herself along the empty sidewalks, the street lamps flickered alight before her, like so many penny candles. Later, how long she didn't know, the same anger drew her up short and breathless on the stoop of the house—*his* house, the house she had driven by just once, weeks ago, when her curiosity about his life away from the college became for a moment unbearable. Anger punched the doorbell, and anger held her stiffly as she listened to his footsteps approach the door.

"Sylvia," he said. "What—"

And then he must have seen her, truly *seen* her—slumped beneath the lintel, her face streaked with tears, the single sheet of paper crumpled against her breasts—for he broke off abruptly. "You're not even wearing a coat," he said. "Are you crazy?"

He seized her by the shoulders and pulled her inside, the gesture unaccountably, inevitably, becoming an embrace. They had stepped across some kind of threshold in her office that day, and now there was no going back. "You're freezing," he said, and she felt her traitorous body warming itself in the circle of his heat. She lifted her face and kissed him hard for a moment, helpless to stop herself. Then, with a wrenching effort of will, she pulled away. That's when she saw the woman standing at the end of the hall: a stout, severe woman clad in loose, blue clothes.

Sylvia met her eyes and took a long despairing breath. "I'm sorry," she whispered.

Thistle stepped back, his face darkening. "For God's sake," he snapped to the woman, "put some tea on! Can't you see she's half dead with cold?"

The woman turned, disappearing silently into the kitchen.

"What's wrong?" Thistle asked. "Is it this?" He reached for the letter.

"No." She drew it away, a question rising unbidden to her lips. "That first day, you said I startled you—"

"Sylvia—"

"Why?"

He said nothing. He stood two feet away, breathing heavily. Crockery rattled in the kitchen. His hand lashed out, snatching the letter. He blanched as he read it, livid with anger, shock—something else maybe, she didn't know what, another facet of that dangerous and brooding intensity she had sensed that first night, spying on him from just outside the circle of light. He crushed the letter into a ball and hurled it away.

"So?" he said.

"Why? What did I remind you of?"

"You reminded me of my wife! Is that what you want to hear? You reminded me of her, standing there in your white dress!" He paused, his hands in fists at his sides. In the kitchen, a kettle began to whistle. Someone set it off the eye, and in the ensuing silence, John Thistle said: "You looked just like her, all those years ago."

"I'm not her— I don't want to be—"

"No, Sylvia." He touched her arm. "Sylvia, you've become more than that to me, infinitely more."

Something twisted inside her. Sylvia lifted her hands. She didn't know what she wanted to do with them. A shadow fell across her face. The woman stood framed in the doorway. "The tea's ready," she said.

Sylvia stepped forward. She could hear her father's voice inside her head, telling her she had to apologize, there were lines one did not cross, the man was *married*. "I'm sorry," she found herself saying, and she could hear her father saying it: "Mrs. Thistle, I just want to say how very, very sor—"

"You bloody fool," Thistle said. "She's not my wife. You want to see my wife?"

He didn't wait to hear her answer. Grasping her by the shoulders, he propelled her down the hall, past darkened apertures where furniture stood in shadowy clumps, past the woman in blue—

—*scrubs, they were surgical scrubs*—

—and through the bright kitchen. Another hall, a darkened stairwell. She stumbled, his hands bearing her up. A light glowed on the landing.

"No," she whispered. "John, please—"

An open door beckoned. A faint unpleasant odor flowed out: a floral mask of disinfectant, and below that, permeating the air and carpet, the furniture itself, the ineradicable stench of human waste. Half-revealed in the dim yellow oval of a bedside lamp lay a woman, wasted, shrunken, unformed as a fetus in her nest of yellowing sheets, whatever beauty she had possessed long ago used up. Staring across the room at her, Sylvia realized she could smell something else, too, an odor she would not encounter again for more than forty years, and which even then, in the sickroom she would share with Louise Philbrick, she would not allow herself to recognize. Yet her undermind would know it, for the stench was unforgettable: it was the ripe pustulant stench of bedsores, of a human body churning mindlessly on, year after year, consuming itself by infinitesimal degrees, no longer truly alive but powerless to die.

"No," she whispered. "No—"

Thistle's hand had gone limp on her shoulder. His face sagged. His mouth hung open.

The nurse appeared at the doorway. "I don't think—"

Sylvia lurched past her. She wasn't strong enough, not for this. She stumbled down the stairs and through the kitchen. The house was hot, unbearably hot. She threw open the door and plunged into the night. The moon hung far above, remote, and wreathed in cloud. The snow was falling steadily now, mantling in silver the empty sidewalk, the uplifted arms of trees, the winter-ravaged world. Sylvia hurried toward the street, leaving footprints in the enameled perfection of John Thistle's stoop.

He caught her on the sidewalk, one thick hand clutching at her elbow. "Sylvia!"

She spun to face him, slipping in the snow. "*What?*"

Snow dusted his shoulders, his unruly thatch of hair. His breath plumed in the cold. "Come inside. You'll catch your death."

"I'm going home."

"Let me drive you then—"

"I'll walk."

She wanted to shake herself free of him, wanted to back away, to flee. She could feel the pull of her own house through the wintry streets, the laundry waiting by the ironing board, the dishes stacked in the drainer, the books neatly alphabetized on the shelves her father had built—the pull of everything safe and familiar. Yet something held her there—the desperation in John Thistle's eyes, the memory of his lips against her own—and for a moment she thought the torsion would wrench her apart.

Thistle must have sensed her conflict, for he stepped closer, pitching his voice low. "You've got to listen to me, Sylvia. You've got to talk to me."

"What's there to talk about?"

"I thought you *knew*. *Everybody* knows."

"It doesn't matter. You're married. Can't you see that? You're married."

"Married?" He flung his hands out in frustration. "It's a word, that's all. The woman I married—she's gone. Don't misunderstand me. I loved her, I *still* love her—but she's been gone for years. That woman you saw upstairs, that's just meat, Sylvia, a shell. The woman I married would've hated everything about this—what she's become, what *I've* become. She was so *alive*, and when, when—" He closed his eyes, he took a long breath. "A part of me died with her," he said, "and now, now for the first time in a decade, I feel alive again. It's like . . . it's like spring, Sylvia. And you feel it, too, I can see that you do. She would have liked that. She would have liked *you*. She would have wanted us to be together."

"It doesn't matter," she said. "What you want, what I want, even what she might have wanted—none of that matters. What am I supposed to *be*, John? Your comfort woman? Your lover? Because that's what people will say, isn't it, people like the one who wrote that letter. That's what they're saying already. That I'm your mistress, your— your whore—" She broke off abruptly, the word—

—*her father's word*—

—hanging between them, irrevocable.

Thistle laughed. "So that's what you're afraid of, what the sniveling Philistines will call you—"

"I'm not afraid!"

"—marriage, mistress, whore—those precious words of yours—they're names, that's all. They're only names, Sylvia. Just words, just . . . human noise. For God's sake, it doesn't matter what people think. Don't you understand that? There's nothing to be afraid of—"

Yet she *was* afraid. Afraid of the vast accumulated weight of decorum, the whispered judgments in the hall, the unblinkered regard of her colleagues, her students, the town itself, Holman, narrow and parochial in its deep-cleft bowl of hills; afraid of these strange feelings flaring up inside her; afraid most of all of John Thistle. He stepped toward her, seizing her by the shoulders as if to shake her—

—as if to kiss her—

—and this time she *did* wrench herself away. She stumbled back a step, and then turned, fleeing, slipping and scrambling to her feet with the same clumsy haste. She stole a glance over her shoulder when she reached the end of the street. He was still standing there, a lone figure in the snow-torn radiance of a streetlight, his hands outstretched. She hesitated a moment, and then the wind picked up, hurling a billowing veil of white between them. When it cleared, John Thistle was gone.

She would see him again when the spring semester got underway—they would nod in the halls or speak if chance threw them together in the elevator—but that was professional cordiality, nothing more. Thistle's wife passed away a year later, and from the departmental talk that followed Sylvia pieced together the rest of his story: a pitted ribbon of asphalt plunging through the wood, a car veering across the yellow line, a cataclysm of shrieking tires and metal. John Thistle had stepped from the smoking wreckage unscathed. The other two victims hadn't been so lucky. The drunken undergrad behind the wheel of the other car had died instantly; and John Thistle's wife (her name was Anne, Sylvia learned) would never regain consciousness. So began the long twilit hiatus of John Thistle's life—the endless negotiations with insurance companies, the grim procession of hired nurses, his wife's slow, irreversible decline. And then, twelve years later, on a bright March morning that found Sylvia spading under a patch of weedy back lawn, commencing the garden that would become her life's substitute for the words she had lost, Anne Thistle died.

The day after the funeral, Sylvia stepped into John Thistle's office for the first time in more than a year. "I just wanted to say I'm sorry," she said.

"Yes, I'm sorry, too," he responded, and that was the end of it.

He didn't return in the fall. In the months that followed, Sylvia heard conflicting rumors—a tenured position at another school, a long-delayed European tour—but she never learned what became of him. In the end, it didn't matter. John Thistle had given her permission to fail as a teacher, and that was all she needed to succeed.

In lieu of the life she might had led in his company, she found fulfillment in the classroom. She began to write again; not poetry, but a study of English folklore, the Grail quest, the Fisher King, the vegetation myth of the dying and resurrected god. She cultivated her garden.

A time came when she rarely thought of that December night, of John Thistle standing bereft in that diminishing circle of light or her homeward odyssey through the frozen dark. On those few occasions when she *did* find herself recalling it, she thought mainly of the utter desolation of the journey, the townsfolk enbosomed in their orderly rows of houses as she made her way alone through streets faërie-struck with snow. And of course she recalled the cold. By the time she reached her house, Sylvia's feet were numb. Her ice-stiffened fingers fumbled the door knob; once inside, enveloped in the womblike heat, she burst into tears.

She woke sick the next morning, fuzzy-headed and full of ill humors. The illness lasted into the new year, and then one January morning she woke with the bright, hard-edged clarity that comes in the wake of fever. She put aside her abortive attempts at verse and sat down to draw up syllabi for the spring.

She would never be the same again.

12

Now, an old woman alone in her hospital bed, Sylvia woke with the same adamantine clarity. A handful of images bubbled up from the cauldron of memory and sleep—that dried leaf slipping from the pages of her single book of verse, John Thistle standing alone in the snow-enchanted street—and for the first time Sylvia found herself examining them critically. Where had that leaf come from? Had such a thing truly happened or had she only imagined it, manufacturing it from the private, inarticulate yearnings of her heart— and if she had, why should she have done so? For that matter, why had she turned away from John Thistle all those years ago? What had she been running from?

But it was an image of Daphne that most haunted Sylvia that morning. She couldn't help recalling the look in Daphne's eyes— that brittle veneer of defiance, of perverse pride in isolation—as she stuffed the quizzes into her briefcase. *Maybe I choose to be alone.* What kind of life was that? Sylvia asked herself, and another voice—

—her father's voice—

—answered that it wasn't her place to interfere. *Live and let live,* her father had been fond of saying. *Cultivate your own garden.* And for the bulk of the morning, Sylvia found herself torn between these opposing impulses, certain only that somehow (how?) she had to make things right between them. As it turned out, however, even that simple resolution had to be delayed. Schaper had decided to send her home.

"Home?" Sylvia asked.

"Home."

"But what happened to me?"

"Syncope, etiology undetermined," Schaper said, and it was these words which Sylvia repeated as she slid into Daphne's car that afternoon.

"Syncope whatsis?" Daphne said.

"Syncope, etiology undetermined."

"And what's *that* mean?"

"It means that doctors are like literary critics," Sylvia said. "Whenever they run into something they don't understand, they give it a fancy name. It means I fainted and they have no clue why."

"I don't like the sound of that," Daphne said.

Sylvia didn't like the sound of it either, but she had resolved not to worry over it. She rolled down the window as they slipped through the quiet streets. It was another windy April day, bringing storm clouds from the east. The rain-drenched odor of spring swept through the car, the scent of sap rising to warm cold limbs, of buds swelling into blossom, the forgotten powers of Earth reasserting themselves as the planet swung round once more into a season of warmth and plenty. A season of life. Yes, life. Sylvia drew the scent deep into her lungs, banishing the taste of the hospital, the bland food, the unvaried rhythm of Louise Philbrick's clotted lungs. Of everything.

For now, this was enough.

Daphne insisted on helping her into the house, on unpacking her little overnight bag and turning back her bed. "Let me warm you some soup," she said. "You must be tired."

But Sylvia wanted to be alone. The house had a dusty, airless quality. It felt worse than uninhabited, it felt dead, and she found herself abruptly anxious to reanimate it, to reestablish her presence among the empty rooms. "I'm fine," she said, ushering Daphne toward the door.

"Are you sure you don't want me to stay?"

"I'm fine, really. Go home, Daphne, you have your own life."

"Right," Daphne said drily, and shut the door.

Right.

Sylvia listened to the word echo in the foyer, recalling too late her resolution to mend fences with Daphne, to talk through once and for all this friction which had arisen between them. Now, before she could reconsider the impulse, she flung open the door. Halfway down the sidewalk, Daphne turned, her face puzzled.

"Come to dinner," Sylvia said.

"What?"

"We need to talk."

"So talk."

"A real talk," Sylvia said. "Come to dinner tomorrow. Seven o'clock. We'll talk."

"You just got out of the hos—"

"They didn't find a thing."

"Sylvia—"

"I won't take no for an answer," Sylvia said, and smiling to take the sting out of it, she shut the door in Daphne's face.

13

Alone, Sylvia moved through the familiar rooms. She opened windows and tested chairs. She fondled the personal talismans on her desk as if she had never seen them before—a brooch Daphne had given her for Christmas; the plaque the college had awarded her for excellence in teaching; a reproduction foliate face cast in gray plaster. Sylvia had brought it home from England all those years ago, a primitive ugly thing, yet she had felt its power even as a girl in the gift shop of some otherwise forgotten cathedral; now, lifting the small gray tile to gaze into the thing's daemonic face, a mask of leaves with feline eyes and an obscenely curling foliate tongue, she felt it once again: the power of the green man, that pagan symbol of seasonal rebirth, itself endlessly renewed in the ornate stonework of cathedrals, in altar screens and gargoyles, looming up in the imaginations of those anonymous Briton artisans long after Roman Christianity had laid official claim to their souls.

Sylvia shivered to think of it.

Setting the thing aside, she plucked a book off the shelf: her second book, the study of fertility motifs in English verse, in which the green man had played a small part. Was that where her interest in the thing had started, all the way back in England? She flipped the pages idly and slid the book back into its slot, her fingers moving already, without her conscious volition, to the book's shelf-mate, the little volume of poetry she had published before she came to Holman. She traced the foil title on the spine. *In Green's Dominion.* How long since she had recalled those words?

Thinking now of her dream, the leaf eddying slowly to the floor from between the yellowing pages, Sylvia started to tug the book from the shelf—

And stopped abruptly.

She didn't know why she stopped.

Her heart hammered in her breast. Her mouth was dry.

She was wasting time, that was all. Fussing over things that had happened a lifetime ago, like a senile old woman. She snorted. Dreams and omens at her age, when she had so much to do. She had meant to assess the damage in the garden before dark, and look! —she glanced out the window—already the light was going out of the sky.

Sylvia tapped the spine of the book decisively, edging it back into the company of its shelf-mates. She shrugged on a sweater, and went out onto the back porch. The clouds had closed in overhead, and the breeze had sharpened, combing through the surrounding woods with a sound like rushing water. She could smell rain coming, a looming premonition of earth and wind, wild and untutored.

A week of neglect. How much damage then?

Moving to the edge of the porch, she surveyed the garden. The clematis slumped where the wind had dislodged it from its trellis, and the verbena, untended, had dispatched green scouts to reconnoiter the river-smoothed stones lining the garden path. The rain had nourished everything. A lid of algae floated atop the birdbath, and weeds crowded the impatiens surrounding the sundial. Still-unstaked tomatoes drooped in flourishing heaps by their more disciplined siblings. Looking at them, Sylvia felt a twinge of anxiety. What had happened to her out there?

Syncope, etiology undetermined.

What did that mean?

That the fainting was a mystery, yes. But that merely begged the question. The fainting, the dizzy spells, the memory lapses which she had withheld from Schaper—were they elements of a still larger mystery? Sylvia felt her thoughts swirling into contemplation of that bleak prospect, like water in the mouth of an open drain.

She wouldn't let herself think of it. She wouldn't.

She turned her mind to more mundane questions. The hammer, for instance. Daphne had retrieved the telephone—Sylvia had seen it, secure on its cradle in the kitchen. Had she also retrieved the hammer Sylvia had been using to drive the tomato stakes? It was worth checking, wasn't it?

Pleased with the practicality of this mission, Sylvia went down the steps and strode purposefully into the gloom. Except she wasn't really heading toward the tomato patch after all, was she? She was already steering toward the back of the lot, toward the bed of annuals where the unearthly weed had lifted its face to the sky. She hadn't allowed herself to look at the thing when she stepped out on the porch, but at some mute inarticulate level, she had known she would wind up there from the moment she had climbed out of Daphne's car. She felt suddenly as if her entire existence, the thousand decisions and indecisions of her days, had been nothing more than a long inevitable arc toward this moment in space and time: the garden windy with storm presentiment and the vile weed that grew there, the great malodorous purple-black blossom, the enormous seedpod in its bed of serrated leaves.

She felt its lure like gravity.

Blood thundered in her veins. She paused, lifting her gaze to the thing at last. It was gone—the weed, the bed of flowers, everything. The wood had overrun them. A great thicket of trees loomed against the storm-tossed sky.

Six days, she thought. Six days.

It was impossible, yet it had happened: the wood had flung out an arm, seizing the flower bed and devouring it. As she stood there peering through the gloom at the black line of trees, Sylvia felt a hinge tear loose inside her, the known world fall away. She must have gone mad. What force could impress the wood itself, what power bid the trees unfix their earth-bound roots?

Thunder purred in the middle distance.

Sylvia lurched forward a hesitant step, then another. And then she was moving as fast as her arthritic legs would let her, nearly running. She stooped beneath a low-hanging bough and moved deeper into the stand of trees, sweeping aside drooping veils of damp greenery. The flower bed. It was there after all, in the sheltering dusk beneath the overarching branches: the soft black earth she had worked with her own hands, the red and white blossoms of her impatiens wanly aglisten in the murk. She gasped, staggering forward another step, and then she saw the weed. It loomed before her in all its grotesque beauty, twisted and huge, impossibly huge, a vast sprawling thicket of growth. Lightning flared in the distance, illuminating the thing in bewildering strobic flashes: a hedge of curving thorns, a tangle of stems as thick as her wrist, a rattling symphony of serrated leaves. She paused, breathless. Around her, the trees stood black and straight against the sky, like sentinel giants. My God, Sylvia thought. My God—

The tiny cut on her index finger throbbed in time with her heart. She felt the strength go out of her legs. She went to her knees, one hand cupped before her mouth. And there, concealed in the snarled network of vines, she saw the remnants of the great seedpod. Easily the size of a man now, the thing had split asunder, spilling its broken halves across the rich loam of her ruined flower bed. An amniotic ichor, glutinous and clear, webbed the shattered remnants. At this level, the glade stank powerfully of decay, a teeming compost of putrid vegetation and new growth.

A drop of moisture slipped through the leaves to kiss Sylvia's seamed cheek, and then the rain began in earnest, pattering steadily against the forest canopy. Still she did not move. She just knelt there, the moist earth cushioning her knees, gazing up at the thing, an incoherent rill of thoughts spilling through her mind. Something had been growing inside the seedpod, something which had at last achieved some awful maturity and which had clawed its way free into the light and air, into the commonplace everyday world, and for God's sake, for God's sake, what could it have been—

What could it have been?

She hung breathless on the question, the night quiring around her. Distant thunder clamored in the heavens. Wind sang through the tree tops. The rain whispered down around her, steady and light, spattering against leaf and bark and stone. And now Sylvia wondered if she didn't hear something else too, an almost subliminal rustle of undergrowth—

—come to me—

—that seemed charged with meaning, with purpose. She pushed herself to her feet, wiping her palms on the thighs of her slacks.

"Is somebody out there?" she whispered hoarsely.

Nothing. Just the wind and rain. Just weather.

"Is somebody out there?" she said again, pivoting, and this time, as if in response, the sky split apart, unleashing a deluge that pummeled leaves from branches and churned the soil into mud at her feet. Disoriented, Sylvia turned to flee, but the house had disappeared. Trees loomed everywhere around her, greenish-black masses against the sky.

Sylvia hesitated. The downpour pasted her hair to her skull. Her sodden clothes hung heavily upon her. She fought to quell a rising tide of panic, but it was already too late: it flooded through her, a frothing cataract of terror that shattered her intricate network of dams and channels, her lifetime of painstaking contingencies. And then she was running, blindly, heedlessly. Rain lashed at her. Limbs whipped out of the darkness to draw lacerating stripes across her outthrust arms. Roots clutched at her ankles. She tripped and went down, her breath labored and distorted.

A cataclysmic streak of lightning unseamed the sky as she clambered to her knees. For a single timeless instant, the world hung in perfect equipoise: the rain, the wind, the whole bruised welter of the night. And there, in the print of leaves against the pewter lid of cloud, Sylvia saw it: a face —

—*was there a face* —

—peering down at her. She saw it. She saw it in the moist shimmering arc of foliage (oh, the curve of that jaw), in the rigid black cicatrix of a branch (that mouth, how like a mouth), in the flickering interstices where two boughs crossed against the sky (ah, the quicksilver gleam of those eyes). She *saw* it. And as she rose to her feet and gazed into that enigmatic face, she sensed the weight of its body as well, its sheer physical reality, invisible but undeniably present beyond the obsidian wall of undergrowth before her. Once again that odd foreboding possessed her: that strange certainty that her life had been nothing more than a long preordained arc angling irrevocably to this moment, this storm-tossed confrontation in the night wood, this now.

Now.

The word chimed in her like a bell, silvery and true, the one true bell she had been waiting all her life to hear and she had never even known it.

The world reeled around her. She could hardly stand upright. Her heart slammed against her ribs. She thought it would tear itself free of her breast.

The storm snapped a leaf off a high branch. She watched it eddy gently to the earth, whipsawed by a twisting vagary of wind.

Sylvia lifted her arms, she stepped toward the thing —

And then the lightning died out of the sky. A peal of thunder smashed the heavens into shards. Stark terror seized her. Turning, she fled wildly into the night.

14

She woke to thunder, a vast cannonade that rattled the window in its frame. Lightning licked at the edges of the room, anointing the beveled frame of her bed, the corner of the chest. Her heart slowed. A dream. That's all it was. A dream.

And yet, it that were true, why did she find herself slipping from between her sheets into that strange flickering gloom? What caused her to snap on the bedside lamp and snatch up the clothes she'd worn home from the hospital?

Her eye found the stain before her hands did, yet she confirmed it all the same, lifting a single dirty finger to her face in dumb amazement, as if she meant to taste it: mud. Mud on the thighs of the slacks, mud on the knees where she had fallen.

What had happened in the interval between the woods and this moment? What? She closed her eyes, she saw it all again. The ruined flower bed, the colossal seedpod, that face peering down at her from the leaves. That face. My God, that face.

Lightning glimmered beyond the window, and against the illuminated screens of her closed eyes, Sylvia watched a leaf drift slowly to earth. In green's dominion. Oh yes, she'd been in green's dominion.

Downstairs then, huddled inside her threadbare robe, she plucked the thin volume of poetry from the shelf at last and let it fall open in her hands. An ancient leaf lay within, a dried shrunken thing, long brittle, long brown.

(In England, it began in England.)

When she touched it, it crumbled into dust.

15

She didn't remember the name of the town, and besides, it didn't matter, did it? It was hardly a real town anyway, just a cluster of weathered buildings perched high among the Yorkshire crags: a news agent, a pub, a handful of mute narrow houses hunched close above the single winding lane. She didn't know why she bothered to stop there at all, except it was late when the coach rumbled into town and she was young enough still to succumb to the incoherent urges of her heart. For her heart *had* spoken, hadn't it?

Yes, she remembered.

Just there, as the coach slowed at the edge of the town, it had spoken. A row of stately yews, the stone facade of a Norman church, and beyond it, rising up in an enveloping wave of foliage, a tract of primeval woodland, ancient oak and ash with the promise of shaded green avenues, the earth fragrant underfoot—this juxtaposition of elements struck some chord within her, and when the coach heaved up before the pub, she had stepped out, that's all.

The coach farted diesel-smelling smoke and pulled away. The street was empty, the first lights winking on as the sun dropped in the west. Sylvia shouldered her pack and went inside.

The pub was dim and narrow. A fire roared in the wide hearth, banishing the chill spring air. Three men huddled over pints at a nearby table, and an old couple ate silently at the bar, watching her ruminatively over their plates. The landlord, middle-aged and running to fat, with a single black tooth in the center of an otherwise flawless smile, leaned on the bar as she swung her pack onto a stool. "What can I get you, then?"

"A room if you have it."

"That shouldn't be a problem. Not exactly hopping here, are we?" Reaching under the counter with one thick arm, he produced a key. "Keep an eye on the tap for me, John," he said to the old man.

Snatching her bag off the stool, he led her up a steep stairwell to a small room with a view of the church and the wood beyond. "Nothing fancy, I'm afraid," he said, "but the sheets are clean. The w.c.'s in the hall here. Come down and have a bite when you've freshened up, why don't you?"

Instead, Sylvia sat on the bed and opened the notebook in which she had begun inscribing her poems. She held a pen, but for a long time she didn't write anything. She gazed at the church and its mantle of woods—was that a prickle of unease she felt?—and let the silence fill her. She wasn't conscious that she had started writing— she didn't know where the poems came from, only that they came, somehow summoned by this green and foreign land where myth loomed palpable as stone behind the comforting tapestry of modernity—but when at last she set the notebook aside, she felt better. She had written it out for now anyway, that faint tickle of anxiety.

Sylvia stood and smoothed the counterpane. Time had slipped away on her. It was full dark, the woods lost in the black well beyond the window. She went downstairs to the common room, empty now but for the landlord polishing glasses behind the bar and the old man nursing a pint of bitter.

She ordered a lager and something to eat.

"You're a Yank, then?" the landlord said when he brought her the food.

"That's right."

"We don't get many Yanks here, eh, John?"

The old man stared fixedly at the mirrored wall.

Undiscouraged, the landlord leaned his elbows on the bar. "Not many Yanks at all," he said. "What brings *you* here, you'll pardon my asking."

Sylvia shrugged. She didn't think an explanation involving her heart's true summons would fly, but she didn't know what else to say. She sipped her lager and thought about it. "Just seeing the countryside," she said finally.

"You hear that, John? Seeing the countryside, she is." The landlord laughed. "I shouldn't think there's much else to see here, but we've got our lot of countryside." He wiped one massive hand on his apron and thrust it over the bar at her. "Graham Massingham."

They shook solemnly.

"Sylvia Woodbine."

"Woodbine, is it? We used to have Woodbines hereabouts, didn't we, John?"

John took a meditative pull on his pint. He licked his lips. "Nah, I shouldn't think," he said.

"Why sure we did. Down the churchyard," Massingham said. He turned to look at her. "Not anymore, mind. I should say the last Woodbine left here two hundred years ago if it were a day. Went to America, maybe." Chuckling, he filled a pint and took a long drink. "What do you have planned for the morning, then?"

"Perhaps I'll have a look at this churchyard."

"The churchyard!" Massingham said. He laughed again. "You hear that, John? The girl says she'll have a look at the churchyard."

But John never said anything at all.

Massingham had been right about the Woodbines. In the churchyard the next morning, under a porcelain spring sky, Sylvia counted six or seven of them mixed among the Slaters, Aldersons, and Worleys. There might have been more; it was hard to tell. The church had fallen into disrepair—crumbling stone drains, broken shingles on the lawn—and the cemetery had not escaped the general neglect. Knee-high weeds brushed her trousers as she moved between the graves and more than one of the stones had toppled over. On those still standing, some names had simply disappeared, so worn that even fingertips could no longer decipher them.

Sylvia worked her way deeper into the churchyard, back toward the broken stone wall and the shaded avenues of woodland beyond. It was like moving backwards in time, the graves older, the inscriptions more often obliterated, the stones themselves crumbling to earth.

Halfway along the back row, a stone's throw from a gap in the wall where a gate might once have stood, she found a trio of Woodbines. Geoffrey and Diana, Rose, the names overgrown with lichen, barely discernible. Massingham's joke came back to her. Maybe he was right, maybe these *were* her centuries-lost ancestors, maybe that was what had summoned her through the coach window—not the yews or the slope of forest beyond the church, but the ethereal behest of some long-forgotten forebear. Maybe she knew this place in her blood. A daft notion, but once you admitted the possibility, . . . well, it made for a more interesting morning.

Take Geoffrey. A blacksmith, perhaps. Or a woodcutter. Yes, she liked that better, a touch right out of the Brothers Grimm. Tiny Rose and her father Geoffrey the woodcutter and her mother—no, her wicked *step*mother, Diana—who one day led the ungrateful little wretch—

Ah, but she wasn't really ungrateful, was she, little Rose? Just lonely and misunderstood. She missed her mother. And of course, she was the apple of her father's eye. *That* was the crux of the problem. *That* was why spiteful Diana took her by the hand one morning, led her through the fallen cemetery gate and far into the pathless wood, and there abandoned her. The villagers scoured the forest for days, but the child never returned. And so this stone had come to be here . . .

But that was wrong, wasn't it? Not a proper fairy tale ending at all.

Sylvia paused. Biting her lip, she stared across the wall at the wood, where an occasional beech rose lithe and graceful as a girl among the grandfatherly oaks. Some of them, the oaks anyway, might have stood so five hundred years or more, she thought— might have stood so when the first stone of the church itself had been laid. She shivered. There was something looming and mysterious in the cathedral gloom beneath those outstretched limbs, something imminent, as if some faërie prince, Auberon himself perhaps, might any moment coalesce from the moted, moss-grown dark. And that was it, of course. Rose had not died. She had been taken for a forest bride, to live happily ever after as the queen of some hidden woodland realm.

Warming to the game, Sylvia threaded her way slowly among the graves, pausing now and again to chip away a patch of lichen with her fingernail, furrowing her brow as she puzzled out the names: here a Gardener, a March, a sole Woodbine amid a row of Dowsons, and there—she paused, a bit perplexed—there, standing oddly alone in a circle of weed-grown lawn, an assembly of identical stones. Two or three of them—there might have been a dozen in all, a little cemetery inside the cemetery—had fallen, ensnared in the ivy that cascaded over the stone wall from the forest. The rest had weathered to anonymity; she could see faint impressions that must have been letters and a raised circular mass that might once have been a sigil, but they were otherwise featureless planes of smooth stone.

Why set them apart like this, though?

Maybe the fallen ones had been better preserved. Sylvia knelt and began to clear the nearest stone, tearing at the flourishing hummock of ivy. Wedging her fingertips under the near edge, she tried to flip it over. It resisted for a moment and then came up abruptly, nearly spilling her into the grass as the clinging verdure at its edges surrendered with a moist tearing sound. She took a deep breath and heaved it onto its back. Insects scurried for cover across the barren earth where it had lain.

Sylvia straightened, panting.

Now then.

This stone too had been badly eroded, but if she brushed away the dirt . . . Her lips pursed as she worked. Slowly, symbols surfaced in the gray stone, black furrows where damp earth packed the weathered incisions. A date—

—fourteen something, could it really be *that old?—*

—and above that a line of letters, most of them illegible. An *l*, a *v*, and further on, unmistakably, *b-i-n-e*.

Something tightened within her breast, making it hard to breathe. The cool spring air felt suddenly clammy. She had started to perspire.

Sylvia dragged her muddy hand across her forehead. A commanding internal voice—

—her father's voice—

—told her to get up, to walk away, to catch the next coach for York. There was nothing for her here. She'd seen enough. Surely she'd seen enough.

But she was done listening to Daddy. That's why she'd come abroad in the first place. To get away from all that.

Besides, it was a coincidence, nothing more. It wasn't even that. It was some other name, meaningless except that she assigned it meaning. It was a poem waiting to happen, that's all, a random oddity awaiting the ordering miracle of language.

The thought calmed her. Rocking on her heels, Sylvia studied the other stones. Maybe it was a trick of the eye, but their inscriptions seemed clearer now. Here and there she could detect discrete letters—an S, a pair of *o*'s, a *v-i-a* all in a row—in the once-illegible grooves.

Unbidden, her lips shaped the name.

Sylvia swallowed. No. On all of them? She could countenance the first coincidence, perhaps, but this—this had to be wrong.

You see what you expect to see, a soothing internal voice counseled. The imagination schools the eye.

Sylvia let her gaze drop back to the monument she had pried up from the earth. She ran her fingers lightly over the raised emblem: some kind of foliate rose, she decided. Except that wasn't right, was it? She bent closer, so close that she could feel a slight chill radiating from the granite. It was leaves, a mask of oak leaves carved in the shape of a human face. The eyes had a faintly feline cast. There was something phallic about the tongue. It lolled obscenely from between the grinning lips, curling upward at the tip.

A ripple of heat passed through her.

Branches rustled at the edge of the woods.

Startled, Sylvia looked up. A man stood on the other side of the wall, half-hidden in the shadows under the trees. "'Tis a green man," he said in a thick Yorkshire accent.

"A what?"

He came a step closer. Sylvia stood, shading her eyes, and peered harder at him, but the emerald woodland murk defeated her. He was lean and tall, she could see that much, and his hair fell in untutored rings around his shoulders, but she couldn't make out any details. She could smell him, though, she realized abruptly: a not unpleasant scent of perspiration and freshly turned earth, the smell of someone who had been working with his hands under a morning sun.

Maybe he was the caretaker. She frowned, glancing at the weed-grown churchyard and the crumbling building beyond. A right shoddy job he was doing of it, then. Someone ought to see about him.

Only then did she register the fact that he had answered her question. "A green man," he'd said. "They all have them."

It was true. Surveying the little cluster of graves, she caught glimpses of that odd, somehow frightening face peering out at her from the weathered sigil atop each stone. Those oddly slanted eyes. That curling tongue.

She looked back at the stranger. "Like in the poem?"

He shrugged. "I wouldn't know about that."

"I studied it in school," she said.

"Aye?"

Now *she* took a step closer to the wall, still peering at him. "*Gawain and the Green Knight*," she said. "The Green Knight rides into Arthur's Court and challenges someone to strike off his head. The catch is, whoever does it has to let the Green Knight strike *his* head off in a year's time."

"And then what?"

"Well—" Sylvia hesitated, abruptly aware that she was alone here, that she knew nothing about this man. Anything could happen, anything at all, as her father had been fond of saying. Yet the tension she felt wasn't exactly fearful, was it? There was something oddly pleasant about it, actually. She found herself taking another step forward, so close she could feel the pressure of the wall against her thighs.

"Go on."

"So Gawain does it. But the Green Knight just picks up his head, reminds Gawain of the challenge, and rides away."

"So he won't stay dead, aye?"

"I guess."

"Ah, well, that's appropriate, isn't it?"

"Is it?"

"The old gods never die," he said.

Sylvia had the sudden urge to step through the fallen gate, just to get a better look at his face. She leaned forward, resting her hands flat atop the wall. "I'm not sure I follow."

"'Twas the Romans, wasn't it?" he said. "Some nights I can still hear their bloody feet marching up yonder road." He made a sound deep in his throat and spat into the trees. "So the old gods died, that's what the Romans thought."

"The old gods."

"Aye, the gods of wood and spring. The forest gods."

She glanced at the grave stone. "The green man?"

"Aye, he's one, he is. But the old gods never really die. They sleep, but sleepers waken, don't they? And people don't forget, not deep in their hearts, they don't. So there he is, the green man, on the stones. Look close, you'll find him on yonder church there, too."

Sylvia cleared her throat, suddenly uneasy with this talk of green men, of old gods waking. She recalled that sense of something impending, something striving to be born in the verdant gloom beneath the trees. A faërie prince, some awful forest king. A deep spring of emotion welled up within her, she had no words to describe it, no words to dam it up. Instead, she knelt and drank of it, the taste rich and strange as wine, a dark bittersweet draught ripe with terror and desire. She was abruptly conscious of the hard ridge of wall against her thighs, at the joining of her legs.

"Come into the light," she said. "I want a look at you."

For a moment, she thought he would deny her request. But instead he did as she had asked, stepping forward out of the shadows, neither faërie prince nor forest king, but only a human being after all, dressed in the practical clothes—the faded trousers and open shirt—of a man who worked out of doors, a man who worked with his hands. She couldn't say how old he was; his long hair, the plain angles of his face, possessed that timeless quality only men seemed blessed with. He might have been twenty, he might have been fifty. She lifted her gaze to meet his eyes, struck by their color, a piercing and fathomless green, like the first bright shout of spring.

"Nothing to fear," he said. "I won't bite."

She turned away, laughing uncertainly. "You looked so strange there under the trees."

He smiled, a flash of white teeth in flesh the color of oak. "You're likely looking enough yourself, aren't you?"

He kept coming as he talked, striding toward her until nothing but the wall separated them. Still she felt that strange tension in the air. She wondered if he sensed it, too. She steadied her hands upon the wall.

He touched her chin with the knuckle of his index finger, lifting it so she had to look him right in the face. "Do you have a name, then?"

"Sylvia." She forced a smile of her own. "Sylvia Woodbine. And you?"

"Jack Bramble."

"Do you live close by, Jack Bramble?"

"Aye, we Brambles have lived along these woods for centuries." And now, unaccountably—had she invited it, somehow?—his hands closed over hers atop the wall. His skin was cool and dry, tough as old hickory. "I know them well, if you'd care to walk a bit with me."

Anything could happen. Anything at all.

Her father's voice.

Sylvia flushed. "I'm expected, I'm afraid. I'm already late, actually."

For the space of a single heartbeat, she feared—

—hoped—

—he wasn't going to release her. Then he did, stepping back and lifting his hands, palms out. He tilted his head and raised his eyebrows, as if he saw right through the lie. "Mustn't be late, then."

"No," she said. "Thanks, though. It was interesting, I'm sure. The green man and all that."

Nodding, she turned away.

"I often walk in this place come evening," he said to her back. "Round midnight, when the moon is high."

Sylvia hesitated. Was that some kind of proposition? "Yes. Well. It was nice meeting you." She nodded again, curtly, and moved away, hurrying past the little cluster of graves and into the broader expanse of the cemetery proper, acutely aware of his gaze upon her. She found herself wishing her trousers weren't so snug across the seat. Except she needn't have worried after all, because—and she found this even more disquieting than his bizarre overture—because when she nerved herself to steal a glance over her shoulder, Bramble was gone. Just gone. As if he had somehow glided sound-lessly back into the trees, as if—

—stop it just stop it—

—he had simply dissolved into his constituent atoms, that celadon murk beneath the forest canopy.

Then her feet struck the sensible macadam of the road, and the glamour that had possessed her seemed to fall away.

But Sylvia remained unsettled the rest of the afternoon. Too restless to write, she leafed idly through her notebook, her mind still entangled in the matter of Jack Bramble, his fathomless green eyes and the feel of his strong hands and most of all the odd melange of emotions he had set off within her, that somehow intoxicating cocktail of apprehension and attraction. There was something else, too, some final enigma that continued to elude her, something he'd said.

What was it?

It was not until she came down for dinner, late, after full darkness had enveloped the village, that Sylvia finally recalled it: *We Brambles have lived along these woods for centuries.* Yet she had not seen a single Bramble among the graves. Not a single solitary Bramble.

She took a seat at the bar, with only the landlord and ancient John for company. "Do you know anyone named Bramble hereabouts?" she asked Massingham when he brought her food.

The landlord shook his head gravely. "There are no Brambles here," he said.

It was after nine by then.

Outside, a silver rind of moon scaled the wall of heaven.

16

No more.

Sylvia lowered herself into a chair. She felt old. She felt so old. She didn't want to remember anymore.

She closed her eyes, she gripped the arms of the chair with palsied fingers, she worried her lip until she tasted blood—anything, anything to anchor herself in this moment. This book-lined room with the pallid light of dawn beyond the windows. This barren house where she had passed her life. This now.

But it was too late for that, wasn't it? She should have known better. Open Pandora's box and anything could fly out. Anything at all.

17

She remembered pushing her plate away and climbing the stairs. The moon peered through the window on the landing, and she paused a moment to look at it, feeling the pull of some ancient, inescapable tide.

Up then, to her chaste maiden's bed, to her thrashing, sleep-tossed sheets. She slept or dreamed she slept, and woke to a hum of shrill expectancy, a silence like a shroud. The moon looked in upon her, and in the breath of wind among the trees she could almost hear a whispered summons. Even before she swung her legs from underneath the covers, even before she threw on her clothes and unlocked her door, she knew with a stark and unremorseful certainty what she was going to do. Anticipation sang in her blood like the sea.

Down the stairs, then, and barefoot into the night. She remembered that, too, didn't she? The moon-frosted street and a gossamer veil of mist in the air and the old man, John, looming up before her from a shadowed crevice in the inn's facade.

She clapped a hand across her mouth to stifle a scream, the sound breaking into muted hilarity when she recognized her assailant.

"You scared me—"

"Go back to your room," he entreated her.

"What?"

"*Go back!*" He closed upon her, his hands clutching at her shoulders. His breath gusted in her face, rank with beer and cigarettes. "For your own good, I'm telling you. You should leave here. You should take the next coach to York."

How lean he was! How dreary and familiar—his face the cratered desolation of some airless moon, his voice the voice of Sinai, gravid with its prohibitions. Why Father! she might have said. An effervescent blurt of laughter escaped her at the thought. She felt giddy as a schoolgirl, apprehended in some harmless prank.

His fingers dug into her. "Listen to me, you don't understand what you're meddling in—"

Sylvia wrenched herself free of him—how strong she had become!—and fled giggling up the street, past the church with its stately hedge of yews and into the neighboring churchyard. She had never felt so alive, so deeply immersed in the world's rich pageant. The fragrant grass caressed her feet, the starry void wheeled above her, the wind bearing down upon her wept with the scent of new-leaved trees. Goosebumps erupted on her arms. Her nipples tightened into hard knots. She lifted her hands to the sky and sighed for the pleasure of the air against her face.

The tombstones in their ordered rows, the ring of grass, the cemetery inside the cemetery—she passed them by all unawares, hesitating at last and for a moment only in that gap that might once have been a gate, when there were gates and borders and passages between, that gap that was now only a gap, a broken place in a bastion that few cared anymore to cross. Yes. She had hesitated. She had hesitated as at the edge of a precipice, encountered unexpectedly in some wild and hidden place. She had hesitated, with the church at her back and the wood before her, her hands outstretched to the stone pillars at either side, drinking in that line of cold demarcation, that wall.

An owl called softly among the trees.

"Yes," she whispered to the sky, and the grass curling at her ankles, and the beckoning line of trees standing dark against the sky. "Yes. I'm coming."

She let go the wall.

She stepped into the wood, the ground beneath her feet buoyant and lush as though someone, expecting company, had unrolled a carpet to receive her. She stepped into the wood, the twilight sanctity beneath the trees. With his name upon her lips—

"Are you here, Jack Bramble?"

—she stepped into the wood.

"Aye, I'm here," he said, and for a moment—surely it must have been an illusion—it seemed that his voice came not from one place, but from many places: the dark ranks of oak and the moss between her toes and the perfumed earth itself.

But no, he was here, here, an emerald shadow moving to embrace her, and she lifted her arms to receive him as she had known she would. There were no words, nothing to say, only the feel of him, this lean strength and the play of muscle under his flesh and his lips upon her lips. Her shirt came open beneath his fingers.

Her trousers pooled at her ankles. For the first time in her life she stood naked in the outer air, with only Jack Bramble and the incurious moon to gaze upon her.

"Jack, no—"

"Shhh. There's nothing to be afraid of."

That done, her protest duly noted in whatever celestial almanac such things were recorded, Sylvia abandoned herself to the moment at last. She let him lower her upon a bower of moss—how soft and welcoming it was, the softest bed she had ever known—and then even that awareness evaporated, there was nothing in the world but his mouth at her breasts, his hand between her thighs.

Yes. She remembered. She felt a single flaring instant of pain as he entered her—such pain that she had by reflex torn free a lock of his hair—and then a slow-rising swell of pleasure, world-girdling, tidal, until at last it overwhelmed her, crested, broke.

She remembered.

And then, only then, with his seed still drying on her thighs and her legs flung open like a common whore's, only then did she understand what she had surrendered, the sole and only gift that was hers alone to bestow, and that to some common stranger.

Sylvia closed her eyes and began quietly to weep.

"Ah, now, lass," Jack Bramble said.

He touched her face, but she would not be consoled. She could not find the heart even to stand and dress herself. She just lay there, clutching his bloody lock of hair in her fist and staring blindly into the trees until at last the character of the darkness overhead changed and she realized she had slept.

A stone was gouging her back.

It was morning. She was alone.

She stood to dress herself, tucking Bramble's lock of hair unexamined into the pocket of her trousers. As she slowly buttoned her shirt, only half-awake and shivering in the cold, gray air, she remembered a dream that had come to her in the night.

In the dream, she had flown, panicked, through a thick and perilous wood. Her muscles screamed. Her breath clawed in her lungs. At last, exhausted, she had stumbled, fallen. Jack Bramble knelt beside her. Jack Bramble extended his hand. "Come away with me," he said. "Come away and be my wife."

And even then—even in the dream—Sylvia had understood that this moment, this single instant in her whole long span of years, was the pivot upon which her life would turn.

A wild longing had risen up within her—to hold his face

between her hands, to taste the fragrant verdure of his breath, to feel once and always those enormous swells of pleasure crest and break within her.

But the world she had known beckoned her home. The wood was wild and desolate.

In short, she was afraid.

"I can't," she'd said.

The words had echoed inside her head as she made her way through the broken gate and the cemetery beyond. They seemed to boom through the thin mist clinging to the church spire, to radiate from the slick pavement of the road as she trudged barefoot back to the inn. *I can't.* Two solid, declamatory syllables of renunciation, prideful and afraid. Yes, afraid. Why not face it after all these years?

Sylvia glanced at the book, still open in her lap. A few powdery remnants of the leaf clung to the pages. Staring at them, she felt a final memory dredge itself from the muddy river bottom of her mind. She had been slumped inside the coach to York, dozing, her head tilted against the chill pane of the window, the big diesel motor throbbing in her bones. Scant hours had passed, but already the memory—

—*no the enchantment it was an enchant*—

—the *memory* of the previous night had taken on such a hazy, dreamlike quality that, in that strange hypnagogic state between sleep and full waking, Sylvia had more than half-convinced herself she *had* dreamed it. Bottomless relief welled up inside her. That's how the forgetting must have begun. Her father had been right. She'd been playing at rebellion, that's all, and finally, there in that nameless cemetery, it had all become too real. So she had fled. From York, she had caught the next train to London, from London the next plane home. It was safer that way. Safer to run, safer to forget, safer to bind it all into orderly measures of verse. Language could contain it.

And events had conspired with her. The coach had lurched, jolting her half-awake. As she sought once again the oblivion of sleep, she had screwed her hands into her trouser pockets, where her questing fingers brushed something unexpected. Opening her eyes, Sylvia had retrieved not the bloody hank of hair she had for some reason—

—*why?*—

—anticipated, but only a leaf, an oak leaf, bruised and bleeding sap.

She remembered gazing at the thing in dull curiosity. It seemed to pulse with some enigmatic significance, but she couldn't say why. She tucked the leaf into her pack—she must have kept it for some reason, after all—and closed her eyes. When she woke again, she was in York.

So that's all it had come to in the end, an old woman alone with her memories, one slim volume of verse, a handful of dust.

I can't.

She could hear those words even now, in the creak of an attic joist expanding or the solemn cadence of the hall clock, measuring out the morning tick by tick. All the empty sounds a house makes when there is no human noise to fill it up.

She thought of Daphne—

—*maybe I* choose *to be alone*—

—and felt a circuit close inside her, illuminating a single sustaining idea.

What kind of choice was it, after all?

The clock chimed ten o'clock. It was Friday. Daphne was coming for dinner. She had too much to do to sit here woolgathering. Sylvia stood and began digging through her desk. When she found the faculty directory, she picked up the telephone and punched in a number.

"Professor Green," she said.

18

The evening started badly.

Daphne had been right about overdoing it. The household chores alone wearied Sylvia. By the time she returned from the market, lugging three swollen sacks of groceries, she felt dizzy. Her heart was beating in a strange swift rhythm and the air shimmered with a glaring, over-illuminated brilliance. She had intended to start dinner immediately. Instead, she went upstairs to nap, woke late, and spent the afternoon trying to catch up.

To top it off, Robin Green arrived early—only ten minutes or so, but enough to catch her putting the final hasty touches on dessert. Clad in jeans and a white shirt, his sleeves rolled back to the elbow, he stood by the sink and gazed distractedly into the lengthening shadows while she iced the cake.

She was obscurely relieved when the doorbell rang.

"That'll be her, I suppose," Green said, drumming his fingers on the countertop.

"Relax. Dinner among colleagues, what could be more

pleasant?" Sylvia smiled. "I'll get the door. Why don't you find something for us to listen to? The stereo's just in here."

Sylvia left him looking at CDs in the living room, and went along the corridor to the front of the house.

"Jeez, I thought you'd never come," Daphne said as soon as Sylvia opened the door. She brushed by in a hurry, a bustling whirlwind of energy that seemed to have touched down in a shop somewhere, snatching half a dozen packages into the maelstrom. She nudged the door closed with her heel, and looked at Sylvia over her laden arms. "I picked up some wine. The doctor didn't say anything about wine, did he?"

"She."

"What?"

"The doctor's a woman. And no, she didn't say anything about wine."

"Well, good, 'cause I brought some. Can you give me a hand with these? My arm's about to break." Daphne shoved a bag at her. "I got red and white both. I can never remember which one goes with fish."

"We're not having fish."

"Well, that's why I got both. And some of the bread you like. And videos. I thought you might want to see a movie."

"We'll see. Let me get that, too," Sylvia said, snatching a video tape that was slipping out of Daphne's hand. "You brought your briefcase? You were planning to work?"

"I'm *always* planning to work, but in this case, I got a couple things from the library I thought you might enjoy. Hang on a sec—" She dug into the leather satchel swinging from her shoulder. "How are you feeling, anyway? I meant to call, but students were in and out of my office all day. And Robin Green, I don't know what's gotten into—"

"Why don't you get the books later, we need to talk—"

Daphne looked up. "You *aren't* feeling well, are you? I *knew* dinner was a bad idea."

"I feel fine, I took a nap. Look—" Sylvia nodded at the briefcase. "—put that down. Actually, I wanted to talk to you about Rob—"

Music started up in the living room, something complex and refined, with lots of strings. Daphne dumped her briefcase and purse unceremoniously on the floor. "Who's here?"

"That's what I wanted—"

But Daphne, still clutching the loaf of bread like a football, was already moving down the hall. Sylvia couldn't see the expression on her face when she came into the living room, but the tension in her shoulders was unmistakable. So was her tone: unimpeachably polite and cold all the way to bone. "Why, Robin," she said. "Sylvia didn't mention you were coming."

Robin Green, standing by the stereo, looked stricken. "Hi, Daphne," he said uncertainly.

Sylvia dropped the videos atop a stack of books she hadn't gotten around to shelving. Robin turned a CD case nervously in his hands. Daphne pursed her lips in a way that indicated a witticism was in the offing, something bright and cutting. "Well—" she began, raising her eyebrows, but Sylvia cleared her throat.

Daphne and Robin regarded her expectantly.

"So you're interested in the baroque composers, Robin?" she found herself saying.

"Oh, that." Robin glanced at the CD case he'd been holding. "Boccherini, is it? It's all right, I guess."

"I think Robin's more post-modern," Daphne said.

"No, no, classical's fine." And then, when no one said anything: "I've always preferred jazz, actually."

Sylvia hesitated, uncertain how to respond.

"Charles Mingus?" Robin added hopefully. "And Sonny Rollins, especially the stuff he did in the fifties. The later stuff . . ." The sentence died on his lips. He shrugged, as if his opinions on the later stuff were a matter of well-established record.

"I'm afraid Sylvia's interests tend to wane after the Renaissance," Daphne said dryly.

They contemplated Sylvia's antiquated tastes for a moment. Robin coughed. He closed the CD case and placed it on the end table.

"Well, dinner smells terrific," he said.

"Yes, Sylvia, what *is* for dinner?"

"We're having a roast," Sylvia said. "But it won't be ready for a bit. Why don't I get us all a glass of wine?"

"I think I'll help," Daphne said. "If you'll excuse us just a minute," she added, looking at Robin.

"Sure—" Robin began, but the door swung shut on his words.

In the kitchen, fluorescent light leapt from the linoleum and the freshly polished countertops. The clock over the sink chimed the quarter hour.

Daphne thunked the bread down on the kitchen table. "How could you? What on Earth were you thinking?"

"I was thinking he might be lonely, he hardly knows anyone here."

"He has friends. He's been at Holman nearly—"

"Well, he can always use another friend, can't he?"

Sylvia held Daphne's gaze for a moment, and then she turned away. She took a bottle of wine out of the bag and nearly dropped it. She was shaking. She couldn't seem to get the corkscrew properly aligned. Daphne loomed in her peripheral vision, but she couldn't bring herself to look up. She didn't want Daphne to see the weakness in her eyes. She didn't want pity, she didn't want anything more to do with hospitals or doctors. "If you're going to help, help," she said. "Don't just stand there looking at me."

"I can't believe you," Daphne said, turning away to collect the glasses.

Sylvia steadied herself against the counter, and took a deep breath. She closed her eyes and swallowed. There. She opened her eyes and positioned the corkscrew. This time, it went in perfectly.

Daphne put the glasses down beside her. "You could have told me. You didn't have to spring him on me like that."

"You're really angry, aren't you?"

"Well, wouldn't you be?"

"What if I *had* told you? Would you have come?"

Daphne grimaced.

"Well, would you have?"

"I already told you I didn't want any part of him."

"You can't even have dinner with him?"

"It's not just dinner, Sylvia."

"Sure it is. Like you said, he's not a bad-looking man, he wouldn't have any interest in you."

The words, hurtful and cruel, slipped out before she could stop them. They found their mark, too. Daphne's mouth dropped open. Her eyes widened almost imperceptibly. She turned her back to the counter and crossed her arms over her breasts.

"That's it, isn't it?" Sylvia said. "You're not afraid he's interested. You're afraid he *isn't*."

"That's not it."

"Then what is it?"

Daphne didn't answer. Sylvia started pouring the wine, the bottle chattering against the rims of the glasses.

"Well?"

"We work together. It could get awkward."

"And so it's not worth the risk?"

"It wasn't to you!"

Sylvia plunked the bottle down hard.

"Yes, and what has that brought me? You envy me? You want to have to hire someone to stay with you when you get old, just so you can live at home? Is that what you want, Daphne?"

"So I should marry myself off to the first man that shows any interest?"

"Has anyone suggested matrimony?"

Daphne rolled her eyes.

"All I'm saying is, it doesn't hurt to talk to him."

"Oh, come on, Sylvia."

"What?"

"Have you *looked* at me?" Daphne said in a whisper, her voice cracking. "How could he be interested in me?"

Sylvia turned, taking Daphne's hands in her own, and peered into the other woman's wide, untrusting face. Daphne had beautiful eyes, cobalt blue—Sylvia had always known that—but she had never noticed the pain in them, the fear and sorrow. How could she have missed it?

It was like looking in a mirror.

"How could he *not* be?" Sylvia said. She found her fingers, unbidden, rising to Daphne's cheek. "I'm not saying this is the right thing. All I'm saying is, give him a chance. Don't be so afraid all the time. There's nothing to be afraid of."

Daphne bit her lower lip. She stood rigidly as Sylvia embraced her. And then, abruptly, she sagged, snugging her face into the crook of Sylvia's neck. In that fleeting instant, holding this fragile young woman who could have been her daughter—who *would* have been, in another, better life—Sylvia understood what she had missed, what she had denied herself.

"You only get so many chances," she whispered. "I *know*. And when they come—" She touched Daphne's chin. "Look at me. When the chances come, you have to seize them. Do you understand me? *Seize them.*"

The words came out with a fury she hadn't expected, and in the aftermath there didn't seem to be anything else to say. She clutched Daphne fiercely for a moment, and then she pushed her away. She held her at arm's length, drinking her in, trying to imprint this moment, this one human face—

—*this poem*—

—on every cell in her mind. Daphne. There was no sound in the kitchen but the steady tick of the clock hanging above the sink.

Daphne shook her head. "Come on," she said. "He's going to think we've forgotten him."

✳   ✳   ✳

For Sylvia, the rest of the night had an enchanted air. No meal had ever tasted so delicious, no candle ever fired such lustrous depths of wine. Light burnished the table in buttery slabs, and the music swirled around her, allegreto and allegro, almost palpable in the mute and fragrant air.

To be sure there had been a measure of awkwardness at the start. The conversation bounced from one obvious topic to another over the wine—how did Robin like Holman? what were his plans for the summer?—but things seemed to slip into a rhythm after Sylvia served the meal. Robin Green was so courtly and low key, so studiously oblivious to the tension in the air, and—yes—so attentive, that he soon dulled the edge of Daphne's anger.

More, Sylvia thought in the glamour of the moment, he charmed it utterly away. Daphne had never been more lovely. Her eyes glistened, her hair shone, she seemed less fat than magnificent, imposing as a goddess in her stature, or a strong, young tree, its arms lifted in defiance to the wind. And her mind—Sylvia had never seen it so quick or elegant.

The evening flagged only once.

Over the second bottle of wine, the talk turned to work. Robin mentioned his dissertation, a study of Middleton, and Daphne said she'd been working on Mary Elizabeth Braddon, which led to a debate about canon formation. Sylvia—who'd come to criticism late, and not entirely by choice—found the whole thing dry as dust.

"But you wrote a book of criticism yourself!" Daphne protested.

"Yes, what was *your* book about?" Robin asked.

So she found herself talking about the Fisher King, the Jack in the Green, and the older underlying archetypes, the ancient vegetation myths of death and renewal that survived in the foliate heads carved on thirteenth-century cathedrals, in the Gawain poem and the annual May Day ceremonies still celebrated at Hastings and Rochester. "The pagan myths are everywhere once you know to look," she said, "even the ecumenical calendar. Easter is May Day in Christian garb, and All Saints Day falls right after Halloween, the Druid holiday of Samhain." She raised her eyebrows. "The old gods never die, they just put on new faces."

"Jesus," Robin said, "you *are* a poet." He gave an exaggerated shudder. "All this talk about ancient rites of renewal gives me the willies. Didn't the Druids used to sacrifice virgins?"

He chuckled, but the joke fell flat, too much an invocation to a guest unseen and uninvited, but always in attendance. Even the music took a funereal turn, adagio largo, a somber rolling cadence that swept back the curtain of years so that for a single exhilarating instant, Sylvia found herself at the edge of revelation, kneeling once again in that strange circle of graves, her fingers lifted to summon from the weathered stone the letters of a name so tantalizingly familiar that she could almost shape the syllables—

"Are you all right?" Daphne said.

And that abruptly the curtain fell back into place.

Sylvia forced a smile. "I'm fine," she said. "I'll just get dessert." She stood, folding her napkin, and by the time she reached the door Daphne and Robin were already talking again.

The kitchen was dim, lit only by the fluorescent bar recessed over the sink. Wind rattled the screen door as Sylvia reached for the overhead light. She paused, her hand lingering at the switch, and then she pulled it away. She crossed in darkness instead, the kitchen silent but for the faraway tinkle of music, and, once, a burst of laughter from the dining room. At the counter, she hesitated again, and then, for the first time all day, for the first time since the dream—

—*it had been a dream it must have been a dream*—

—she drew back the curtains. Her own face, greenish and wan in the glare of that one flickering light, floated disembodied atop the glass. With trembling fingers, Sylvia reached out and snapped down the fluorescent's switch.

Her face hollowed into darkness, ghostly and strange. Beyond it, like a photo swimming up through a tray of chemicals, the night summoned itself into being, a chiaroscuro of moonlight and gusting shadow: first the rigid black pillars of the porch, and then the moon-struck eye of the birdbath, gazing blindly from the garden's center, and finally the ragged fringe of woods, the trees stark against the opalescent sky.

Sylvia realized she'd been holding her breath. She exhaled, misting the window. As the foggy crescent evaporated, the trees materialized once again, clearer now—

—*closer*—

—and she sensed suddenly the magnitude of the forest, its weight and density, its dumb intent. It loomed there, encircling not just the house or the scant streets beyond, but the whole world: all the aggrieved forests girdling the Earth, waiting to assert their dominion once again. Ah, but waiting for *what*, that was the question.

Sylvia leaned closer, so close she could feel a slight chill radiating from the glass. She sensed something else out there, didn't she?

A green and piercing intelligence peering back at her from the trees. She stepped back. Her finger throbbed. She could hardly draw breath. The wind kicked up again. It sounded almost like a voice crying through the trees, the words indistinguishable. If she could only get a little closer—

The overhead light went on.

"Sylvia?"

She came to herself, her hand outstretched to the back door. She had no memory of crossing the room. Daphne stood on the other side of the kitchen.

"Are you all right?"

"I'm fine."

"What are you doing in the dark?"

"The screen door was blowing," she said. It was all that came to mind.

"Oh." Daphne lifted her eyebrows. "Well. Let me help you with dessert."

"Yes," Sylvia said. "Do."

She cut the cake while Daphne got out plates, and then, Daphne holding the door for her, she slipped back into the dining room, the dessert tray held before her like an offering. Robin Green stood to meet her, smiling. Sylvia saw his eyes move past her to Daphne, brightening, and everything else fell away, these strange spells and the weed and the wood, all the burdens of history. The music brightened. Color flooded the room. Her feet seemed barely to touch the floor.

The cake was buttery and rich. Light shimmered in every surface. The air buzzed through her veins like wine. And though the conversation moved on to more mundane topics—funding and faculty politics and students held in mutual disregard—Sylvia could hardly follow it, she was so intent on drinking everything in, on seizing it and holding it fast, this intoxicating pageant of the senses, this abundance. Outwardly everything seemed normal—she nodded, she smiled, she put in an occasional remark—but inwardly, inwardly she sang.

And then—too soon—it was late.

Robin Green left first. As they stood watching his car disappear beyond a screen of trees, Daphne said she'd help with the dishes. "Forget it," Sylvia said. "I'll do it in the morning." But Daphne insisted, and Sylvia succumbed—pleased, actually, at the prospect of a little more time. And this too was a small miracle of the senses: the hot, clean fragrance of the soap, and the shining dishes stacked away still warm in their accustomed cabinets. "This was my mother's china," Sylvia said. "I want you to have it someday."

"Don't be ridiculous," Daphne said. "You're not going any-where."

They didn't say much after that, not until Daphne got ready to go. But on the stoop, with her purse slung over one shoulder and her briefcase over the other, Daphne clutched Sylvia fiercely.

"I'm sorry I was angry," she said. "This was a good night—"

"You don't have to—"

"I *do*. I felt something, a spark. I never would have given it a chance." She gave Sylvia a squeeze and stepped away. "You sure you're okay? You gave me a scare in the kitchen."

"I'm fine. I promise."

Daphne smiled. "Good. I'll call you tomorrow then. And thanks, Sylvia."

She touched Sylvia's hand, smiled, and went down the stairs. At her car, she turned around. "You ever find the word, Sylvia, the one you were looking for?"

Had she? Sylvia supposed not. But it was all too easy to imagine a world in which she might never have had to look in the first place. She looked at Daphne. "I found two of them," she said abruptly.

"Yeah? What are they?"

"Choose life."

Daphne laughed. "Not exactly a description of your state of mind, that."

"It could have been."

Daphne opened the car door, but she didn't get in. She stood there, gazing solemnly at Sylvia while she thought it over, and then she nodded. "Good night, Sylvia."

"Good night."

Daphne slid into the seat and closed the door. A moment later the headlights came on, dazzling Sylvia. The car backed into the street and pulled away.

Sylvia didn't go anywhere, though.

She just stood there, listening as the sound of Daphne's car faded into the distance. She just stood there, listening to the wind.

19

The night was dark and rich and cool, and though Sylvia knew that she should go back inside—she wasn't well, the evening had tired her—there was this matter of the wind. It swept down from the wood in a perfumed rush, laden with the splendor of the season, the spendthrift beauty of new-budding limbs, the promised languor of some woodland bower, mattressed thick and soft with moss. Yes, and there was a voice, too, just as she had thought in the kitchen. *Come to me*, it entreated her.

She could hear it clearly now, this summons from the night wood, coaxing, earth-succored, drawing her down the crumbling steps of the stoop, and along the path to the back garden, the path she had made with her own hands, cutting away the turf and leveling the mulch and placing each white river-smoothed stone with the care of a poet, laying down a path of words. How they shone, those bordering stones, bright against the omnipresent dark.

The house rose above her. She glanced up, the yellow windows, foursquare and orderly, beckoning her back—back to the dishes stacked neatly in the cupboards, back to the carpets so freshly vacuumed that you could still see patterns in the nap where no human step had fallen. But she resisted. She focused her gaze on the path. She kept her feet moving until she reached the side gate.

The garden lay on the other side, a tangle too long unattended, flanked on three sides by a forbidding wall of trees. Had they crept forward or had she only dreamed it—the woods, the vile weed, and all the rest, vanguard of some encroaching senility? It was a frightening thing either way, yet she felt no fear, not anymore. She felt . . . what exactly? A bottomless yearning, that's all. A loneliness so deep and wide that she could hardly plumb it.

"Are you there?" she whispered.

The wind touched her face.

Sylvia lifted the latch and swung the gate open. She stepped through, thinking of that other gate, that gap that might have been a gate when such things still existed, gates and borders and travelers between, and she didn't bother closing it behind her. She didn't bother with the path either. She struck off across the garden instead, planting her feet firmly in the mulched beds and crushing flowers underfoot, so that fragrant eddies swirled around her and drew her on. The woods loomed closer, higher, deeper than she had ever known them, spilling across the lawn in bold profusion.

Holman's clocktower began to chime when she reached the edge of the trees, and there she hesitated at last, stealing a glance back at the house as the old fear rose up inside her once again. John Thistle had been right. She'd been afraid, she'd always been afraid. And of what? Life, that's all. Just life. All this time running away. She'd wasted all this time. The thought was like stumbling across a dark pearl on some broken shore, something so unexpected, so black and revelatory that it took your breath away. What a paltry thing it was, fear.

She turned away.

She looked up. She squared her shoulders.

The forest held its breath and listened. She sensed something peering out at her from the green darkness, something ancient and abiding.

"I'm coming," she said, and now, without looking back, she moved into the wood, past the ruined flower bed and past the snarl of thorns where the great seedpod rotted into earth, inward, gliding among the trees, her feet silent on the moss-grown earth, always inward, penetrating deeper and ever deeper into the emerald shadows that awaited her (they had always awaited her), so that when at last she stole a backwards glance not even the faraway gleam of the house was any longer visible.

She paused then (how her finger throbbed!), not knowing why but knowing that she had done her part in penetrating to this consecrated glade, knowing too that something there awaited her and drawing breath in silent expectation when it began at last, when a deliberate shadow—

—*a man she had known it would be a man*—

—*but it was not a man nor had it ever been, it was a*—

—shadow, detaching itself from that cathedral gloom, began to flow slowly toward her, attended by a musk of earth and leaf and sap but newly risen. Yet it was a man, after all, and she knew him, did she not? She had caressed that curving jaw, she had gazed into those eyes. Her mouth had kissed that mouth. Yes, and hungered now to kiss it yet again. Sylvia stepped forward to embrace him, she lifted her face to his, his name—

"John—"

—already taking shape and departing from her lips as air even as she realized her mistake. For there was a face beyond that face (it was Jack Bramble's face) and yet another beyond that and another and another (there were always more faces, there always would be), so many ephemeral masks and only one true face, as old as time and unwived in its season, and questing always for its vernal bride.

The old terror seized her then, words rising unbidden to her lips—

"No, no—"

—and she would have fled, but she did not have the strength. He was strong. He was too strong: the hands at her shoulders and the arms drawing her close and the lips pressing firmly to her own. Then she was kissing him back, eagerly, with all the pent-up yearning of a lifetime, and as she opened herself to receive him, she understood what she might have come to know all those years ago, in the green and hungry embrace of Jack Bramble, had she only permitted it: she did not want words, she had no need of them. And so she surrendered at last—life, words, everything—a green thought in a green shade, enrapt in green and leafy silence.

Story Notes

THERE'S A PRETTY GOOD CHANCE YOU
wouldn't be reading this collection if it wasn't for "The
Resurrection Man's Legacy." Published in July 1995, three years
after I left the Clarion Writer's Workshop at Michigan State
University, it landed me on the final Nebula ballot. I didn't win
(and why should I have? I was up against some of the real masters
of the genre that year, including Ursula LeGuin, Jim Kelly, and
Mike Resnick. In this case, it really *was* an honor to be nominated).
But the story *did* get reprinted in the Nebula anthology for that year,
which found its way to Hollywood, where the story has since been
optioned several times for development as a motion picture. More
important, the boost in confidence enabled me to get moving on a
stalled novel, which has since seen print as *The Fallen*.

It's a fairly auspicious record for a story that got bounced—and
justifiably so—from just about every market in the field. Part of the
problem with that failed first draft was that I was still discovering
what the story was about. It had come to me—as stories sometimes
do—in the form of a title: "Resurrection Man." I must have stumbled across the phrase in its literal meaning somewhere—it has
roots in the 19th century, when it was used to describe the grave
robbers who stole freshly buried corpses for sale to medical
schools—but it seemed from the first to possess a metaphorical
significance which I couldn't quite pin down. When I finally did

figure it out, I still faced the problem of compressing the action—which spans decades—into the limited scope of a short story. The initial draft—the one that collected all the rejection slips—was told in third person, and moved chronologically through Jake's life: roughly one scene every four or five years, resulting in a kind of narrative whiplash for the reader, who barely had time to get comfortable with the characters before they were all half a decade older. The story didn't achieve any kind of unity until I rewrote it using a first-person retrospective narrator, in which carnation it sold the first time out.

In her introduction to the story, then-editor of *Fantasy & Science Fiction* Kris Rusch flattered me deeply by saying that it combined the feel of Ray Bradbury and Isaac Asimov. I think that this is an insightful comment, for in rereading the story now, I can see that it is as much about the golden age of science fiction—twelve, or so the old joke goes—as it is anything else. After all, I was about twelve years old myself when I discovered Bradbury and Asimov on the shelves of the Princeton Public Library, and those early reading experiences in the genre literally shaped my life the way Ford and his love of baseball shape Jake's life.

In that respect, the story is less speculative than nostalgic. It trades on baseball's love affair with its own mythic history almost as unashamedly as it trades on the science fiction fan's longing for an old-fashioned future populated not with cyberpunks, nanobots, and dark matter, but with the essentially humanlike robots who gave Susan Calvin such fits—a future that somehow made sense. And so it's set in a slightly "alternate" and more innocent past—a past in which baseball history alone remains unchanged, a past that never fell under the nuclear shadow, a past in which we could come to love our machines rather than fear them. That, ultimately, is the central irony the piece effects: the tragedy arises not out of Jake's decision to leave behind the machine which has become a parent to him, but out of the machine's inability to understand the complex web of emotions the boy has woven around it. It is, after all, just a machine—and while Jake understands this fact, it cannot ameliorate his grief.

Jake's decision is finally the wheel upon which the entire story turns. In that sense this story is of a piece with the other stories in this book; until I started putting this collection together, I didn't realize just how many of my stories hinge upon the fraught relationships between children and their parents. That relationship is, in so many ways, both good and bad, the central relationship in our lives—the one from which everything else radiates. And so I dedicate this one both to the literal parents who encouraged me to follow my dream of writing, and to the community of science fiction writers—Asimov and Bradbury among them—who gave me the dream in the first place.

"Death and Suffrage" embodies one of those weird coincidences between history and fiction that occasionally crop up. Finished the October prior to the 2000 Presidential Election—an election that really *was* decided by the Supreme Court (the reference to the controversy in Florida was added later, at the request of *Fantasy & Science Fiction* editor Gordon Van Gelder)—this one seems to confirm the dictum that the writer of fiction can no longer compete with the strangeness of contemporary reality. It's also an example of how completely a writer's intentions can go awry. In keeping with the pun in the title, I intended this one to be short and light: What if the dead really *could* vote? Ha, ha. But somewhere along the way it turned long and very dark indeed.

When it was first published, in *Fantasy & Science Fiction*, it occasioned an irate letter from a reader opposed to the story's stance on America's gun culture. At the time, I chose not to respond—mainly because I felt that the story was about a lot more than gun control. As I wrote, I came to see that it was really about Rob's emotional journey—his growing understanding of the value of human relationships and the way that understanding forces him to re-evaluate his views of the political process. I believed then—and I believe still—that fiction driven by purely ideological goals is likely to be very poor fiction indeed.

In retrospect, however, I think it was a mistake not to respond to that letter—and one of the advantages of being a writer (there are a few) is the opportunity to revise your mistakes. About one thing, my correspondent was right: whatever else "Death and Suffrage" might be about, it is also, undeniably, about gun control. What's more, the death of Dana Maguire was inspired by a real crime—the murder of six-year-old Kayla Rolland, shot on February 29, 2000, by a classmate who found the weapon in his uncle's bedroom. Gun control probably would not have prevented her murder: the gun in question was illegally obtained, and, as gun control opponents quite rightly point out, those who are inclined to disobey laws are unlikely to surrender their illegal weapons.

Still, at least one of the guns used by the killers at Columbine High School was purchased legally. Limiting access to guns—

especially the semi-automatic weapons favored by spree killers, many of whom are law-abiding citizens until they snap—may well lower the mounting body count. My correspondent also quibbled that we can't compare the death rate by handguns in the United States to those in other industrialized nations in part because the US death rate is inflated by firearm suicides. I can't help wondering why anyone bothers making such distinctions—the mortician certainly doesn't.

The fact is, there's a fundamental problem in using a gun for home protection. Burglars are unlikely to stand politely by while you unlock the gun cabinet and get the bullets out of the safe. For a gun to be of any use at all in such a case, it must be loaded and ready to hand. Those facts make it all too likely that the gun will be used on another family member in a moment of anger—or that it will fall into the hands of a child.

As of this writing, Kayla Rolland is still dead.

In the early nineties I was teaching English at the University of Tennessee, home to the famed "body farm." Founded by forensic anthropologist William Bass, the body farm was designed to gather data about the processes of decay as a means of improving criminal and accident investigations. It's a simple premise—dump donated bodies in a fenced-in area so that forensic scientists can observe the results under controlled circumstances—but it has proved to be highly effective: Dr. Bass and his protégés have become widely known for their investigative expertise, and the body farm has inspired more than its share of fiction, including a best-selling novel by Patricia Cornwell.

Around the same time I became aware of the body farm, I found myself teaching college composition out of a writing text that included a debate on animal rights. In the course of the debate, one of the participants, a medical ethicist, pondered a future in which anencephalic children—infants born without a brain—are hooked up to life support in order to provide handy donor organs. The two ideas—body farm and wards full of living dead organ donors—must have lodged somewhere deep in my subconscious, for in the summer of 1997 "The Anencephalic Fields"—with its literal farm of bodies—bubbled up fully formed and begging to be written.

In the rural West Virginia where my paternal grandmother grew up during the first decades of the twentieth century, home births and family cemeteries were still the rule, and the events of "Home

Burial" really happened—to a point. As a young girl, my grand-mother had a neighbor who really did pass the time during her pregnancy by sewing clothes for her unborn child. The neighbor in question really did have a stillborn baby, her husband really did bury the baby before she regained consciousness, and she really did insist that he dig up the body to clothe it properly.

The rest—excluding the title, which I stole from Robert Frost—is pure invention. The Bible salesman has no basis in reality (though subscription book salesmen were not uncommon in rural America in the final years of the nineteenth century). Ditto the ghostly cries of the buried baby and the final scene, where Rachel digs up the body herself. This is, in fact, a considerable improve-ment over the source material. I can remember listening to my grandmother's story with a kind of trembling fascination as a child, only to be inevitably disappointed by the conclusion, in which she admitted that the proposed disinterment never took place—an early and perhaps formative experience in the comparative paucities of reality as measured against the riches of the imagination.

Like "Home Burial," "Quinn's Way" grows out of family history—in this case my father's stories of growing up in Princeton, West Virginia, during the Depression and the Second World War. Those readers who know the Princeton of that era may recognize some of the landmarks in the story—among them the Grand Hotel, the Court House, the Bluehole, the Stull house, and the monkey chained to the post. I want to talk about that monkey for a moment. Even as a child listening to my father's stories, it struck me as an especially telling detail, for in its casual and wholly unthinking cruelty—imagine the life that poor monkey must have led—it seemed to undermine the nostalgia my father obviously felt (and still feels) for the town of his youth—the nostalgia we *all* feel in one degree or another for those chapters of our lives which are irretriev-ably closed but for the all-too-often self-serving gaze of memory.

It troubles me, this story. It enshrines the stories of my father's youth—the stories which have come to play such a central and defining role in my own imagination—and yet it casts them all into doubt by exposing, relentlessly, the hypocrisies and horrors which surround us every day, which existed then, as now, despite the lying voice of memory. Like memory itself, Jemmy E. recoils from those horrors; he joins the circus, he flees into the idealized world of a boy's fantasy (though this world, too, has its horrors). But Henry Sleep—and the story itself—insists that we must never run. It is a subtle act of rebellion, this story. And that troubles me. It troubles me that a story about fathers, based so much on *my* father's past—the father who has been, and remains, the single closest, most influential, and enduring friend I have—it troubles me deeply that this story should have at its heart such a monstrous father, and that there should be so many such fathers in the whole sweep of these stories.

There are other acts of rebellion here—and against other fathers. Many readers will rightly recognize "Quinn's Way" as an *homage* to the writer who most influenced me—Ray Bradbury—and to his finest novel, *Something Wicked This Way Comes* (others will say that this is not his finest novel, that *The Martian Chronicles* is his finest novel, or *Fahrenheit 451*; but they are wrong). Yet it has always bothered me that the heroes of that novel, Will Halloway and his father Charles and his best friend Jim Nightshade, should face the darkness in themselves only to escape unscathed back into the light. There is darkness, of course, and there is light, but none of us—none of us—come through unscathed. Jemmy E. does not escape, not really, and neither does Henry Sleep. And neither will you. But like Henry, we can all be strong at the broken places—which is the best line in the story, and which is stolen from another, and finer writer, Ernest Hemingway, who also had issues with fathers (the final line is stolen, too, from Robert Frost; all writers are unregenerate thieves, and the ones who deny it are also liars).

Two other notes in closing: those who've read my novel *The Fallen* will recognize the names Sauls Run and Henry Sleep. The Henry Sleep of this story is not the Henry Sleep of that novel, and the Sauls Run of this story (or the other stories I've written and have yet to write set in towns named Sauls Run) is not the Sauls Run of that novel. I can't say why that is, except to tell you that both the novel and the story were conceived around the same time, and the muse insisted that those were the names and one does not argue with the muse. Henry Sleep is me, of course—in the same way that Nick Adams was Hemingway—and no doubt he will crop up again somewhere along the way, as Nick Adams did, and when he does he will be someone else. And, of course, he will still be me.

Finally, there is an irony in the fact that this story—which is about the secret stories hidden in the lies we so often tell ourselves—has its own secret history, which I will not divulge here. But I dedicate it to my wife, Jean, who lived it. And who knows.

"Touched" is the first story I wrote that felt fully formed—that seemed, somehow, wholly and originally mine, rather than a

pastiche of influences and borrowed techniques. The historical setting—West Virginia coal country soon after the turn of the twentieth century—was at least a full generational remove from the West
Virginia in which I grew up; but I knew well the kind of rural people who inhabited that world—stoic, impoverished, frustrated, and
yet fiercely proud. "Write what you know" is the oldest advice there
is on the craft of fiction, but writing "Touched" felt like a revelation
all the same. For the first time—the examples of Clifford D. Simak,
Manly Wade Wellman, Zenna Henderson, and Ray Bradbury
notwithstanding—I understood that my own rural experience could
resonate in the contexts of science fiction and fantasy.

The story itself finds its origins in the Appalachian superstition
that a mentally deficient child is compensated with other gifts.
When I found myself wondering what such "gifts" might include,
my subconscious almost immediately served up the story's core elements—a Down Syndrome child with the ability to resurrect the
dead, who struggles to understand his gift amid the labor turmoil
that marked the West Virginia coal fields during the 1920s (students
of labor history will recognize the story's climactic gun battle as a
thinly fictionalized version of the Matewan Massacre, a confrontation between United Mine Workers organizers and union-busting
Baldwin-Felts detectives that left ten people dead on May 19, 1920).
As compelling as this scenario was, however, the idea seemed
fraught with pitfalls—not least among them, what one was to do
with the resurrected corpse once it had achieved reanimation. I
could understand why W. W. Jacobs never opened that door in
"The Monkey's Paw." So I turned my attention instead to a consid-
eration of what would motivate such a character *not* to use his gift—
and as a result the narrative turned inward, upon the knotty terrain
of familial conflict and sibling rivalry.

None of this resolved another problem the story posed: how
to tell it? It seemed to me that it should be Jorey's tale, yet every
attempt to root it in his perceptions ran aground. Third person seemed too objective, too far removed from his center of
consciousness—I wanted the reader to experience first-hand his
isolation and loneliness. First person attempts resolved into stream-
of-consciousness incoherence. Though I dislike experimental
narratives as a rule, I finally settled on second person because it is
just unusual enough to suggest the subtly alienated quality of Jorey's
everyday experience. We see lucidly through the pane of a second-
person narrative, yet everything is oddly distorted by the novelty of
the technique. I omitted the quotation marks for the same reason:

in Jorey's world, all sensory experience comes in at the same level of priority. Everything is equally important (or unimportant).

Finally, I should note that "Touched," like several of the stories reprinted here, was revised for inclusion in this collection. The changes, which are minor, eliminate an instance of auctorial intrusion in the final paragraphs: story notes aside, stories should not be in the business of explaining themselves, and in the first published version of "Touched" I made the mistake of not trusting my readers to "get it" without signposts pointing them in the right direction. Purists who object may seek out the original and compare for themselves; for my money, this is the superior version.

Like "The Resurrection Man's Legacy," "The Census Taker" came to me as a title. It was conceived in the summer of 2000, when our own census was very much in the news, and grew into its present form over the months that followed. My neighbor at the time had taken on a temporary assignment seeking out non-respondents, and I remember asking him a few questions about his work. But anyone with any real knowledge of the census will no doubt find all sorts of inaccuracies (who knows, for example, if census takers really have a master list of surveyed territories, as Lucas Dixon seems to? I don't know, that's for sure).

Readers who've lived in Louisiana may note other inaccuracies having to do with Cajun culture or the bayou. The Alligator King, for example, is wholly a fabrication of my imagination (but not, I think, an unlikely one). While I've spent a few weeks doing touristy things in New Orleans—ogling the drunks on Bourbon Street and drunkenly providing ogle-fodder in my turn—I have little experience—check that: no experience—of rural Louisiana. And the one time I ate crawfish, they put me off my feed. Yet I *do* have a lot of experience with rural Appalachia, and I submit to you that rural people all over the country are very much the same in their stoicism, their self-reliance, their mingled insecurity and pride. Scratch the surface of one of Stephen King's trademark Maine Yankees, and you'll find someone who looks an awful lot like the denizens of William Faulkner's Yoknapatawpha County.

Still, inaccuracies are inaccuracies, and critics have every right to harp on them.

That's okay. Let me be honest here: I tried, but I didn't try very hard. One of the reasons I've never been a very successful academic is that I loathe research, so I tend to do what writers do: make it up. And that's okay, too—because the story isn't really about the surface tenor of life in the Atchafalaya. The story is about the inner lives of the human beings who live there. The story is, once again, I'm afraid, about fathers and sons, and I'm certain—check that, too: I'm almost certain—that I got that right.

If I didn't, you have every right to gripe.

"Exodus" is an oddity in a couple of ways. One, it was written at what, for me, is white-hot speed (I started it on May 16, 1995, and finished it two days later). It is also—unlike most of the stories here, which exist in the hazy border country where science fiction, fantasy, and horror come together—inarguably *science* fiction, my own small contribution to the honorable tradition of science fiction stories which project a current trend to its logical, if unhappy conclusion—"if this goes on . . ." stories. The "this" in this case is actually several trends—the demographic shift toward an older population, the exponentially increasing life span Americans can reasonably expect, and the current system of providing senior citizens (a mealy-mouthed euphemism if there ever was one) with some kind of government pension. Your social security dollar does not go into a "lockbox" investment, despite the insistence of certain recent presidential candidates to the contrary; it actually subsidizes the present generation of retirees. It does not take any great acuity to see where these facts ultimately lead us.

A second impetus for the story came from reading John Keats's poem "Ode to a Nightingale," where the speaker addresses the eponymous bird this way: "Thou wast not born for death, immortal Bird! / No hungry generations tread thee down." The passage seemed ironically appropriate—given the trends in place, it seemed to me, we were looking more and more at a future in which a subsidized leisure class would exist at the expense, literally, of younger, and hungrier, generations. In fact the working title of the story was "Hungry Generations," later dropped in favor of the current "Exodus" both because the first title seemed too obvious and because the story had grown into something more than a simple screed on the perils of American social policy. In the actual writing it had become an examination of the *true* cost of aging—the human cost.

When "Cockroach" was conceived (pun very much intended) in 1995, I was four years married and had no intentions of becoming a father. By the time the story was published in December 1998, my wife Jean and I had not only experienced a miscarriage of our own, but were six months into a second pregnancy. If it had been gratifying to discover that my research on the physical effects of pregnancy proved accurate, it was more than a little disturbing to learn that in imagining Gerald Hartshorn's anxieties about his impending fatherhood, I had managed to map the psychological terrain with some accuracy.

My daughter was delivered under emergency circumstances in March 1999. Our first sign that something was very wrong indeed came early in our eighth month of pregnancy. By the time Jean was correctly diagnosed as suffering acute fatty liver of pregnancy, an extremely rare condition that strikes perhaps one of fifteen thousand otherwise healthy pregnancies, she was already experiencing liver failure. Her kidneys began to fail soon afterwards. The subsequent two weeks—as our extended families gathered bedside—were harrowing. I am happy to report that at this writing, almost four years later to the day, both Jean and Carson, our daughter, are completely healthy. I am happier still to offer this story in belated dedication to the doctors who pulled her through, Sarkis Chobanian and Perry Roussis.

I'm glad I wrote it when I did. I do not think I could write it now.

"Sheep's Clothing" is among my favorite stories because it so distinctly *doesn't* fit here. It's hard science fiction—or as close to hard science fiction as I'm likely to come anyway (though the hard science fiction markets, *Analog* and *Asimov's*, both bounced it, so maybe I'm wrong about that).

I undertook it largely because the core idea—contrived as it is—struck me as, well, just really kind of cool. The actual execution of it was an absolute bear, however—mostly because I couldn't get my head around the science of it. True hard science fiction fans will demur, of course, and say that there isn't any real science there. And they're right. What I meant to say is I couldn't get my head around faking up the science plausibly enough to make readers buy into the story.

Fortunately, I happened to be attending Clarion when I conceived the idea in June 1992 (typically for me, the story wasn't finished until January 1994). Cory Doctorow, who has since gone on to considerable fame in the science fiction world, happened to be among my classmates, and Cory throws off more genuine speculative ideas in the course of a ten-minute conversation than I am likely to generate over the entire span of a lifetime. So thanks to Cory for helping me fake up the science convincingly—and thanks, especially, for the robot.

I should add that "Sheep's Clothing" is actually the culminating piece in a series of linked stories which I had planned to turn into a novel. Unfortunately, I've never gotten around to writing the other ones—mainly because, well, I can't get my head around the science in them either.

You out there, Cory?

"In Green's Dominion" gestated longer than any other story I've written. The first drafts date back to October of 1993; the idea is a year or two older. I finished the final revisions on August 29, 2001. Mostly what I did in between was start the story over and over, usually once or twice a year; each time I ran into a brick wall about twenty pages in.

Like "Exodus," this one grew out of a striking image in a poem —in this case, Andrew Marvell's "To His Coy Mistress," a seduction piece on the theme of *carpe diem* ("Seize the day"). The speaker of Marvell's poem informs his potential mistress that if they had all the time in the world, his "vegetable love would grow vaster than empires, and more slow." As mortals, however, the poem argues, we haven't the luxury of time: lovemaking should never be delayed lest the Grim Reaper *interruptus* our *coitus* in the most unpleasant of ways.

This is an admirable sentiment, and one I wholeheartedly endorse as a general life policy—but the line and the poem stuck with me at some deeper level, too. Apparently, I'm not the only one, for other fantasy writers have mined this particular vein for inspiration—most notably Ursula K. LeGuin for her novella "Vaster Than Empires, and More Slow," and Peter Beagle for *A Fine and Private Place*, both classics. It's worth wondering why the poem has proved so memorable to writers of the fantastic.

One answer, I think, is that science fiction and fantasy, by its very nature, takes literally what so-called "mainstream" fiction touches upon only at the level of metaphor. At some level, of course, language is *all* metaphor—so interesting things happen when you approach it this way. When I read "To His Coy Mistress" I found myself thinking what "vegetable love" might *literally* mean. From any logical perspective, the question is intrinsically ridiculous—which is one of the reasons it took me so long to write the story. I could never find a framework sufficient to sustain the idea.

And then I saw an open call for an anthology called *The Green Man*, to be edited by Ellen Datlow and Terry Windling. The title steered me toward a body of English fertility archetypes that proved to be the very framework I needed. Once I tapped that root myth, the story, then called "Vegetable Love," grew into something more than another iteration of the *carpe diem* theme. It became also a meditation on the tensions between order and chaos, between civilization and the natural world, between sexual impulse and puritanical morality, between, especially, art and life. It became a story *about* stories—and how the ordering impulse of story-making can insulate us in ways both constructive and destructive from the risky circumstances of human existence. In the process, the story grew too long for the Datlow/Windling collection; however, Ellen *did* end up buying it for *SciFiction*. She also suggested that I change the title.

Some personal thanks are in order; also, a few words of acknowledgment. In naming Sylvia's innkeeper, I borrowed the surname of my own English landlady and lifelong friend, Siobhain Massingham; similarly, Schaper is the maiden name of my medical advisor for this and other stories, Sherrie Bohrman. Some readers may note literary debts, as well, especially to Robert Holdstock's 1984 World Fantasy Award-winning novel *Mythago Wood*, Jethro Tull's classic 1976 album *Songs from the Wood*, and John Crowley's incomparable fantasy *Little, Big*. Though I ultimately made no direct allusion to "To His Coy Mistress," I *did* quote from another Marvell poem, "The Garden." Finally, I wish to thank W. W. Norton & Company for permission to quote from E. E. Cummings's poem "All in green went my love riding," and Indiana University Press for permission to use as an epigraph the opening stanza of Mark Musa's masterful translation of Dante's *Inferno*.